THE
MENDING
String

CLIFF COON

MOODY PUBLISHERS
CHICAGO

All Scripture quotations, unless otherwise indicated, are taken from the *Holy Bible, New International Version*®. NIV®. Copyright © 1973, 1978, 1984 by International Bible Society. Used by permission of Zondervan Publishing House. All rights reserved.

Library of Congress Cataloging-in-Publication Data

Coon, Cliff, 1934-
    The mending string / by Cliff Coon.
        p. cm.
    ISBN 0-8024-4084-3
    1. Teenage girls—Fiction. 2. Children of clergy—Fiction.
3. Fathers and daughters—Fiction. 4. Conflict of generations—
Fiction. 5. Secrecy—Fiction. 6. Clergy—Fiction. I. Title.

PS3603.O58M46 2004
813'.6—dc22

2003024136

1 3 5 7 9 10 8 6 4 2

Printed in the United States of America

To Lucille,
God's gracious gift, my wife and friend,

and

To our children,
Steve, Catharine, David, Patricia, Tim, and Chris,
who helped teach me openness and companionship.

He will turn the hearts of the fathers to the children,
and the hearts of the children to their fathers, . . .
Malachi 4:6a

A C K N O W L E D G M E N T S

A book is seldom written without the help and encouragement of others. I have been fortunate to have many companions on this literary journey; I have not been lonely. My heartfelt gratitude to . . .

Doug Rumford who first challenged me to write,
The Christian Writers Seminars in Castro Valley and the
Mount Hermon Christian Writers Conferences
for training and inspiration,
Launa Hermann, Dianne Smith, Jon Drury, John Vonhof,
and Steve Lim of the Bay Area Writers Critique Group
for hours of careful listening and constructive criticism,
Dale Wellcome for use of his laptop computer,
Revs. Greg and Marsha Roth, pastors and friends,
for their understanding and encouragement,
NAEN Ministries for compassion and prayers,
My family for reading and my wife
for rereading and rereading and . . . ,
My agent, Les Stobbe,
for insightful suggestions and invaluable help,
Michele Straubel, Amy Peterson, LB Norton, and Pam Pugh,
for their work at and for Moody Publishers,
who made every step of this project thoroughly enjoyable.

PROLOGUE

In May of 1973, Clayton Loverage built the only privacy fence in Springdale, Illinois. He bought a posthole digger, twelve bags of concrete, twenty pounds of galvanized nails, and enough costly California redwood to construct a barrier all the way across the backside of his rectangular lot. The fence was six feet high, ninety feet long, and sturdy enough to last fifty years. He planted Boston ivy along its length, fronted by a dense row of thorny roses. The fence was not an actual barrier to his property, however, for one needed merely to walk to the end and step around it to reach the other side. Although well constructed and beautifully landscaped, to a town that prided itself on openness it was an eyesore. People drove by just to view the monstrosity that was out of place in what had once been nicknamed Friendly Town, U.S.A.

Clayton was the new pastor of Springdale Church, and he and his family had moved into town four weeks earlier. To some it seemed that he built the fence in response to the young woman who, at about the same time, moved into the house behind his, but no one was ever sure.

That young woman was Miss Caroline Merkle, the new English teacher at Springdale High School. She was taller than half the men in town, with a stately manner and trim figure. Her long auburn hair, often woven into a chignon, glistened with streaks of copper and bronze. She might have been a highly paid fashion model, except as far as anyone could see, she had forgotten how to smile. The women of Springdale soon observed that she wore only green—stylish green suits, green skirts and blouses, green belts and shoes, jade brooches and emerald earrings. Everyone noticed her classic 1950 Chevrolet Bel Air hardtop, the body a rich forest green, the top a silver-green, polished to rival the brilliant chrome of the grille and bumpers.

The Loverages quickly made friends with Springdale. Clayton joined the Rotary Club and made a point of contacting the mayor and police chief, having coffee with city council members, and attending civic functions. Although quiet and reserved, his wife, Joyce, opened their house to church members and neighbors. Clay, Jr., who was ten, and Dan, eight, joined the Little League, and four-year-old Linda, pretty and precocious, won people's hearts before they even knew the rest of her family.

Caroline Merkle, on the other hand, made few friends. Within two months she had fenced in the other sides of her property, presumably to contain her Rottweiler. She hired a gardener to maintain her yard, and spent many weekends in Chicago. She socialized only at the Kingswood Country Club, where she played tennis and led a weekly book discussion group. Otherwise, she was simply the striking Miss Merkle who drove the Bel Air and taught English at Springdale High.

After several years Clayton Loverage's eyesore was overgrown with Boston ivy, and the white floribundas blossomed from spring until fall. No one drove by to see it anymore; few talked about it or even thought about it. Its offense faded to a whisper, then a faint echo that almost died out.

O N E

When Ellen Loverage needed to be alone, she went to Miss Merkle's house. On such days she came directly home from school, grabbed a few dog biscuits from her dresser drawer, and headed out her back door. Edging behind an ancient row of white roses and raising the thick, tangled stems of Boston ivy, she pushed back a rotting board in Father's old fence and squeezed through. After pacifying Rolex with a few pats on the head and a biscuit, she retrieved a key from its usual spot under the potted hosta, quickly unlocked the door, and stepped into peace and solitude.

In Miss Merkle's library she slid a book from its ornate slipcover, adjusted the stereo to a whisper, nestled into her usual spot on the plush Persian carpet, and leaned back against the brocaded settee. Perfect. Absorbing hours of reading lay ahead. Good music. No chores. No phone to answer. No homework.

When the clock chimed a quarter to five she replaced the book, pushed the OFF button on the stereo, smoothed the carpet where she'd been sitting, and left. Another biscuit and a few more pats on the head to assure Rolex that all was well, and Ellen slipped back through the fence. Miss Merkle would get home around 5:15, Father at 5:30.

NO ONE ELSE KNEW about Ellen's sanctuary. The previous summer, while relaxing in the backyard hammock, sipping lemonade and reading, she had heard Rolex's gleeful half-yip, half-bark. Through a knothole in Father's fence she watched Miss Merkle toss sticks and balls for her dog to fetch, now and then substituting a leather bone for him to chew on. After freshening Rolex's water bowl, she climbed her porch steps to go inside. Finding her door locked, she tilted a large terra cotta pot, picked up a key, and unlocked the door.

Everybody has a hiding place for an emergency key. The Loverages' was under the decorative rocks next to the entryway. Ellen felt a little uncomfortable with her unsought knowledge, but it was no big deal. She no more thought of entering her neighbor's house than of trying out for the cross-country team.

And she never would have entered Miss Merkle's house if she hadn't needed to get away from Father and his things. The aroma of his coffee in the morning and the redolence of his leather recliner greeted her when she came home from school. His stodgy music played at breakfast and dinner, and each day ended with his ten o'clock news. Mom's touch still lingered throughout most of the rooms, but in the living room, where Ellen liked to read, the pictures and plaques, the furniture, the clocks, and the carpet were all his. Nothing in the house had her own touch, except for her bedroom, which was on the dark side of the house, and the laundry room, which Father hadn't entered for years. Even the kitchen was his, because he dictated what he wanted for breakfast and dinner, and she had to keep it cleaned according to his specifications.

The event that pushed her through the back fence and into

Miss Merkle's house happened near the end of her sophomore year. She had hurried home from school to finish the last chapters of *The Power and the Glory* before Father got home from work. He wasn't sure she should be reading the book, but it was on Miss Merkle's recommended reading list. Ellen opened a cold can of Pepsi and settled into Father's forbidden recliner. He wouldn't be home for two hours. It was the most comfortable chair in the house, and she often read there when he wasn't around. After all, if he let her sit on his lap when she was little, why couldn't she use his empty chair now?

About four o'clock, she heard his car pull into the driveway. He was home early. She hurried upstairs to her bedroom, but as soon as she got there she knew she was in trouble—on the end table next to his recliner sat her Pepsi, sweating and coasterless. It was too late to rescue it; he was in the house. She looked at her watch: 4:03. Within two minutes he'd call her name. She went into the bathroom to wait.

"Ellie!"

4:06. A minute slow. "Be right there, Father." She let him stew a little longer.

"Ellie, come down here!"

"Just a sec, Father." She peered into the mirror and saw the same boring pie-face draped with straight, mud-puddle brown hair. Thick, rimless glasses, supported on a petite upturned nose, reflected back at her. Her older sister, Linda, had used up all the Loverage family good looks. She flushed the toilet, ran the faucet awhile, and lingered another minute before sauntering downstairs—4:12. Father stood at the bottom of the stairs with his hands on his hips.

"You were in my chair."

A wonderful father-daughter greeting. He could at least start with a simple hello.

"I was reading, Father." She reminded herself to stay cool.

"Haven't I provided enough places in this house for you to read?"

Ellen purposely stopped in the middle of the staircase,

knowing it made him uncomfortable to look up at her. "Yes, but your chair's so comfortable. I didn't think you'd care."

"Why would you think I'd changed my mind since the last time you sat there?" He maintained the same pose at the bottom of the stairs.

Father was a pair of triangles, his head with its broad forehead and pointed chin perched on a broad-shouldered, hipless, athletic body.

"I never sit there while you're home. I don't think it should make any difference if you aren't here." He wouldn't buy it. A rule was a rule.

"Ellie, you know the rule about my recliner. Don't sit in it! What part of that don't you understand?" He waited, as though he expected an answer. "And the Pepsi?"

"That was a mistake, Father. I'm sorry. I should have used a coaster."

"Ellie, one act of disobedience always leads to another. Big sins grow from little ones."

She could get his sermons in church; he didn't need to preach at her.

"If you hadn't sat in the chair, you wouldn't have left the can there. It could ruin the end table."

She stared at the ring of water surrounding the can. "Sorry. I'll wipe it up."

"No, I'll take care of it. It's best if you stay away from my things." He shifted his feet and narrowed his eyes as though he were aiming a rifle. "There's one more thing. Do you know what it is?"

"Yep."

"You mean yes?"

"Yes, Father."

"Well, what is it?" he demanded.

"You think I ran upstairs when I heard you coming."

"Disobedience is bad enough, carelessness with the Pepsi might be overlooked, but running upstairs hoping I wouldn't notice is deception."

"It might have worked if it hadn't been for the stupid Pepsi." Why did she say things like that? Now she'd uncapped his geyser. He'd raise his voice slightly, but his language would remain exemplary, always under control.

"That's enough, Ellie. You're adding insolence to everything else. You're grounded again, for a week. Come straight home after school. No activities in the evenings or on the weekend. We'll talk about it seven days from now and go over the rules again."

"Thanks, Father." She couldn't conceal the sarcasm in her reply.

"Make that two weeks. I don't know what I'm going to do with you. I didn't have this trouble with your brothers and sister." He turned abruptly, picked up his briefcase, and strode to the front door. "I'll be home at the regular time. I expect dinner at six."

She was still on the stairs as he hurried into his study, then out the front door. He had probably come home just to grab something he'd forgotten, and now was late for a 4:15 meeting. It would be her fault, of course. She tried to resettle herself in his recliner, but she couldn't get comfortable with the Pepsi can still signing its white-ringed signature into the varnish. Well, let it sign. He'd accepted responsibility for it and hadn't followed through.

Back in her room, she stretched out on her bed and imagined the peace she might find in Miss Merkle's house.

IT WAS SOON AFTER the Pepsi incident that Ellen began going into her neighbor's house. It was too easy. If Rolex was in the backyard, Miss Merkle wasn't home yet. Besides, the kitchen light was on when she was there. Ellen always checked. Surprises could spell disaster.

Rolex was never a problem. She'd made friends with all of Miss Merkle's watchdogs, Rolex and his predecessors, Bulova and Hamilton. All three were Rottweilers, marked copper-red and black, standing three feet high, their barks resounding like cannons. When they were puppies she'd talked to them and fed them biscuits through the fence. When Rolex was a puppy, she'd loosened one of the boards so she could pet him. Miss Merkle's backyard was safe from all intruders except her.

The first day Ellen went into the house she was as tense as a set mousetrap. As she had expected, the key lay under the hosta pot. It slid into the lock and turned effortlessly. She replaced it, in case she had to leave in a hurry, wiped her feet on the mat, and tentatively stepped inside. She thought that any second Miss Merkle might walk in. Maybe she was already there. Every squeak, every noise, was a butler announcing her presence.

From the moment she stepped through the door she knew she was in Elysium. Mom's country style decor was all right, but this was elegance. Not of luxury, but refinement and taste. The kitchen was lined with dark wood cabinets. In its center stood an island, its top a cutting board composed of black, brown, red, and tan hardwoods inlaid in a geometric pattern. Stainless steel pots, pans, and utensils were suspended over the island and from pegs above the stove. The floor was tiled, and a garden window overlooked the backyard.

On that first day Ellen had turned and left quickly, frightened and guilty. She had no business being in that house. Everybody—Father, her sibs, Miss Merkle, her classmates, the people at Father's church—would be scandalized if they knew. It was too risky. She swore she'd never go in there again. It was best to leave with the knowledge that Miss Merkle's house was wonderful. She didn't need to see any more of it.

ELLEN DIDN'T RETURN to Miss Merkle's house until after Labor Day. Every time she thought about what she'd done, she was chagrined. She, Ellen Loverage, the pastor's daughter, trespassing. Unthinkable! How could she have been so stupid?

The second time she entered the house was after another

fight with Father. This time it was about music. His range of what was acceptable was as narrow as a tightrope. Old church music, a little classical, some golden oldies, that was all. Anything else was sinful or, if not sinful, unedifying. Father loved the word *edify*.

She was lying on her bed reading and listening to a CD by Angels of Light, a contemporary Christian group, purposely keeping the volume low so it wouldn't bother him. After a while Father knocked and, before she could reply, opened her door. His upper lip had a slight curl and his nose was wrinkled, as if he were sniffing burnt cabbage.

"What's that noise?"

"What noise?" She turned back to her book.

"That so-called music."

"That's my CD player."

"All I hear is Babel. What's it supposed to be playing?"

"It's a song called 'Breath of Heaven.' Mostly verses from the Psalms."

"I can't understand a word."

"It's an unknown tongue called English, Father. Would you like me to interpret?"

"It's loud and repetitious."

"You mean like the 'Hallelujah Chorus'?" She still didn't look at him, but out of the corner of her eye saw him take a deep breath.

"Ellie, this is just noise. If the message is covered up, there's no message."

"You mean like when Mrs. Ritchie sings at church? She warbles so much she sounds like a howler monkey."

"Ellie, that's not fair. Adele Ritchie has a trained voice. Everyone understands what she's singing."

"The kids don't. We get a lot more out of Angels of Light."

"Where'd you get that CD, anyway? It's not yours, is it?"

"I got it for a dollar at the Salvation Army thrift store."

"I don't want it in my house."

"Why? I like it." She tried to sound innocent, wounded. "It's just words from the Bible. You can't object to that."

"Ellie, if you mix pure, sweet honey with pesticides and puree it in a blender, you still can't drink it. You can't keep feeding your mind this stuff. You should listen to something that will edify your soul."

After Father left, Ellen looked over the rest of the CDs in her rack. She chose the one he'd just given to her for Christmas. *To Ellie,* he'd written on the cover, *To edify your soul and light your way. With love, Father.* She'd listened to it once.

She put it in the boom box and adjusted the volume, not high enough to bother anyone in the hallway. Then she laid the boom box on the floor, speaker side down, and placed her thick dictionary on top of it. Father's study was in the room below. The floor and ceiling acted as a giant sounding board to vibrate his pictures crooked and ripple his coffee.

That ought to edify his soul. She locked her door, settled back on her bed with her book, and waited.

A few minutes later he was back upstairs, rapping on her door.

"Yes?" she answered sweetly.

"Ellie, can you turn it down a little? I'm trying to work on my sermon."

"Sure, Father." She lowered the volume just enough to be noticed. "How's that?"

"A little more." It was not a suggestion, but a command.

She cut off another thin slice of volume. "That okay?"

"I'll try it."

"Let me know if there's a problem." She moved the boom box to the center of the room, piled a couple of schoolbooks on it, and went back to reading.

Five minutes later he rapped again. "Ellie, do you think you could turn it down a little bit more? I still can't concentrate."

She pushed the OFF button.

"I didn't want you to turn it off. That's good music."

"Don't worry about it. I wasn't listening anyway. I can

16

study better without it." She leaned back against the pillow, gave a long, satisfied stretch, and continued reading *The Sound and the Fury.*

After a while, she went to her desk and unpinned her calendar from the wall. She'd promised herself she'd leave home when she turned eighteen. That would be June 13, 1997. Today was January 21; a year and five months to go. She calculated the days—510. At five hundred and the other hundreds she'd celebrate by treating herself to a double sundae smothered under chocolate syrup, chopped almonds, and mini-marshmallows. She highlighted the days on her calendar and went back to reading.

AFTER THE CD INCIDENT, Ellie started going to Miss Merkle's house regularly. She knew she was breaking the law. If she were caught, she'd be in big trouble and Father would be mortified. But she wasn't doing anything morally wrong— she promised herself never to take so much as a cashew or mint from the crystal candy bowl on the coffee table. She was simply taking advantage of peace and quiet that would otherwise go unused.

When she went into the house she was extremely careful. Mondays and Thursdays were best because Miss Merkle had regularly scheduled meetings at school on those days. Still, she checked on Rolex and the kitchen light. During the winter months she walked carefully on the stones around the edge of the lawn so as not to leave footprints.

It was the contrasts between her house and Miss Merkle's that fascinated Ellen. Persian carpets and throw rugs over polished hardwood floors instead of wall-to-wall carpets. Tile in place of linoleum in the kitchen and bathrooms. Walls decorated with stylish wallpaper instead of off-white paint with stenciled geese parading around the top of the wall.

Mom had collected carvings and figurines of cows; Miss Merkle's Hummel figurines were locked in a large china cabinet behind thick, beveled glass. Crystal and cut-glass figurines were everywhere. Floor and table lamps lighted the Loverage house; Miss Merkle had a few of these plus chandeliers and wall lamps mounted on sconces. Their religious and Rockwell prints looked tawdry compared to her original florals and pastorals. Their Melmac and stoneware paled in comparison to Miss Merkle's navy blue and gold filigreed bone china.

Miss Merkle's house greeted her with the scent of lavender. Melodic chimes announced the time. Sofas, chairs, tables, magazine racks, serving ware—expensive but not gaudy, tasteful but never flamboyant.

The room Ellen always went to was the study-library. Shelves of hardcover books covered two walls. Most of these were in their own slipcases, as though meant to last hundreds of years. There were no paperbacks, no throwaways. Everything Miss Merkle recommended in class was there, and much more, from Homer to Hugo to Hemingway. It was better than the city library, because everything Ellen put her hands on she wanted to read. The room was a blissful haven with all the literary delights she could desire.

A second reason Ellen spent her time in the study-library was that it was next to the garage. Because Miss Merkle always opened the garage door electronically from about a block away, there was more than enough time for Ellen to slip out the back door and through the fence. She was always careful. No one suspected. It was easier each time.

TWO

Clayton Loverage sat in his office at Springdale Church, rocking back in his black leather chair and scanning his schedule for the day. His polished mahogany desk sank into a royal blue carpet and was lighted by two small chandeliers. Except for a telephone, pictures of his wife and four children, and an open Bible, his desk was clear.

The office was spacious enough for a meeting of thirty people. On one wall oak shelving displayed bound books and mementos presented to him by missionaries; behind his desk a large olive-wood cross reminded everyone of the focus of the church. Two framed pictures, Jesus on the road to Emmaus and Jesus healing a leper, set off another wall. In the back of the office a door led to a bathroom, complete with shower. Clayton considered his office comfortable, but not ostentatious. If one served the God of the Universe, he explained, it was right to invest in quality. Because the Bible tells us to be good workmen, we should buy the products of the best craftsmen.

Clayton was thirty-seven when he'd arrived in Springdale; now he was fifty-nine. After finishing seminary, he'd studied two years in Germany, earning a doctorate from the University of Darmstadt. This was followed by associate pastorates at medium-sized churches in Texas and Missouri, before he took on the challenge of the Springdale position.

When he first considered the church it was dying, only a year or two from complete collapse. The average Sunday attendance and the average age of the parishioners were almost the same, about sixty-five. Only a handful of children attended Sunday school, dragged there by parents or grandparents, and teenagers were overlooked. The deteriorating sanctuary, the church sign obscured by overgrown shrubs, and the weed-infested parking lot spoke of a church in its death throes. While everything cried for resuscitation, Clayton saw two things in its favor: it was in the middle of a prosperous section of town, and it was located on eight acres of land.

Although the church was a rehabilitation project, Springdale was an ideal place to raise a family. The school system rated among the best in the state, and unemployment was low. Drawn by a major rail line and an interstate highway, companies waited in line to fill the new business and industrial park. Slums were nonexistent, and the crime rate was far below the state average. A community college was to be built within five to ten years. After carefully considering the advantages and disadvantages of accepting the pastorate of a declining church in a small town, he presented the opportunity to Joyce. Years in urban areas had left her longing for a small-town atmosphere. After weighing the pros and cons and praying about it together, they accepted the challenge of Springdale Church.

Now his church was the largest in the county. The new sanctuary, filled twice every Sunday morning, seated four hundred. The high school group numbered almost two hundred, the junior-highers about 150. He led a team of five pastors, and six people worked in the office. As one of the most successful small churches in the country, Springdale Church was once featured in *Today's Christian* magazine.

As for his children, Clay, Jr. pastored a medium-sized church in Fort Worth, and Dan worked with start-up computer companies in Silicon Valley. Recent stock splits had made him wealthy. Linda, after graduating from Wheaton College, taught high school math in Aurora. All three were still in the faith, happily married, and living productive, satisfying lives. Added to that were the grandchildren Clay, Jr. and Linda had given him.

And then there was Ellie, born five years after their arrival in Springdale when he and Joyce were forty-two. Always her own master—or was it mistress?—she was the most headstrong child he'd ever known, defying all the theories of child-raising that humankind had ever devised.

EACH WEEKDAY CLAYTON woke at 6:30, showered, shaved, dressed, and straightened his room in time to be at breakfast at 7:00. After eating, scanning the newspaper, and giving Ellie last-minute instructions for the day, he drove to the church to spend the next hour in his study reading the Bible and praying. That hour had become a willing obligation, usually a pleasure, rarely a duty. Sometimes emergencies came up, but to skip because he wanted to sleep in or because he wasn't in the mood was forbidden. God honored faithfulness, even when one's mind was distracted and one's heart was troubled. Those first sixty minutes, immersed in the Word of God and bathed in prayer, were essential.

His staff began trickling in at half past eight, and the next half hour he invested in the minutiae of office details. The usual questions about announcements for the bulletin, meeting times and places, and office responsibilities had to be answered. More importantly, he used those minutes before nine o'clock to bond with his staff, to exchange anecdotes and feelings, and to learn each other's likes and dislikes, joys and sorrows.

Just before nine o'clock he retreated to his office and scanned his schedule again. Tuesday, April 9, 1996.

9:00 Joe Nunes, Central Paving/parking lot expansion
9:30 Plan Sunday's worship service with Nate and Wilson
11:00 Sermon preparation
1:30 Visitation at Good Samaritan
3:00 Jack Brandt/JubiLatte Coffeehouse
4:30 Springdale High to discuss Ellie

He looked forward to most of it. The first two involved people he could work with, and sermon preparation was his joy and passion. He'd eat his lunch while he studied and wrote. Hospital visitation was usually a pleasure, although often disquieting. After that, however, his day went downhill. A meeting with Jack Brandt often resembled a forced march through the Sahara, and he had no idea why the high school counselor wanted to talk about Ellie.

THE FIRST PERSON he ran into at Good Samaritan was Adele Ritchie, a member of his church. She was wiry, six feet tall, and had kinky pumpkin-orange hair that made him suspect she was Little Orphan Annie's mother. He was convinced she dyed it until he had recently noticed strands of softening gray. Clashing with her hair, stoplight-red lipstick outlined a small, slightly puckered mouth. True green eyes perched a little too close together above a thin, slightly hooked nose. He could not easily overlook Adele, nor did he want to.

Several weeks after arriving at the church, Adele let it be known that she had a trained operatic voice and was available for solos. Trained at Juilliard, she had then spent fifteen years in New York. When she was almost forty and realized her musical career was going nowhere, she dropped everything to study nursing at Fordham.

Clayton had talked Wilson, the music director, into letting her sing. She nearly shattered the stained-glass windows; the preschoolers plugged their ears with their fingers while the older kids snickered. Her voice may have been suitable for opera, but its volume and vibrato, and her exaggerated gestures didn't suit a church in Springdale, Illinois. He asked to meet with her in his office.

"Adele, about your solo last Sunday . . ." he began with trepidation.

"Yes! You liked it!" Her eyes were bright, and her puckery little mouth was stretched into its broadest smile.

"Well, I liked it well enough"—he had to be careful not to lie or offend her—"except that our sanctuary is rather small. . . ."

"Too loud?"

"Well, yes, a little. And the Latin . . ."

"I had a feeling it was too formal."

"And the congregation's not used to gestures. . . ."

"My, I got everything wrong, didn't I?" She put her face in her hands.

"No, no. Your motivation was perfect, Adele. You sang from your heart to the Lord; that's what counts. Maybe you'd like to talk with Wilson. Together you could figure out what's perfect for both your voice and our church."

Adele had responded graciously, saying she was very flexible and was anxious to be guided to a more appropriate singing style. Now she sang with a subdued operatic flair. The children still giggled, but at least some of the congregation appreciated her efforts.

Clayton considered Adele a prime example of God's grace. In her New York years she had made token appearances in operas and musicals while cruising through two husbands and numerous lovers. Contacts with Catholics and Episcopalians at a Brooklyn hospital turned her heart toward God, and she ended up working in a hospital and attending a Presbyterian church in Havre de Grace, Maryland. It was there she married Eric Ritchie, and a few years later they moved into the old Schroeder estate west of Springdale.

Adele was one of Good Samaritan's three head nurses. She was competent and authoritarian—some would say bossy—and ran such a tight ship that the hospital staff simultaneously revered and despised her.

"You're late," she announced to Clayton. "You should have been here four minutes ago."

"There was a major earthquake and a landslide on First Street," he quipped, "and I had to fight my way through a flock of killer sparrows. Next Tuesday I'll be here at 1:56 to make up for it."

Anyone listening to their acrimonious comments would think they were enemies, but in truth Adele was one of his treasures, a hard-nosed, worldly-wise parishioner whose faith and commitment could never be doubted. She had become his friendly inquisitor, lagging behind at the end of services to make humorous, critical, or insightful comments. Just before Christmas she'd caught him off guard with another one of her offbeat questions. "If the male parentage of a child can be traced through DNA analysis, and Jesus was conceived by the power of the Holy Spirit, what would the Holy Spirit's DNA analysis look like?" She hadn't waited for an answer, but hurried off, leaving him with a ridiculous question that rattled around in his head the rest of the week.

"It's best to avoid unexpected catastrophes, but I sympathize," she said to him now. "There's been a devastating flood in the B hallway. If you're going to see Wally, you'll have to go all the way around. You think you can manage that? Or should I call for a guide and a wheelchair?"

"I'm tough, Adele. Even if I have to swim down B, I'm going to see Wally," he said, hurrying off.

"I didn't like the third song last Sunday," she called after him.

"I know you didn't."

"How'd you know? Did it show on my face?"

"No, you hid it very well. I didn't care for the music either, so I knew you wouldn't."

24

"Why do we sing those things then?" she asked.

"Because a lot of the younger people like them. I try to keep it under control."

"My friend George Frederick Handel is weeping."

"For the music perhaps, but we can all sing the words to the glory of God."

WALLY FITCH, Clayton's long-time fishing partner and confidant, probably wouldn't hang on another week. He'd been a clerk at Western Sporting Goods when Clayton first moved to Springdale, and was soon taking him fishing out at Braxton Reservoir, where he kept a small rowboat. He attended St. Thomas Episcopal when the weather wouldn't allow him to fish. Over the past twenty years they'd fished together hundreds of times, usually at Braxton, sometimes at other lakes and reservoirs in the area. The old man empathized with Clayton's worst frustrations and deepest emotions. Now he lay in Good Samaritan with thyroid cancer, so weak he struggled to speak. Wally made being a pastor a pleasure. As always, through his pain, he asked about the church, Ellie, and the rest of the children. As Clayton spoke softly, Wally's blinks became longer and longer until he drifted off in a sedated sleep. Clayton stayed by his bed, wending his way through memories of fishing trips and conversations that contained more wealth than Fort Knox.

After a while, Wally rolled over to face him and said, "Clayton, I have all day and night to lie here and think and daydream and pray. One of the things I've thought about is leaving you my boat and shed out at Braxton. It's okay with my kids. They don't know a minnow from a marlin and don't care."

"Wally, you don't have to—"

"Oh hush, let a dying old man do what he wants." His smile was weak and beautiful.

Near the end of their time together, Clayton opened his

Bible to read the Twenty-third Psalm. After the first few words, Wally held up his hand and stopped him. Then, in a crepe-paper voice, he quoted the rest of the Psalm word for word and, as he finished, dropped off to sleep. Clayton said a silent prayer over him, maybe the last one he'd ever pray with his old friend.

Bella Belinsky, on the other hand, was her usual complaining self. Her second language was Gripe. In some ways she had a right, Clayton thought, for her life had been a caravan of misfortunes. She'd endured three marriages, and her last husband had suffered five years with lung cancer. Last year her teenage grandson, whom she was raising alone, was killed in a spinout on Bull Creek Road. She owned an array of ailments, real and imagined, that kept Springdale doctors employed, guessing, and intimidated. For the twenty-two years he'd known her she'd been a grumbler, and now that was intensified by real illness.

As Clayton sat by her bed she blathered on about the nurses, doctors, her family who never came to see her, her HMO, Medicare—nobody was doing anything right, no one cared. When he told her that he cared, she shooed him off like a fly and said that he didn't count because he was getting paid to care. When he said that Jesus cared, she asked why, if Jesus cared so much, He hadn't protected her grandson, and why He wouldn't cure her diver-tickle-itis.

As he left the hospital, he wondered what he would be like if he were a sick old man. Would he be able to handle pain? At fifty-nine he'd probably lived three-quarters of his life, and in only eleven years he'd be in his seventies! Joyce had been gone two and a half years. She'd been in a lot of pain those last six months, but had never complained. What an angel. *God, thank You for that woman*. He hoped he'd be like her and Wally when he was sick. God preserve him from dragging everyone down as that Belinsky woman did.

Clayton arrived at JubiLatte Coffeehouse at 2:55 to find Brandt waiting for him. Eleven years earlier he'd been delighted when Jack and Shirley Brandt showed up at his church. Within six months they had both assumed leadership roles. Jack taught a Sunday-morning Bible study that quickly grew from twenty to fifty attendees, and Shirley, who was trained in marriage and family ministries, set up a Christian counseling center. They led a Thursday-evening Bible study in their home and were active in outreach to visitors. Except for one unfortunate incident in which five-year-old Ellie had grabbed and nearly unscrewed Shirley's nose, he had gotten along well with them during those first months. They were a little opinionated at times, but some opposition was healthy. What more could a pastor desire from parishioners?

Eight months after the Brandts moved to Springdale, however, Clayton was given an ominous glimpse of the future when he lunched with Walt Logan, their former pastor from Fort Collins. Logan avoided specific accusations, but his warnings were unmistakable. Although Walt never doubted the Brandts' faith or the sincerity of their deeds in the church and community, he had found that everything was an issue for them—from obscure doctrinal points to the color of the carpet in the foyer. They had their say on every issue and believed that their opinion, simply because it was *their* opinion, was right. They thrived on power struggles and relentlessly lobbied people behind the scenes.

At the time, Clayton had defended the Brandts. He wasn't looking for people to parrot his viewpoints; lively discussions were healthy. He could handle any personality problems that might appear. Logan warned him again, saying that he had never been so relieved as when Jack Brandt announced his new position with the police department in Springdale. A plague of locusts had ended and healing of the land could begin.

Within a few years, Jack was elected to the church's ruling board, and Clayton felt the plague of which Logan had spoken. Most people were delighted, because Jack was indeed a solid Christian who had the time and dedication to provide leadership for many years. And it was true, the man was all that. Like Walt Logan, Clayton seldom doubted Jack's faith or sincerity; but as the parishioner carried out his thorough, efficient work, he seemed to sow discord instead of harmony.

Brandt's irregular hours with the police department freed him to meet people any time of day. With breakfasts, lunches, cups of coffee, ball games, and hunting and fishing trips, Jack garnered support for his side of every issue. Furthermore, Shirley, with her involvement in counseling, Bible studies, exercise classes, and growth groups, was equally effective among the women.

Intentionally or not, their highly regarded visitation ministry served as a subtle tactic to sway people to their points of view. And, as Walt Logan had warned, no issue, major or minor, escaped their interest and influence. It was impossible to stay ahead of them, because they seemed to be tireless and omnipresent. Jack especially irritated Clayton. His persuasion appeared gentle on the surface, but often implied that if you disagreed with him, you might be opposing the will of God.

After ten years he considered Jack Brandt both an enigma and a paragon of Christian living. No person at Springdale Church, or at the other two churches he'd served, was as dedicated. Besides being on the church board and teaching, he had a visitation ministry to the sick and dying that would shame most pastors or priests. He always wrote notes and letters of condolence in times of tragedy or loss. The Brandts not only tithed to the church but gave generously to many Christian organizations. And somehow Jack squeezed in time to work with Boy Scouts, Little League, and camping programs for underprivileged youth. Clayton once heard a city council member say, "When I consider what it means to be a Christian, I think of Jack Brandt. Now there's a man who practices what he believes."

It was hard to criticize such a man, and, indeed, Clayton had never done so publicly, but shared his frustrations only with Wally and Joyce. He realized that he himself might be jealous and resentful. In a very real sense, without the burdens of administrative duties and sermon preparation, Brandt was outpastoring him. But the man believed so firmly in his own rightness that he left no room for anyone to differ with him. His incessant lobbying and the sheer volume of his arguments left no breathing space, and Clayton was suffocating. There hadn't been one day since Brandt had become firmly entrenched at the church that Clayton wasn't fighting wildfires on four or five fronts that seemed to have been ignited and fanned by the man. Despite biblical commands to forgive and avoid being judgmental, he occasionally envisaged Brandt as a hundred-eyed Argus bent on destroying him. God forgive him, but he couldn't escape such thoughts.

The time at JubiLatte exceeded Clayton's worst fears. After fifteen minutes of friendly chitchat, Brandt hinted at his agenda.

"Pastor, how long have you been in Springdale?" It was clearly a rhetorical question.

"Since spring of '73. Twenty-three years. Why do you ask, Jack?"

"That's a long time. You're comfortable here, aren't you?"

"Yes, Joyce loved it here. I'm very thankful for our town and our congregation."

"You're an exception, you know. Most pastorates last less than six years."

"Yes, I know. But there are no rules for how long a minister should remain with a church. Two years, twenty years. I believe God has different plans for every congregation."

"Sometimes new blood and renewed enthusiasm are helpful. Don't you think so?"

"We must balance enthusiasm with maturity and experience."

"That's true, as long as that maturity has kept up with the times. Even a mature Jonathan Edwards wouldn't stand a chance in late twentieth-century ministry."

"I pray that we meet the needs of our congregation, Jack. Do you think we are failing to keep up with the times?"

"I think you've done a wonderful job in Springdale, Pastor, but there's always room for improvement."

"No person or system is perfect. We have a broad range of needs in our church. It's difficult to meet them all."

"We should always review our priorities."

"I try to do that, Jack. Thank you."

"And I will try to help you."

Clayton stared at the wonderful-terrible man sitting across from him. Brandt wasn't making small talk; he was subtly outlining an agenda. If he thought enough about something to mention it, it was already part of his action plan. And that meant there was already some movement afoot to remove him from the pastorate. Brandt was surely soliciting support from key people, one-on-one. How did one counteract such tactics?

They parted with smiles painted on their faces and blessings flowing off their tongues, both knowing that the first salvo of a major battle had been fired.

With Brandt's time bomb ticking away, Clayton found it difficult to shift his focus and worry to Ellie. He envisaged Jack having coffee with someone at that moment, arguing that an almost-sixty-year-old man wasn't qualified to lead a family-oriented congregation. He was suddenly tired and not up to a life-or-death struggle with Brandt.

A meeting about Ellie was the last thing he needed. It was always the same thing: a teacher had tried to get her to do something, and Rock-of-Gibraltar Ellie had refused.

None of the other kids had given him any trouble. Clay, Jr., Dan, and Linda had done what was expected with no arguments. Ellie, on the other hand, was born shaking her head no. She had been a colicky baby who bawled and fussed from the minute she opened her eyes. Every night he and Joyce took turns holding and patting her, pacing the floor, sitting in his recliner or Joyce's rocking chair. Usually it did little good, and they'd end up letting her cry herself to sleep. After a year and a half the colic finally disappeared but left a residue of stubbornness and independence. It was as though his little girl was born claiming veto power over decisions that involved her, and when she cast her vote, no power on earth could change her mind.

As he waited at the school for the teachers, he recalled the recliner episode of several months ago. Although he had said he would take care of the Pepsi can, he suspected she'd noticed he forgot when he left in a hurry. Now a white water ring marked the spot where condensation had damaged the varnish. He'd refinish the end table someday. On the other hand, the water ring might serve to remind her of her disobedience. Then again, maybe not. Ellie was Ellie.

THE MEETING WAS NOT as bad as Clayton expected, just a routine concern from the teachers that Ellie wasn't living up to her potential. She was getting her usual A in English, but in all her other classes she hovered around C minus. At that rate she would pass and graduate next year, but her teachers were frustrated, convinced she could do much better. Mrs. Moreno, her counselor, warned that a GPA of 2.2 wouldn't get her into much more than a community college.

Mr. Wicker, her math teacher, had the most to say. "Dr. Loverage, your daughter is one of the most focused pupils I've had in twenty-five years. She can do anything she sets her mind to. . . . Let me show you some of her recent tests. I don't grade on a curve. Taught math long enough to know what to expect from my students. A score of 90–100 gets an A, 80–89 a B, 70–79 a C, and so on."

He placed a test paper on the table so that all three could view it and pulled a yellow pencil from behind his ear. "Look at this. Twenty problems, each worth five points. Ellen finishes the first fourteen and quits. She does nothing on the last six. Sits there, fiddles with her pencil, doodles, daydreams. She gets all fourteen right and earns a seventy, a low C.

"Now look at this one." He laid a second test paper on the table. "Ten questions, worth ten points each, but I add a difficult extra-credit problem at the end worth another ten. Ellen finishes the last six, the harder ones, and then works the extra-credit problem. I'm watching her. With about fifteen minutes left she just quits and stares out the window. She gets her usual seventy."

"That's Ellie," Clayton said. "I hope you don't think you've failed her, because I don't blame the teachers or the school system for what's going on."

"Do you have any idea why she does it?" the teacher asked.

"I think she delights in not meeting others' expectations," said Clayton. "She gets C's because everyone expects her to get A's. She needs to prove something by ignoring everyone's wishes and feelings and catering to her own. I've watched her do that since she was two years old."

When he found out that Ellie wasn't in trouble, his mind wandered, drifting back to his talk with Brandt. He half-listened while Mrs. Moreno suggested heart-to-heart talks, psychologists, extra jobs, groundings, and incentives. But she didn't understand: Ellie couldn't be bought, convinced, reprogrammed, or coerced. He'd have more success rearranging the Great Lakes.

Clayton left the conference feeling agitated but relieved. Ellie wasn't in big trouble, just the usual. In a perverse way he was pleased that she could deliberately get the grades she wanted. He wondered if she could get exactly ninety-fives if she set her mind to it.

THREE

It was almost midnight as Jack Brandt drove his usual patrol around Springdale. Today his shift ran from six in the evening until two in the morning. At 9:55 he stopped by Jubi-Latte for his usual just-before-closing cappuccino; now he circled up First Street, out to where Bull Creek Road took off to the south, back into town, past the Circle K next to the interstate, up and down the numbered streets to Eleventh, back and forth on the tree streets to Elm, over to the industrial park, and out Highway 22 past the access road to Braxton Reservoir and Kingswood Country Club. Nothing much ever happened. He was fortunate to be in a town with a low crime rate, and he hoped to keep it that way.

The patrol took about twenty-one minutes, and he'd driven it so often he could spot anything unusual. He knew what time Luella Ricci shuffled down her driveway to retrieve her morning newspaper, which days Ruth Arnold took her afternoon kindergarten class on a walk, the cars he'd find leaving The Ale Keg when it closed at two. Almost everyone's car and many of the license plates he knew by heart, and he routinely checked unfamiliar cars at the Circle K.

Some of Jack's best thinking was done on patrol. He could concentrate on his work, missing nothing, while at the same time reviewing what was happening at home and church. He was thankful God had given him that kind of mind. Tonight all he could think about was Springdale Church and his meeting that afternoon with Clayton Loverage.

When he and Shirley arrived from Fort Collins eleven years ago, they'd found what looked like a thriving, Bible-based church. Membership was exceptionally large for a town the size of Springdale, the youth program was vigorous, and the budget was substantial and stable. He and Shirley had immediately poured themselves into the life of the church to make it even more dynamic.

It hadn't taken long, however, to see that the church's most glaring deficiencies centered around its senior pastor, Clayton Loverage. No one questioned that the man was an effective leader and an excellent communicator, but like most older seminarians, he was incapable of adapting to the times. The adage about old dogs and new tricks was coined with him in mind.

From what others said, Loverage had resisted computers, and the battle to modernize the sanctuary with a console-controlled sound system and overhead spotlights had lasted five years before he gave in. Now he hung on to the old hymns as though they were composed by the apostles. As the years slipped by, the pastor slipped further behind the times until he had become an anachronism.

Although on the surface Loverage seemed personable and outgoing, he was as cold as Antarctica, shunning all attempts at friendship. Meeting with him one-on-one had never gone well. He claimed to be open-minded, but changing his mind on an issue was like bending an I-beam. Furthermore, his self-proclaimed expertise in family relations was a charade; his own daughter was out of control and manipulated him like a pull toy. And it was no surprise. Jack recalled that there had been a scene soon after their arrival, when the little girl had behaved very rudely toward his wife, and the pastor hadn't even made his daughter apologize.

As might be predicted, the church was stalled in the doldrums. Attendance was down, and members were leaving for newer, more modern churches on the outskirts of Springdale and nearby Longwood. Giving was down, and the youth program was declining. These were the first symptoms of a fatal illness, and Jack felt led to do something about it.

What was happening to Springdale Church was the concern of many others, kindred spirits not confined by established margins, not afraid to try something new. A group of them had been meeting for almost three years, praying for Loverage and the church, sharing what an ideal church might look like, even reviewing names of dynamic young men to lead Springdale Church into the twenty-first century. His group was not interested in a power play, but only in advancing the Kingdom of God. They had wrested a few changes out of Loverage, but those were too few and too slow in coming.

During their last meeting, at the home of Bill and Susan McAfee, the group had decided to act decisively. Vickie Unger, a young mother, broke the ice.

"We've been meeting for almost three years now. I think it's time we approached Dr. Loverage about leaving. It's either that, or Mark and I will start driving to the new Bible church in Longwood."

"Just demand he resign?" said Steve Benchley. Steve taught second grade, and he and his wife, Debbie, had moved to Springdale in the summer of '93. The whole group knew that *demand* and *resign* were exactly what Vickie meant. As soon as the words were mentioned, it was as though a dam had broken. They all wanted to talk at once.

"We've already talked to him about getting a young associate pastor, and nothing's happened."

"Nothing will happen unless we make it happen."

"We meet, and talk, and pray . . . we're together on this . . . we know what's got to happen."

"But we're not an official group."

"We might as well be; we've been together three years."

"This is the only group in the church where everyone agrees."

"We can go on praying forever, but sometimes God uses those who pray to carry out His work."

"Maybe one of us could meet with him . . . speak for the whole group."

"Then, if he still refused to listen, we'd all meet with him."

"We should pray about this some more."

"We don't want a church fight."

"Sometimes there has to be pain to have growth."

"Let's wait a month."

"We can't wait any longer. One of us could at least talk with him."

"Who knows him best?"

"Jack, you've been here over ten years. You know him pretty well. Do you think you could say something?"

"Well, maybe Shirley and I . . ." He knew they'd reject that.

"One-on-one would be better. You're good at that."

"Don't give an ultimatum, Jack. Just mention something about . . . well, about retirement. He's almost sixty. Maybe he's been thinking about it and will jump at the suggestion."

"Some retirement community would jump at the chance to get a big name like Loverage."

"I think he wants a fatter retirement package."

Jack had let the talking run its course, making no effort to organize or control them, as long as they were heading in the right direction. As they talked, both their conviction and enthusiasm grew. He knew they would come back to him. He was the logical person to speak with Loverage.

That afternoon he'd finally had his opportunity. It hadn't been easy. When he told Loverage that most pastors stayed at a church for less than six years, the man turned expressionless. Like a marble bust of Caesar, his face betrayed nothing, but Jack knew from the way the pastor answered that the message had hit home.

"God doesn't set term limits for pastors," he had replied pointedly, "and I expect to remain at Springdale Church until I retire." *That* was the problem! But retirement was still six years off, and in the meantime the church would continue to weaken and lose ground.

Loverage still had a lot of backing, especially among the older generation. Those people should have their say, of course, and it was important to provide something for them, but almost by definition, they were not the future of the church.

He didn't want to hurt Clayton. The pastor was a good man, but he was coasting to his retirement on the momentum of his success in the seventies and eighties. In his mind, Jack likened the pastor to an old horse that had pulled his load up a hill and now was sauntering toward the barn, his mind filled with visions of hay, carrots, and sugar lumps. The old steed wore blinders, and couldn't see a radical new world that had sprung up around him. Even if he could see it, he probably wouldn't know how to react.

But Jack Brandt couldn't stand idle and watch his church fail. It was the same pattern he'd noticed with Walter Logan back in Fort Collins. This time, in Springdale, he determined to do something about it. His recent talk with Loverage was a start, but if nothing came of it, he'd have to apply more pressure.

FOUR

Maria Villanueva rode in the backseat of her own car, bracing her feet against the floor, gripping her youngest son's arm. Beside her, Osvaldo sat hunched over, biting his lip and staring at the speedometer. Eighty-five, ninety, ninety-five. Ramon, an older son, rocketed down the interstate, ignoring the blackness of the night and the ice warnings. He had grabbed her keys and planted himself in the driver's seat, and she could do nothing but let him drive. Raphael sat next to him, feet on the dashboard, opening cans of beer for himself and his brother.

Although Ramon had been in two wrecks already in his young life, he had learned nothing. Even when his brother Raul was killed in an accident, Ramon refused to slow down.

"Ramon, please. The roads are slippery," Maria pleaded, knowing it would do no good. She hoped a highway patrolman would stop him.

"Mama, you said you were in a hurry to get to Illinois. I'm just trying to help."

"You could help more by slowing down. This is not a

video arcade game." She felt the car accelerate, his message that he was in control.

"Give Mama a beer, Raphael. She needs something to calm her down."

Why do they say that? They know I haven't had a drink in ten years. She ignored them and stared out the window. Red taillights dappled the darkness ahead of them, but they were catching and passing everything, just as they had done for the last three hours.

For many months before they left Socorro, Maria had prayed that God would help her move from New Mexico. She had been there all her life, and she wanted to get away, far from all the people and places that had treated her badly. Being a waitress hadn't earned enough to cover rent and keep food on the table, but she didn't know how to do anything else. She'd be stuck waiting on tables until her skin shriveled and her teeth rotted.

About a year earlier her cousin Pedro, a successful businessman in St. Louis, had visited his New Mexico relatives. She had always enjoyed talking with Pedro because he listened and took her seriously. When she said she would like to get out of New Mexico, he told her there was a job waiting in Illinois if she ever decided to come. She couldn't remember what business he was in. Some kind of manufacturing; it didn't make any difference. If she didn't go, she'd regret it the rest of her life. So she had prayed and saved her money. Two months ago she'd bought Miguel Garza's old Chevrolet for $300. She was sure that was an answer to prayer. Miguel said it would get her to Illinois if she were careful.

They had left Socorro later than she had planned, heading north on the interstate before turning east in Albuquerque. Now they were in the Texas panhandle. Behind them a huge February sun slid below the horizon, leaving a tarry black sky that hid the stars. Yesterday a storm had descended on the Southwest, depositing two inches of snow that was at the mercy of a chilly, swirling wind. Maria wondered why it couldn't have waited a few more days. Now as they tore down the interstate, she pictured herself in a coffin-shaped luge.

They were approaching an interchange when it happened —a terrible clanking, like boys running iron rods across a wrought-iron fence. Ramon skillfully controlled the car, stopping it on the gravelly shoulder of the highway.

He turned and glared at her. "Mama, see what you've done? You buy a cheap car and it breaks down. Now we're stuck in the middle of the desert."

"You drive too fast," she said softly. She didn't want a confrontation.

She had heard that clanking sound before. The car had thrown a rod, whatever that was, and was totaled. She had only $150 to buy gas and food until they reached Illinois. Car repairs weren't in her budget.

Through the wind, they trudged back to the interchange, a cluster of two gas stations, a twenty-four-hour restaurant that catered to truckers, and a sleazy motel. Ramon said he'd try to get the car fixed, and he grabbed her purse and left with Raphael. She and Osvaldo wandered penniless into the warmth of a convenience store.

An hour later Raphael hurried into the store and whispered that the car was fixed, but they had to hurry. Outside Ramon sat at the wheel of a 1988 Honda.

"Sorry I can't do better than this, Mama. Hurry, get in."

"No. I don't ride in stolen cars."

"Hurry, Mama, don't argue with me!"

"No. Take the car back."

"If you don't get in, we'll leave." He meant it for a threat; she hoped it was a promise.

"Leave, then. But give me my money."

"It's gas money, Mama. You said so yourself." He flung the purse back at her but kept her wallet. "We'll race you to Springdale. That's where you're going, isn't it, Mama?"

"Why don't you just go back to Socorro!"

They hadn't heard her, but it was just as well. The Honda

bolted onto the on-ramp of eastbound I-40 and disappeared with every cent she owned.

MARIA AND OSVALDO would hitchhike to Springdale. She had never done it, too dangerous, but what other choice did they have? The man at the convenience store said they couldn't hang out there any longer. She would never go back to Socorro; all her hope lay ahead in Illinois. She stayed near the pumps at the Texaco station, watching for drivers who looked nonthreatening. She asked an older man and a young couple for a ride, but they ignored her and drove off. When a young man said he'd take them a little way, Maria accepted his offer. A little progress was better than standing around the station. He took them about twenty miles before turning off the freeway. It was as far as he could go, he said. It was almost ten, and he was supposed to be home. There was nothing at the interchange—no gas station, no store, no motel. It was dark, and a cold wind moaned through the roadside tumbleweeds. Thanking him, she and Osvaldo headed down the on-ramp to take their place beside the freeway.

Now she was stuck in a frozen, black desert in Texas without a penny. *God, do You call this an answer to prayer? Why aren't You taking care of Your children?* Had she misunderstood what God had wanted her to do? Had she just followed some silly whim, some mirage that would soon vaporize? She was furious with Ramon. He had ruined her car and taken her money. She wished he'd stayed in Socorro; he was nothing but trouble. But she was angry with God, too. He shouldn't have let her come, or He should have kept her car running. Now she and Osvaldo were going to freeze to death.

Before they reached the roadway, she was trembling. Her wool sweater might as well have been lace, and her scarf and gloves were threadbare. Her legs were bare and her tennis shoes so flimsy she could feel the pebbles under her feet. Osvaldo wore only a summer windbreaker and clenched his teeth to keep them from chattering.

God, I don't even know how to hitchhike. She waited for the cars to come, and then stepped out a little to hold out her arm. But they came so fast, it was dark, and she was only a blur. Maybe she'd do what girls did in the movies and lift her skirt a little. No, she'd rather die. But Osvaldo was freezing. He needed to be inside.

The cars and trucks passed like bullets, mocking her with the droning *eeee-yow* of their approaching and speeding by. Soon her feet and legs were so numb they felt like croquet mallets, and she could hardly lift her arm to beckon. Osvaldo, looking frightened, tried his luck. A few vehicles slowed down momentarily before racing on into the darkness. Maria thought about lying down in the ditch off the side of the highway and curling up around Osvaldo so they could get some sleep. In the morning they might get a ride.

O God, I am so cold my arms and legs have forgotten how to move. Please, God, make someone stop. Send one of Your angels to us, God. Save Osvaldo. He is a good boy. God, I want to be warm. I want a nice, warm cup of hot chocolate.

A truck was coming. Maria stepped clumsily onto the asphalt to get into the beam of his headlights and held both arms as high as she could lift them. In a split second of eye contact she saw him hesitate. The brakes screeched and dust rose from the gravelly shoulder as the driver braked and halted the huge truck. She tried to run, but her feet had no feeling, and she fell. Osvaldo helped her, and they both limped toward the passenger door that the driver pushed open for them. She looked up at the driver, but couldn't speak.

"Lady, you'd better get in here. This ain't no night to be hitchin' rides on the interstate."

She couldn't climb, couldn't move another step. Her breath was gone, her lips paralyzed. She stared at him blankly.

"Here, let me help you." He got out and circled the cab to help them. Osvaldo was almost in by the time he reached them.

"You're next, lady."

All she could do was stare at him. He had a big grin on his face that she couldn't trust. She had seen it before, too many times.

"Lady, you can't stand here all night. I gotta get movin'. I'll help you in."

Slinging her over his shoulder like a Raggedy Ann doll, he hoisted himself onto the running board, plopped her into the seat next to Osvaldo, and slammed their door.

The warmth from the heater welcomed and caressed her. She breathed it, rubbed it into her fingers, wriggled it into her toes. It tasted like hot chocolate with marshmallows. As feeling returned, she began to cry. She hadn't realized how scared she'd been. Now, for a while, she and Osvaldo were safe, at least from the cold.

Finally Maria relaxed enough to look over at their rescuer. He was in his early forties, thin and wiry. A blue-and-white bandanna was tied across his forehead, and a graying ponytail dangled on the back of his neck. Skinny arms covered with tattoos emerged from a sleeveless leather vest. A skull-and-crossbones tattoo on his cheek emerged through three or four days' growth of whiskers. A can of Pepsi dangled from a plastic cup holder hanging from his window.

God, I prayed for an angel, and You send me a Hell's Angel. But thank You for the warmth, and keep Osvaldo and me safe from this man.

"What's your name?" the man asked gruffly.

"Maria," she answered, "and his name is—"

"He can talk. What's your name, boy?"

"Osvaldo," her son said softly. "What's yours?"

"Spike."

"You have a nice truck, Mr. Spike," said Osvaldo. "Thank you for picking us up."

"Mr. Spike!" The man swore good-naturedly. "Ain't nobody called me that before." He looked at Maria and nodded toward the thermos that rolled on the floor among soiled newspapers and girlie magazines. "Want some coffee? Got it in

44

Phoenix this morning, but it's still warm. You can use the cap."

The coffee tasted stale and bitter with age, but to Maria its warmth felt like steaming Christmas cider. Osvaldo tasted it and made a face.

"What's the matter, Osvaldo, can't take hard liquor?" Spike reached under his seat and pulled out a Pepsi. "Here, try this."

"Thank you, Mr. Spike."

"Prefer beer, but learned a long time ago it don't mix with drivin' trucks. How'd you end up on the side of the interstate?"

Maria told him everything—Ramon and Raphael, the car, her new job. She even told him she had no money, not one cent. If he was going to rape or kill her, it didn't matter what he knew. Maybe he had a soft spot in his heart.

"So you have no money and you're going to Springdale where your cousin has a job waiting for you? Sounds like you're hallucinating."

"He told me to come," she replied.

"Okay, tell you what. I'm goin' to St. Louis, then on up to Chicago and Milwaukee, and the freeway passes close to Springdale. I'll let you off at the interchange. You don't have to worry about no more rides from here to Illinois. Are you up to riding straight through?"

"Yes. You're the driver." She hesitated. "Don't you need to sleep?"

"I might stop at a rest stop near Oklahoma City or Tulsa and sleep a bit in the truck. You can sleep too if I don't snore too loud."

The rest of the way to Springdale was an education for Maria and Osvaldo, especially Osvaldo. Osvaldo sat wide-eyed and openmouthed, hearing an anthology of stories that Maria had sheltered him from for years, as Spike took advantage of his captive cabmates. The truck driver talked about everything—brothels in New Orleans, combat in Vietnam, gambling on horses in Santa Fe and dogs in Corpus Christi. Nothing was off-limits. Half of his stories were sensual; all of them were liberally seasoned with swear words.

Maria figured he'd forgotten his passengers were a woman and her teenage son and not motorcycle buddies, but she let him ramble, too grateful for the ride to complain. She would explain some things to Osvaldo later.

Three times only they stopped at convenience stores for food. Spike's capacity for holding urine seemed infinite, and Maria was wise enough to drink very little. Osvaldo learned to do the same after having his eyes nearly pushed out of their sockets from his first Pepsi and an expanding bladder. Spike paid for everything.

"I haven't had so much fun in years," he assured them. "I'll hafta get a girlfriend again to ride with me, so I'll have someone to talk to."

They arrived at the Springdale interchange at ten in the morning on February 16. Spike stopped just before the off-ramp, and they climbed out. Maria thanked him sincerely. He gave her a twenty-dollar bill, saying it was ungentlemanly to leave a lady there with no money. Osvaldo called him Mr. Spike and shook his hand. Then the trucker drove away, waving and honking his horn, heading north toward Chicago and Milwaukee.

Despite all his bawdy stories and earthy language, Maria had been able to relax. She thought how tense she would have been if they'd ridden with Ramon and Raphael. Her own sons! How could they have turned out like this? She hoped they had decided to return to Socorro.

It was cold and sunny as they walked the mile into town. They passed a concrete sign that introduced Springdale to the world.

SPRINGDALE, ILLINOIS FRIENDLY TOWN, U.S.A.	
POPULATION	7351
FOUNDED	1833
ELEVATION	542
TOTAL	9726

At a Circle K she asked directions to Megatronics, where her cousin had said a job was waiting. Four more blocks down First Street toward town, turn left at Giant Foods onto Locust, then three blocks. They couldn't miss it.

Sitting in the parking lot at Megatronics in a nearly new Taurus were Ramon and Raphael. They wore new, warm jackets, and each held a can of beer.

"Mama, you're late." Ramon tossed her wallet with her driver's license and credit cards at her. "Here, you'll need this to cash your payroll checks."

MARIA SAT WITH Osvaldo in the reception room of the Springdale division of Megatronics. The receptionist said that Mr. Platt would see her in a few minutes. Maria could see his door with the gold plate on it. Omar Platt, Manager. His blurry silhouette moved behind the frosted glass windows. Her cousin had made the job sound so definite. Come anytime in the next month, he had said; the job will be waiting for you. What if this Mr. Platt had never heard of her? What if there was no job? She'd be stranded in Illinois, broke and without a car.

At last the door opened and a short, balding man with a tiny line of mustache approached her.

Maria stood up nervously. He looked friendly, but she couldn't be sure.

"Good morning, Mrs. Villanueva."

She was reassured when he held out his hand to greet her.

"And I assume this is your son."

"Yes, this is Osvaldo. He is sixteen."

"I hope you had a good trip from New Mexico."

"Pretty good," she said. "We just got here a few minutes ago. Did Pedro call you? He's my cousin."

"Yes, I talked with Pete, Mrs. Villanueva. We have a position open for you. I hope you don't mind assembly work."

"Anything is fine. Do I start today?"

"There are several things to take care of first." He motioned her to sit down, and he sat across from her. "Pete said you might need a place to stay, at least temporarily."

"I will find something."

"There's a two-room house near the depot that you can rent. It has a large kitchen–living room area and a bedroom with a bathroom. You can have it for $200 a month, unfurnished. That is very reasonable for Springdale."

"Two rooms is enough. I will take it, but I can't pay rent yet." Two rooms were enough for her and Osvaldo. She hoped Ramon and Raphael would find a place of their own.

Mr. Platt gave her an envelope with a key in it—*14 Depot St.* was scrawled on the outside—and said Pete would take care of the first month's rent.

"Your beginning pay is $11 an hour. After one month, if all goes well, it will increase to $11.50. After six months, $12. It that all right?"

It was wonderful. The most she'd ever made in New Mexico was $8.25. Full medical and dental benefits for her and Osvaldo would begin after sixty days. She'd never had benefits before.

Mr. Platt gave her forms to fill out and took her on a tour of the plant. The assembly room was large, brightly lit, and very clean. Rows of people, mostly women, sat on stools or stood next to a slow-moving conveyor belt. Music played softly in the background, occasionally interrupted by a voice on the intercom. He said she would start out by supplying parts to the assembly line, and later she could learn to assemble the electronic components.

"Do you have any questions, Mrs. Villanueva?"

"No. Everything is fine." Vacations, sick leave, nothing made any difference, as long as she had a job. "What time should I be here in the morning?"

"This is Thursday. Why don't you start on Monday? That will give you a few days to get settled. Our hours are seven to four. Be here about five minutes early. Is there anything else I can do for you?"

"No." She wanted to say everything was wonderful. Pedro had come through on his promise. She would have to phone him in St. Louis to say thank you.

Mr. Platt dismissed himself, saying he was honored to have a relative of Pete's at Megatronics. "And Osvaldo," he added, "you'd probably like to check in at the high school. When you leave by the front gate, it's three blocks to the right."

Maria painstakingly filled out the forms and gave them to the receptionist. When they left, Ramon and Raphael were waiting in the parking lot.

Yes, everything was wonderful, except for them. They would never change. There were too many years of arrogance and rudeness, of run-ins with the police, of jail time. Something terrible was going to happen to them someday.

Maria told them she was walking to the school to register Osvaldo, but she didn't mention the house. She wanted to get there first so she could claim the bedroom.

It took two hours to enroll Osvaldo at Springdale High School. He was to start the next morning with a battery of tests. The counselor said she would have his records faxed from Socorro, but she was sure he'd be behind the schools in Illinois. He would have to work hard to catch up. He might even need a tutor.

When they left the school, Maria was relieved not to see Ramon and Raphael. *They've probably gone to St. Louis. That's where the action is. They can't waste their time in Springdale. We'll get settled into the house. It will be good to lie down and rest . . . even if I must lie on the floor.*

That evening they found a free dining room that was sponsored by Bethel Temple. Since Maria had to make her twenty dollars last until her first paycheck, at least they wouldn't have to spend money on meals. She was feeling weak and Osvaldo looked exhausted, although he never complained. At the dining room they met Mr. Santori, who was the pastor, and several volunteers. By the time they left, they had two old sleeping bags, a cart full of groceries, and the promise that someone would come by to take them on errands the next day.

Back at the house she and Osvaldo sat on their sleeping bags and leaned against the wall. She began to weep softly.

"Mama, what's wrong?"

"Nothing, Ossie. Everything's right."

"Why are you crying?"

"I'm happy, Ossie. This was the most wonderful day of my life since I was a child."

Mr. Spike, her new job, a good house with heat, the free dinner, new friends—God watched over His children, and sometimes He even sent His angels.

The next few days she kept an eye out for the blue Taurus the boys were driving. It was only a matter of time until they came back to Springdale. As predictable as the thunderstorms that swept over Socorro, they would always return to make her life miserable.

FIVE

As the moon regulated the tides, so Father's schedule governed the times for breakfast and dinner. At 7:00 A.M. and 6:00 P.M. he expected the table to be set, the meal prepared, and his coffee freshly brewed. On the first of every month he conducted his synchronizing ceremony, making one- or two-minute adjustments to align every timepiece in the house with his watch. Behind his back this fetish had become a family joke, with even Linda and Clay, Jr. using terms such as Mr. Greenwich and Loverage Mean Time, and speculating about his making adjustments to the atomic clock. Ellen, however, appreciated this extreme punctuality, because she could depend on his being out of the house by 7:23 every weekday morning and leaving for church by 6:44 most evenings. She also had a good idea when he'd return.

She and Father usually ate dinner in silence, as though they spoke different languages. After Mom died he'd stopped talking about what was happening at church, and he'd never been interested in the books she was reading. Occasionally they visited safe areas, such as how Clay, Jr., Dan, and Linda were doing, but that involved the mere passing of information, never opinions or feelings. Sometimes, out of necessity, they'd bring up household matters. The furnace man was coming Tuesday afternoon at 4:00, he'd say; make sure you're home. He used to tell her what he wanted for dinner, but lately that was left to her discretion. Once he asked if she'd like to accompany him to a marriage seminar he was leading in Omaha, but she declined. A weekend at home by herself was a mini-vacation she couldn't turn down.

That evening Ellen knew Father would be obliged to say something about the conference with Wicker and Moreno. A decent dinner would help his mood, but she didn't want to heat up leftover tuna casserole again. Sandwiches were easy, and, although he might ask how she made them, he never complained.

On one side of giant sesame seed buns she spread garlic butter; on the other side, a thin layer of Aunt Laura's raspberry chutney. Over these she added strata of finely shredded red cabbage with a trace of chopped cilantro in ranch dressing, sparse sprinklings of cinnamon and nutmeg, two slices of Gruyère cheese, and quarter-inch slabs of turkey breast. She wrapped them loosely in Saran wrap and nuked them in the microwave for thirteen seconds to soften the cheese. On name tags she printed: *Mount Ararat Delights. Recipe from Anatolia, circa 1577.*

At 5:50 she heated frozen succotash, his favorite vegetable dish, and poured applesauce into a bowl. She set the large dining room table for two, using laminated place mats with scenes of steepled New England churches and green plastic napkin rings with cow decals on them. To pass Father's inspection, knives and spoons had to be on the right side of the plate, perpendicular to the edge of the table, parallel to each other, with the knives' blades turned inward. Forks lay to the left, next to the napkins. Her glass and Father's coffee mug sat above the knives, with small fruit bowls above the forks. She was tempted to turn her own knife blade outward, but Father would notice. It wasn't worth the hassle.

As she set the table, she thought about the two of them just sitting there, eating together for fifteen minutes, anxious to go their separate ways. They were like two oscillating circles, touching but not part of each other. She didn't mind the quick, silent dinners, because then there was less chance for his interminable advice and righteous judgments. She'd already heard his entire tape; now everything was a rerun.

Nevertheless, she knew that their silences weren't good—two people, night after night, saying so little. But she didn't know how to fix it, or whether she wanted it fixed. Maybe their minds just didn't fit together, like two oddly shaped jigsaw puzzle pieces. Father "fit" with Clay, Jr., Dan, and Linda. Why was she so different?

She wondered what Father thought about these tedious evening meals. During the last year he'd seemed more businesslike than unhappy, finishing his meal between 6:14 and 6:17 and immediately returning to his study. Sometimes he'd tell her the meal was good, but most of the time he'd wipe his hands on his napkin, fold it on its creases, place it on the left side of his plate, and stand up to say something like, "Well, back to work. Got a lot to do." Did it bother him that father and daughter ate in silence?

She couldn't blame him entirely for their lack of conversation. He used to question her about school, or church, and occasionally bring up sermon topics or political issues. He probably blamed her that they hadn't gotten anywhere, but he had to share the blame. He didn't want to *know* her; he only wanted to *change* her, to discover her wrong thinking and then set her straight. She didn't want to be a little lump of clay on his potter's wheel. Trim a little here, press there, shape here, flare there, inscribe here. After firing, he could present a miniature Clayton Loverage to the world. Ellen didn't want to be Clayton Loverage, or a miniature of anything. It was easier not to respond at all.

She wondered if he were truly happy. Before Mom had died, Ellen had never questioned Father's happiness or her own. She clearly recalled the lively mealtimes when all the kids were home. Even now, when they came home for visits, there was a constant stream of chatter. Clay, Jr., Dan, and Linda were smart and outgoing, and dinner discussions were spirited. The Bible, religion, politics, sports, school—anything was fair game. They laughed, joked, teased, even argued good-naturedly until Father issued his final judgment on the matter and the conversation shifted to another topic.

After the others had left home, Ellen used to discuss things with Father, but even then their dialogue was always strained. After Father made one of his final pronouncements, she would still speak up and disagree with him or bring up a related question. He considered her reluctance to drop a subject a sign of rebellion.

"Ellie!" he'd say, raising his voice on the end of her name.

"Yes, Father?"

"Don't argue with me. It's right here in the Scriptures." He'd reach behind him and grab his Bible off the buffet as though it were a club.

"Father, I know what it says, but I don't think one sentence covers all the possibilities."

Those sharp *Ellie's* and barrages of Bible verses intimidated her. How dared she argue with God? Father was a pastor. He'd gone to seminary. People flocked to Springdale Church to learn from him, and he traveled all over the country giving seminars. But as she got older, she began to see their discussions as one-way streets, and she was always going against the arrows.

It was easier to say nothing, to find her own streets and let him go motoring off wherever he wished. Father knew the Bible so well that she couldn't discuss anything with him without ducking and fending off a hundred other verses he'd hurl at her. She wished he'd stop the verses and just talk, really talk, not about issues, but about . . . well, about life, about fishing with Uncle Claude, high school, meeting Mom, living in Germany, or just about fooling around when he was young.

When Father was really low, he sighed a lot, filling his lungs deeply and slowly, then audibly releasing his breath. Sometimes she could hear him through the walls of his study. The sigh seemed to have a question mark after it, like "sigh-h-h-h?", as though he were asking whether it was all worth it. Once she'd tried to get him to talk.

"You sound tired, Father. Are you all right?"

"Of course, Ellie. Why do you ask?"

"That was such a big sigh. I thought maybe—"

"I'm doing fine, Ellie. Just a little tired." That evening he'd left the table quickly, passing on her freshly baked French apple pie.

She knew he must still miss Mom. They'd been devoted to each other for almost forty years. Now he was alone, and there was no one to share his thoughts, no one to sleep with. Her touch was missing. Compared to Mom's creative, tasty meals, her own were dishwater and sawdust. Outside of home Father had the church and his seminars to keep him going, but at home he had nothing, not even his daughter. No wonder the most exciting room in the house for him was his study.

At 5:58 she put Father's favorite CD into the stereo and adjusted the volume. The melody sounded like "Great Is Thy Faithfulness," but she wasn't too sure about old hymns. If hymns weren't playing at dinnertime, Father couldn't lift his fork. At 5:59 the coffee finished perking, and she filled his favorite mug. He liked his coffee hot out of the pot, not standing for five minutes. As the living room clock cuckooed six, Father's study door opened and he emerged to sit in his captain's chair at the head of the table.

Father always said grace, so she bowed her head, but she didn't close her eyes. Twice each day, seven hundred times a year, Father said almost the same thing. Was it a prayer, or did he just press the button on his tape recorder?

"Our gracious Father in heaven," he intoned, "thank You

for this food and the hands that have so lovingly prepared it. Thank You for Your bountiful blessings and tender care. Teach us to love You and to obey Your commands. Give us wisdom and courage to seek and follow Your will for our lives. We ask this in Jesus' strong name. Amen."

Ellen whispered her expected amen. If she didn't, he'd ask whether she had laryngitis. She'd grown up saying amen after table grace, but it sounded better when the whole family was still living at home. Father and Mom sat at the ends of the table, Clay, Jr. and Dan on one side, Linda and she on the other. When Father finished with grace, like a family choir they'd echo his amen.

Clay, Jr. was sixteen and Dan fourteen when she was born. They seemed more like uncles than brothers. Linda was ten years older than she, always the big sister, preening her, showing her off. People teased her parents about Ellen's being an afterthought. She once overheard Father refer to her as a child of his old age, but he quickly added that she was a gift from God. Tonight he was probably trying to convince himself that was true.

Near the end of the meal, Father finally spoke up. "How's your math coming, Ellie?"

"Oh, about the same. You know how it is."

"You're not going to fail, are you?"

"No way. I'll get a C."

"You can do better than that."

"I know."

"Then, Ellie, why don't you?" He raised his eyebrows like old-fashioned window shades.

"Because I'm not into math. I don't like it."

"Ellie, you need to do your best in everything, even when you don't like it. We've discussed this before."

True, and she'd disagreed with him each time. "Father, the square root of 117 and the volume of a sphere don't do much for me, and I've never heard you mention those in a sermon.

The time I waste studying math can be used for something more productive."

"Such as?"

She wanted to ask him if theology was more productive than math. This was going to end in a quarrel like everything else. "Reading," she answered.

"Ellie, you can't make a living reading."

"No, but I like to read. Maybe I'll teach English someday."

"High school? College?"

"Maybe high school. Like Miss Merkle. I think she's neat. We should have a neighborhood barbecue sometime and invite her."

He gave her a look she'd never seen before, something between embarrassment and hurt. Father was friendly with all their other neighbors but, except for school conferences and a few neighborhood crises, seemed to avoid her English teacher. Whether deliberately or not, Father's fence functioned as a moat that discouraged friendly contact, and even Mom hadn't known her backyard neighbor very well.

Without saying a word, Father pushed back his chair and went into his study. Ellen finished her sandwich and applesauce before clearing the table. At least she wouldn't have to eat the succotash.

THE NEXT MORNING Clayton skipped breakfast at home and drove out Highway 22 to Piney's Diner. He needed time alone, away from the house and the church. Everything moved to the rhythmic ticks of Brandt's time bomb, and he had neither the know-how nor the will to disarm it. Now Ellie's stubbornness and careless academic effort were sure to add to his problems. In a small town, everyone knew who the good students were. If she'd just try her best, he'd back her 100 percent, but he had no room for deliberate mediocrity.

From the time she was a toddler, Ellie had been stubborn.

He'd learned that confronting her at church was a lose-lose situation. He might win a Pyrrhic victory in a minor battle, but there was so much damage control that it wasn't worth it.

He remembered one Sunday when she refused to stop reading a book she'd found in her kindergarten Sunday school class. Joyce was anxious to get home because she had a roast in the oven. First he told Ellie it was time to leave; then he informed her firmly; after that he demanded she leave; and finally he commanded her to get out of the chair, close her book, and get in the car. He might as well have been speaking Serbian, because she didn't budge a millimeter, just continued scanning the pages of her newly discovered treasure. Finally, under the watchful eyes of three Sunday school teachers, he pried her little fingers from the book, tucked her under his arm, and carted her out of the room, feeling as though he were carrying a gunnysack full of yowling, kicking raccoons.

Ellie never took part in church activities anymore. The only service she attended was on Sunday morning; she skipped the high school Sunday school class and all other youth activities. He could hear the hens cackling. "Why, he can't even get his daughter to attend youth group, and he has the nerve to set himself up as an expert on the family."

The day of her last spanking still haunted him. He couldn't remember what she had done, but it obviously called for punishment. He had taken her up to her bedroom and explained why he was going to spank her. She should have known better, he told her; after all, she was eight years old.

"Father, I'm not going to cry this time," she had said. Her aqua eyes, refracting through her Palomar lenses, pierced him. She was too young to say such a thing. "You told those people at the seminar that when you spank your child and she doesn't cry, it's time to stop spanking and to try something else. I don't want to be spanked anymore, so I'm not going to cry."

He turned her over his knees. He always spanked with his hand; it was more personal that way, because he felt pain along with his child. He gave her ten swats—no sound. Ten more, a little harder—not a whimper. The little girl's will contested against his. Ten more—nothing. He stopped counting. It felt as though he spanked for five minutes before he heard Joyce at the door.

"Clay, please." Joyce was crying. He was spanking Ellie and making his wife cry!

When he stopped, Ellie stood up straight and gave him a look he would never forget—frightened, defiant, triumphant. "There," she said, "now you can't spank me anymore."

He left Ellie's bedroom, pushed past Joyce, and fell exhausted on his own bed.

Since then, he had never seen Ellie cry. Sometimes he thought she was so deep into her own world, so intent on doing only what she preferred, that her feelings had been anesthetized. She seemed like an observer of the world, not a participant. She *read* about grief and joy, struggle and compassion, he knew, but they had little to do with her.

He had seen it when Joyce died. The evening before the memorial service, the family gathered at home and spent the evening reminiscing. Clay, Jr. and Linda related story after story, some of them humorous, most just things that had happened. He and Dan chimed in occasionally with special memories. Ellie sat listening, impassive, never saying a word or changing expression. Even when Clay, Jr. and Linda prodded her, asking her about her favorite memories of Mom, she responded by shaking her head and remaining silent. The laughter and the tears of the others didn't faze her.

At the memorial service she remained unmoved. Almost everyone shed a few tears, because Joyce was much respected and beloved, but Ellie was stoic, maintaining the sphinxlike countenance she'd worn the evening before and throughout her mother's illness. The memorial service, the ride to the cemetery, the graveside service, the reception at the church, the ride back to the house—always the same stolid, molded face, as though she were putting up with what was happening and couldn't wait for it to end.

At home, she'd gone straight to her room. She was tired, she said, and it was late. The next morning, she fixed breakfast for everyone as though nothing major had happened. Maybe that was what fiction did to a person. Reading about others' problems, fears, and emotions was vicarious living; it desensitized one to the real world. Maybe, the same way she knew a novel wasn't true, she thought life wasn't true, but merely a story, a fantasy. Literature was making her all eyes and ears and no heart.

As he left Piney's, Clayton went over their brief discussion from the previous evening. He had made a token effort to talk to her about grades, all the while knowing it was pointless, and she had responded in her predictable blasé way. He could do or say nothing, absolutely nothing, to change her. It was too late. He wouldn't put it past her to follow through on her promise to move out the day she was eighteen. Where would she go? She had no money. Maybe she'd be absorbed into the drug culture of Chicago or New York or San Francisco, but that didn't seem like her. Would she go to college? He had no answers. His only recourse was prayer.

At times like this he ached for Joyce. He could lean his head on her shoulder and tell her things weren't going well with Ellie. She'd understand. Now, without Joyce or Wally, there was no one in the world to empathize with his frustrations.

Joyce had always been more lenient than he toward Ellie. She didn't consider the child's grades important as long as she passed. "Don't worry about it, Clay. One of these days, she'll start doing real well. Some kids have a harder time adjusting to this world than others."

Sometimes Joyce's easygoing attitude bothered him, but for yesterday's talk with Ellie about grades, it would have worked best. Even when he didn't agree with his wife, her words calmed and reassured him. Last night she would have said, "Now, Clay, I'm sure Ellie's doing what she thinks best. And Ellie, we'll try harder on the next exam, won't we?" The whole event would have blown over as though it had never happened.

Joyce, Joyce, you were a good wife. I made the right choice; no one could have been better.

As he parked in his reserved spot in the church parking lot, his mind drifted off to their days at North Texas State. He'd met Joyce in his sophomore year at an InterVarsity Christmas party, and they married a year and a half later. It would have been forty years in June, and he still thanked God for her every day. Loving, hardworking, a good mother, an obedient wife—there was never a need to press the obedience issue—she was the perfect foil for him.

Joyce had been sensitive to his moods and always had a remedy for what was bothering him. Although somewhat shy and introverted, in the privacy of their home she was a wonderful mimic. She would suddenly slip into her imitation of Grandpa Mahler, Sally, Adele Ritchie, and even Police Chief Riley and soon have the whole family howling. One summer when the boys were home from college, she mimicked Shirley Brandt so perfectly that the whole family, even Ellie, ended up on the living room floor kicking their feet, holding their stomachs, and wiping gleeful tears from their eyes. Joyce wasn't mean-spirited and never said an unkind word about anyone, but she had that rare knack of pinpointing blind spots and idiosyncrasies, and making them acceptable, if not lovable.

Joyce had been insightful and sympathetic to the members of the churches he had led, often seeing and feeling things he missed completely. While he caught facts, Joyce intercepted emotions. Over the years, he'd trained himself to listen to her, for she had seldom been wrong about people. He missed her so much. Maybe Ellie would turn herself around, as Joyce had always claimed, but some kids never did and went on to ruin their lives. He didn't want that to happen to one of his children, and he was sure that Ellie was in danger.

He could hear Joyce saying, "But Clay, she's a good person. She hasn't gotten into any trouble with the law. She doesn't drink or do drugs, and she's not into sex. She's just different from the other children."

Yes, as different as kerosene and marmalade. He opened his car door to go to his office, but dreaded the thought of facing his long-time secretary, Sally Biggs. Bless her caring heart, the first thing she'd do was ask about the conference at the high school the day before. He wasn't in the mood to talk about it, so to avoid lying to her, or telling the truth, he circled out of the parking lot and drove to JubiLatte. His first meeting wasn't until ten o'clock. He'd read awhile and think some more before starting his day.

My God, why did You give me such a child?

LATE IN THE DAY, after a second contemplative trip to JubiLatte, he'd made up his mind. Yesterday's conference at school and his lack of success in talking to Ellie had finally tipped the scales. He found himself disqualified. He couldn't honestly stand up in front of a group of parents, look them in the eye, and pretend he had answers for every child. He'd preached a dozen sermons on not being a phony, and he wasn't going to be one now.

He buzzed Sally.

"Yes, Dr. Loverage?"

"Will you come into my office for a minute, please."

"I'll be right there."

Sally settled into the chair to the right side of his desk, pad and pencil in hand.

"Sally, my next parenting conference is in September, isn't it?"

"Yes, at Pine Cove. Then there's one at Covenant Community near Milwaukee in January."

"I want you to cancel those. I'm sure they can find another speaker, even at this late date. If they can't, tell them I'll do something on husband-wife relationships."

She reached over and touched his arm. "Ellie?" she asked.

"Yes, but I don't want to talk about it. Not today anyway."

"I'm sorry, and I understand. I'll keep praying."

"Thank you, Sally. You're a jewel."

After Sally left, Clayton paced his Ellie-path, as he called it, from the bathroom door around his desk to his office door. Moving helped him think.

Thousands of people had been helped by his seminars. How many kids had chosen the right path because of what he'd taught their parents? How many relationships had been rescued? But there must be other Ellies out there, kids who didn't fit the formula. Had some parents tried what he'd said, only to find out that it didn't work? He felt he'd helped more people than he'd failed, but he couldn't do it anymore. Not until he'd worked things out with his daughter.

Except for English, Ellen thought school was a drag. She liked Mr. Wicker, her algebra teacher, but saw no purpose in imaginary numbers or the quadratic equation. Math was easy but as boring and useless as memorizing the St. Louis white pages. It was the other way around in history, where she found the subject fascinating, but the teacher's drone would lull a windmill to sleep. Biology and German were okay, but during class she often drifted into the more pleasant streams of literature. As for PE, it should be eliminated from high school curricula.

At times even English was tedious, especially grammar, diagramming, and punctuation. Miss Merkle referred to these as the nuts and bolts that held the language together—absolutely essential even though they might be dull.

Ellen recalled Grandpa Mahler's German word for boring: *langweilig.* Long-while-ish. The perfect word. She could endure Miss Merkle's *langweilig* mechanics as long as she returned soon to writing and literature. It was like putting up with car maintenance in order to satisfy one's love of driving.

The students at Springdale High knew Miss Merkle as a tough, straitlaced English teacher who would have the Easter Island heads speaking correctly if they were in her class. Common advice around the campus was to stay away from Merkle if you wanted any sort of life outside of school. She'd prepare you simultaneously for college and the mortuary.

Ellen thought of Miss Merkle as young, although she knew she must be about Father's age. Clay, Jr., Dan, and Linda had all taken honors English from her and considered her a benevolent slave driver. Miss Merkle used to hire Clay, Jr. or Dan to help her move furniture and stack firewood in her shed, and she always paid them very well. The only time she'd seen Father talk with Miss Merkle outside of school was when heavy winds caused a branch from their elm tree to crash over the back fence. Father repaired the fence, removed the branch, and cut it up. Other than that, her parents seemed to ignore their backyard neighbor.

Her radiant coppery brown hair, which was always woven into a crown, probably flowed past her waist when she let it down. She was willowy and, whether walking or sitting, her back was straight as a Puritan's pew. She always stood while teaching, towering over the students as she traced a path in front of the whiteboard. The authority in her rich, contralto voice and her sheer enthusiasm for language and literature kept her classes orderly.

Ellen tried to picture Miss Merkle as a teenager, riding in the same classic car she drove around town now, sitting next to a good-looking boyfriend. She must have been very beautiful, like a model or an actress. She might have been the descendant of a royal family, one day destined to be queen.

The students knew Miss Merkle had never been married, because at the beginning of each semester she issued her usual pronouncement. "I am not a Ms.," she would say, pronouncing it *Mizzz*. "A Ms. is a person who doesn't want others to know whether or not she's married. I have never been married, and I probably never will be. So in writing and orally, please address me as Miss Merkle."

Each school year there was fresh speculation about Miss Merkle's secret love life. The reason she went into Chicago so often was to meet some senator, CEO, movie star, or famous writer. Someday it would all come out in the press. Others thought she went into Chicago because she was gay. It didn't matter to Ellen. Miss Merkle could be whatever she wanted as long as she made literature and creative writing come alive. Ellen's theory was that Miss Merkle was so dedicated to literature and to her students that she had no time for romance.

One of the things Ellen appreciated about Miss Merkle was the way she decorated her classroom. Instead of the clutter of student papers and book covers found on other English teachers' walls, Miss Merkle used ornately framed scenes from classic novels and portraits of authors, such as Victor Hugo, Charlotte Brontë, Fyodor Dostoyevsky, and Edith Wharton. She had hundreds of pictures and changed them every month to inspire her students and to keep the same intimidating faces from hovering over them.

Last semester they had studied Russian literature, and Tolstoy, Dostoyevsky, and Pasternak hung on the walls. Miss Merkle gave her students a choice of one of three novels to read and report on: *War and Peace, Crime and Punishment,* and *Dr. Zhivago.* The class moaned when they saw the size of the books and joked about renting a forklift to haul them around. Most of the class didn't read any of them, but bought Cliff Notes or read summaries on SparkNotes.com.

Ellen, however, couldn't get enough of the Russian authors. *Crime and Punishment* was so good she read *The Brothers Karamazov.* After *War and Peace,* she read *Anna Karenina.* All were in Miss Merkle's library, elegantly bound and beautifully illustrated. During the fall semester she read seven Russian novels, living them, relishing their details, intricacies, and depth. While other students had their football games and parties, Ellen was satisfied with her world of rogues and villains, tragedy and triumph. Wasn't it better to be shaped by the great minds of literature than the hollow heroes of sports and entertainment?

For her Russian literature report she chose *Dr. Zhivago*. First she read Miss Merkle's bound copy, then she bought and read a paperback edition, highlighting important passages and writing notes in the margins. After that, her report was easy to write— merely summarize the book's plot, describe its main characters, and speculate about the message the author was trying to get across. Most of the other students' reports were stamped out with cookie cutters. No matter how they rearranged, paraphrased, and plagiarized, their reports sounded phony and cheap, like the tinny electronic music at video arcades.

Ellen heard from Mr. Wicker that her *Dr. Zhivago* report had caused a minor stir among the faculty. Some doubted she had written it. Too lengthy, well-written, and original, they said, beyond the scope of a high school student. But Miss Merkle had stood up for her, saying it was more likely the report was beyond the scope of some high school teachers. She told Mr. Wicker that Ellen's report was a "symphony."

Now, in the spring semester, they were studying English authors—the Brontës, Eliot, Dickens, Conrad, Austen. They were great, although Ellen still preferred the Russians. She completed her report on *Middlemarch* before the semester was half over and then read another seven novels.

LATELY ELLEN HAD actually been looking forward to algebra. It was still as *langweilig* as ever, but Mr. Wicker had asked her to tutor a new student, Osvaldo Villanueva. Osvaldo, his mother, and two older brothers had moved to Springdale from New Mexico, and lived in a small bungalow on Depot Street. Mr. Wicker usually assigned boys to tutor boys, but as he said to Ellen, "You aren't listening anyway, so you might as well be doing something useful."

Osvaldo was short and chunky, with a face round and flat as a platter and a mouth set in a perpetual grin. His large, brown-black eyes, magnified through rimless glasses as thick as her own, darted continuously, trying to absorb everything around him—but he was too shy to look directly at her.

Ellen had no idea what to expect from him. She quickly found that Osvaldo could add, subtract, multiply, and divide simple numbers, but beyond that he was lost.

"Yo no comprendo," he said.

She didn't know whether he wasn't very bright, had forgotten all his math, or had been promoted indiscriminately by his schools in New Mexico. At any rate, he needed to catch up in decimals, fractions, ratios, and square roots before he could start thinking about algebra.

"Well, you're going to *comprendo,* if I have anything to do with it," she said, as they sat like two owls at the tutoring table in the back of the room. "Let's start with fractions." She drew a large circle.

"Now, this is a pizza, Canadian bacon with pineapple and extra cheese."

"Make it pepperoni and sausage," he said.

"Pepperoni, sausage, salami, even liverwurst, if you want it."

"No liverwurst."

"Now we'll cut it into twelve pieces," she said, slicing it with her pencil, "and I'll give you three. Three twelfths, right? And I'll take three for myself."

"You can eat that much?"

She ignored him. "Now between us we have six twelfths, and that equals one half the pizza. Got it?"

Ellen learned that Osvaldo was the youngest of six boys. He was born near Hobbs, New Mexico, but for years his family had roamed the state while his mother looked for work. They finally settled near Socorro, where his father got a job as a custodian at the New Mexico School of Mines. By then his three oldest brothers had moved out. He saw them only a few times after that, once at Raul's funeral.

Shortly after they settled in Socorro, Osvaldo's father was diagnosed with lung cancer, probably from forty years of smoking. Despite good treatment in Albuquerque, he died within nine months, leaving Osvaldo and his mother penniless. Maria had moved to Springdale when a rich cousin assured her of an assembly-line job at Megatronics.

Ellen began looking forward to her visits with Osvaldo. He was the only boy at school or church she could talk with, and he found unexpected ways to make her laugh. One day in algebra, she noticed Osvaldo sliding his glasses up and down his nose. After a while she realized he was copying Mr. Wicker. When the teacher's glasses slid down his nose, Osvaldo made his own slide down. When the teacher took his off quickly to write on the board, Osvaldo ripped his off. When he put them back on, on went Osvaldo's. He maintained a serious, absurd smile the whole time.

Ellen couldn't help herself: she got the giggles. She thought she was going to explode. The more Osvaldo carried on, the more she knew she was going to start snorting and roll on the floor any minute. Finally she dashed out of the room.

She made it to the girls' restroom, but erupted as she burst through the door. Nancy Morgan and Alicia Robertson stared at her as she entered a stall.

"What's wrong with her?" she heard.

"Maybe she's on drugs."

That evening, as she thought about the giggling incident, she decided that she liked it. Despite her embarrassment, it had felt good, like swigging a cold lemonade on a hot summer day. But she had to watch herself, and Osvaldo. She wasn't going to let him do that again, at least not in class.

ELLEN CAME HOME from school to find a new recliner, complete with strong bovine odor, in the living room where Mom's rocking chair had always stood. Its dark brown leather matched Father's recliner, but it was smaller and not as plush.

The two chairs posed like male and female of the species *Reclinus loveragiana.* Obviously Father's way of remedying the chair problem. He probably thought he was doing something wise—maybe it would become an illustration in his parenting seminar.

When she tried it out, it felt lumpy and its leg-rest mechanism didn't work smoothly. She served herself a large bowl of corn chips, opened a Pepsi, and settled into Father's chair to read a few chapters of *Pride and Prejudice.* She'd thank him for it. What else could she do? But couldn't he have let her choose the style and color? Or better yet, just let her use his when he wasn't home? Why was that so difficult? The chair probably cost him $600. He could have saved the money.

On Saturday morning Father, as usual, was in his study applying the finishing touches to his sermon. Ellen settled into "her" recliner with *Don Quixote,* postponing the inevitable vacuuming and dusting until she'd finished at least fifty pages. Reading was like being in a cave at Mammoth. Although she knew there was a world outside, it was distant and unreal. Phones or doorbells had nothing to do with her. She rode with Don Quixote and Sancho Panza over the Spanish plains, unaware of a growing clamor in the street.

Then she heard Father. "For Pete's sake, Ellie, are you deaf? Don't just sit there! What's going on anyway?"

He flung open the front door and peered down the street toward the noise. "It looks like Cary's dog's loose and terrorizing the neighborhood."

Cary? Did he mean Miss Merkle?

"Couldn't you tell something was wrong?" he yelled back into the house. "I could hear it all the way in the study. Phone and tell her the dog's out." He retreated to his study.

Ellie exhaled. Why didn't he phone? He was the one on his feet.

"Miss Merkle's in Chicago for a book signing," she called, getting up and going to the door.

"Okay, I'll phone animal control."

Ellen looked down the street at Rolex. The reddish brown markings on his chest, feet, and above his eyes contrasted with the deep black on the rest of his body. He barked like a Howitzer at everybody he saw, and she couldn't tell if he was poised to attack or just wanted to play. She wasn't sure he wouldn't bite a child's arm off. Parents were herding kids inside for protection.

Ellen rushed to her bedroom, grabbed a few dog biscuits, and strode down the middle of the street toward the dog. A few seconds later he was wriggling with contentment as she scratched his ears and neck. She led him around the block to Miss Merkle's house, talking to him and feeding him biscuits. Miss Merkle's gate was slightly ajar; Rolex had obviously wedged himself out to explore the neighborhood. Ellen took him into the backyard, rubbed his back, and scolded him gently while he tried to lick her face. She left through the front gate and walked around the block to her house.

She arrived home just as an animal control van and a police car pulled up. Father stood in the doorway. "Everything's okay, Father. I took Rolex back to his yard. I guess Miss Merkle left the gate open."

She recognized the policeman as Jack Brandt from church. Father said Mr. Brandt was an exemplary Christian, but Ellen found him too cocksure, like a used car salesman. His skin reminded her of cork, and his cheeks were so ruddy that he might have rouged them each morning. Little lobeless ears pressed close to his head and supported hairy thickets that screened what he heard. She imagined him carrying a sackful of masks that he adroitly whipped on and off, as needed. Meet-the-visitors, pat-the-kiddies-on-the-head, kiss-up-to-the-teenagers, sweet-talk-the-old-ladies, say-an-eloquent-prayer— one for every occasion. Besides, he was the husband of Mrs. Brandt, with whom she'd been feuding for years.

While looking up *brannigan* in the dictionary one day, Ellen had discovered the word *brant,* defined as "a wild goose of the genus *Branta* that breeds in the Arctic regions." Ever since then, she had thought of Jack and Shirley as male and female brants.

She and the female Brandt had gotten off to a bad start eleven years earlier. It was one of the couple's first Sundays at church, and someone was showing them around. Ellen was sitting in the kindergarten Sunday school room reading a book; probably the tour guide had pointed her out as Dr. Loverage's youngest daughter. She looked up at a pair of huge blue eyes above a nose so long and pointy that, if it were painted yellow, would make its owner look just like Big Bird's sister.

The stranger, whose lips formed a bright purply Cupid's-bow, leaned over to pinch Ellen's cheeks. "My, aren't you a darling, moonfaced little girl!" she exclaimed.

Whether from instant dislike, hurt feelings, or self-defense, Ellen had reached up, grabbed the lady's nose, and twisted it with all her might. Afterwards Mom and Father tried to get her to apologize to Mrs. Brandt, but she refused. Who was going to make Mrs. Brandt apologize to her for pinching her cheeks and calling her moonfaced? Besides, she wasn't sorry; she wished she gotten a little more goose flesh under her fingernails.

Since that time, she and the female Brandt had never spoken to each other. At first, when they met in a hallway or on the church patio, Mrs. Brandt looked askance at her down her long nose, silently declaring her disapproval. Now, when they couldn't avoid each other, Mrs. Brandt smiled woodenly, with all the sincerity of a smiley face. They just plain didn't like each other, but that was between them. Father didn't need to know.

Now she stood on her front porch with Father, looking at Officer Brandt's I'm-in-charge-here mask.

"Good morning, Clayton. You called about a vicious dog loose?"

"Yes, I made the call. The dog was in the street, and I thought it might attack a child. The matter's taken care of; it's back in its yard."

"Did it go back by itself, or did the owner come after it?"

"Ellie took it back. You know Ellie, don't you?"

She acknowledged him by rubbing her nose.

Officer Brandt raised his eyebrows. "You?"

"Gentle as a bunny," she replied. She had almost said gentle as a goose.

He sighed and donned his burdens-of-the-world-on-my-shoulders mask. "Well, I still have to fill out a report. Clayton, I'll have to ask you a few questions. Want to get everything accurate in case anything else comes up." He looked at her. "Thanks for your help, young lady, but be careful when you're dealing with strange dogs. They aren't all bunnies."

Ellen went back to her recliner, where Don Quixote and Sancho were waiting.

AT DINNER THAT EVENING the air was heavy and strained, as though gasoline fumes were present, and a single spark might create an inferno. Father's short, terse grace meant that he was getting ready to confront her about something. As they ate in silence, Ellen tried to think of what she might have done.

Halfway through the meal, Father lined up his silverware neatly by the edge of his plate and folded his arms. "Ellie," he said firmly, clearing his throat, "why did you go after Miss Merkle's dog this morning? You heard me say I was going to call animal control."

What? Couldn't he be proud of her? She might have saved a child's life. "We both did what was needed, Father. You made the call; I went after the dog."

"If you had asked to go after the dog, what do you think I would have said?"

"You'd have told me not to."

"Exactly," he replied. "Now, Ellie, look at me."

That's what he did when he came to pivotal points in his sermons. "Now look at me, Beloved," he'd say to the congregation, "for what I'm going to say could affect you for all eternity." Then he'd speak slowly, deliberately, driving home his point.

Ellen took off her glasses and focused on his right cheek. That drove him crazy, and she could always blame it on her poor eyesight.

"Knowing—that—I—would—forbid—you—to—do—that." He paused to let his words sink in. "Why—did—you—go—after—that—dog?"

He thinks he's made a coup de grâce. She wanted to answer him by mimicking his staccato cadence, but didn't dare. "Because, Father, I couldn't stand the thought of a kid being ripped to shreds while we stood around waiting for animal control to arrive. I had to do something."

"Ellie, you're not qualified to handle vicious dogs. It might have attacked you."

"It might have, but it didn't. Nobody was hurt. I did what I had to do. Everything turned out all right." *Criminy, he's making a felony out of nothing.*

"It didn't look too good with Brandt today. He considered my phone call a false alarm."

Heaven forbid that Father lose face in front of a member of his congregation. "I didn't mean to make you look bad, Father. I'm sorry."

"I can handle that, Ellie. I'm more concerned about your rejection of my authority in this family. God gave me that authority, and I mean to carry it out. When you know my wishes and you deliberately disregard them, that is wrong. That is sin, Ellie, sin!"

Sin! Deep, black, soul-staining sin! All I did was take a loose dog back into its yard.

"Somehow you've gotten it in your head that you know more than anyone else. Well, your guardian angel was watching over you today; otherwise there might have been a disaster."

She wanted to say that maybe one of the children's

guardian angels had urged her to go after Rolex, but her father's burners were already turned too high. "I'll try to remember, Father."

After dinner and cleanup, Ellen returned to her room, locked her door, and lay back against her pillows, but she couldn't reenter the world of Don Quixote and Sancho Panza. Two things bothered her. First, Father had referred to Miss Merkle as Cary, as though he'd known her for a long time. She knew the teacher's first name was Caroline. But Cary? Why would Father call her that?

Second, wasn't "sin" just a little strong to describe her going after Rolex? She understood why he felt embarrassed under Officer Brandt's interrogation, but she had done something all the adults in the neighborhood had been afraid to do. Couldn't he give her some credit?

Father accused her of thinking she knew more than anyone else. Well, in this case, she did. He didn't have all the facts; she knew she could handle Rolex. He didn't have a clue. For a change, couldn't he just trust her? Was it so hard for him to accept the fact that she was competent? She was sixteen! She'd learned *something* in life. But he always thought he knew best, and never tried to see her point of view.

For some reason, she was reminded of the ballet fiasco in first grade. Over her loud protests, he had stuffed her into a leotard and driven her down to Lydia's Dance Studio.

It wasn't that she didn't like ballet or didn't want to dance. It was just that, in all the recitals and children's ballets she had seen in books or on TV or in real life, she'd never seen a dancer wearing glasses. Much less thick, rimless glasses like hers. And she had to wear them, or she'd run into the other dancers and they'd laugh at her.

If she said that to Father or Mom, they'd say it didn't matter what the other kids thought. But it did matter. Furthermore, she was fatter than the rest of the girls and didn't want them to see her in tights or a tutu. She wasn't as fat as Billy Bolger, but some boys at school said Ellie was a nickname for

Ellie-phant. When she pictured herself dancing in a leotard, all she saw was a sky blue elephant prancing around the dance floor bumping into everyone. So she took off the leotard in the backseat and pushed it out the window. It was either that or a big scene at the dance studio.

Father should have trusted her and not demanded she take lessons. On the way home from Lydia's she prayed that he would put his arms around her and tell her that he was sorry and it was okay if she didn't want to take ballet. But back at home he'd spanked her until she cried.

Tonight, after the episode with Brandt, he'd pounded on her again, only verbally. Well, it wasn't going to work. Going after Rolex was the right thing to do, and she didn't have to justify it to him or anyone else. She picked up *Don Quixote,* turned on her stereo, and hoped for some good, long hours of reading.

SEVEN

During the next week, Ellen's mind was tethered to the Rolex incident, and she couldn't wander off into a book or a daydream without it tugging at her. Father had forged a major case of disobedience out of nothing. In an emergency one acts without asking permission. She could understand why Brandt's questioning had spun his dials, but he shouldn't have taken it out on her. If Mom were there, she'd have calmed him down.

She and Mom had always been on good terms. They could talk for hours about school, about growing up on a farm in Texas, about making plum jam—anything that didn't involve a judgment or an opinion. Ellen had given that up when she realized Mom never gave her own opinion, but always parroted Father. No matter what the subject, at the slightest shadow of controversy Mom pushed her submit-to-your-husband button. And the two shall become one. Unfortunately, that one was all Father.

Mom couldn't stand to see her and Father arguing. Usually during their disputes she would leave the room, but occasionally she resorted to diversionary tactics, like a killdeer flopping on the ground, feigning a broken wing, to distract attention from her chicks in a nearby nest. Once when she and Father were going at it, Mom cut her finger with a paring knife and gave a little shriek. Father rushed to her immediately, and their argument came to an abrupt halt. It wasn't a big cut, little more than a prick, but Ellen knew she had done it on purpose.

Ellen couldn't comprehend why Mom had thought it was wrong to openly disagree with her husband. She didn't need to verbally attack him or make him look bad; she could merely say, "Another way of looking at this is . . ." Then again, she wished that just once she could have heard Mom say, "You know, Clayton, sometimes I think you're a big bag of prunes." Mom would say it gently, of course. She wondered what Father would have done.

When Ellen was in the second grade she'd caught the tail end of one of her parents' discussions. It was probably an argument, but she wasn't sure.

"But, Clay, we haven't seen them for fourteen months."

"I know that, Joyce, but I'm overwhelmed at church, and this is a bad time to leave."

"Then I'll take Linda and Ellie and go. I can drive that far. Besides, Mom and Dad are expecting us."

"No, you won't. We'll go this summer. Maybe take an extra week."

Mom's eyes were red, and a small handkerchief lay on the table. But when she noticed Ellen standing in the doorway, her voice grew suddenly cheery.

"Good morning, Ellie. Father and I were just discussing Thanksgiving. We're postponing our trip to Grandma and Grandpa's until summer when there will be more things for you to do."

"What's for breakfast?" She didn't let them know she was mad at both of them.

As it turned out, she never saw Grandpa Mahler again. He had a stroke in April and died in May. Even as a seven-year-old she wondered whether Mom ever pointed out to Father that they'd missed their last chance to see Grandpa. No, she probably hadn't. That wasn't something Mom would do.

It had always been like that. Mom and Father both seemed happy, and she was glad they didn't fight with each other the way some of her friends' folks did. But she wondered whether the price wasn't too high for Mom. Did she sell her true self, and even truth itself, for tranquility? She loved her mom dearly, but she wasn't sure she'd ever known the real Joyce Mahler Loverage. And now she never would.

A week before Mom died, they'd had their last real conversation. The hospice nurse had just left, and Ellen had gone into Mom's bedroom to see if there was anything she could do for her. Mom lay on her hospice bed, the light blue bathrobe Father had given her for Christmas draped over her bony shoulders. Chemotherapy had left her gaunt, and patchy tan fuzz replaced shoulder-length, golden brown hair. Scooped-out cheeks and parched lips begged for ice chips, and weary eyes yearned to close in long, restful sleep.

Despite Dr. Kirshner's prescriptions, Mom was in a lot of pain, but she never complained. When Ellen entered the room Mom smiled feebly, and pushed the button to elevate her head a little.

"Sit down, Ellie." She nodded toward the edge of the bed. Her voice was a wispy cloud the sun would soon burn away. "You and your father. You don't get along. Sometimes you make him furious."

"I don't mean to, Mom."

"But you know when you're making him angry, don't you?"

"Sometimes. Not always." That was the truth; she didn't always know.

"Then Ellie, don't push him. You don't need to do that, even when you're sure you're right."

Ellen hesitated. This was not the time to argue with Mom. "I should just agree with him?" she asked meekly.

"Ellie, winning isn't everything. Look at the big picture, honey, not just whether you're right or wrong." Mom was exerting herself, almost out of breath. "If you win an argument, it's not just your father who loses. So do I, and a lot of others. And he can't minister as well to the people at church. Sometimes his arguments with you affect his sermons."

Good sermons depended on winning arguments?

"But sometimes he *is* wrong, Mom," she said, trying to hold back her tears. She didn't want to talk about this. "He should just admit it, and not let it spill over into the rest of his life."

"And maybe, Ellie, just maybe, he's being outfoxed by a sharp teenage daughter whom he doesn't understand."

As her mother's words dropped to a whisper, Ellen bent closer.

"Ellie Loverage is a little different from anyone he's dealt with. Are you still planning on leaving home when you're eighteen?"

"I want to."

"That's only three years off. Father needs you to play by his rules for the next few years. Do it for me, for all of us . . . for yourself. An exercise in self-control, if nothing else. You don't need to respond, Ellie. No promises. Just think about it, real hard."

"I'll think about it, Mom." What else could she say? She took Mom's hand and gently rubbed the loose skin that covered her twiglike fingers.

"I love you, Ellie," Mom whispered and closed her eyes. A tear trickled down her cheek and fell on the pillow.

"I love you too, Mom," she said before her throat grew so tight she couldn't say another word.

During the next week Ellen spent hours beside her mother's bed, and they exchanged words of appreciation and love. But that was their last mother-daughter talk, and it was chiseled into her brain. Obey Father; don't stand up for what you know is right; sell yourself for peace; arguments aren't worth the effort they take; winning means nothing; everyone loses when you argue, even the people Father ministers to.

She couldn't be true to herself and honor Mom's words at the same time. The best she could do was to use the memory of that conversation as a restraint to temper what she really felt like saying.

The four days between Mom's death and the memorial service were a living hell. Ellen moved like a zombie, carrying out her duties mechanically, listening to a stream of anecdotes that triggered a myriad of others in her mind. She wanted to share hers with someone, and she almost did the evening her brothers and sister had sat around reminiscing, but she wasn't good with groups, even her own family. If she started to talk, she'd cry and be humiliated. If Linda had invited her to go for a Coke, she would have said a lot. But as it was, she just sat and listened, blinking tears from her eyes, never quite swallowing the hard lump in her throat.

She held on through the memorial service and reception, steeling herself against hugs and syrupy sentiments. But at home, after she'd told everyone good night, she closed her bedroom door, threw herself on her bed, and pressed her face hard into the pillow so she could barely breathe. She hammered her fists on the mattress, kicked her feet, and wept for a long time. She didn't want anyone to hear her, yet she wanted someone to knock on her door. She never wanted to see her family again, but she wanted to throw her arms around them and tell them everything she felt. But no one heard, no one knocked, and she spent the night alone wondering what it would be like with just her and Father at home.

SEVERAL TIMES THAT WEEK Father brought up the encounter with Rolex and Jack Brandt, asking her the same questions and spouting his same line about his being the authority in their household. She knew he was fishing for an apology, even if it was just a weak "sorry," but he wasn't going to get it.

Despite what Mom had asked her to do, she wouldn't apologize simply to keep the peace. If she were truly sorry or even not sure she was right, she might apologize, but in this case she'd be lying. That was like forcing little kids to hug and make up after a spat when it was obvious they weren't sorry at all.

Several weeks passed before Ellen returned to Miss Merkle's house. She needed to be alone, not just in her own house, but someplace new and fresh. Mom's words still haunted her, but even if Mom was right about submitting to Father, she wasn't going to do it. Her circuit boards wouldn't allow it.

Relaxing on the carpet in Miss Merkle's library, Ellen completed a history assignment and started on Dickens's *Bleak House*. A classical music station played softly in the background. She was beginning to recognize some Mozart and Prokofiev. At four-thirty she returned the book to its case and punched the OFF button on the stereo. She wanted to look around the house a little before she left. She didn't mean to be a snoop, but she was curious. Drawers, closets, everything personal was off-limits. She just wanted to see how Miss Merkle decorated, and examine her interesting artifacts and souvenirs. Today she'd go into the bedroom. She'd never been there before. She took her history book with her.

The bedroom was what she expected. Plush ivory carpet, a four-poster bed, a magnificent hand-stitched quilt in whites, blues, and purples, pillows and bolsters on the bed, twin chests of drawers, and an antique nightstand. A full-length mirror hung on one wall with large floral paintings mounted on each side. Like the rest of the house, the room was beautiful without being gaudy.

As Ellen glanced around the room, a picture on the nightstand caught her eye. She walked over and picked it up. *What? That looks like Father when he was a teenager. I've seen that photo somewhere before. It has to be him!*

As she stared at the photograph, the rumbling of the garage door and Rolex's barking startled her. Miss Merkle was early. Ellen knew that would happen someday. Now she'd find out if she'd planned things right. Miss Merkle always pressed the opener a block early.

Ellen left the bedroom door slightly open, just as she had found it, and calmly stepped out the back door, making sure it was locked behind her. Rolex demanded his usual biscuit and a quick pat. Then Ellen strode swiftly across the lawn and squeezed through the back fence. There was plenty of time. Ellen waited several minutes until the back door opened and Miss Merkle called Rolex into the house.

Good news and bad, she thought. Good, because she didn't have to worry about Miss Merkle surprising her. Bad, because the photograph on Miss Merkle's nightstand sure looked like Father.

FROM THE TIME Clay, Jr. was two years old, Clayton had reserved one evening each week for his family. The members of the church knew Tuesday evenings were unavailable for meetings or appointments of any kind, and, except for serious accidents or illnesses, they should not call him. He reminded them that pastors were busy people, sometimes so busy they neglected their families. He had no intention of doing that. For over thirty years he'd set an example for his congregation and those who attended his family seminars.

Although he realized that some people and families were more laid back than others, he recommended that parents keep a tight schedule on their family nights. A lackadaisical attitude told your children they were unimportant, but promptness honored them.

On his own family nights, dinner was served punctually at six o'clock. Joyce prepared one of the children's favorite meals and served pie à la mode for dessert. He wanted dinner to be finished by six-thirty so the Loverage family night could begin and he'd have several valuable hours with his children.

While Joyce cleaned up after dinner, they started their activities. When the children were young, they played Uncle

Wiggley, Chutes and Ladders, and Memory. Later Monopoly, Clue, or Risk lasted from a few hours to several days. Clay, Jr. and Linda thrived on competitive games, whereas Dan was into action figures and building—superheroes, Johnny West, and Legos. Clayton often found himself on his hands and knees building forts and castles and playacting heroic scenes. Every second was well invested.

When the older kids were in high school, family nights shifted to the living room, where they discussed everything from school to politics to religion. Joyce served coffee, hot chocolate, and occasionally popcorn, and joined them when the kitchen was cleaned.

What he didn't tell people at church or at his seminars was that his youngest child considered Tuesday evenings a bother. She participated when they read stories, but the older kids tolerated stories only so long before their impatience demanded a game or an important topic of conversation. It didn't matter to Ellie; she was unaware of what Tuesday evenings were all about, and preferred to read alone.

When Ellie was young, the older kids sometimes coaxed her into playing board games, but it never turned out well. Between turns her mind wandered, and Linda and Dan chafed at her slowness. Even after she spun a dial or rolled the dice, she moved her piece almost randomly, without thinking. Winning or losing meant nothing to her. Relieved when a game was finished, she hastened back to her little rocker to gaze into a book, absorbed in pictures and words, oblivious to the fun the others were having.

After the older kids left, family night disintegrated. Subtly, Ellie let him know she had no interest in games or conversation. Now, with Joyce gone, Clayton didn't attempt a family night. He still stayed home on Tuesday evenings and stressed the importance of family evenings at marriage and family seminars, but he now used the time for study and sermon preparation.

The same thing had happened with family dinners. With the other children, evening meals were never squandered, because he deliberately gave them value. Their half hour together was a time for sharing and asking questions. His children needed to think, to give reasonable, concise answers, and to raise questions of their own. The only things they could take for granted, he told them, were God's love and the Bible. Everything else was open to questioning.

All the time invested in Clay, Jr., Dan, and Linda had paid off, in Clayton's assessment, but nothing worked with Ellie. Starting a conversation was like storming an impregnable fortress. The moat was wide, the drawbridge up, the gate a meter thick, and armed soldiers peered over crenelated walls.

But he hadn't failed from a lack of trying.

"Did anything interesting happen at school today, Ellie?" It was a simple enough question.

"No."

Okay. He'd give her the benefit of the doubt. Maybe nothing interesting had happened. "What are you studying in history?"

"U.S."

"U.S. what?"

"U.S. history."

"What part of U.S. history?"

"Twentieth century."

"First World War? Second? Korean?"

"No."

"Well, what then?" One concrete fact! That was all he wanted. By now Clay, Jr. and Linda would have been jabbering like mynah birds.

"Politics."

"Which politics?"

"U.S."

"Who was president during this period you're studying?"

"Lots of guys."

"Could you name one?"

"Roosevelt."

"So you must be studying the Depression or World War II."

"Theodore."

He stopped and claimed victory in a minor skirmish. Ten questions to produce one insignificant fact.

Since Joyce's death, every evening had been the same. He would have talked about any subject—school, hobbies, movies, religion—but she was like wet kindling, and his matches caused no more than a fizzle. In his family seminars he'd always stressed communication. If you don't know what the other person is thinking and feeling, you aren't communicating. Now the parenting expert was a failure, at least as far as his younger daughter was concerned. And he didn't have the foggiest idea what to do about it.

JUST AFTER SPRING BREAK, Mr. Wicker left a message on Clayton's answering machine. "Dr. Loverage, I need to talk with you about Ellen. I can meet you tomorrow at five at Jubi-Latte. Let me know if you can make it."

More Ellie problems. He wants to meet outside of school hours, outside of school. Now what? He left Wicker a message that he'd be there.

Clayton arrived at JubiLatte at 5:00; Wicker didn't show up until 5:11. By the time he got his drink it was 5:16. Clayton always carried sermon notes or a book when there was a possibility of waiting. Time was too precious to be wasted.

After the usual greetings, Clayton got to the point. "You have something to say about Ellie?"

"This is very unofficial. My job is to teach math, not to interfere in private matters."

"Private matters?"

"About six weeks ago I assigned Ellen to tutor another student. She doesn't participate in class discussions, so I thought I'd let her do something useful."

"How'd she take to that?"

"Better than I could have imagined. She's brought him up to speed in six weeks."

"Him?"

"Well, that's what I wanted to talk to you about. His name's Osvaldo Villanueva. He moved here from New Mexico with his mother in February."

"Are you're telling me Ellie's getting involved with this Osvaldo?"

"I don't know about 'involved.' I see them together in the halls and in the cafeteria—no reason to believe they're more than friends. But you know kids."

"What do you know about the boy?"

"Nothing negative. Very quiet, shy, although I've detected some clownishness in him lately. But it's not Osvaldo I want to warn you about. Last Tuesday night after Jack Brandt and I played racquetball, he mentioned something about a new family on Depot Street. Says the older brothers are nothing but trouble. They have an arrest record in New Mexico. Jack might give you a full rundown."

Just what he needed, another meeting with Brandt.

They talked another five minutes about Osvaldo before moving on to Ellie's math grades. Wicker wasn't worried about her anymore. She was learning, but not letting anyone know.

"There was a day when she was tutoring Osvaldo that she ran out of class with a panicky look on her face."

"Was she sick?" Clayton asked.

"I assumed so, but Osvaldo didn't seem too concerned and had a funny grin on his face. I think something else was going on. She's never given me any behavior problems, so I didn't pursue it."

Ellie hadn't mentioned either tutoring anyone or getting sick. Why should she? He wasn't included in her world.

Osvaldo Villanueva, huh. Clay, Jr. married Cathy Johnson. Dan married Beth Miller. Linda, Alan Davis. Leave it to Ellie to be different.

THAT SAME AFTERNOON, Maria Villanueva relaxed in her two-room clapboard house on Depot Street. She brewed a cup of coffee and collapsed into a rickety folding chair, relieved to sit down after being on her feet most of the day.

She opened her paycheck envelope. Four hundred and ten dollars for a week's work on the assembly line! After taxes! And in another few weeks health and dental benefits would begin. Maybe there was a tiny bit of hope . . . if Ramon and Raphael didn't cause trouble.

What was wrong with those boys? They had learned nothing from their arrests in New Mexico or time in juvenile hall. Someday someone was going to shoot them, or they'd land in prison for twenty years. *God, my little boys are so mixed up. Can You help them change? Fix them on the inside so they don't steal anymore and Raphael doesn't go after girls.*

She rolled up her check, wrapped it tightly in Saran wrap, and pushed it deep into the mayonnaise jar, which she set back in the refrigerator. Until she could go to the bank, the check was safe. Ramon and Raphael hated mayonnaise.

Around five o'clock Osvaldo arrived home from school. He was whistling. It sounded like a song she'd heard at church. He wasn't much of a whistler, but he was a good boy . . . so far.

"Hi, Mama." He kissed her on the forehead.

"Hello, Ossie. How was school today?"

"I'm caught up in math. I don't need a tutor anymore."

"That's good. I'm proud of you."

"Not so good, Mama."

"Why? You don't want to be tutored forever."

He gave her a sly smile and raised his eyebrows. "With this tutor I would."

"Oh-oh, Ossie. You be careful. You know how much trouble you can get into with girls." He was her only son who hadn't gotten into sex before he was sixteen. "What's her name?"

"Ellen."

"Is she a nice girl?"

"I think so. Her father's a pastor. I want you to meet her."

That was the first time Maria had heard one of her sons say that.

"I want to meet her too," she replied. But she didn't want the girl coming to her sparsely furnished, two-room house. They had only two wooden folding chairs and a wobbly card table. "We could meet in town after work or on the weekend."

"We're going to have lunch Saturday."

"Ossie, you don't have any money. How can you take her out?"

"She's going to make sandwiches, and I'm going to bring dessert and lemonade. We'll go to Schroeder Park if it's warm enough. I was hoping you could make a cake."

"I'd be glad to, *mijo*." She stood on tiptoe and kissed him on his cheek.

Osvaldo sat in their other folding chair, took a paperback from his backpack, and opened it to a bookmark in the middle.

Maria looked over his shoulder at the tiny print. "Such a long book," said Maria. "What are you studying?"

"I'm reading it, Mama." He showed her the cover.

The Hobbit. She didn't even know what a hobbit was. She studied her son. He had never read anything longer than a comic book. "This Ellen must like books," she said.

"Yes, Mama. She likes them very much."

E I G H T

On Saturday, Osvaldo rang the Loverage doorbell at 12:25. Clayton liked punctuality, but being five minutes early wasn't a bad trait. He'd asked Ellie to stay in her room until he'd finished talking with Osvaldo. Establishing ground rules showed he cared about his daughter, and he hadn't frightened off any of Linda's suitors. He wouldn't be surprised, however, to find Ellie eavesdropping.

A chunky teenager in thin-kneed jeans, a faded blue windbreaker, and large rimless glasses stood at his door. Straight black hair, parted in the middle, fell over the boy's ears, and he clasped a large brown grocery bag in front of his chest. He was probably no more than five feet four with a pre-Columbian face.

Clearly, he wasn't going to say anything, so Clayton spoke up. "I assume you're Osvaldo."

"I came to get Ellen," said Osvaldo shyly.

Clayton could hardly hear him. He opened the door wider and stood back. "Come in, Osvaldo. I'm Dr. Loverage, Ellie's father." He put out his hand, and the boy shook it mechanically, as though slowly pumping water. "Come in, come in, I want to talk with you."

Osvaldo entered tentatively, his eyes darting around the entry hall, trying to take in everything at once. Clayton led him into the living room, offered him Ellie's recliner, and sat in his own.

Osvaldo stood in front of him, smiling and clutching his grocery bag. Ellie had probably warned him about a pre-date interview.

"Have a seat, Osvaldo. Here, sit right here." He pointed at a straight-backed chair next to his recliner. Osvaldo sat on the edge with the bag on his lap, but did not lean back.

"Now, young man, tell me about yourself. I like to know who my daughter's having lunch with."

"We moved here from New Mexico." Silence. "You're Ellen's father?"

"Yes." Of course. Who else did he think he was?

"We came in February. It was cold."

"And you live by the depot?" Clayton was working hard to get something out of the boy. It occurred to him that Osvaldo might be as uncommunicative as Ellie.

"Yes, our house is small, but better than New Mexico. We have heat."

"And you live with your mother?"

"Mama's name is Maria. Sometimes my brothers sleep there." The poor boy was squirming. For him this was an inquisition.

"Do your mother and brothers work?" Clayton knew the answers. He just wanted to make the boy feel comfortable.

"Mama works assembly line. She makes something for computers."

"How did you get here from New Mexico, Osvaldo?" Maybe that would help him relax.

"At first we drove. Mama had an old Chevrolet. Maybe 1960. But it broke down in Texas."

"Then what did you do?"

"My brothers stole a car."

Clayton swallowed hard; this was something he hadn't known. "And you rode the rest of the way in a stolen car?"

"Mama said no. Ramon and Raphael came in the car. Mama and I hitchhiked. It was cold."

"Hitchhiking's dangerous, Osvaldo. Did you have any trouble?"

"Mama prayed. She said God would protect us. But we waited a long time in the snow. Finally Mr. Spike drove us all the way."

"Mr. Spike?"

"In his truck. Mama prayed, and God sent Mr. Spike."

"So you believe in God, Osvaldo?"

"Yes."

"Where do you go to church?"

"Mama and I go to Bethel Temple."

That was a charismatic church on the south side of town, near the new industrial park. Clayton respected its pastor, Mr. Santori.

"They helped Mama get some furniture."

"How about your brothers? Do they work?"

"No. They don't even try to help Mama. At first she walked through the snow to get to work."

For fifteen minutes they talked about how Osvaldo liked Springdale, school, and Maria's job. Osvaldo had finally set the bag on the floor and leaned back in the chair. But Ellie was probably fuming. The boy hadn't come to talk with him; it was unfair to make him and Ellie wait any longer. He seemed okay, at least as trustworthy as some of the studs who had dated Linda.

"Just two more things, Osvaldo, before I call Ellie. I want you to have her home by five o'clock, and I don't want any touching on this date. Do you understand that?"

Osvaldo nodded yes.

"By the way, where are you going for lunch?"

"Ellen said Schroeder Park. She's bringing sandwiches."

"Ellie makes interesting sandwiches. What do you have in the bag?"

Osvaldo picked up the grocery bag and needlessly opened it. "Lemonade, and Mama baked a cake. Would you like a piece? It's chocolate."

ELLEN AND OSVALDO walked the eight blocks to Schroeder Park. The spring weather brought people out to work in their yards, mowing, pruning, and planting. At the park, the playground swarmed with children swinging, sliding, crawling through plastic tunnels, and digging in the sand, while their mothers watched and visited nearby.

They stopped at the granite monument in the center of the park and read the inscription, "1918. To the sons of Springdale who gave their lives in the Great War." About twenty names were engraved below, including one that read Edmund Leo Schroeder. Embedded in a walkway around the monument were other plaques honoring Springdalers killed in World War II, the Korean War, and Vietnam. All the tables were filled with picnickers, mostly families, so Ellen and Osvaldo sat on a patch of fresh spring grass under a tall red oak just breaking into leaf.

Ellen spread out Mom's red-and-white checkered oilcloth while Osvaldo poured lemonade into Styrofoam cups. On the oilcloth she laid two sandwiches wrapped neatly in waxed paper, tied with orange and green ribbon, and labeled, *Pilgrim's Delight, Massachusetts, circa 1623*.

"Pilgrim sandwiches?" said Osvaldo. "This is April, not November."

"I know, but I served these to Father last Thanksgiving, and he thought they were great."

She had used two pieces of fifteen-seed bread, one spread with cranberry sauce, the other with pumpkin pie filling. Between were layers of turkey dressing, thin slices of yam, a sprinkling of leftover corn, and thick slabs of dark turkey meat from the deli.

Osvaldo took a bite and said, "We didn't have anything like this in New Mexico."

After they finished their apples, they decided to read before having Maria's chocolate cake for dessert. They were slowly making their way through Dickens's *The Old Curiosity Shop*. Osvaldo liked the story, but had trouble with vocabulary. When they came across a word he didn't know, they'd stop and Ellen would define it for him, if possible. He preferred that Ellen do all the reading, but she wouldn't let him get away with that.

"You need practice," she said. "The best time is when you're with someone who wants to help."

As they read, Osvaldo saw Ramon and Raphael coming toward them. "Uh-oh. Those are my brothers—don't argue with them, Ellen. They just want an excuse to start trouble."

"With all these people around us, they can't do anything, can they?"

"They cause problems anytime, anywhere."

The brothers sat down, Ramon next to Osvaldo, Raphael next to Ellen. They were both taller than Osvaldo, but still no more than five feet eight or nine. They had the angular features of Maria, and would have been nice looking, but for their walk and general demeanor.

Raphael put his hand on Ellen's leg to help lower himself to the ground. He didn't smile, but leered, and he seldom looked away from some part of her anatomy. Ramon seemed to be the leader of the two.

"So, little brother, you didn't invite us to your picnic."

"It's not for you," replied Osvaldo.

"Ossie, don't you remember when we took care of you? We even changed your stinky diaper once."

"This is not for you. You should leave."

Ramon moved closer to Ellen. "You, girlfriend, what's your name?"

She said nothing, but gazed absently toward the playground.

"Did you forget your name, girlfriend?"

She wasn't about to answer him.

"She doesn't know how to talk, little brother." He nodded toward the grocery bag. "What you got there?"

Neither she nor Osvaldo answered.

"Give it to me. I'll find out." Ramon reached between them and seized the bag.

"Raphael, we're in luck. They saved chocolate cake for us." He took the four pieces out and handed two to Raphael. "Did Mama make this, little brother?"

Silently Osvaldo and Ellen watched Ramon and Raphael devour all four pieces, lick their fingers, and wipe them on Osvaldo's jacket.

Ramon nodded toward Ellen. "Let me see your book, girlfriend."

She stood up, grasping the book, glad to escape Raphael's attention. They might take the chocolate cake, but they weren't going to touch her book. If they came near her, she'd scream so loudly the whole park would be alerted.

"Little brother, your girlfriend isn't very nice. What does she have, a porno book, and she doesn't want to corrupt her boyfriend's nice brothers?"

Followed by the three boys, Ellen walked to the playground. They wouldn't bother her there with all the mothers and children nearby. She sat in a swing, ignoring the frowns of some young mothers nearby.

Ramon and Raphael stayed for only a few more minutes.

"Thanks, little brother," Ramon said. "We'll have to have another picnic soon."

THE NEXT TIME Ellen returned to Miss Merkle's house, she went immediately to the bedroom. As she entered the room, she saw herself in the full-length mirror and paused.

Not much to look at. Face too round. Eyes too big, too far apart. Thick lenses that made her look like a great owl. Mud-puddle brown hair straight as a laser beam. The Washington Monument had a better figure. Here she is folks, Miss Ellen Loverage, Miss Less-Than-Average of 1996.

Why did Linda get all the good genes? Boys had started coming around when she was in the eighth grade. Linda was class valedictorian and voted most likely to succeed. What did it matter, though? Ellen wasn't going to jump through a bunch of hoops just to get her picture scattered throughout the yearbook.

She walked back to the nightstand and picked up the photograph. It sure looked like Father. The same triangular face, dark hair, that surfer's wave in front. Look at those eyes . . . that's how he smiles when he greets people after church. The guy in the photo was seventeen, maybe eighteen or nineteen. She knew it was Father, but what was Miss Merkle doing with his picture on her nightstand?

Back in the library Ellen settled into her usual spot on the floor next to the sofa. She was beginning to like Miss Merkle's classical station. Today she was starting *Sense and Sensibility*. Austen wasn't one of her favorite authors, but she was okay.

How strange it was that she could lounge in Miss Merkle's house. It was so easy to read here, without any distractions. The only thing she was doing wrong was using valuable space that would otherwise be wasted. She'd never steal anything from Miss Merkle's house, not even a lemon drop.

She left promptly at 4:45. Everything was in order, as usual. She was doing it right, and she'd never get caught. But the picture on the nightstand was bugging her. She'd have to check Mom's box of photos. It was eerie. Either that was Father, or he had a long-lost identical twin.

CLAYTON SAT WITH Jack Brandt in the far corner of JubiLatte Coffeehouse. While he sipped a small black coffee,

Brandt drank a large frappuccino. A lilac just coming into bloom brushed against their window, reminding him of the fresh spring weather and his aborted plans to fish at Braxton Reservoir that afternoon. After his talk with Wicker, he needed to get the scoop on the Villanuevas.

Brandt was in a hurry. "I ran the Villanueva family through the computer. Ramon's barely nineteen, but he's been arrested eight times in New Mexico. Two car thefts. Three DUIs. Two for breaking and entering. Raphael, he's twenty, arrested seven times. Same kind of stuff, plus he's been picked up three times as a suspect in rape cases. Both have spent time in juvenile facilities, and Raphael some time in jail. I found no violations outside of New Mexico, although they've been questioned several times in southern Illinois for burglaries. Small stuff."

"What about Osvaldo?" asked Clayton.

"Nothing. At least not yet. I wish I could say the same thing about his mother."

"Why, what's she done?" He was surprised.

"First I'll tell you about her husband, Fernando Villanueva: Three arrests between 1962 and 1968. Convicted in 1969 of being an accessory to an armed robbery in which a night watchman was killed. Served a full twenty years, the last seven at Los Lunas. Maria Villanueva was picked up numerous times between 1969 and 1986 for soliciting. Arrested and brought to trial three times in the seventies for prostitution. She was a call girl in Albuquerque and Socorro, catering to servicemen and college students. Convicted each time, but always given probation."

"I didn't want to hear that."

"You asked."

"Nothing since '86?"

"Nothing on record. Why are you asking, Pastor? You've obviously had contact with these people."

"Ellie had a date with Osvaldo."

"Not good."

"He seemed like a nice kid."

"If she were my daughter, I'd break them up before they got serious."

That wasn't as easy as it sounded. "I'd like to give the boy a chance—"

"Pastor, he's living with three people with records. The whole county's watching his brothers. It's only a matter of time until they make a mistake."

"I'd like to talk with Maria," said Clayton, remembering how fondly Osvaldo spoke of her.

"Don't meet with her alone. It wouldn't look good. Remember, she's a prostitute."

Clayton resented Brandt's giving him advice. As a minister, he knew how to handle such situations; he never placed himself in a compromising position. He seldom allowed himself to be one-on-one with a woman, even when counseling. If he did, it was in his office with his staff nearby.

Jack hurried off on an emergency call, leaving Clayton to sip his coffee and think over what the police officer had said.

Osvaldo was probably sixteen. Born around 1980, while Maria's husband was in prison. Maria was arrested for prostitution. No telling who Osvaldo's father was. Maybe she didn't know . . . or know who had fathered Ramon or Raphael. . . . But she prayed and attended Bethel Temple. All his life Clayton had preached that people could change. That was the Christian message. Mary Magdalene had been a prostitute. *All right, Lord, I choose to give Maria the benefit of the doubt until I learn differently.*

He'd arrange to see her as soon as possible.

LATE IN THE SPRING Clayton reluctantly yielded to members of his congregation who were lobbying for topical sermons. He suspected that Jack Brandt was behind this supposed groundswell, but wasn't sure. Clayton had always preached directly from the Scriptures, believing that all topics worth preaching on would be covered sooner or later. Now, against his better judgment, he had departed from this expository style to present a sermon series on truth.

The subject of truth had been on his mind for several years, and this was an opportunity to organize and record his thoughts. The material conveniently lent itself to a four-week series that he could present just before school let out and attendance foundered in the summer doldrums.

During the series he stressed that lying is, in a sense, trying to make oneself God. As God spoke and everything from gnats to galaxies leapt into existence, so people try to create their own worlds by lying them into existence. A person strives to create a world that suits his or her fancy by coaxing others to believe it—pure legerdemain or, if you prefer, slight-of-tongue—and if the lie is believed, then presumably, it becomes truth. No one escapes this desire to be a little god. By outright lies, half-truths, omissions, and innuendos, we all, to some extent, twist truth so that the listener understands something other than what truly is.

Clayton had sat at his desk one morning, indulging his imagination. He pictured himself standing in front of his congregation and daring to illustrate his points with an example they'd never forget: "Now take our friend Jack Brandt," he'd say, "a man highly skilled in constructing falsehoods from fragments of truth.

"Several years ago Jack brought up the idea of adding a staff position at our church for marriage and family counseling and implied that his wife would be available for the position. Because that has long been my area of expertise, I considered the position superfluous and, trying to be tactful, told him I'd have to think very seriously about it before favoring such a move. I was astounded the next Sunday when one of our deacons said he was pleased that I was 'thinking very seriously' about appointing Shirley Brandt to lead our marriage and family ministries. Our friend, Jack, did not misquote my words, but he misrepresented my meaning."

Clayton chided himself for such thoughts; they contained the seeds of bitterness. Maybe he had been protecting his own precious territory and not thinking about the good of the congregation. By education, demeanor, and Christian commitment, Shirley Brandt was thoroughly qualified, but the thought of having a Brandt entrenched in the church office complex made him quake.

The series went well, and people were making insightful comments and asking questions. That meant they were listening and the messages were striking home. Maybe Brandt was right about people wanting topical sermons, or maybe Clayton had just done a good job in his presentation. At any rate, he'd think about a second topical series in the fall, maybe around Thanksgiving.

On each Sunday of his series, as he greeted his exiting congregation, the orange-haired presence of Adele Ritchie lurked in the vestibule, waiting to impart her pithy, significant comments. After the first sermon she told him he might think differently if he worked at the hospital. Sometimes very ill people needed to hear an optimistic prognosis to keep them fighting for their lives. If you told them what was going to happen, they'd give up all hope and die quickly. What do you do with truth when it destroys one's last fragment of hope? After the second sermon, she said she was angry at him because his sermon the previous Sunday had caused her to sleep like a twig. And after the third, Adele again waited with her stern, mischievous countenance.

"Well?" he said. The word may have sounded cross to someone passing by, but both Clayton and Adele knew it was packed with respect and appreciation.

"I don't need your sermons," she replied.

"Just as I suspected. You've reached perfection."

"I never lie," she replied, staring at her feet. "Haven't done so in years. If I'm tempted to tell the least little falsehood, I feel this terrible grabbing in my heart." She looked up at him, clutched the front of her dress dramatically, and staggered off toward the parking lot. Such compliments encouraged him.

His final sermon in the truth series dealt with the need to occasionally confront people with the truth. When Adele lingered again at the end of the service, he wondered what her response would be.

"You're not going to like this," she said.

"Try me. I'm tough."

"It's you and Ellen."

"What about us?" What did the sharp-minded Orphan Annie know?

"You and Linda were always hugging and talking with each other, but you and Ellen never look at each other unless you're telling her to do something. Your relationship is shaky, isn't it?"

He didn't have to talk about this with anyone; it was between Ellie and him. But he had to say something. "Somewhat."

"Does that mean kinda sorta shaky, or real and awful shaky?"

"We have some problems to work out, Adele."

"Well, you don't have much longer to do it. I think you're fortunate to have a daughter who's not getting into trouble, and who cooks, launders, and cleans the house. You'd better treat her like a queen."

He couldn't respond without going into hundreds of details, so he stared helplessly at her.

"I mean it, Pastor. I was that teenager once, and I bailed out of home when I was seventeen. I'll be thinking about you two." She touched his arm gently and walked to her car.

THE LOVERAGES HAD never been big on photographs. They'd snap them, look at them once, and then stash them in Mom's photo boxes. So when Ellen asked her father for some family pictures, he had to think for a while. Then he went to his bedroom and retrieved a shoebox tied neatly with blue ribbon, another of Mom's unexpected touches. He wiped the dust off the box and handed it to her, then left for a missions committee meeting at church. She settled in at the dining room table, hoping to solve the mystery of the photo on Miss Merkle's nightstand.

Going though the photos was like maneuvering through rows of barbed wire. She was snagged by pictures of herself and her siblings and hooked by photos of Mom and Father when they were college students. It was hard to think of them as ever being young.

As though she were in a time machine, the pictures moved back through the years as she worked to the bottom of the box. She saw Mom's black-and-white high school graduation picture. Pershing High School, class of 1954. Her golden brown, shoulder-length hair curled outward, and her contented smile was what Ellen would always remember.

She found pictures of Father posing in his basketball and baseball uniforms or standing by cars with high school buddies. But there were none of him with girlfriends. She couldn't believe he hadn't been popular. He'd probably removed them all for Mom's sake.

Then she saw it! The same picture as on Miss Merkle's nightstand, except smaller. She felt sick. Father belonged to Mom; his picture didn't belong in anyone else's bedroom. It didn't make sense; it was non sequitor, like discovering that Eleanor Roosevelt had dated Tom Hanks! She slipped the photo into the book she was reading. She'd compare it side by side with Miss Merkle's.

She replaced the photos, oldest ones on the bottom, retied the ribbon, and set the box next to Father's office door.

On the Thursday before school let out, Ellen went back to Miss Merkle's house one last time before summer vacation. She went straight for the bedroom, and with the afternoon sunlight streaming through the window, she needlessly compared them detail for detail. There was no doubt about it.

Well, Father must have known Miss Merkle when they were young. No big deal . . . it was a small world . . . they just happened to end up in Springdale. She wondered why he'd never mentioned it. She turned the frame over, bent back three tabs, slipped the photo and backing out together, and checked the back of the photo.

> *Dear Cary,*
>   *May the years ahead of us be as precious as the last two.*
>   *I will love you forever.*
>   *Clay*

Cary! That's what he had called her when Rolex got loose! She read it again, not knowing whether she should faint, weep, scream, or laugh. Father and Miss Merkle! Emotions swirled in her head. Her hands trembled as she slid the photo and backing into the frame. She re-bent the tabs, wiped her sweaty fingerprints from the glass with a tissue, and set the picture on the nightstand.

Ellen left the house immediately, her perfect sanctuary tainted. She may resent the way her father thought he had all the answers, she may argue with him, but she had always respected his character.

It must have been a high school fling. Puppy love. What happened in the past was over. Father and Miss Merkle! It was the dumbest thing she'd ever heard!

Early in June, on the Friday that school let out, Clayton finally met Maria Villanueva. In a short note, he had invited her and her family for dessert. Although he'd written *family,* he hoped Ramon and Raphael would not come.

Maria bore little resemblance to her Mayan-faced son. Thin as a pencil, she wasn't over five feet tall. Her ebony hair shimmered with traces of silver and was drawn back into a tight ponytail. High cheekbones set off intense black eyes that examined him, asking *Who are you? What do you want from me? Will you harm me? Can I trust you?* He imagined her years earlier as a flamenco dancer, castanets snapping rhythmically as she enchanted a circle of leering men. Now she looked worn, as though she'd danced through the night on into the morning. He couldn't help thinking about the fact that she was, or had been, a prostitute.

In his years at Springdale Church, he'd known of two former call girls on the membership roll. There was hope for everyone. He greeted Maria warmly, reminding himself of his duty and privilege to show her the love of Jesus. He hung their coats in the closet and led them to the dining room, where Ellie was dishing up her recipe of peach cobbler à la mud, as she called it, with sauce so thick it handled like putty.

Clayton offered a simple grace. "Our Father, we thank You for this food. We ask You to bless it and to bless our conversation. Thank You for new friends and good fellowship. Amen."

"Would you like coffee, Mrs. Villanueva?" he asked. "Some decaf is ready."

"Yes, thank you."

"Do you take cream?"

"Yes, thank you." She kept her eyes focused on her cobbler.

Clayton poured the coffee. "So, how do you like Springdale, Mrs. Villanueva?" If there was going to be any conversation, it was up to him. Was he expecting Ellie to help?

"It's nice," Maria answered.

"I understand you just arrived from New Mexico."

"February 16."

"Osvaldo mentioned that you had a hard trip."

"My car broke down."

"So Osvaldo told me. Tell me about the trip, Maria. I'd like to hear."

Maria spoke in words almost whispered. Like a frightened little girl she told him about her Chevy throwing a rod, and Ramon and Raphael stealing a car. Then she described hitchhiking, the freezing cold, and the ride with Mr. Spike. "I prayed for God to send an angel to help us, but He has very strange angels." She glanced up at him with a shy smile.

"God often surprises us, Maria. Maybe you helped the truck driver as much as he helped you."

"Do you believe in God, Dr. Loverage?" For the first time that evening, her gaze was steady. Her dark eyes held him firmly.

"Do I believe in God?" Clayton echoed her question, startled. "Of course, Maria. I am a pastor." What kind of an answer was that? He sounded like a pompous fool.

"I knew a pastor in New Mexico who said he believed in God, but he didn't."

"I've met a few of those myself, Mrs. Villanueva. It's sad. It's essential to believe in God."

"And that Jesus died to take away all the bad things we do."

"I believe that. Is that what you believe?"

"I do now. I didn't always. It took me a long time." She touched the plain wooden cross she wore as a necklace.

"And you, Osvaldo?" he asked.

"I believe like Mama."

"Do you love God?"

"Yes."

"Do you pray to Him?"

"Yes."

"Do you read the Bible?"

"Sometimes."

"Do you like to go to church?" He caught an aggravated look from Ellie.

Back off, Father, she was saying. *You have no right to grill him . . . he's our guest . . . leave him alone.*

"I like the music and the singing," answered Osvaldo, "but sometimes the sermon is boring and I go to sleep."

Clayton smiled. "When I was your age, I sat through some boring sermons . . . and I've probably given my share. How about your brothers, do they go to church?"

Maria looked down and answered nervously. "No. They don't like church. I pray for them."

"What are their names?" he asked, though he already knew.

"Ramon and Raphael."

He took a small notebook from his shirt pocket and jotted in their names. It was his prayer list, to-do list, and a place to jot ideas for sermons and seminars. "Do they live with you?"

"No."

"Maybe they can come with you for dinner sometime," said Clayton. Trying to be polite, he knew he sounded insincere.

Almost imperceptibly, Ellie shook her head and rolled her eyes.

"No. That wouldn't be good," replied Maria.

The rest of the evening they talked in safe areas about Maria's job, school, and the weather. After the dessert, while Maria helped Ellen with the cleanup, Clayton showed Osvaldo his study. Osvaldo was especially drawn to a series of etchings of Jerusalem, gifts from a friend who had visited the Holy Land.

THE NEXT MORNING at breakfast Clayton reminded Ellie of his rules for dating. One date, maximum, each week on Friday or Saturday evening. Home by 11:00 sharp, unless he specifically gave her permission to stay out later. He was to know how to get in contact with her at all times. To be sure, he'd buy a cell phone she could take on her dates. She was not to ride in anyone's car unless he approved. No movies, drinking, drugs, dancing, or necking. And she was to stay away from the Villanuevas' Depot Street house and avoid Osvaldo's brothers.

He admitted that his rules were a little old-fashioned, but at least they were easy to understand. The older children had given him no static. He wasn't too sure what Ellie would do, and he didn't know how he'd react if she pushed him on an issue. He watched for her reaction.

"Okay," she said, giving a slight shrug.

"Okay what?"

"Okay. That sounds fine. No big deal."

"I'm serious, Ellie. I don't want you stepping over the lines."

"What would happen if I accidently got home at 11:05? Or accidently had sex?"

110

He knew that Joyce and Linda had talked to Ellie about the details of sex. He had no problem presenting the moral principles to her, but the details were better explained woman-to-woman. "You can't," he answered.

"Can't what?"

"Can't 'accidentally' have sex."

"People get carried away," she replied.

"Then it's not an accident. Stay away from the current. For seventeen years you've had a mind of your own. No one can make you do anything you don't want to. Now it's time you take some of that stubbornness and turn it into a strength."

Ellie nonchalantly spread jam on her toast, but she'd been working on the same piece for a long time, so he knew she was attentive.

"Set your limits ahead of time," he continued. "You've heard that before. Talk about it with Osvaldo. You don't have to do anything you don't want to." *But maybe she wants to.*

"Father, we aren't even thinking about sex. He's never kissed me, never even held my hand. We're just friends."

"Let me tell you what temptation's like, Ellie."

She slouched into her resigned posture.

"I've been there, and I remember when I was seventeen." Sam Houston High School, 1953–1954. Sometimes it seemed as though it happened yesterday. But now he was preaching again, and she probably wouldn't listen. He'd make it quick and shut up. "You know what shrink-wrap plastic is, don't you?"

"What's that got to do with temptation?"

"Sometimes I've tugged, twisted, pinched, and bit, but haven't been able to tear the wrapping from a package. But if I make a tiny cut in the plastic, I create a weak spot, and it tears away like tissue paper. A person's resolve is exactly like that plastic, Ellie. You resist and think you've got it under control, and then bingo, there's a weak spot, and you don't have any resistance at all. That happens, especially with sex."

111

He'd said his piece, and it was time to bail out. He wished he could tell her about some of his own failures. Maybe then he could get through to her. "Do you understand what I'm saying, Ellie? I don't want to see you in trouble."

"It's a nonissue, Father. You didn't even have to mention it."

ON THE FIRST SUNDAY afternoon of summer vacation, Ellen was deep into *Les Miserables* when Father suggested that they ride out to Braxton Reservoir. He wanted to walk the partially completed trail that rimmed the lake. The whole area, including the forest that stretched several miles back toward Kingswood Country Club, was destined for state park status in the next few years. She would rather stay home and read, but he asked her to do so few things with him that she felt obliged to go. She hoped he just wanted some father-daughter companionship, but he probably had some issue to bring up.

Before they'd walked five minutes, he'd slipped into his preacher mode and began carrying on about the Great Designer who had made the trees, flowers, animals, etc., etc. Everything was God's handiwork.

He kept pointing and talking as they walked. Since he had all nature to choose from, he'd probably go on yapping until the sun cooled off. She wondered, if what God made was so wonderful, why Father didn't pause to look and listen. They passed a huge oak tree, its randomly twisted branches embracing the sky, and she wanted to stand back and absorb the magnificent structure. Awe was called for, not rhetoric. But Father had to talk about acorns and galls and mistletoe and the birds that benefited from the oak, all being part of God's master plan.

A meadow of white, yellow, and purple wildflowers affected them the same way—she wanted to kneel in amazement and curiosity; Father felt compelled to preach. Everywhere they saw swallows and sparrows, jays and woodpeckers, hummingbirds and hawks, but she couldn't hear them because of his continuous drone.

Father, shut up! she wanted to scream. *You've had the floor a long time. The birds and trees have something to tell us. I know you're smart, but I've learned all I can from you!*

"Have I ever told you about the monarch butterflies, Ellie?" He sensed nothing from her, but rolled on obliviously.

Yes! Yes! Thirty-one million, Brazilian times.

"Did you ever wonder how they fly here from Mexico or South America? And they always end up in the same areas, sometimes in the same groves of trees covering less than two acres. And they're the offspring of the ones that made the trip south. How do they know where to go?"

Well, I'll tell you . . .

"Well, I'll tell you how. God wired their little brains so they know just the right time to leave and the way to go. Even the winds don't blow them off course. The Master Navigator embedded a unique navigational system in their little heads. That, Ellie, is a miracle."

And it's the same with each of us . . .

"And it's the same with each of us. Deep inside, in our hearts, in our souls, we know we should turn to God."

But we are not like the animals . . .

"But we are not like the animals. They're programmed to fly to Mexico, but we have free will. We can choose to follow God or turn our backs on Him."

Hey, Father, why don't you let me give your sermons? We are sorry that Dr. Loverage is sick today, but in his place we are highly honored to have Ellen Loverage, trained in theology and homiletics at 472 Meadowlark Lane Seminary under the guidance, of course, of the distinguished Dr. Loverage, otherwise known as Dr. Aphorism.

As Father talked on, she reached down and picked up some acorns. God had made them the perfect size and shape—perfect for stuffing in her ears. She was tempted, but she didn't dare. Father was on top of his world, doing his thing. She'd let him chatter on, but he was talking only to himself. . . .

When they were nearly back to the car, Father paused for a few seconds and cleared his throat . . . his signal that he was about to say something important. At last, the reason he'd asked her out to Braxton.

"Ellie, I think you should get a summer job."

Her goal for summer vacation was to read. Miss Merkle had given her advanced English class a list of the one hundred best novels, based on the personal preferences of two hundred English professors, librarians, editors, and publishers. It was an excellent guide for one who was serious about literature. Ellen had already read about twenty on the list and hoped to read at least ten more during the summer.

"I thought about it," she told him, "but it doesn't fit my plans." She saw the here-we-go-again look on his face.

"And what are your plans?"

"I have ten books I need to read, maybe more."

"I want you to get a job, Ellie. Your brothers and Linda had jobs between their junior and senior years. You need to accept some responsibility."

"Father, I am responsible. You tell me to set goals for myself and then do everything in my power to meet them. I've set my goal for this summer; now I will meet it."

"I was talking about useful goals, Ellie, not reading library books."

He said "reading library books" as though he were picking up roadkill. There was going to be an argument. She wondered if she could stay cool.

"Father, I consider reading classic literature a furtherization of my educational goals." She couldn't help herself. After telling herself to be cool, she had immediately baited him.

"Furtherization?"

"I didn't think you'd notice." She watched him take a deep breath and tighten his lips into his get-firm-with-her line.

"Just when did you start setting educational goals? I must have missed something when I checked your report card."

This was how disagreements escalated into wars. "I've achieved every goal I've ever set in education. A's in English, C's in Math, C's in French, etc., etc."

"Anyone can meet a goal if it's set low enough. It's like setting the high jump bar at one foot. You should be able to do some reading this summer in addition to holding down a part-time job."

"Maybe next summer, Father. This summer I'll concentrate on reading."

"I talked with Mr. Cox at Giant Foods. He said you can work as an inventory clerk for $6.25 an hour."

"No thanks."

"I want you to start buying some of your own school clothes."

"Don't worry about clothes. I have enough for next year." Her jeans and sweatshirts still fit, and she could use some of Linda's old things.

"If you get your driver's license, you'll need money for insurance and gas."

One by one he was trying to pry her fingers off her goal. "Then I may have to wait a year to drive, Father. I'm very serious about my goal for this summer."

"And I'm serious about your working. I don't want you sitting around all summer. Think about it, Ellie, and get back to me tomorrow. Pray about it. You're old enough to pay a little of your way in this world."

Pray about it? She hated it when he told her to pray about something. She didn't mind praying; she did it all the time, actually. But when Father told her to pray, it usually meant he had already received instructions from God, and she needed to pray to verify them. It never occurred to him that she might pray and receive a different answer. On the other hand, the time was coming when she'd have to earn her own way. No big deal. She'd do it when she had to.

"There's time for that later," she replied. "Maybe next summer."

He took another deep breath and shook his head ever so slightly.

Gosh, I'd hate to have me for a daughter. Maybe someday God will give me a child just like me. Maybe Father got a little girl who behaves just like he did. Maybe this is all a bunch of hogwash.

WHILE ELLEN SPENT the summer reading, Osvaldo painted houses. He told her he needed a job to help his mother. They would have enough money if it weren't for his brothers.

"I hear them in the middle of the night," he told her. "Two o'clock, three o'clock. They go into Mama's bedroom."

"They just take her money?" Ellen asked.

"At first they demanded it; now they just grab her purse and take it."

"Does she always have money?"

"She has to. If they don't find money, they dump out all the drawers, even in the kitchen. It's easier to give them money."

"She should call the police."

"She's says they're her boys, and she could never call the police."

"But they're robbing her."

"She feels guilty because she wasn't a very good mother to them, that she robbed them when they were little."

"But it can't go on."

"I know. They used to want forty dollars, now they want eighty or a hundred. Last week when I got home from school I found Mama crying. They'd found her hiding place in the mayonnaise jar. Ramon left a note. 'Dear Mama, For all the times we begged you to help us and you didn't. Thank you for $410. You are very generous. P.S. Don't make your hiding place so hard next time.' Sometimes I'm so angry I want to kill them. Mama says to be patient; it can't last forever."

"She shouldn't take her checks home, Osvaldo."

"She didn't know what direct deposit meant. In New Mexico she always got checks or cash. Now her checks are going to the bank, and she has an automatic teller card she leaves at work. If she brings it home, it's in her bra or taped in the toilet tank."

Osvaldo's house-painting job had come about through a recommendation from Mr. Wicker. Mr. Edgar Pettigrew, who owned Rainbow Painting, was sixty-nine and found it hard to do the prep work, like scraping and sanding. He needed a sharp, hardworking young man as his partner, he said. Osvaldo worked eight to ten hours each day, six days a week, for seven dollars an hour. Mr. Pettigrew even took time to teach him how to drive so he could run errands for him.

Osvaldo was making more money than his mother, at least for the summer. Each payday he went directly to the bank to deposit his check in his mother's account.

FOR ELLEN, THE SUMMER was a time for reading and waiting. Because of Miss Merkle's irregular summer schedule and Miss Merkle's friends showing up to take care of Rolex and water the houseplants, Ellen's reading sanctuary was off-limits. It didn't matter. She had plenty of books to read and most of the day at home without Father. The "Merkle mystery," as she called it, could wait. In the fall she'd find out more about the photo on the nightstand without alerting Father or anyone else.

She usually had two books going at once, one at home and one at the library. At church she overheard Father tell Mrs. Ritchie that his daughter was spending the summer plowing through books. She'd wanted to speak up and say she wasn't plowing, she was sailing. She envisaged herself as a passenger on a ship with Austen, Dickens, Conrad, Faulkner, Hugo, Brontë, Dumas, Eliot, Kipling, Tolstoy—and they were giving her a tour of history, human nature, heroism, cowardice, valor, love. She wouldn't trade it for anything.

She wanted to tell Father that if he'd had his way she'd be working part-time at Giant Foods, or McDonald's, or Buskirk's Department Store earning, at most, $120 each week. Reading was worth far more than that. Some of the world's finest minds tutored her, and Father wasn't paying a cent, not even for school clothes, car insurance, or gas money.

Sometimes she wondered why it was so hard to get along with Father. She loved him, and she never questioned his love for her. And she didn't feel neglected. He'd certainly spent enough time with her when she was younger, and he tried to spend time with her now. She knew he wanted what was best for her and was raising her to be a Christian and a credit to his family. She couldn't argue with that. She'd have the same goals for her own kids.

No, this whole mess wasn't about love; it was about control. All over the country he had expounded his theories on raising kids. He taught parenting as though it were a math class. *A* plus *B* divided by *C,* all multiplied by love, was supposed to produce happy, productive, well-balanced children. And it worked most of the time. She was proud of Father's parenting seminars; people spoke highly of him. She'd sat through enough of them that she could give them herself.

The only thing wrong was that his formulas were too restrictive. They didn't allow for $x, y,$ and z factors that needed to be included, and maybe some p's, q's, and r's, and a few square roots, irrational fractions, and imaginary numbers. If he were in charge of the Museum of Life, its walls would be hung with geometric figures and blueprints, not paintings.

Well, in 334 more days she'd be out of here. She hadn't been a star pupil at the Clayton Loverage Finishing School, but she was tired of the professor and anxious to move on to new things.

T E N

On Sunday afternoons throughout the summer, Clayton observed Ellie and Osvaldo as they sat in his living room. Occasionally they tried chess, cribbage, or some other game, but these were always abandoned in favor of art books, CDs, short stories, and poetry. If the weather was good, they strolled to Schroeder Park or to Bud's Burgers for a soda, and late in the afternoon, after pie or ice cream, Osvaldo walked home to spend the evening with his mother.

Theirs wasn't a typical 1990s teenage romance. How many teenagers enjoyed spending an afternoon in the girl's living room with a nosy father nearby? Maybe they *were* just friends, or perhaps this was a glacier-speed romance, moving slowly toward intimacy as surely as a billion-ton river of ice inches down a valley.

What's the matter with their hormones? When I was that age I should have had my hands tied behind my back to keep me out of trouble. Linda and her boyfriends worried me more than Ellie and Osvaldo. If I were not here and left them alone, maybe nothing would happen . . . maybe.

Clayton liked Osvaldo, but doubted he was the right person for Ellie. His motives for this thinking puzzled him, because one of the themes of his preaching was that race and social position made no difference. Latino, African-American, Native American, Middle Eastern, Caucasian, Asian—all were equal in God's eyes. Prejudice of any kind was unworthy of a Christian. So, why did he have his doubts about Osvaldo?

To be honest, he *was* bothered by that flat, round face; it reminded him of paintings of the Mayans who had first welcomed Cortés, only to fall under his sword. More than that, however, he was afraid of Osvaldo's seedy family background and the looming specters of Ramon and Raphael. More rumors had circulated throughout the summer. They were suspected of dealing drugs in New Hope, but a search of their car and Maria's house had turned up nothing. He'd seen them driving around Springdale in a BMW, but Brandt told him they had proper registration. Raphael had been questioned about a rape in East St. Louis, but no charges were filed.

What did Ellie see in Osvaldo? Why was it she could talk with him for hours when she couldn't talk with her father for two minutes? He wanted to pin all the blame on her, but he was no longer sure of himself.

What were the best times he'd ever spent with Ellie? Some of their vacations were wonderful, especially when they camped and took long family treks. When she was little, she loved hiking the creeks, jumping from rock to rock to see how far she could go without falling. When the water was deep, he carried her on his shoulders. Recently, when they walked the new trail at Braxton Reservoir, they had a wonderful time, and he'd been able to explain a lot of things to her, especially about the monarch butterflies. She hadn't said much, but he knew she was taking it all in.

But the times he remembered best were when he'd read to her. When she was little she sat on his lap, nestled her head into his shoulder, and insisted on turning the pages. If he read a book four or five times, she nearly memorized it and corrected him when he made mistakes, real or deliberate. "No, Father," she'd say delightedly, "not four wishes, only three." Once he tried outfitting Snow White with glasses. "Father, Snow White doesn't need glasses; she had good eyes." She loved the stories so much, she cried when bedtime came.

When she was a little older he'd read all the Winnie-the-Pooh stories to her. Milne could build up suspense when there was no suspense at all. Everyone except Pooh, Tigger, Eeyore, and their friends knew what was going to happen. When he neared the end of an episode, Ellie held her hands over her mouth to keep her giggles in check, and kicked her feet in anticipation.

When she was older, they'd read Lewis's Chronicles of Narnia, all seven of them, taking turns reading chapters. She loved Lucy, Susan, Edmund, Peter, and, of course, Aslan, and talked about them at dinner or when they rode in the car. When he tried to explain some of the stories' deeper spiritual concepts to her, however, she refused to listen, squinching her eyes tightly and clamping her hands over her ears. The stories were only stories to her, and she didn't want them contaminated with lessons and morals. But he had persisted; there were things to be explained that she might miss. In hindsight, he wondered if it might not have been better just to let Lewis's seeds germinate in their season.

Now it was Osvaldo who had gained the right to sit and read with Ellie. Today they were reading O. Henry's "The Gift of the Magi." A good choice; there was enough moral teaching in it to make it worthwhile. Clayton leaned against the refrigerator and listened as Ellie read. He knew the outcome, but the suspense in Ellie's voice caught him, and he wondered what Osvaldo was thinking. The boy had probably never heard the story before. It was like listening to a tragic, adult Winnie-the-Pooh story. Clayton knew what was going to happen, but couldn't wait to hear it again. Wonderful!

He walked back into his study, scolding himself for

eavesdropping. But he envied the young man from New Mexico who got to listen and read to his daughter.

MARIA KNEW THAT someday it would happen: The boys would be desperate and come to her for money, lots of it. She stood against her old refrigerator, gripping a dishtowel. They sat on the edge of her rickety card table, facing her. Its legs could crumple and they wouldn't care.

It was near the end of summer. Between Osvaldo's paychecks and hers, they had saved about $3000, the most she'd ever had in her life. Mr. Pettigrew was going to sell them his '85 Camry for $2800. Osvaldo said it was a good deal: the car was worth four or five thousand, and Mr. Pettigrew had taken good care of it, and in a week or two it would be theirs. She could drive to work, and Osvaldo could help her by running errands.

"Mama, something's wrong," said Ramon. "You didn't leave us money in the mayonnaise jar. Where are you hiding it now?"

He was lean and angular and looked just like her, the same high cheekbones and dark brown eyes. His raven-black hair was combed straight back. But his good looks were tarnished by the smirk on his face. He was going to tease her before he got tough. That was his way. Her own son, the baby she had held in her arms. *Yes, the baby you abandoned a hundred times to go to the bars. You made him like that. You made all of them bad except Osvaldo.*

"No more money, Ramon. It's time you get a job and earn your way." It was just talk, putting off his inevitable coercion. "You too, Raphael. You're smart. You both could get good jobs, if you wanted to."

Raphael did not look at her, but sipped on a can of beer and cleaned his fingernails with a knife.

"Mama," said Ramon, "we already have good jobs. We just need a little capital to buy some materials. We thought our mama would be glad to help us."

"What is your job? You have no job."

"We're in the happiness business. Your Mr. Santori makes people happy. So do we."

"Mr. Santori preaches the Gospel. You should listen to it."

"We preach our own gospel, Mama, and people flock to us. We have a bigger congregation than Mr. Santori. But we need a little money to keep it running."

"I have no money for you."

"Mama, don't lie to your boys." Ramon did all the talking. He'd always been good at it. Raphael was his marionette, except when it came to girls.

"I'm not lying, Ramon." She had no money *to give him.*

"Between you and Osvaldo, you must bring home eight or nine hundred dollars each week. You can't spend all that money, Mama, and your boys are in need."

She glanced out the window at his fancy car.

"No, Ramon. No money this time."

"Mama, you hurt me deeply. But come close, I will tell you a deep, dark secret."

Maria leaned back hard against the refrigerator. He scooted the card table closer to her. Now it was coming, the pressure, the arm-twisting. She shook her head before he started speaking.

"Mama, this house is bad for cars. There is something in the ground that causes them to stop running, maybe even fall apart. It's the air around here, that's it. It's too pure for cars. I wouldn't park one here for anything, Mama. It will just fall to pieces, or vanish."

"I can get along without a car. I've done it most of my life."

"And another thing, Mama. I saw it on TV this morning. The guardian angels are on strike. They're refusing to protect people until God gives them better harps. It would be too bad if one of those angels were Osvaldo's."

So that was it. They will threaten their brother to get money. But she wouldn't give it to them this time! She'd take

Osvaldo away. Tomorrow, the next day. They'd go to Florida or New York.

"I have to think about it," Maria said. She would pray, and God would help her.

"Mama, we'll drive you to the bank."

"It's past five o'clock."

"Doesn't matter. There's an ATM."

"I requested a forty-dollar maximum withdrawal."

"Mama's getting smarter, isn't she, Raphael?" Ramon stood in front of her; Raphael still sat on the card table, looking bored.

Lord, please help me. Keep him from hurting me. Change my poor boy's heart, and Raphael's, too. And don't let Osvaldo come home until they leave.

"But Mama, look at me! We need money real bad. Real bad, Mama! You gotta give it to us. Do you understand? Tomorrow, we'll come back tomorrow. If you love us, you better have $2000. And Mama, I hope Osvaldo makes it home all right."

"I pray he will, Ramon. To Jesus the Christ I pray he will."

MARIA WAITED FOR Osvaldo to get home. Usually he was there between five-thirty and six, but sometimes he worked late. She had never worried about him before. She wanted to have dinner almost ready when he came. To keep busy she mixed garlic and basil in butter and spread it between slices of French bread. She chopped sausage and celery to add to packaged macaroni and cheese and made peach cobbler à la mud from a recipe Ellen had given her.

She puttered in the kitchen, occasionally lifting the curtain to look down the street, hoping to see Osvaldo walking toward the house. She tried reading an old magazine she'd found, but articles on home decorating and insurance for the elderly were meaningless. She wished she had a phone; then Osvaldo could tell her if he were going to be late.

Once she went into her bedroom and knelt by her bed. *O God, don't take my boy from me. I'm sorry for everything I've done. Don't make him pay. Give him an angel. Give him ten angels.*

She went back into the kitchen, sat at the card table, and opened her Bible to the Psalms. She loved Psalm 91. Sometimes she thought of it as Psalm 911, the emergency Psalm. "He who dwells in the shelter of the Most High will rest in the shadow of the Almighty. I will say of the LORD, 'He is my refuge and my fortress, my God, in whom I trust.'"

She read on. "He will command his angels concerning you to guard you in all your ways." There it is! Ramon had better not make fun of God's angels, or they might strike, and it will be a different kind of strike from what he expected. *O God, be with Osvaldo . . . and Ramon and Raphael, too.* She read the Psalm over three times.

Around seven-thirty, a vehicle pulled into her driveway. Through the curtains she saw a battered white van with ladders strapped on top. On its door she read RAINBOW PAINTING. She nudged the front door open and peered through the crack. Osvaldo climbed out of the van.

Thank You, Jesus.

An old man emerged from the driver's door. He was tall and walked with deliberate, jerky steps. He was skinny and white—white skin, white hair, bushy cotton-ball eyebrows, white overalls, white shoes. The only things that weren't white were the splotches and speckles of paint that decorated him. When he turned to the side, she noticed his painter's cap with its long yellow bill. Osvaldo was right. With that bill, his jerky steps, and his whiteness, Mr. Pettigrew was a speckled stork, a rare species found only in Springdale, Illinois.

Osvaldo introduced him.

"I'm sorry we're late, Mrs. Villanueva," the old man said. The bill of his cap moved with the rhythm of his speech. "We were only an hour from finishing the job, and I didn't want to stop. I'm sorry if you were worried."

"I'm just happy to see him. Are you all right, *mijo?*"

"Of course, Mama."

"And Mrs. Villanueva, tomorrow we have to leave early for a job in Alton. Would it be all right if Osvaldo spent tonight at my house so we could leave early?"

She didn't like the thought of spending the night alone, but at least Osvaldo would be safe for another day. "Certainly, Mr. Pettigrew. Shall I fix him a lunch?"

"I'll take care of him. We should be back by six-thirty or seven."

"I hope he's not giving you any trouble, Mr. Pettigrew." She knew he wasn't. It was just something to say.

"Best worker I've ever had. He's one in a thousand, Mrs. Villanueva. You can be proud of him."

After they left, Maria knelt by her bed and thanked God for His speckled angel.

ELLEN WAS DISAPPOINTED when Osvaldo decided to stay with the Pettigrews and could no longer walk to her house in the evenings. The old man and his wife lived in a two-story, five-bedroom house three miles west of Springdale. Their children had moved out years earlier, and now a parade of grandchildren marched in and out during summers and holidays, thriving on the attention of doting grandparents.

"I stay downstairs, in the back bedroom," Osvaldo told her. "The kids stay upstairs."

"What kids?"

"James and Molly. They're six and seven. They call me Uncle Oz and think I'm a wizard."

Like Mr. Pettigrew, Osvaldo never worked on Sundays, but went to church with his mother. Saturday evenings and Sunday afternoons, however, were reserved for Ellen. On weekends Mr. Pettigrew let him use the painting van, as long as he stayed in Springdale. If it wasn't raining, Ellen and Osvaldo walked to Schroeder Park for a picnic, then returned home to play games or read to each other. They talked about the coming school year, what they'd do after graduation, what it was like living in New Mexico. He taught her a little Spanish, and she taught him new English words. Osvaldo liked to tell her about the Pettigrews and his job.

"I call them the Eds," he said one Sunday afternoon, referring to his employers.

"The Eds. Why the Eds?"

"Edgar and Edna. Have you ever seen them?"

"I've seen Mr. Pettigrew. He looks like a white straw."

"Mrs. Ed looks like a jumbo jawbreaker. One evening I read to James and Molly about Mr. and Mrs. Sprat."

"Who?"

"Mr. Sprat didn't eat anything with fat in it, and Mrs. Sprat—"

"Oh, you mean Jack Sprat."

"And I started laughing and couldn't stop—but I didn't want to tell them that the Sprats reminded me of their grandparents."

"What did you say?"

"That it would look funny watching them lick their dishes."

It was obvious that Osvaldo enjoyed working with Mr. Pettigrew. The old painter made him work hard, and by the end of the day his shoulders ached and he was drenched with sweat. "Aching muscles and sweat feel good," he said, "and besides, I'm making money for Mama."

Osvaldo's job was preparation. First he trimmed back the trees and shrubs touching the house they were painting; a few of the larger shrubs he bundled and pulled back with staked ropes. Next he removed loose paint and dirt using a high-pressure water nozzle, followed up with wire brushes, putty knives, and sanders, if necessary. Finally he used the pressure sprayer again, welcoming its cooling mist in the summer sun. All Mr. Pettigrew had to do was follow him a few hours later and paint. He sprayed the walls, eaves, and gutters, but preferred using a brush on the trim.

Mr. Pettigrew explained everything to him as though it were Nobel Prize research, delighting in the wide varieties of paints, brushes, surfaces, and painting techniques. Ellen listened patiently as Osvaldo enthused about all he was learning.

"It's important not just to cover a surface, but to get the paint into the tiny pores."

And "You have to clean the brushes, rollers, and spray nozzles every time you use them, so they'll last."

And "Mr. Pettigrew says if you're going to be a painter, you must treat your customers and equipment right."

Ellen thought of her messy room, where nothing was cared for except her books.

And "If people are paying good money, you owe them a good job. I pretend I'm going to own their house someday."

She heard echoes of Father: *If a job's worth doing, it's worth doing well.* She wasn't sure she wanted Osvaldo to sound like Father.

"Once I made a bad mistake," said Osvaldo.

"What did you do?"

"I missed a whole section of wall I was supposed to scrape. I must have been thinking about you." He winked at her.

"What did Mr. Pettigrew do?"

"He got mad. We waited a couple of days for the paint to dry; then he made me do it over again. He wasn't really mad though, just upset."

"What's the difference?"

"Mr. Pettigrew helped me never to make that mistake again. Someone who was mad would terrorize me into not doing it again."

Osvaldo told her how he made Mr. Pettigrew smile by leaving "things" for him to find. One day it was a sketch of a monarch butterfly on a wall that had been scraped and power sprayed. The next day Osvaldo taped a giant, blue dragonfly to the wall; after that he drew two hearts and an arrow that said Edgar loves Edna. Every day, wherever they worked, he left something new—a package of tangerine Lifesavers, a picture of Abraham Lincoln, a drawing of a caterpillar, a beautiful maple leaf, Gothic letters reading *Jesus Loves You*. Every day was a surprise. Mr. Pettigrew never acknowledged what he found, and Osvaldo never asked.

DURING THE SUMMER, while Osvaldo was staying at the Pettigrews', Ramon and Raphael never returned to Maria's house, although she expected them at any time. She knew they were watching for Osvaldo. Each night she feared they might burst into her room to demand more money. She resolved not to give it to them. If she did, they would crave more, and there would be no end to it.

She didn't like being away from her boy, but she had no choice. She sensed deep in her bones that Ramon and Raphael would return, and Osvaldo was helpless before them. She didn't dare buy a car. The boys were right, the air around her house was not good for cars, but it was the air that hovered around them like a poisonous aura. Now she was saving her money for something else: Osvaldo would go to college. He had done well at Springdale High. Two A's, four B's, and a C. Ellen Loverage may have helped him, but her boy was smart. Next semester he would do even better.

But she missed him. She needed someone close to her to make her smile.

On Labor Day weekend Ramon and Raphael came back. They were waiting when Maria arrived home from work. Her back window was shattered. There was no car, and they were dressed in old Levi's and worn-out shirts. They both rocked on the back legs of her two folding chairs, hands locked behind their heads. She took her purse into her bedroom, rinsed her face, and drank a large glass of water. Her gallon of fresh orange juice was empty, the container lying on the floor near the refrigerator. They watched her silently.

"Good afternoon, Ramon, Raphael," she finally said. "You've made yourself at home."

"This *is* our home, Mama," said Ramon. "We'll be living here for a while. I need a key."

"This is not your home. It's mine."

"What's yours is ours, Mama. I remember you told me that."

"A long time ago, Ramon, when you were young. Now I've changed my mind."

"Mama, let me put it straight. We need to stay here for a while. Not for long, maybe a month, maybe two. I'll sleep on Osvaldo's cot; Raphael gets the couch. Osvaldo can sleep on the floor."

"No."

"Mama, you have no say in the matter. You can't stop us. You have no phone and no car. Osvaldo's a fuzzy duckling. He can't do anything."

"No."

"Mama, remember the story of the Prodigal Son? He comes home and his father greets him with kisses and throws a big party. But I come home . . . no hugs, no kisses, nada, only a cold shoulder. That's not very Christian, Mama. It's enough to make me bitter."

"That prodigal would have had a different reception if he'd swaggered home acting smart and demanding money. He was sorry for what he did, Ramon. That's the difference between you and him."

"But, Mama, I am truly sorry—sorry you didn't give us money the last time we were in need. Look at the trouble you caused us, Mama. Now you owe us big time."

"I owe you nothing except my love and prayers."

"Forget those; they're cheap. Just give me a couple thousand dollars, and we'll get out of your hair forever. Maybe we'll go to California."

That sounded like too good a bargain. Two thousand dollars to ship them to California forever. Osvaldo could move back home, and they could save more money and buy a car. But she didn't trust Ramon. He never told the truth.

"Love and prayers will do you more good."

Raphael spoke. "When does Osvaldo get home?"

She didn't answer.

Raphael opened the cardboard box where Osvaldo kept his things. "Nothing, Ramon."

Ramon checked the closet. All that was left was a pair of Osvaldo's paint-spattered tennis shoes that Maria kept forgetting to throw out.

"Where is he?" demanded Ramon.

"With friends," answered Maria. They'd have to find out from someone besides her.

"Then there's plenty of room for two honored guests."

What could she say? They would stay no matter what she did or said, at least for a few days.

"What are you fixing us for dinner, Mama?" said Ramon.

"You may eat whatever you find. I'm having coffee."

"Don't make it hard on us while we're here. The happier we are, the happier you will be."

Maria felt as though she were entering a murky tunnel, with twisting, tortuous turns constricting to nothingness. Tomorrow she would run away. She would go to work, leave in the middle of the morning, and go by the bank. Then she'd get Osvaldo and they'd leave town. But Ramon was smart; he might be watching, and then he would get her money. There had to be another way, but she was so poor at figuring things out. He was always a step ahead of her.

It was good that Osvaldo was not with her. He would not know anything was wrong until tomorrow night when they ate at Ellen's house. But all that was for tomorrow. Right now she needed to go into her bedroom and pray.

DURING THE SUMMER Ellen had missed the library of beautifully bound books and the solitude of Miss Merkle's house. Once in a while she talked with Rolex through the fence and gave him dog biscuits. She didn't want him to think she was an intruder the next time she went into the yard.

The house now had a different meaning to her. Superimposed on the beauty and peace was the mystery of Father's relationship with Miss Merkle. Without question they had known each other a long time ago. But what, if anything, had been going on since then? She made up dozens of scenarios involving Father and her English teacher. Some were as innocent as having dated once in high school; others were racier, and she didn't like to dwell on them. It was like seeing a few minutes of a movie and then having the VCR break. There was more to find out, and, rightly or wrongly, she was determined to investigate.

Late in the summer she found Mom's senior yearbook in a box in the basement, and, that evening, brought it to the dinner table. Books at mealtimes were forbidden, but the flak would be worth it.

"Ellie, you know the rules."

"I wanted to show you a darling picture of Mom. It won't take long." How could he object to that? She had earmarked a picture of the Girls' Honor Society in which Mom and ten other smiling girls posed in a line. She wore a plain white blouse and a plaid skirt that came almost to her ankles. All the girls had on white bobby socks and oxfords. Her shoulder-length hair curled under slightly in a pageboy. "Mom was really pretty, wasn't she?"

Father moved his chair to a corner of the table so they could look at the book from the same angle. He slowly turned the pages, pointing out pictures of Mom in the school orchestra and on the badminton team, as well as some candid shots with her friends.

"I didn't know Mom in high school, Ellie, but yes, she's beautiful . . . just my kind of girl."

"When did you meet her?"

"In our freshman year at North Texas State, at a Christmas party."

They turned to the back of the book and read the auto-graphed messages, some dripping with sentiment, others humorous. After a while he set the book aside, and they finished dinner in silence. When he stood up to go to his study, Ellen asked her question.

"Father, I'd love to see your yearbook. Do you know where it is?"

"Stashed away someplace, Ellie. I doubt if I could find it." He turned away, as if to avoid more questions, and started carrying dishes into the kitchen. He seemed agitated. "If I run across it, I'll let you know."

"Maybe it's in the basement. There are a lot of boxes down there."

"Don't go poking around," he warned. "Everything's sealed, and I have things organized just the way I want."

"I'd like to see what you looked like when you were a teenager."

"You've seen pictures of Mom and me when we were engaged."

"That's not the same. Everyone looks weird in high school."

"That was too long ago. I didn't think anyone would care to see my high school photos again."

"I'd care."

"If I run across it, I'll let you know." He left quickly for his study.

ELEVEN

Someone had warned Maria that Illinois summers were humid, but at the time that didn't sound like clammy, muggy, sweltering. Her little house had no air conditioning, and because she was afraid to leave her windows open at night, her rooms felt like a sauna. Years ago she'd been in a sauna in Albuquerque and couldn't understand how anyone enjoyed sitting in a hot fog, inhaling scalding vapors, unable see the person next to her. Now she lay sweating on the sheets, praying and humming hymns, hoping exhaustion would overcome the steamy darkness, wishing the night would disappear so she could go to the air-conditioned assembly room at Megatronics.

If she got up at six o'clock she had enough time to dress and gather up beer cans, liquor bottles, and fast-food wrappers, and to fix a lunch before one of the other assembly workers picked her up at a quarter to seven. To save time she'd tried making her lunch the night before, but the lunch never made it through the night. As she left the house, she often saw Ramon on Osvaldo's cot and Raphael sprawled on the couch. They'd come in the middle of the night, never thinking to be quiet. If they needed to use the bathroom, they'd burst into her room, talking and joking. To them she was another piece of furniture.

From somewhere the boys got a large TV and VCR. Several weeks later a satellite dish that received over 200 channels showed up. Who needed to watch that many channels? A computer occupied her old card table in the kitchen, and often in the mornings video games glared at her.

Maria was relieved that she seldom saw them awake. From what she could tell, they slept late and stayed home during the day, but when she got home from work, they were usually gone. During the night, however, the loud banging and raucous voices started again. Sometimes other men came with them; a few times she heard women's voices.

This morning, after finding extra TVs, stereos, computers, and other items, she banged angrily around the kitchen. Ramon awoke, perched on his elbows, and glared at her.

"Not so much noise, Mama. What's wrong with you?"

"Ramon, what is this stuff? Where did you get it?" Meaningless questions, her only way to protest.

"Don't worry about it, Mama. We're in the distributing business now."

"Do your distributing someplace else, not in my house."

"Mama, some day *People* magazine will do a feature on us and you'll be proud. Two disadvantaged Latino boys from the slums of New Mexico, whose mother was a prostitute, make good."

It was better to say nothing. Don't approve; don't disapprove. They knew how she felt. When she complained, they made it hard for her.

She was thankful Osvaldo was living with the Pettigrews, among good people and away from his brothers. Ramon and Raphael couldn't influence him any longer, but they might harm him physically. The only thing good about their "distributing business" was that they were too preoccupied to torment their younger brother.

Working with Mr. Pettigrew was good for Osvaldo. The old painter referred to him as his partner and sent him on errands to the hardware and paint stores, going over to New Hope to pick up paints, brushes, and rollers. Each week Osvaldo seemed taller. A growth spurt, Maria thought. When school let out, he was five feet four; now, three months later, he was five-seven. He would always be chunkier than his wiry brothers, but over the summer he'd lost much of his baby fat, and his boyish face had lengthened. She was pleased that his smile and lively eyes remained the same.

All of her other boys had been lazy, but Osvaldo was a worker. In addition to working for Mr. Pettigrew, he was painting a mural for Adele Ritchie at her estate west of Springdale.

He told her about Mrs. Ritchie, a tall, bossy, pumpkin-haired lady.

"One day she got angry at me," he said.

"Why, what did you do?"

"I drew a little pencil butterfly on the wall . . . for Mr. Pettigrew."

"Were you supposed to do that?"

"It doesn't matter. We paint over it."

"But she didn't like it, Osvaldo. You shouldn't—"

"But she wasn't really angry, Mama. She just pretends like that. She wants me to draw a whole wall of butterflies and leaves, in color."

"Do you know how to do that?"

"She showed me a picture of a branch covered with monarch butterflies. Mr. Ritchie took it on their first anniversary trip, in Mexico. It's beautiful."

"Ossie, you aren't trained—"

"Mama, she's teaching me, in the evenings after work. She told me she knows a thing or two or even three about art. And she likes the way I paint. She told her neighbor that an authentic Mexican Indian was painting her mural. Am I an authentic Mexican Indian, Mama?"

"I don't know, Ossie. My mother was Chihuahuan Indian, and my father was Spanish and Serbian. I don't know about your father."

"Is there any way to find out?"

"No, Ossie, no way to find out." She wondered if he was thinking about her husband, Fernando, or about his real father. She'd said very little about her past life, but he was old enough to figure things out. "Where are you painting this mural?" she asked him.

"On the gardener's shed, where I drew the first one."

Although Maria was proud of him, she was unhappy that it meant he had even less time to spend with her. After working with Mr. Pettigrew, he drove straight to Mrs. Ritchie's. He even missed some of the dinners with the Santoris. Daylight lasted until about eight-thirty, and Mrs. Ritchie rented a bank of lights for him so that he could continue after dark. She told him that it didn't matter if he wasn't finished before school started. The mural was a big job, and he should take as much time as he needed to do it right.

When Mrs. Ritchie went back on night shift, she left notes for him, suggesting improvements or praising him for what he'd done the evening before. By the time school started he'd completed most of the butterflies, using every free minute he had, sometimes painting after sunset using the lights she had rented.

One of the high points of Maria's summer was when Osvaldo took her to the Ritchie estate to view his mural. On a long trailing branch hung a cluster of black and orange butterflies almost covering the foliage. The branch looked as though it were swaying in a mountain breeze. Osvaldo had painted that! Where did he get such talent? Not from her. If she tried to draw a butterfly, it would look like a twisted paper clip. Maybe from his father, whoever that was.

When school started, Mrs. Ritchie was so pleased with his

work that she gave him a check for $800 and said he could finish the mural during his free time that autumn. She called him the next Diego Rivera and promised to recommend him to her friends. That same evening Maria and Osvaldo walked to the bank to deposit his check in her account. On the way home, they celebrated at Bud's Burgers. He had a double cheeseburger, a double order of curly fries, and a giant root beer, while she had a scoop of vanilla ice cream and a cup of coffee.

On the last Friday of summer vacation, when they ate with the Loverages, Maria saw a different side of Osvaldo as he talked about the mural. Usually he sat quietly through the meals, but that evening he chattered on about Mrs. Ritchie, Mr. Pettigrew, monarch butterflies and their two thousand-mile migrations, painting murals, painting houses, and maybe, someday, studying art. Nobody could keep him quiet. Nobody wanted to.

At the end of the meal, Osvaldo and Ellen went for a walk in the warm summer air. They were going to the library, he said, to find out about Diego Rivera.

OSVALDO'S FULL-TIME WORK with Mr. Pettigrew ended, and with the blessing of the Santoris in the next-door manse, Osvaldo moved into the basement of Bethel Temple. As a part-time custodian he mowed the lawns and kept the Sunday school rooms clean. On Mondays and Wednesdays Maria joined him for dinner at the Santoris', and on Fridays they ate at the Loverages'. Osvaldo never went to the Depot Street house.

Ellen was pleased to have two classes with him, math and Spanish. Mrs. Moreno, his counselor, had thrown in Spanish as a "freebie" to help him elevate his GPA. Now Ellen had to reconsider setting her goals so low, when she knew she could do better. How could she encourage Osvaldo to get good grades when she got no more than seventies? Life was simpler when she didn't have to worry about other people.

Father, true to his word, gave Ellen no money for clothes. She started school in the faded jeans and sweatshirts she'd worn the previous semester. Twice she tried wearing Linda's castoffs, but they never felt comfortable.

Several weeks into the school year, Osvaldo took her shopping at the Salvation Army thrift store. She found a dark blue skirt and a white blouse with blue and yellow flowers embroidered on the front and fine blue piping on the sleeves and collar. Nothing fancy, but they felt right. They were new, as far as she could tell, and a bargain for eight dollars. Osvaldo paid for them.

"An early Christmas present," he told her.

"It's only September."

"Then maybe a Thanksgiving present, or Halloween, or Labor Day. It doesn't matter. I want to buy them for you."

The next Sunday during the church service Mrs. Ritchie passed Ellen a note. *I must see you afterward. I have something important to tell you.* She signed her name *Adele.*

Everyone knew that Mrs. Ritchie was rather odd. Besides the pastor, she was the only person everyone, from little kids to tottering seniors, knew by name. Now she was writing cloak-and-dagger notes to a teenager. What could she want with Ellen?

In the narthex after church, Mrs. Ritchie pulled her aside. "Ellen," she said, "you look wonderful in that outfit."

"Thank you." She didn't know if Mrs. Ritchie meant it or not.

"And I've always admired your hair, it's so . . . so . . . straight. You've probably noticed my hair has a little curl to it."

How was she supposed to answer this woman? "Sometimes I wish I had more curl."

"Blue is definitely your color. It highlights the golden tones in your hair."

"Um. Thank you." Ellen frantically searched for some

compliment she could return. Finally she said the only positive thing she could think of. "Father really appreciates the feedback you give him after church."

"He doesn't repeat it to anyone, does he?" She looked shocked.

"He used to tell Mom. Now, sometimes he tells me, but that's as far as it goes."

Mrs. Ritchie moved her purse to her other arm and sidled closer. "And how are *you* doing, Ellen?" she said furtively.

"What do you mean?"

"I know that you cook and take care of the house for your father. Are you doing all right?" She looked concerned, as though she cared.

"I'm doing okay. I don't do as well as Mom, but I try to keep up."

"Well, Ellen, I notice and I'm proud of you. I wish I'd told you sooner. You're one of my favorite people, you know."

"Thank you, Mrs. Ritchie. I like you too." She didn't know whether she really liked the lady or not, but she liked what she heard, and Mrs. Ritchie didn't sound like a phony.

That evening at dinner, Father asked about her new clothes. When he heard that Osvaldo had bought them for her at the Salvation Army, he had a fit. "You went shopping at the thrift store with Osvaldo?" His voice was a note or two higher than usual.

"Father, I found a lot of nice things there, and they're inexpensive." It looked as though another argument was unavoidable. She couldn't even buy her clothes where she wanted.

"Was Della Mathews there?"

"The lady from church with the blue-gray bouffant? Yes, she helped me pick things out. She's very nice."

"I'm sure she *is* very nice, Ellie, but her tongue wags like a flag in a hurricane. By now the whole church knows you're buying your clothes at the Salvation Army."

"That doesn't bother me."

"Well, it bothers me, and Mom would have been appalled."

It was unfair for him to play the Mom card. Besides, Ellen didn't believe that Mom would have been "appalled."

"I don't want you to go there anymore. I'll arrange some way for you to earn money for your clothes."

"No."

"No what?"

"I've finished my summer reading, so I'll work if you want me to, but I'll buy my clothes anyplace I please." She had raised her voice, lost her cool. But he made her so mad. Now she couldn't stop herself. "There's nothing you can do about my clothes unless you rip them off of me. You don't care about me. All you care about is how you look to the people at church. Well, there's no way in the cosmos you can stop me from shopping anyplace I please."

He put his hand on her arm and looked at her with his intense preacher-to-congregation face. "Ellie Loverage, I forbid you to buy your clothes at thrift stores."

Something broke inside her. He'd pushed her beyond being mad . . . to being indifferent. "Get used to it, Father," she said calmly. "Where I shop isn't going to hurt you, me, the church, or anyone else. The only thing that's being injured is your pride, and you can afford to lose some of that."

"Ellie! Stop it!"

She was startled. He'd never yelled at her before.

He took a deep breath, blew it out slowly, and seemed to calm down. "Ellie, that is no way to speak to your father. I'm trying to do what is best for all of us. I know I'm not perfect, but I'm still the . . ."

Authority. Say it, Father, au-thor-i-ty.

He didn't go on, but bit his lip and stared hard at her. "Now I want you to go to your . . ." He paused, wiped his forehead with his napkin, then paced slowly through the dining room, into the kitchen, and back.

She wanted to tell him he couldn't discipline her anymore. He thought he'd seen stubborn, but he hadn't seen anything yet. Two hundred and seventy-one more days and she'd be out of here, away from him.

He finally stopped pacing, stood behind her, and placed his hands gently on her shoulders. His fingers were so icy she almost cringed, and his voice was soft and trembling. "Ellie, I want you to go to your room . . . choose a book, any book, and bring it to the living room and read to me. I'll phone the church and tell them I won't be there this evening. I'll see you in five minutes." He massaged her shoulders for a few seconds, then went to his study.

What was he trying to do? Win her with kindness? Well, he'd certainly caught her off guard. Choose a book? She'd make it long and crammed full of imagery. How about *The Hobbit?* She'd find out what effect Bilbo Baggins had on him.

In the living room Father had settled into his recliner with his coffee. On the end table next to her female recliner stood a frosty glass of lemonade—on a coaster, of course. He stood up and moved the floor lamp so that it illuminated her book.

"We haven't read for a long time," he said.

"Maybe since the fifth grade when we read the Chronicles of Narnia."

"Let's try again. We won't have many more chances. If you get tired, I can take over."

She read for about an hour, and Father listened intently, sometimes leaning back with his hands clasped behind his neck, his eyes closed. The words flowed like a fast-moving creek. She loved reading Tolkien, and envisaged herself and Father as invisible companions of Bilbo, meeting Gandalf and the dwarfs, helping the hobbit steal the troll's purse. By the end of chapter 2 she knew he was hooked.

CLAYTON HAD MADE a priority of reading his Bible before going to sleep. He didn't have to read very long, but he needed to end the day as he started it, reading the Word. This evening he climbed into bed with two books. He'd read his

Bible, but first there were a few details in *The Hobbit* he wanted to clarify. He opened to chapter 1.

Clayton woke just after one o'clock, his bed lamp on, *The Hobbit* lying beside him on top of his Bible. Dutifully he opened his Bible to Psalm 23. God would understand if he didn't read more than one short psalm. He read slowly, meditating on each verse. Then he turned out the light, rolled over, and immediately went to sleep, dreaming about the adventures of Bilbo and Gandalf in the valley of the shadow of death.

ON THE SECOND Thursday and Friday in October, parent-teacher conferences were held at Springdale High School. The students celebrated a mini-vacation, their last break before cold weather set in. While Osvaldo took advantage of the time to work with Mr. Pettigrew, Ellen looked forward to two days of reading. Father was going to see her counselor, Mrs. Moreno, at four o'clock on Thursday, but it was a routine conference and Ellen's presence wasn't needed. She'd made it through the first six weeks of her senior year without any problems. Her grades were decent; she even had a *B* in Mr. Wicker's math class. It was just as easy to make 80s on every test as it was to make 70s. Maybe next semester she'd present him with 90s.

The all-day conferences meant that Ellen could safely read at Miss Merkle's house all day until about five-thirty. To be on the safe side, however, Ellen planned to leave at four. She was in the middle of Hugo's *The Toilers of the Sea* and looked forward to long hours of peaceful reading.

That afternoon, however, she had trouble concentrating. Father's photo was down the hall, on a nightstand, staring at her through the walls. She went into the bedroom and picked up the five-by-seven. *Father, Father, what's going on? You don't belong here.* She slipped the photo from its frame and read his words again.

May the years ahead of us be as precious as the last two. I will love you forever. Clay. It was wrong! She didn't want him writing love notes to anyone but Mom, even if it had been forty years ago.

Setting the photo back on the nightstand, she noticed some books lying on the narrow shelf underneath. A blue and yellow spine near the top caught her eye—Sam Houston High 1954. That was it! Father's high school yearbook—or rather, Miss Merkle's. She sat cross-legged on the floor, leaned back against the spread, and started turning pages.

Seniors, Class of '54. Lane, Lee, Locicero, Loverage. There was Father. Same long, triangular face, his hair parted on the right, a big lumpy wave in front. She flipped over to the next page to the *M*'s. Merkle. Caroline Merkle. She looked like a 1950s movie star with long, wavy, shoulder-length hair curled up at the ends. Her English teacher! Beautiful.

She turned back to the beginning of the book and scanned pictures of the principal, teachers, and class officers. There was Father—Clay Loverage, Student Body President. And Caroline Merkle—Student Body Secretary. On every page she looked for Father and Miss Merkle. Father on the basketball and baseball teams. Caroline Merkle, cheerleader. She couldn't imagine her English teacher jumping, swinging her arms, and yelling. She studied the candid photos. In one Father and Miss Merkle had their arms on each other's shoulders; the word *Lovers* was printed underneath. The two of them at the school carnival, at the homecoming dance, at a beach. On the awards pages she found Most Likely to Succeed—Clay Loverage. Valedictorian —Caroline Merkle. Best-looking couple—Clay and Cary.

She read the notes scribbled in the free spaces. *Dear Cary, You've been a true friend since fourth grade. Great to hear about you and Clay. You're the luckiest girl in the world. Love, Nancy.* And another: *Dear Cary, The best always deserve the best. I couldn't be happier for anyone. Alicia.* On the teachers' page she read: *Dear Caroline, You are an outstanding student, a pleasure to have in my class. Best wishes to you and Clay as you attend college. It will be tough, but I know you two can make it. Harry Montague.*

On the back page she found Father's note. She felt guilty reading it; it was private, not meant for her eyes. *Dear Cary, I love you. You're the only girl I've ever had. I started with the best, and I'll soon be married to her. God has brought the most wonderful person in the world into my life. I'll love you forever. Clay.*

She read it again. The words were wrong. It should read Joyce, not Cary. At marriage and parenting conferences she'd heard Father talk about Mom being his true love since he was young. How could he have written these things to Miss Merkle?

She flipped back through more pages of the yearbook. The two of them were everywhere. In the choir. She was on the swim team. Father was on the debate team. She had been homecoming queen. Clay and Cary. Cary and Clay. Congratulations. Best wishes. The perfect couple.

Ellen sat on the floor, stunned and bewildered. It was like watching a TV movie with the power switching on and off and the sound track messed up. High school sweethearts? Serious enough to plan a wedding? Now, forty years later living next to each other in a town a thousand miles from their high school . . . when Father had been happily married to someone else?

When Ellen closed the yearbook and returned it to the nightstand, it was almost three o'clock. She'd been sitting there an hour and a half. She went back to the library, but photos and cryptic notes obscured Victor Hugo's words. Like giant waves, thoughts about Father and Miss Merkle crashed against walls she had considered firm.

Father and Mom and their wonderful marriage. Now the specter of Miss Caroline Merkle was etched on their wedding pictures. She wished she'd never found out. She should have stayed out of Miss Merkle's house, and especially her bedroom. But who would have dreamed it? It was impossible! She knew there had to be a logical explanation. There just had to be.

The next afternoon Ellen returned anxiously to Miss Merkle's house. She went directly to the bedroom to look at the stack of books on the nightstand. Something of importance besides the yearbook might be there. Underneath the yearbook she found three photo albums. Two of them contained family pictures, photographs of Miss Merkle with her parents and two younger sisters. Ellen thumbed rapidly through a blur of birthday parties, beach trips, holiday gatherings, and silly poses without finding anyone who looked like Father.

The third album, however, was all Father. On the first page was written in calligraphy *Clay and I*. After that followed page after page, picture after picture, dozens of them, of Father and a young Miss Merkle taken when they were in high school. Every picture was captioned. "At the lake." "Football game with Lincoln High." "Jenny's birthday." "Grandma and Grandpa's anniversary." "Church conference at Faith Meadows." "With Denny and Brenda at the fair."

Okay. So they were high school sweethearts. Everybody thinks they're in love when they're in high school. It's strange that it was Miss Merkle, but stranger things have happened. And I don't blame Father for not wanting anyone to know about it. I wonder if Mom knew? But it's his business, not mine or anyone else's. It doesn't change anything at home. It's just one of those weird coincidences.

She returned to the library and relaxed while she read *The Toilers of the Sea*. At four-thirty she checked the house to make sure everything was back in place and left.

Just high school sweethearts. That's all they were. No big deal.

ON SUNDAY THE *Springdale Gazette* ran its weekly feature about citizens of Springdale and featured Miss Caroline Merkle, English teacher, Springdale High School. Ellen pored over the article, noting names and dates. Graduated from Sam

Houston High School, Houston, Texas, 1954; attended Rice University 1954–1958, graduating summa cum laude; attended graduate school at Southern Methodist University, 1958–1963, earning an M.A. in English Literature; taught high school English in Dayton, Texas, 1963–1966; taught at North Kansas City High School, Missouri, 1966–1973; came to Springdale High School, 1973.

The places sounded too familiar. She had never paid much attention to where Father had been pastor before he and Mom moved to Springdale, but she'd heard him mention Kansas City and Dayton. For him and Miss Merkle to end up in Springdale by chance was one thing, but three places?

That evening, while Father was at church, she went into his study and got down Mom's old Bible in which she'd recorded family information. Clay, Jr. and Dan were born in Dayton, Texas; Linda in Kansas City. The years matched perfectly. Father and Miss Merkle had lived in the same cities most of their lives!

Her mind raced through a dozen scenarios she didn't like. Father might be stuffy and controlling, but she loved and trusted him and couldn't accept that he might be involved with her English teacher. She *wouldn't* believe it. Not Father.

TWELVE

Maria felt helpless as Ramon and Raphael slowly took over her house. If it were only she, she'd disappear to Florida or Texas, someplace far away; but every time she hinted that she might leave, the boys made threats. They'd discovered that Osvaldo stayed in the basement of Bethel Temple, painted with Mr. Pettigrew, and worked on Mrs. Ritchie's mural. They knew it all and threatened it all.

"Mama," Ramon would say, "we love you so much we don't want to see you move away. You have to stay here to protect Osvaldo, Mr. Santori's church, and Osvaldo's girlfriend. You wouldn't want anything to happen to them, would you?"

"God's watching them, and He's watching you, too."

"We'll give Him a good show, Mama. Maybe we'll make a fiery sacrifice out of the painting van, or—listen, Mama, you'll like this—we'll use black paint to create nighttime for Osvaldo's butterflies."

They were ridiculing God. *Oh, my Lord, forgive my boys.*

"And, Mama, pretty soon you'll have chubby Osvaldos crawling around your house, wearing thick, Coke-bottle glasses. Osvaldo doesn't sleep at Bethel Temple, he sleeps with his girlfriend."

On another occasion Ramon talked to her about the need for silence concerning their "work."

"Mama, I'm concerned that you might say something about the business we've set up in our house."

"You mean *my* house, don't you, Ramon?" It was a futile statement, a feeble protest, but her only way to fight back.

He shrugged his shoulders. "Your house, my house, it doesn't matter. Just listen to me. To ensure competitiveness, you must be very quiet. Do you understand me, Mama?"

"I hear what you're saying, Ramon."

"But do you understand me? I don't want bad things to happen to Osvaldo or your friends. We have partners who guard secrets and wouldn't like to hear that you've been talking."

"I know perfectly well what you mean."

"Then think about it every day, Mama, every minute. Go to work, to your silly church, to your dinners. Do your thing, but remember, you live in a cozy, private bungalow with your two loving sons. We want to keep it that way."

God, I am cornered and have no place to turn but heaven. I can't talk to my boys. They stopped listening so long ago. They didn't learn to love me when they were little; now it's impossible. They are wild, unruly stallions doing what they please. It is my fault, but they know what they're doing is wrong.

God, for the hundredth time I ask You to forgive me. I know I'm forgiven, but I can't help asking again and again. Forgive me, God, and make my life better. But more than anything else, protect Osvaldo.

The boys now used her bedroom for their "distribution operation," as they called it. Most of the boxes contained electronics stuff, but they also had U-Haul and beer boxes. Once she saw a loop of a necklace hanging out of one. At first they stored things only in the living room, but when she refused to buy opaque curtains, they moved all their boxes into her bed-room. Now only a narrow path wound to the bathroom and to her bed. She had no space, no privacy. Without moving boxes she couldn't reach her clothes in the closet or open the dresser drawers, so she kept a few things in a small locker at Megatronics.

She stayed away from the house as much as possible, caus-ing the boys to complain that she didn't love them enough to fix a decent meal. The best days of the week were Mondays and Wednesdays, when she and Osvaldo ate with the Santoris. Olga was her best friend, and they could talk for hours with-out growing tired of each other. One of the Santoris' five chil-dren had not turned out well, so Olga understood her anguish over Ramon and Raphael. Maria never mentioned the dis-tribution operation at her house.

She also enjoyed dinner at the Loverages' on Fridays, al-though more for Osvaldo's sake than her own. Pastor Lover-age was a nice man, but she didn't know how to talk with him. He asked lots of questions, and they talked about church and Jesus, Osvaldo's school, and New Mexico, but it wasn't like being at the Santoris'.

Ellen was a nice girl for her son, and she enjoyed seeing them together. Four months earlier, they'd looked like chil-dren, but over the summer they had matured rapidly. Now they were a young couple. She liked the way they were so natural together, listening to music, playing games, reading. In these modern days of fast, quick romance, when anything and everything was acceptable, they seemed very old-fashioned.

She thought about her own life as a teenager in New Mex-ico, with parents who drank so much they forgot to love her. Her father used to take her to smoky back rooms of saloons where he drank and played poker. When she was twelve, after he'd lost badly for the evening, he sent her upstairs with one of the men. She'd run away from her parents when she was fourteen, mostly at their urging, and for the next twenty-five years she had always been in trouble.

She hadn't taken good care of any of her other boys. No wonder they all turned out bad. If her husband, Fernando, hadn't gotten mixed up with drug dealers, things might have been different. He wasn't a bad person, but he could be talked into anything by his friends . . . and he had the wrong friends. He hadn't killed anyone—he didn't even own a gun—but a state trooper was killed, and Fernando had been with the men who did it. At the trial he didn't have a good lawyer. Twenty years later, when he got out of prison, he was a confused old man she hardly knew, but she took care of him because he was her husband. Before he got lung cancer, he worked a little as a night janitor at the college in Socorro, but most of the time he lay on the couch watching TV.

Now she was in Illinois eating in the beautiful homes of pastors, and a pastor's daughter and Osvaldo liked each other. What would Fernando, or her other sons, think about that! Ramon and Raphael made fun of Osvaldo and Ellen, but maybe they were jealous or didn't appreciate something good when they saw it. Ten years ago, before she became a Christian, she might have made fun of them too. Priests and pastors and chaplains had never impressed her, and if any of her friends had eaten dinner at a clergyman's house, she would have ridiculed them. But now, three nights each week she dined with pastors, and they liked and respected her. And they liked Osvaldo, too. He was a wonderful boy who loved her and treated her nicely. Praise be to the Lord Jesus.

Church on Sunday mornings was the other wonderful time of the week. What freedom to stand and sing, lifting her hands to the God who loved her and saved her. The singing never lasted long enough. Some of the songs made her want to laugh, and others made her cry.

Hide me in Your Rock, my God,
Shield me with Your hand,
Keep me safe from storm and foe,
Lead me to Your promised land.

Hear my cry, have mercy, Lord,
Forgive my sins, I pray;
Wash me clean, renew my life,
Lift me up today.

Lift me up, lift me up,
Lift me up, I pray.
Lift me to Your precious Rock,
Lift me up today.

"Lift Me Up" was her favorite. She loved the words and the melody, and sang it all day long at work. And as she sang, she prayed. *O God, hear my prayer, be my Rock, lift me up. Be with my Osvaldo. Keep him safe from sin and from his brothers. And be with Ramon and Raphael and make them good.*

Deep inside she prayed for peace for herself. What was going to happen with the "operation" at her house? She knew what was going on. Would the police arrest her for helping her boys? Would a policeman knock on her door and take her to jail again? Would she ever find peace and have a house where she could invite a neighbor for coffee or have grandchildren come to play? *It's time for that, isn't it? O Lord, help me, help me, help me.*

AFTER SCHOOL BEGAN and Ellen knew the teachers' schedules, she went to Miss Merkle's house as often as she could. Soon late fall and winter storms would blanket the lawn with snow, and Rolex would be left in the house all day. On one occasion the previous winter she'd found him in the house, and he was so friendly she couldn't relax with him inside. While she read, he wandered about the house, returning to offer her slippers and frayed leather bones. She didn't know where they belonged and felt uncomfortable leaving them in the library. She would have to be careful. If the snow was deep enough for her to leave tracks, she wouldn't come. She didn't dare leave the slightest trace of a path from the fence to Miss Merkle's back door.

One Friday near the end of November, she entered Miss Merkle's house after school and headed for the library. First she'd finish her science homework, then read a few chapters in Hawthorne's *The Scarlet Letter.*

Before she opened her science book, however, she wanted to check Miss Merkle's bedroom again. She would look through the photo album for the umpteenth time and reread the captions she knew almost by heart. She was tempted to search closets and drawers for more clues about Father and Miss Merkle, but that would be crossing the line she'd set for herself.

As she entered the bedroom she noticed a white binder lying among the lacy pillows on the bed. On the cover, within a filigreed border, a picture of Father as a teenager stared at her. Miss Merkle had obviously been looking through it the night before. Inside, transparent plastic sheets contained notes and letters from Father to Miss Merkle, Clay to Cary.

She turned the pages quickly to get a sense of time. The first pages were dated 1952 to 1954, when they were in high school, but the last few letters were written when Father was at North Texas State and Miss Merkle was at Rice. The final entry in the binder was dated January 21, 1956. Father and Mom were married in June of that year. Ellen read slowly.

Dear Cary,

This is the hardest letter I have ever written. I write with remorse and shame, but with the conviction that I am doing what is right for both of us. In earlier letters I alluded to what was happening. When we were together at Christmas I tried to tell you how I felt, but you did not hear me. When we saw each other on New Year's Day, you didn't understand what I was saying. Now I write what is final and irrevocable. I've prayed about it, and it has weighed on my mind for months. It is the only thing I can do—

In June I will marry Joyce Mahler.

I know this hurts you, Cary, and I am filled with sorrow and guilt. When we were together, I never lied to you. All of my promises were sincere at the time. I never led you on to take advantage of you. But when I came to North Texas State, I realized that I didn't love you enough to be your husband. Our weekends in Galveston will always haunt me. I accept full responsibility for those and ask your forgiveness. I am sorry and expect to carry a burden of shame the rest of my life. Please forgive me.

I wish you happiness.

Clay

As she reread the letter she heard a key turn in a lock and the front door open. The garage door opener hadn't made its grinding announcement. Miss Merkle must have come home early and parked in the driveway, and now the house was a trap! Maybe she would just dash in, get something, and leave. Ellen felt a sudden panic, but reminded herself to keep cool. Everything was going to be all right. She laid the binder among the pillows, dropped to the floor, and rolled under the bed. Miss Merkle would probably leave in a few minutes, and everything would be all right. Otherwise she'd have to wait until her teacher was in the bathroom or something and try to sneak out. Her chances of leaving undetected were still good.

She scooted back against the wall, next to the headboard. The dust ruffle hung almost to the carpet; there was no way Miss Merkle would see her unless she looked under the bed. She could hear her in the living room. Any second she might come into the bedroom.

Then she heard a man speaking in a low whisper. "Yeah, that's good." "Here, take this." "Now, lay the tablecloth between them." She heard glass shatter and visualized the curved panes of the china cabinet. The Hummels! The fragile figurines clinked together roughly as they were bundled into a tablecloth. The jangling of silverware lasted only a few seconds.

There were at least two men, and they moved quickly from the living room to the dining room to the library. They weren't bothering with the TV, VCR, stereo, or computer. They entered the bedroom, moving swiftly, efficiently.

Where's Rolex? Why isn't he barking? What if they look under the bed? They could rape me or kill me! God, don't let them look. Make them blind. I'm so sorry. I'll never come here again, never, never. Please, please, please, don't let them see me. Make them go away.

She pressed herself against the wall and curled up into a ball and took slow, shallow breaths, fearing each might rumble through the room and betray her. Her heart pounded rapidly, drumming through her temples, pulsing to her toes, threatening to vibrate the foundations of the house. Droplets of sweat trickled down her forehead and neck, and her hands were chilled and clammy.

The men apparently spread a sheet on the bed. Miss Merkle's exquisite crystal music box sang a weak complaint when tossed on the bed, and figurines protested melodically. Ellen watched two pairs of shoes move about the room from the dressers to the closet to the nightstand. She stared at the strip of light between the dust ruffle and carpet, waiting for a face to appear.

The men's tennis shoes were dirty. Sometimes they stuck under the bedspread close enough so she could touch them. The white ones moved the quickest, and the tense, confident voice above them hissed directions. The black shoes, which obeyed the voice, were speckled with yellow and white. On the toe of the right shoe was a round gray dot drawn out in a long smudge. She'd seen it before.

Impossible! Those were Osvaldo's old painting shoes. His brothers must have stolen them, or maybe some tramp had scavenged them out of the garbage. Osvaldo's not a thief.

God, this is the worst day of my life. Make me invisible!
Please, get me out of here! I promise never to come back.

As soon as the men finished with the bedroom they left the house, firmly closing the front door. Ellen wanted to rush to a window to see if one was Osvaldo, but she couldn't move. She lay trembling, afraid someone was still there or that they would return. If she tried to leave, they'd surprise her in the hallway or the kitchen, and there would be no escape. She closed her eyes and listened. She heard little creaks and clicks, probably house noises, but she wasn't sure. She waited a long time, until she was sure they had left.

She finally dared to scoot out from under the bed and glance around the room. The music box was gone, the jewelry box lay upside down on the floor, and fragments of a crystal figurine littered the dresser. She didn't know what else was missing or broken. She didn't care. The binder lay among the pillows, and Father's eyes followed her to the door, making her feel ashamed, for him and for herself. She didn't want to see the binder again; she'd already seen too much. She just wanted to escape that house forever.

She slipped out the back door. Rolex lay sprawled on the grass, either dead or stunned. After squeezing through the board in the fence and under the Boston ivy, she breathed deeply, relishing the safety of her own backyard. Then it hit. She stopped abruptly and fell to her knees, her head to the ground. Her science book! In the library. Ellen Loverage emblazoned on the cover. She should go back and get it, but she couldn't. She'd never go into that house again! She trudged to her room, closed the door, and waited for the police.

THIRTEEN

As Jack Brandt patrolled First Street near the freeway, the call came about a burglary at 473 Starling Lane. The resident, Caroline Merkle, was at Vesta Davidson's house, 485 Starling. He knew Buzz Rossiter would respond quickly in another car.

Brandt found Caroline Merkle on her neighbor's couch, pale and trembling, a damp cloth on her forehead. In his formal, official manner Brandt assured her that everything was under control and she was safe. Anyone who had been in the house had undoubtedly left.

"Rolex! Something's happened to my dog."

"Where was he?"

"In the backyard. I just know he's been poisoned or shot."

"We'll check on the dog first, Miss Merkle. We have a vet on call."

"The first thing I saw was my amethyst decanter, on the tile, broken. And all the drawers were open, and I know my silverware is gone." As she rambled on, mixing important facts with trivial asides, guesses with fears, he jotted down notes to be entered later into his laptop.

When Rossiter arrived, they checked the perimeter of the house and found Rolex whining feebly in the backyard. In a few minutes Dr. Stone had the dog in the back of her SUV and was on her way to the clinic. After making sure no one was inside, Brandt and Rossiter began their routine investigation.

Caroline Merkle walked with them through the front room mentioning missing items: the amethyst decanter was beyond hope, a Higbee panel thistle vase was missing. When she saw the china cabinet in the dining room, she collapsed onto one of the chairs, leaned over, buried her face in her hands, and rocked gently. Between tears and groans Brandt caught fragments.

"The Hummels! . . . eighty-six . . . boyfriend . . . started 1953 . . . Houston . . . irreplaceable! . . . invaluable."

When she became pale as ivory and he thought she might faint, he called the paramedics to take her to Good Samaritan. Later, when she was feeling better, they could inventory the house.

Brandt and Rossiter spent the next half hour completing their investigation. The burglars were knowledgeable and efficient, taking only small, expensive items, not bothering with the TV, stereo, or computer. A partial shoe print was found near the back door, but nothing at the front. While Jack began his report, Buzz collected fingerprints from the rooms the burglars had ransacked. With the station's new computer and a little luck, they'd have answers by evening, or the next morning at the latest. It was more likely, however, that the prints were useless, belonging only to Caroline Merkle. Professionals wore gloves.

As Brandt checked out the master bedroom, he saw a white binder on the pillows with a photograph on the cover. Crazy—it looked like a young Clayton Loverage. It was unprofessional, but he couldn't resist. He turned its pages and saw notes and letters addressed to Cary from Clay. He wanted to know more, but Rossiter might walk in and want to know what he was looking at.

Near the end of their investigation, the dispatcher reported a rumble among teenagers at the strip mall on the south side of town. Buzz, who liked action better than detailed investigating, was anxious to get going. Brandt agreed to close up the house and submit the preliminary report.

At a little after seven o'clock he was ready to leave and lock Miss Merkle's house. He had been thorough and intuitively felt something would come from the investigation. He had a strong hunch the Villanueva brothers were involved, although they usually went for electronic items. But the real find was the binder full of love notes. In light of his recent concerns about Loverage and Springdale Church, this wasn't a coincidence. The Bible promised that all things work together for God's glory. God's hand was on him and had led him to the binder. He was at that place at that time for a purpose, but he needed to know more. Before locking the front door, he went back into the house. A few minutes later he left with a binder concealed in a grocery bag.

ELLEN LAY ON HER BED stunned the rest of the day, not even coming down at five-thirty to prepare Friday dinner for Father, Osvaldo, and Maria. In one hour everything in her life had unraveled. Father had been intimately involved with Miss Merkle! One of the burglars might be Osvaldo! And maybe, probably, the police or Miss Merkle would find her science book. She endlessly replayed the terror of watching feet moving around the edge of Miss Merkle's bed and knowing that any second the dust ruffle would lift and leering eyes would find her. She was afraid to close her eyes, afraid the burglars would come into her own house next.

She didn't want to see Father, Osvaldo, the police, or anybody. She wanted to wake up and find that it had all been a nightmare. She felt like Job, whose world had crumbled in a day. How could three things hit her so hard, one after the other? She should run away, to Chicago, Milwaukee, or New York. Nobody would find her. She'd be a waitress, find a cheap apartment, start over. But that was stupid. She had no money, and the police always found people who ran away . . . unless something bad happened to them. She didn't want to run away or stay in Springdale, go to sleep or stay awake, stay in her room or go out. She wanted to cry, but she'd used up her tears. She could only lie on her bed and try to erase the paralyzing dream from her brain.

If she were a suspect in a burglary, what would Father do? It would sabotage his standing at church. And even if she could prove she wasn't involved in the burglary, she'd still have to explain why she'd been in Miss Merkle's house. What would Clay, Jr., Dan, and Linda think? And what about Miss Merkle? Could she look her in the face again?

She could hear the gossip at school. "Ellen Loverage! The pastor's daughter! I knew there was something sneaky about her, always so quiet and smug." What would the newspaper say? "The daughter of a Springdale pastor was questioned Friday evening in connection with the burglary of her English teacher's house. A senior at Springdale High School . . . " Of course, they couldn't divulge her name, because she was a minor, but the whole town would know how to fill in the blank. There was no way this could end well.

And Osvaldo? She wouldn't believe it. Those were his shoes, but not him. His brothers were the burglars. He wouldn't cheat in class if it meant passing or failing, so why would he rip off Miss Merkle? Maybe his brothers had made him do it by threatening to harm his mother. But no! It wasn't him. Not Osvaldo.

At a little before six o'clock, Father arrived home. When he knocked on her door, she said she was sick and couldn't come out. Sometimes, when she had her period, she felt sick. He was sympathetic and asked if he could fix something for her or bring her medicine from the drugstore.

"Get some rest and don't worry about Maria and Osvaldo," he told her. "I'll take them to the buffet at Piney's."

Later in the evening she tried reading *Notre Dame de Paris,* but Quasimodo and Esmeralda's adventures and dilemmas were camp skits compared to what she faced. She lay on her bed until midnight, her mind never breaking free from the events of the afternoon, but extrapolating them into what might happen. Rolex was dead; Osvaldo would stand trial for burglary; she'd end up in juvie; Miss Merkle hated her; Father would have to leave Springdale Church. If she went back to school, the hallways would be gauntlets for the other kids to lash her with their tongues.

Near midnight she undressed and flung her clothes against the wall. She didn't want to touch anything that had been in Miss Merkle's house. She'd wash her clothes ten times before wearing them again. She took a long shower, washing her hair twice and scrubbing her body until there was no hot water left. She brushed her teeth until her gums ached, and finished off the antiseptic mouthwash.

Back in her room, she looked for a place to think. Her bed was too familiar, too comfortable, and she'd made too many bad decisions lying there. Her dressing table chair was too stiff and hard and reminded her of an electric chair. Finally she lay facedown on the floor, her nose pressed against the hardwood, her hands clamped over her ears. She needed to sort through what had happened, and she couldn't afford to be comfortable.

What had gone wrong? There was no use trying to convince herself that she was just unlucky and the whole mess wasn't her fault, that she'd been in the wrong place at the wrong time. That was the problem—there was no right time for her to be in a wrong place. In her mind the words *Wrong Place* appeared in gigantic flashing neon lights.

Somehow she had convinced herself that it was okay to relax in Miss Merkle's house. Her motives had been pure; she hadn't the slightest temptation to harm or steal. But her resolve not to steal even an after-dinner mint was little consolation. Her care and planning had been perfect: know Miss Merkle's schedule; always leave in plenty of time; leave everything in the house exactly as she found it; have a plan in case her teacher came home early. So what had happened? The unexpected.

At one o'clock she got up off the floor, stiff and aching, and tried listening to CDs, watching TV, reading and studying, and daydreaming, but still every thought was stampeded by the events of the day. Finally she picked up her Bible, let it fall open near the middle, and started reading Psalm 23. *The Lord is my shepherd. . . .* She read on blankly, using up the time. She knew the words, but they didn't speak to her. In desperation she continued reading. Psalms 24, 25, 26 . . . Then she came to Psalm 31.

> *In you, O LORD, I have taken refuge;*
> *let me never be put to shame;*
> *deliver me in your righteousness.*
> *Turn your ear to me,*
> *come quickly to my rescue;*
> *be my rock of refuge, a strong fortress to save me.*
> *Since you are my rock and my fortress,*
> *for the sake of your name lead and guide me.*
> *Free me from the trap that is set for me,*
> *for you are my refuge.*
> *Into your hands I commit my spirit,*
> *O LORD, the God of truth.*

Someone, maybe King David, had been stressed out, was in some kind of trouble big time. He had talked to God about his hopeless situation, and just laid it all out. She knew all of that stuff. *O God, this is different! You know I didn't steal anything, but I am not innocent. Walk with me, God, pick me up and carry me. Let it turn out all right.*

Into Your hands I commit my spirit, O Lord. She knew those were the words of Jesus from the cross, but she had never known what followed them . . . *the God of truth.* Father had given a sermon series on truth, and she had sat bored every minute. Now she saw it in a new light. Truth is what *is,* what really *is,* eternally unchangeable. A person's past—all the things done, said, or thought—is unchangeable, embedded in the firm matrix of time. People may rationalize what they've done, or try to ignore it, but God knows. Truth cannot be hidden from God because He *is* truth.

Okay, God. You gave me a stubborn streak. Make me stubborn with the truth this time.

IT WAS TWO O'CLOCK Saturday morning when Maria heard the boys come in. They were hungry, and went straight for the refrigerator. *There it is, boys, everything I'm having for lunch tomorrow. I might as well give it to you, because you'll take it anyway.* She heard them gulping down the milk, knowing they would leave none for breakfast. *That's okay, boys. Cereal tastes like sawdust when I try to eat it with you sleeping a few feet away from me anyway.*

The boys began moving boxes. *More items for "distribution." God, when will it ever end?* As she listened, she realized they were not moving things into the house, but out of it. She got up, tiptoed to her window, and peered out at a van in the driveway, instead of a car. She hurried back to bed, knowing they could burst into the bedroom any second.

She had barely settled herself when Ramon kicked the door open. She rolled over to face him and rubbed her eyes.

"Mama, you are going to be so sad," he said.

"I'm sad every time I think about you," she replied.

"Then you will be sadder. Raphael and I are going away for a while."

"I wish you safe journeys," she said with little feeling. "Where are you going?"

"You don't need to know."

"Good, don't tell me."

She got up and put on a threadbare pink bathrobe. "Do you need something to eat before you go? I will fix sandwiches." That might make them feel guilty.

"Make it quick, Mama. We're in a hurry," said Ramon.

As the boys carried boxes, TVs, computers, and other things to the van, Maria made sandwiches, using all of her bread, peanut butter, jelly, and sliced cheese. It didn't matter if it was gone. She was celebrating. But inside she was weeping because she might never see them again. *My boys! God, forgive me. They didn't have a chance. I was never a mother to them.* On a napkin she scrawled some words and shoved it into the grocery bag along with the sandwiches and two apples. *Dear Sons,* she wrote, *please forgive me for not being a good mother. I love you forever. Mama.*

Maria watched as they pulled out onto Depot Street, not bothering to look back at her. She went inside, threw herself across her bed, and wept.

Just a couple hours later, she was startled awake by a loud knocking at the door. She saw the blinking red lights of the police car through her bedroom curtains and headed for the front door. *The boys had an accident. Maybe there was a shoot-out. They're hurt or dead. I don't want to know.* She cracked open the door.

"Mrs. Villanueva?" asked the policeman.

"Yes."

"I'm Officer Rossiter. Officer Harrick's on the other side of the house. I have a warrant to search your house. We don't want to inconvenience you, but—"

"You may come in, officer." What else could she do? They had a warrant.

"Thank you, Mrs. Villanueva. Is anyone else here?"

"No, I am alone."

The officer walked through the house and took several photographs in each room. He did a cursory check of the cupboards, refrigerator, and the oven. Under the sofa he found dirty socks, old paint-splattered tennis shoes, underwear, beer cans, dust bunnies—Maria was embarrassed. The shoes were Osvaldo's, but Raphael had left the rest. She watched the policeman jot some words on his pad.

He asked if he could check a small chest of drawers she had in her bedroom. Certainly. There was nothing in it, just some personal items.

As he looked through the drawers, he found a small paper bag, opened it, and took out a crystal figurine partially wrapped in a napkin.

"How long have you had this?" he asked.

"What is it? I've never seen it before."

He handed her the napkin. Four letters were scrawled on it. *MAMA*. Probably Ramon. Maybe Raphael. She didn't know.

She asked to see the figurine. It was the first present either boy had given her. It was probably stolen, but one of them had thought about her. She held it tenderly, hoping she wouldn't start crying in front of the policeman. It was beautiful. And it was an angel. Another angel from God, she thought, given to me by one of my boys. She handed it back to the policeman.

"I'll have to keep this for a while, Mrs. Villanueva. I hope to return it to you when the investigation's over."

She knew she'd never see it again. That was all right. She'd keep the napkin forever.

IT WAS AFTER FATHER arrived home from church on Sunday afternoon that the doorbell rang. The chime should always be the same, but this time it sounded ominous, and she knew it was the police. She heard voices, and soon there was a knock at her door.

"Ellie?" Father's voice was tense and inquisitive.

"Yes, Father?"

"Are you feeling well enough to come out? Officer Brandt wants to ask you something."

"Give me a few minutes."

She brushed out her hair and put on a clean white sweatshirt, using it to buff her glasses. She could at least look decent for her inquisition. This was it. After this her life would be different—at home with Father, at church, at school. She shot an arrow prayer, pleading that God would help her tell the truth, and went out.

In the hallway Brandt's sugary voice wafted up the stairwell—small talk, clichés, weather, the St. Louis Rams—as if nothing important was happening. The man was a molasses machine with its spout stuck open. If he'd been born a hundred years earlier, he would have sold snake oil to pioneers. Although Father never criticized him, rumors circulated around church that he and Father verbally jostled for leadership at church meetings. That wasn't going to happen here; he wasn't going to jostle her. This may be his investigation, but she was determined to tell her truth in her way, not his.

From the bottom of the stairs she saw Father standing near the fireplace at the far end of the living room, his back to the officer, his arms folded. The policeman had settled comfortably into Father's recliner with a smug, papier-mâché countenance and was looking toward Father. They hadn't heard her coming. She walked straight through the dining room and stood directly in front of Jack Brandt. As she approached, he cleared his throat and started to speak, but she held up her hand to stop him.

"Officer Brandt, if that's a recorder you've got with you, you'd better start it. I'm going to tell you exactly what happened at Miss Merkle's." She didn't wait for his response but continued speaking, looking directly at him. He pushed a button on the recorder.

She told the whole story, from beginning to end. Discovering the key. Rolex. Her first visits to the house. The books she'd read. Walking through the house to admire Miss Merkle's china, Hummels, cut glass, and figurines. She insisted she'd never taken anything, not a lemon drop, a cashew, or a sip of water. She confessed that she was guilty of borrowing the space and serenity of Miss Merkle's house. In detail, she related the events of Friday afternoon: hearing the burglars enter, hiding under the bed, listening to the shatter of glass, imagining the Hummels being carelessly scooped up. It was two men, she said, one wearing black and the other white tennis shoes. The black shoes were spattered with paint with a long strip of gray on the toe of the right shoe.

Father did not look at her as she spoke, but kept his eyes on the carpet as he paced between the fireplace and the dining room. Occasionally he shook his head slowly, as if to say, "I can't believe this." Then he stopped his pacing and stared at her as though he'd never seen her before. Each time she looked in his direction, he met her eyes. She had never seen that look on his face. It wasn't anger or pain or frustration, but something else. As she continued to talk, he continued to stare.

Then he did something that sent shivers up and down her spine, through her mind, and into her heart. He paced nonchalantly behind Officer Brandt, clenched his fist, and gave it a pump, as if to say, "Atta girl, Ellie. Nice going. I'm proud of you." She thought she saw tears glistening in the corners of his eyes.

When she finished she felt completely drained, emptied. It was time for Brandt to leave so she could be alone.

"Now there are just a few more things I'd like to ask you, Ellen," said Brandt.

"No, that's all I have to say. I'm sorry."

"To complete my investigation, I need to know whether—"

"Officer Brandt"—Ellen started toward her bedroom—"all the dungeons of Dalmatia couldn't make me add a comma to what I've said, so you might as well leave."

He followed her through the dining room to the stairwell. "Ellen, this will only take—"

"Jack," said Father, "it's not going to happen. You can talk to her tomorrow."

"Out of respect for your position at the church, I won't press this matter tonight. I hope you're aware I could take her to the station for further questioning. I'll call you in the morning, and we can get on with this." He adjusted his fake smile and with a meager bow, bid them good-bye.

As soon as the front door closed, Ellen nodded slightly to Father, gave him a faint smile, ascended the stairs, and firmly closed her door.

JACK BRANDT LEFT dissatisfied. Ellen Loverage's statement was far more than he'd hoped for, but it left an acrid taste in his mouth. Over the years he'd heard and seen enough confessions so that he could spot a phony, and he had no doubt the girl was telling the truth. Only a master con artist could fake the look in her eyes and the conviction in her voice.

What galled him, however, was that she had turned his investigation into her own performance. She had caught him off guard, and he had carelessly lost control the moment she opened her mouth. She'd treated him like a Boy Scout, not a police officer. No one had done that before, and he wouldn't let it happen again. If she hadn't been Loverage's daughter, he would have hauled her in and booked her on the spot. The science book Miss Merkle found would justify that.

As he drove to the station, he went over what he had learned. Ellen was guilty of entering Merkle's house. She was there during the burglary, but her under-the-bed vantage point supplied little information. The tennis shoes, one pair with paint on them, might be important. In the morning he'd question her more about the shoes and the men's voices.

He also wanted to pursue the connection between Ellen and the Villanueva brothers. Both Wicker and Loverage had mentioned that Ellen dated Osvaldo, but did she have contact with the other brothers? Ramon and Raphael Villanueva had recently been questioned about similar burglaries in Mt. Vernon and Decatur, but nothing could be traced to them. They left no fingerprints.

The good side of the incident was that it helped solidify his case against Loverage's pastorate at Springdale Church. As he'd said many times, he didn't have anything against Loverage personally. He was a fine man under whose leadership the church had flourished, and the congregation had a right to be proud. Up to this time, his character had been beyond reproach, but Loverage's time had passed. He was still running a church and preaching in the style of the sixties and seventies, and these were the nineties. Change was essential, and Loverage wouldn't, or couldn't, see it. You can't power a 1996 SUV with a Rambler motor; it just doesn't work.

He wasn't sure what he should do with the information he'd found in Merkle's binder. Those love notes were written so many years ago, almost before he was born. They were private and truly none of his business. It was a chance in millions that he'd stumbled across them. Yet he had, and it was so amazing that God had to be behind it. During the past few days, he'd spent a lot of time in prayer, at home and on patrol. He didn't want to do anything wrong. But he knew that he had in his possession the means of "retiring" Clayton Loverage.

His talk with Loverage the previous spring, in which he'd obliquely suggested the pastor move on, had proven fruitless. Loverage had no intention of leaving before retirement, and in the meantime, was making no effort to modernize the church. The worship service continued in its old-fashioned grind, forcing a modern, fast-paced congregation to sing centuries-old dirges. Loverage still emphasized foreign missions in the face of urgent needs within their own community. His sermons might be excellent Bible studies, but they failed to address the needs of a changing congregation. And occasionally the pastor was divisive, speaking out against abortion and death-with-dignity. He personally agreed with the pastor on these issues, but there was no reason to divide the congregation. How could Springdale Church expect to attract and hold a younger generation?

The church was becoming polarized. Old-timers, who remembered Loverage in his heyday and probably contributed the most money, felt a strong loyalty to their pastor. A few ac-knowledged it was time for a change, but argued that Pastor Loverage was nearing retirement age and would step down in a few years. They had advised Jack not to rock the boat.

But support for modernization was burgeoning, and now his group was meeting at least once a week. Every chance he got, he talked about the church's need for an associate pastor, one who could come alongside Loverage to uphold him in areas where he was weak. Then the church could get a glimpse of young, dynamic leadership.

He was intrigued by how the information from the Merkle burglary might affect the situation at the church. For starters, it would not look good when the congregation learned the pastor's daughter was sneaking into a neighbor's house to find peace and quiet. What was going on in the marriage-and-fam-ily expert's household to make the girl so desperate?

Second, Ellen was hobnobbing with the Villanueva family, which had a mile-long police record. While he knew nothing about the youngest brother, the mother's record was shady at best, and it was only a matter of time until the older brothers slipped up. If they were involved in the Merkle burglary, Ellen's association with the family would look suspicious.

Third, there was an undeniable connection between Loverage and Caroline Merkle. He had to be careful with that information. He shouldn't read too much into it . . . or too lit-tle. He might never discover if something was going on presently, but that didn't matter; the binder was indisputable proof that they had been lovers at one time. Furthermore, why were they now living so close to each other? It was unlikely that it was a coincidence. But he wanted to be fair to Loverage and Merkle. One word about their relationship might destroy them and damage the church.

He reminded himself that God had a purpose in leading him to the binder, and that he had only the best interests of the church at heart. He and Shirley would pray about this, alone; the information stopped with them. He abhorred the thought of igniting wildfire gossip. Such blazes were bright and exciting, but so uncontrollable they caused untold damage. Occasionally, however, they were useful in burning away the chaff.

Perhaps he could personally mention something to Loverage about Caroline Merkle. He wouldn't threaten him—that would be blackmail—but merely drop a few words, a few seeds, to start him thinking. Maybe Loverage would arrive at his own conclusion that it was best to leave Springdale. By gently confronting the man, he might both rescue the pastor's reputation and set the stage for renewal at the church. He'd pray some more, but it was becoming clearer what he should do.

FOURTEEN

After Jack Brandt left and Ellie went to her room, Clayton retired into his study, sat heavily in his swivel chair, and randomly opened his Bible. Words from the Psalms drifted past his consciousness like autumn leaves on a stream. Isaiah was no better, and the Gospels, the very words of Jesus, seemed like stagnant pools. That was wrong, and he felt ashamed, but he was numb. He tried praying, but found his mind switching paths, first walking with Ellie, and then confronting Caroline Merkle or Jack Brandt. He didn't even know what he should be praying.

What he really wanted was to talk with Ellie, to find out how she was feeling and what she was thinking, but he knew she wouldn't allow it. How had he let this happen—his own daughter erecting barricades to keep him away? It was futile to knock on her door. She had sent him a strong signal that she wanted to be alone.

He went upstairs and gazed down the dark hallway toward her room where light fanned from the base of her door onto the carpet. He tiptoed to her door to find out what she was listening to. It wasn't her usual fare, but a gentle ballad.

> *My Lord, You know I've lost my way,*
> *I cannot see, it's hard to pray,*
> *I wear a shroud of agony.*
> *Please carry me, O carry me.*
>
> *Each day I wander in a maze,*
> *A labyrinth of dead-end ways,*
> *A map of dread uncertainty.*
> *Please carry me, O carry me.*
>
> *Convinced I am an afterthought,*
> *An accident, with troubles fraught;*
> *I question whether I should be.*
> *Please carry me, O carry me.*
>
> *My God, I long to understand*
> *Your ways, Your paths;*
> *Lord, take my hand,*
> *And lead me through this mystery.*
> *Please carry me, O carry me.*
>
> *O blessed Savior, hear my cry,*
> *I cannot live, but fear to die,*
> *Each day brings grief and misery.*
> *Please carry me, O carry me.*
>
> *O Shepherd, draw me close to You,*
> *With rod and staff, help me be true.*
> *And if I want to wander free,*
> *Please carry me, O carry me.*

The lyrics were a little depressing, but the prayer was right. The song was sung in mild tenor with velvety soprano providing muted background harmony. The vocalists were accompanied by piano, folk guitar, a fiddle, occasionally a flute or recorder, and a faint percussion. At least it wasn't the pounding beat she usually preferred.

He tiptoed back to his study, wondering what this Merkle incident was doing to his daughter. He'd been proud of her as she gave her statement to Brandt. Maybe she should have waited for legal counsel before she did it, but that wasn't Ellie's way.

Now that she was alone again, how was she feeling? Was she distraught? Crying? Stoic? Or reading her precious books? Was she aware of the enormity of what she'd done and its possible consequences? He needed to talk with her. As her father, he should demand that right. Several times he started upstairs to knock on her door, only to remind himself that it wouldn't do any good. This wasn't the time. Finally he went into the living room, resolved to anchor himself to his recliner.

As he replayed the scene with Brandt, it dawned on him that Ellie had stayed in her room for almost forty-eight hours waiting for the police to come. If she'd eaten anything, it was while he was at the church. She must have been anxious the whole time.

And what was she thinking when she grabbed control of Brandt's interview? Clayton bet nobody had done that before. Brandt was a controller, at church, at work, and probably at home, but tonight Ellie had usurped that role. In the middle of her statement, Clayton had wanted to cheer. Now he wished he could hold his daughter in his arms and tell her how proud he was. All her stubbornness wasn't necessarily bad. He wished he could stand up to Brandt like that at church. *Jack Brandt, I have something to say; you're going to sit there, with your lips zippered shut, and listen. I'll let you know when I'm finished. Maybe I'll even let you say a word or two.*

What was Ellie feeling when she gave her statement? Shame? Embarrassment? Anger? It didn't sound like defiance. She spoke resolutely, reflecting something that burned deep within her, but she was good at camouflaging her emotions . . . or he was poor at reading them. Maybe the same thing had happened when Joyce died.

And why had Ellie dared go into someone else's house? Was it so difficult for her to be in her own home? She could have read here just as well as at Cary's place. He wasn't sure he wanted to know the answer to that question. He'd *give* her his recliner if he thought it would help. He could convert Dan's old room into a library for her, with a recliner, a stereo for her CDs, and an end table for all the varnish stains her heart desired. He'd buy all the books she wanted to read.

What did I do to deserve a child like Ellie . . . what did she do to deserve a father like me?

ELLEN HAD CLOSED the door to her bedroom, aware she was leaving Father standing speechless. Any second he'd rap, insisting that they sit down right that minute and have one of his heart-to-heart, father-to-daughter talks to get to the bottom of things. He'd tell her what was right and wrong, pointing out that she had sinned in the eyes of God and needed to repent. She already knew that; she just didn't want to hear it from him. If he insisted on talking, she'd clam up so tight he couldn't pry her open with the Jaws of Life.

After fifteen minutes, she knew he wasn't coming, and she was grateful. She'd done six months' worth of talking in the last hour, and now she needed solitude. She wondered how much he knew about his own photo on Miss Merkle's nightstand, the photo album, and the white binder. What would he say if he knew she'd seen them, or knew that he'd had an affair with Miss Merkle? She had to talk with him sooner or later, when the time was right.

She'd been surprised when he stood behind Brandt and pumped his fist. He had never encouraged her so much, and she wanted to thank him. She knew how Clay, Jr. or Dan must have felt when he cheered them at their basketball games. She knew he was proud of her.

She thought how unreal it was to have entered a house that wasn't her own; it must have been someone else, not her. When she reviewed her rationalizations, she understood them, but they were flimsy. All she had to hang on to was that she had meant no harm and hadn't taken anything, but that wasn't much. She wasn't comforted by the fact that she'd been unlucky, tripped up by the unexpected.

People handle the expected. Something happens a certain way 99.9 percent of the time, so people think it's going to happen that way 100 percent of the time and plan accordingly. Then bingo, the one-in-a-million occurs, and they're done for. That's what happened when Steve Belinsky was killed in a spinout on Bull Creek Road last year. He'd taken that curve a thousand times without a problem, but he hadn't planned on a gravel spill earlier in the day. His tires didn't grip, and two seconds later his neck was broken. It wasn't his fault there was gravel on the road, but it was his fault he was driving too fast.

She lay on her bed, thinking about Father. She had known he would be furious if he found out, but she hadn't thought about what it would do to his career if she were caught. Half the people at church were busybodies, growing plump on a steady diet of gossip. This would be one of the juiciest tidbits they'd had in years, and in their generosity they'd share it with everyone they knew. By tomorrow morning everyone in Springdale would know something. When the rumormongers got through with the story, she'd be leading a gang of thieves operating out of St. Louis, responsible for most of the break-ins around Springdale.

No matter what happened to her, Father would be hurt. Suddenly she felt protective toward him. Although sometimes she couldn't stand him, she never doubted her love for him. She wasn't out to destroy him; in fact, she was proud of him. She knew he had done a good job at the church and was highly respected in Springdale and around the country. She thought it didn't matter if her relationship with him wasn't so great; that was between the two of them and no one else.

Brandt had looked so smug in Father's recliner, as though he owned it. No one belonged there but Father . . . and her, when he wasn't home. But there the man sat with an inane grin on his corky, rosy-cheeked face. She'd never liked him. His smiles, handshakes, good-natured laughs, and lengthy pompous prayers were nothing but cotton candy. She'd heard that he favored getting a new pastor. It wasn't going to help Father that his daughter was caught breaking into a house.

She took her Bible from the nightstand and lay on her stomach on the floor, resting on her elbows. Psalm 51. She knew all about that one—David's Psalm after he'd committed adultery with Bathsheba and killed her husband. *Have mercy on me, O God, according to your unfailing love; according to your great compassion blot out my transgressions. Wash away all my iniquity and cleanse me from my sin. . . .*

She turned her CD off and read the Psalm all the way through, three times. She lay on her bed and jumbled her prayers with the events of the last two days until she pulled the bedspread over herself and slept.

CLAYTON AWOKE EARLY from a troubled sleep, fatigued and depressed, his body unsatisfied. He wished he could pull the blankets up around his neck, bury his head in his pillow, and sleep through the day. He shuddered at the thought of dealing with disgruntled parishioners, hypochondriacs, and lean budgets.

Duty, good ol' duty, prodded him to get up and read his Bible and pray, as he'd done each morning for the past thirty years. But thoughts from the night before elbowed into his consciousness. Ellie's words thrust themselves in front of Bible verses and prayers before they could be read or uttered. He devised plans and strategies for dealing with her problems, only to discard them as ineffective and worthless.

Still, he *had* to talk with her, to say something, even if it failed to penetrate her thick armor. He could help her through this whole mess, if she would only let him. Would she try to maneuver through a labyrinth of police and legal procedures by herself? That would be just like her, obstinate and independent.

It was Monday. She wouldn't dare go to school, would she? He should knock on her door and insist they talk. But they'd probably end up arguing, or she'd sit like a monolith allowing him to give his spiel. How had it ever gotten to that point? He didn't even know his own daughter. The only thing they did together was eat meals in stony silence. Soon she would finish high school and be off to college or adventures unknown, out of his life forever.

He wanted to run away today, spend the day fishing. Wally had left him his rowboat and the run-down shed at the western end of Braxton Reservoir. In only twenty minutes he could be sitting in his favorite cove, enjoying the scenery. With the sun bright and the leaves in full color, it was an autumnal kaleidoscope. He didn't even care if he caught anything, as long as it didn't rain and no one was around to badger him. He needed time alone to examine this burden that had been heaped onto his shoulders. But going to Braxton would be irresponsible, like playing hooky on exam day.

The more he thought about fishing, however, the better he liked the idea. Jesus had fished when He was on earth. He'd even climbed into a boat and set out from shore to avoid dealing with the crowds. There was nothing wrong with getting away for a while. He wasn't running away from his problems, just seeking a few quiet hours to refresh his spirit. He'd tell Sally where he was; she had his cell phone number.

But there was Brandt. He was going to contact Clayton and Ellie that morning, probably first thing. That was the way he operated.

Clayton thought about asking Ellie to go fishing with him, but why would she go with him today, the first time in six years?

Right now she was probably in her room thinking up ways to avoid him. He wouldn't blame her if she decided not to go to school. While both old and young gossiped behind one's back, kids were more likely to confront a peer face-to-face. He'd give Ellie his blessing to skip. He'd ask her to go to Braxton with him. All she could do was say no. They could have breakfast at Piney's on the way. No one would bother them there.

He sat on the edge of the bed and tried to pray again, but the words still failed to come. Finally he rationalized that everything churning in his head was a prayer, hundreds of big and little prayers stuffed into a gunnysack and tossed up to God. *That's the best I can do this morning, Lord.*

Clayton put on old khakis, boots, and a plaid shirt and went into the kitchen. He ground Columbia Supremo and brewed his usual four cups, pouring a cup for himself and the rest into the thermos. In the local section of the *Gazette* he found a short article about the burglary at Caroline Merkle's house. An investigation was underway; no one had been arrested. He wondered what the Tuesday edition would say.

Ellen came in about seven, her usual time for going to school, dressed in her customary blue jeans, white sweatshirt, and sneakers.

"Good morning, Ellie." He folded his newspaper and laid it on the table.

"Morning, Father."

"I'm thinking about going fishing at Braxton today. Would you like to go with me?"

"I should stick around. Mr. Brandt wants to talk with me this morning."

"I could leave a message with Sally that we're at the reservoir. I'll take my cell phone."

She paused. "What kind of sandwiches do you want for breakfast?"

Sandwiches? Breakfast? "What'd you say, Ellie?"

"To take to the reservoir. What kind of sandwiches do you want?"

She's coming! It was her way of saying yes. He almost told her to forget the sandwiches. They'd have breakfast at Piney's. *Stuff it, Clay. Don't disagree with her; don't even suggest another plan.* "Anything you can find in the fridge. You make great sandwiches. I'll get some gear together."

"Don't take anything for me. Oh, but may I borrow one of your hats? I think it's going to be sunny today."

As they started out, Clayton resolved not to say anything about Miss Merkle's house, Jack Brandt, or how Ellie was going to handle talk at school. Like uninvited passengers waiting to be noticed, those questions rode in the backseat. He felt he was forsaking his paternal duties, but for this day he didn't want to use the direct approach. *Tie your tongue in a square knot, Clay. Talk about what she wants to talk about, and forget the advice unless she asks something directly. Can you do that for just one day, or is that too hard for you?*

They rode to Braxton in silence. At the reservoir, while he dragged Wally Fitch's rowboat, the *QE XIII,* to the shore, Ellen gathered several rocks from the beach. They climbed into the boat and in silence he rowed to a small, isolated cove, shaded by scrubby willows and taller hickories and oaks. Redwinged blackbirds and sparrows skittered among the branches, and a few stray ducks bobbed along the shore. Finally he let the boat drift and prepared his fishing line. He watched as Ellen unrolled a piece of string, tied a rock to one end, and hung the line over the edge of the boat. He reeled in his line, cut another piece of string, and tied one of her rocks to it. If she was going to catch fish with rocks, he would do the same thing.

After a long silence, Ellen spoke first. "I'm worried about Osvaldo, Father."

"Osvaldo?" Of all the things she might say, this was not one he had expected.

"Those were his tennis shoes I saw Friday. I could tell by the paint on them. But I'm sure it wasn't him."

"I don't know him very well," he said, "but from everything I've observed, he wouldn't do something like that."

"Yeah. Just like I wouldn't go into Miss Merkle's house."

Clayton paused before he answered, afraid of frightening her thoughts away. Finally he replied, "I've done some things I've regretted all my life, Ellie. I understand."

"Every word I said last night was true, except that I didn't say the shoes belonged to Osvaldo. Do you think I should have?"

He couldn't remember the last time she'd asked him for advice.

"No. It's Brandt's investigation. Let him ask the questions. But if he asks, tell him the truth." *Careful, don't preach at her.*

"I think I'll miss school this week. Only three days anyway. Thursday is Thanksgiving."

"I'll write a note to Mrs. Archambeaux."

"This is better than being at school. I'm glad I'm here."

"We won't be here much longer, Ellie. Here comes Brandt with the game warden. They think they're pursuing dangerous criminals."

A large patrol boat swung into the cove, slowed down, and pulled alongside, rocking the little rowboat in its wake.

Jack Brandt yelled over the rumble of the motor. "Clayton, you knew I wanted to talk with Ellen this morning. Why did you take off?"

Before he could answer, Ellen shouted, "I can't hear you! What'd you say?"

"I'm not talking to you, Ellen. I'm talking to your dad," he yelled a little louder. "Why did you take off when—"

She rounded her hands to form a megaphone. "I still can't hear you, Mr. Brandt. Can you please turn the motor off?"

The warden reached over and flicked the power switch.

The instant the motor died, Ellen began. "Mr. Brandt, I'm really disappointed in you. You could have reached us by cell phone and we would have been anyplace in town in fifteen minutes. You know father-daughter relationships are more important than anything you have to ask me. Why don't you just tell me when and where you want me to be, and I'll be there. I'm sure the warden has better things to do than chase a pastor and his daughter."

Clayton listened to his daughter, dumbfounded. He had tried to teach his children civility and diplomacy, especially toward their elders. Treat others with esteem. Don't embarrass them or make them feel inferior. But here was his daughter telling one of Springdale's top policemen that she was disappointed in him. Anger flashed across Brandt's face. Clayton had seen that look before at church meetings, and he knew what it meant: Brandt would do something to get his way.

"Pastor, I'm just trying to help your daughter," said Brandt, never acknowledging Ellen. "But I'll need a little cooperation. You and Ellen can have your father-daughter chat in Springdale."

"What time do you want to see me, Mr. Brandt?" asked Ellen.

He checked his Palm Pilot. "Ten-thirty, at the station. That gives you an hour."

"Plenty of time," she said. "We can leave our lines in the water a little longer."

"You might check fishing licenses before we leave, Warden," added Brandt. "Nothing personal, Pastor. Routine procedure."

Clayton pulled his license from his shirt pocket and handed it to the warden, who checked and returned it. "And yours, young lady? You have one, don't you?"

"I'm not fishing," she replied.

"You're sitting in the boat holding a line that's going into the water. In my book, that's called fishing."

"This is just a piece of string with a rock tied to the end of it. I change the rock every once in a while to give the fish something new to look at. I have no interest in catching them."

"Well, pull your line out of the water so I can see this unique way of fishing."

Clayton watched his daughter slowly pull up her line and hold the string high, the rock dangling, dripping, over the water. "This is one of my prettiest rocks, Warden. Do you want to look at it up close?"

"No, that's okay, young lady. That's a new one to me. No bait, no catch, no violation. You'll have to admit it looked suspicious."

"Sorry. I don't mean to cause problems."

On the way back to Springdale Ellen served the sandwiches, uncovering the end of one for her father so he could eat while he drove.

Bread, butter and mayonnaise, catsup, mustard, a dab of horseradish, pickle relish, lettuce, American cheese, Swiss cheese, plenty of ham and turkey, finished off with a layer of Rice Krispies. *California Deli Crunchies,* the label said, *Recipe from Santa Monica, circa 1951.*

"Great sandwich, Ellie. As good as the ones Mom used to make. I like them crunchy like this. What did you put in it, water chestnuts?"

"No. Rice Krispies."

"Oh, of course . . . my blossoming gourmet."

They rode in silence almost into Springdale. He had things to say, but he'd pledged himself to silence. He bit his lower lip and chewed on his tongue, restraining himself. Finally he needlessly cleared his throat and said, "You know what we'd better do, Ellie?"

"Yeah, find a lawyer. Do you know one?"

"We could try Bill McAfee. He goes to our church."

"I don't know him."

"Fiftyish. About five foot ten. Shiny head. Round face, always smiling. Wife's Susan. Mom and I used to be good friends with them. Maybe we should have seen him this morning instead of fishing."

"No. Fishing was more important. I'm saving my string for the next time we go."

FIFTEEN

At the police station, Clayton listened to Ellie's terse, matter-of-fact replies to Brandt's questions. They added little to her statement from the previous evening, but at least she was talking—giving polite, concise answers. When Brandt asked about the shoes, she repeated the description she'd given the previous evening. He didn't ask if she recognized them. To his questions about the men's voices, she replied that only one of them had spoken, giving orders in a throaty whisper. She didn't think he had an accent, but she wasn't sure.

"You said there were two men. How did you know the second person wasn't a woman?" Brandt asked.

"I don't know for sure. I assumed it was a man by the feet."

"You shouldn't assume, Ellen. It can get you and others into trouble."

"Do you think it was a woman?" she asked.

"I make no assumptions. And I want to remind you that I am asking the questions."

Clayton watched his daughter's face turn distant and

defiant. Up to that point the interview had been, at best, tenuous; now Brandt had broken his frail strand of communication, and the interview was essentially finished.

"Now, Ellen, what time did you enter Miss Merkle's house?"

"It's on the tape."

Clayton felt a vague satisfaction in watching Ellie apply her stone-cold treatment to someone else.

"No, it isn't. I have the transcript right here."

"I said, right after school."

"What time is 'right after school'?"

"Figure that out," she replied.

Clayton felt suspended between embarrassment and pride.

"Ellen, don't be difficult. I'm trying to help you," replied Brandt, turning pages of the transcript. "Are you sure you never took anything from Miss Merkle's house?"

"It's on the tape."

Brandt continued with his questions, checking them off one by one, writing notes as he went down his list. How many times had she entered the Merkle house? How had she managed to handle the dog? How long had she known about the loose board in the fence? Had she loosened the board? Did anyone else know about the key? Had she made copies of the key? Had she ever visited with Miss Merkle in her house?

Although he asked his questions patiently, Ellie either shrugged her shoulders, referred him to the tape, or told him to wait until they secured a lawyer.

"We'll have to search your house, Ellen. You know that, don't you?"

"Get a warrant and be my guest," she said sweetly.

He looked at Clayton. "I assume someone will be there at three?"

"You can reach me anytime at church or by cell phone. I'll be there," answered Clayton. He wouldn't speak for Ellie.

Brandt clicked off his recorder. "Ellen, it is a privilege working with you. You've been most helpful. But let me suggest you secure the lawyer you keep referring to."

"Officer Brandt," she replied, "it is the highest pleasure assisting you with this investigation, and I am honored you desire to visit my home."

"By the way, Pastor, I appreciated your sermon series. We need to hear more about truth."

"Thank you, Jack. And don't forget I also stressed that truth without compassion is sterile."

ON THE WAY HOME from the police station, Clayton stopped at the office of Bill McAfee. McAfee had practiced law in Springdale for fifteen years, first as a county deputy district attorney, now as a county-appointed defense attorney in criminal cases. He and his wife, Susan, had attended Springdale Church since arriving in town. Their two children, Joel and Debbie, were now in high school. Bill had served two terms on the board of deacons; Susan taught Sunday school and sang in the choir. They were among the church's largest contributors.

The McAfees, like the Brandts, lived what they believed. They served once a month at the free dining room at Bethel Temple, and annually sponsored a dozen inner-city kids to summer camps in Wisconsin. Bill led a Boy Scout troop, and every Thanksgiving Susan collected food for the needy. At one time the McAfees and the Loverages had been very close, but after the Brandts arrived in Springdale, they had drifted apart.

As he and Ellie entered McAfee's office, Clayton felt uncertain. But why should he doubt? McAfee—and Brandt, for that matter—would help Ellie, not work against her. Nevertheless, he was bothered that the two men were so close.

The receptionist greeted them warmly and notified the attorney of their arrival.

McAfee sat in a huge, customized swivel chair and smiled across his polished black walnut desk. Not a paper clip was out of place, the in-box was empty, and a vase of miniature yellow roses accented a family picture. Plain, cushioned chairs awaited them. He offered them coffee and a soft drink.

"Now then, what can I do for you, Pastor?" he began.

Clayton summarized the incident at Miss Merkle's house, stressing that Ellie had no part in the burglary, although she admitted entering the house. He said nothing about Brandt or the police investigation. McAfee listened politely, nodding to show understanding, now and then asking a few key questions.

"I'd like to hear more," he finally said. "I'll treat you to lunch at The Pink Turtle in New Hope. We can talk about this on the way, if you wouldn't mind waiting a few minutes." He gestured toward the reception area. "I have to make a couple calls before I leave."

Soon they were headed for New Hope, Clayton and McAfee in front, Ellie in the back of McAfee's black Mercedes.

"I'd like to represent you, Ellen," McAfee said, looking at her in the rearview mirror. "Your dad and I have been friends from way back. Why don't you go over things from the beginning? I want to hear it in your words."

Ellen said nothing.

"Ellie, did you hear Mr. McAfee?" Clayton glanced over his shoulder and saw his daughter's straight, tight-lipped mouth and narrowed gaze. They were in trouble.

No answer.

"Ellen, perhaps we can get started if I ask a few questions," said McAfee. For the next few miles he asked questions, patiently, painstakingly. When had she started going to Miss Merkle's house? Why had she started going in the first place?

Ellie looked at the magazines in the pockets behind the seats, out the side window, out the rear window. She was riding in a different vehicle, in a different state, in a different country.

After a half dozen questions had gone unanswered, McAfee scolded her. "Ellen, I'm trying to be patient with you. If I'm going to represent you, I must know what's going on. You and your father came to me in good faith. I assumed you

190

trusted me. You have nothing to fear. I promise to do what's best for you, but we've got to work together. If you don't talk with me, I can't take the case."

With her glasses off, Ellie stared blankly ahead and deliberately shook her head. McAfee could see her in the rearview mirror.

"Aren't you going to say anything to her, Pastor?" asked the attorney.

"I'm sorry, Bill. We'll find someone else," he replied. There was nothing else he could do.

McAfee pulled into a gravel driveway and turned around.

Clayton was frustrated and disappointed, but Ellie was unreachable, in a private soundproofed compartment. What made her arbitrarily decide she didn't like someone, then cut the person off as though he didn't exist? He wanted to lecture her, punish her, but he didn't dare. They had connected for a few minutes that morning at Braxton, and that connection was as tender as a seedling. He had to protect it at all costs.

After a while he asked, "Bill, is there another lawyer you can recommend?"

"You might want to try F. Lee Bailey," he replied. "He knows how to handle difficult clients."

They rode back to Springdale in icy silence.

When they got home, Ellie arranged for the Villanuevas to eat with Father and her rather than the Santoris. She apologized to Mrs. Santori, explaining that there was an extremely important matter that had to be discussed.

Clayton ordered two large pizzas to be delivered at six-thirty. Osvaldo could handle the pepperoni and sausage alone; he, Ellie, and Maria preferred Canadian bacon and pineapple. While they waited for the pizza to arrive, they sat in the living room sipping Coke and Mountain Dew. Ellen repeated the statement she'd made to Brandt. When she admitted her guilt in entering Miss Merkle's house, Maria dabbed the corners of her eyes.

Ellie apologized to them, saying she was sorry to have

broken their trust, and asked for their forgiveness. At her mention of the paint-speckled tennis shoes, Maria looked shocked and bit her lip. Osvaldo squirmed in his chair and took his mother's hand.

When the pizza came, Maria helped Clayton set the table and pour more drinks. Ellen stayed with Osvaldo in the living room, her head resting on his shoulder as he gently held her. Clayton hadn't seen physical contact between them before, although he'd have been amazed if there had been none. *My youngest child, whom I love but don't know; the one who walls me off, or maybe I wall her off. I don't know anymore.* He put his hand in his pocket and felt his fishing string. He caressed it with his fingers and promised himself that he'd do anything not to blow it this time. They had made a tiny start.

After dinner they returned to the living room and talked. Osvaldo related the rumors swirling around school. At first, all that was known was that Miss Merkle's house had been burglarized by a St. Louis gang operating in the area.

"All the bad talk started after lunch, just before fourth period," Osvaldo said.

"What did you hear?"

"I saw Debbie McAfee in the hallway, with her friends circled around her. I kept hearing Ellen's name. They were all crazy."

"Debbie goes home for lunch," Ellie inserted.

"They bugged me until school was out. Said you'd robbed Miss Merkle and had been robbing people for years. They wanted to know if I helped you."

"Did you say anything, Osvaldo?" asked Clayton. *Poor kid. A lot of people pay when we do something wrong.*

"I didn't open my mouth." He was talking to Ellie. "They said you thought you'd get away with it because you were Miss Merkle's favorite. They talked about the other burglaries you'd been in on, and asked me where you stashed the loot. It was all crazy, and they enjoyed it so much. I wanted to sting them, like a scorpion. I was glad to find Mama's note about eating here tonight. I would have come by anyway. Does any-body want that last piece of Canadian bacon?"

While Osvaldo talked about school, Clayton thought about his church. If rumors were flying around the high school, by now they were in every home in Springdale. He was angry with McAfee. He must have gone directly home and started talking. He didn't blame McAfee for being frustrated with Ellie, but there was a matter of confidentiality.

How would this affect his standing at church? How many of his congregation would understand, or at least sympathize with, what he and Ellie had to go through?

Coincidently, his sermon for the next Sunday was about coming alongside those who are hurting, whether they deserve to hurt or not. None of us deserves the favor of God, he would tell them, yet He is there despite our countless failures. We pay lip service to grace, but show little of it to others. He wouldn't mention Ellie directly, yet he knew everyone would fill in the blanks with her name. Many would criticize him for preparing the sermon with Ellie in mind.

Let them assume; it didn't matter. He was proud that his daughter wasn't running from her guilt. In her unique way, she had clearly grasped the concepts of truth, confession, and repentance. If people didn't show her they cared, maybe she'd drop out of church. In a way, he couldn't blame her. He thought again of the rumors at school. *Everything was going to come out sooner or later, but confounded McAfee didn't have to open his big yap! Help me, God. I don't want to hate him.*

The doorbell rang, interrupting Clayton's thoughts. It was Jack Brandt . . . looking for Osvaldo.

MARIA STARED IN DISBELIEF at the policeman. Too many of them had come to the door for her sons. All of them —Raul, Jaime, Alfredo, Ramon, Raphael—stealing, speeding, drinking, fighting, assaulting women. But not for her baby; not for Osvaldo. He hadn't stolen anything. *Stay away from my boy!* she wanted to scream. She didn't trust the police, any police, anywhere, when they thought they had a suspect. They asked too many tricky questions. If Osvaldo was going to say anything, he'd have a lawyer by his side.

"I have a few questions to ask Osvaldo Villanueva," said Brandt. "Officer Rossiter is in the squad car. This should only take a few minutes."

Maria stepped in front of Clayton. "I am Maria Villanueva." She pronounced her syllables distinctly, feistily. "My son will not answer your questions. I will get a lawyer."

"There are a few important matters to clear up. This will take only a minute."

"I'm sorry. No questions. Good-bye."

"Mrs. Villanueva, it's not as easy as that. I need to interview Osvaldo, and if I can't do it here, I'll take him to the station."

"He has the right to remain silent. He will say nothing."

"We both know he has that right, but I'm only asking a few questions. This is not an arrest."

"What are you going to ask him?" She stood in the doorway, solid as Gibraltar, blocking the policeman's way.

"I want to know where he was Friday after school," said Brandt.

"Osvaldo, tell the policeman where you were last Friday after school. Then he will go away."

"Studying at the library. Then working with Mr. Pettigrew," he answered.

"There, now you can go," she said.

Brandt ignored her. "Did anyone see you at the library, Osvaldo?"

"Maybe the librarian. I checked a book out."

"That's two questions. Now go. Go away," she demanded.

"Osvaldo, I have some tennis shoes I want you to look at," said Brandt.

"No! Osvaldo, don't answer him. He will get you in trouble. You go away now, Mr. Policeman. I'll get a lawyer. Then you can ask Osvaldo questions."

"I'm sorry, Mrs. Villanueva. Osvaldo needs to come with me to the station. The interview will go better there." He radioed Buzz Rossiter to come in.

"Jack, I will stand by Maria and Osvaldo," said Clayton. "You don't have to do this. Let them get their lawyer. You won't help anyone by taking the boy to the station."

"It's just a precaution, Pastor Loverage. His brothers skipped town. There's a warrant out for them. We don't want Osvaldo to disappear."

Maria recognized the other policeman. Saturday morning he had taken the crystal angel, and yesterday evening he'd come back after Osvaldo's old tennis shoes. He was nicer than Officer Brandt, but he was still a policeman. Ramon and Raphael had taken Miss Merkle's things. One of them had worn Osvaldo's shoes, and one had left the angel. She'd tell them that and get this over with. But she needed a lawyer first. It wasn't good to just start talking. The police believed only what they wanted.

"Osvaldo," she said, "go with the police, but do not say anything. I'll be there as soon as I can."

CLAYTON FELT HELPLESS. Now both Ellen and Osvaldo needed legal advice. The only lawyer he'd worked with in the past ten years was Bill McAfee, but he wasn't about to call him. He might have to find a lawyer outside of Springdale. Should Ellen and Osvaldo have the same one? Did Brandt really have evidence to connect Osvaldo with the burglary, or was he just trying to get information from him?

He felt Maria touching his arm. "Pastor Loverage, where is your phone? I will call Mr. Santori. He will know what to do."

He wanted to tell her that he could handle this. He was the pastor of the largest church in the county, the pride of his denomination. Mr. Know-It-All. Mr. Competent. Mr. Give-It-to-Me-I-Can-Do-It. But he couldn't even choose a lawyer from his own congregation. Bill McAfee! He could have done better choosing randomly.

"Maria," he said, "please use the phone in my office. Ellie will show you. The telephone book is in the top drawer."

Mr. and Mrs. Santori met Clayton, Ellen, and Maria at the police station. Mr. Santori was thin, wiry, and full of energy. His hair, which was beginning to gray, was thick and combed back, so that he looked as though he were walking into a fierce wind. His eyes were keen and busy. The weather was still warm enough for him to wear a short-sleeved Hawaiian shirt and khakis.

Olga Santori was not much taller than Maria, but stocky, with neatly coiffed reddish-brown hair. She wore an inexpensive blouse and slacks and greeted Maria affectionately, as though she were her sister.

Clayton knew Mr. Santori through the pastors' association that met once a month to discuss and pray about local problems. He respected the way Bethel Temple's free dining room served the homeless and hungry on Tuesdays and Thursdays. That's where Clayton sent many down-and-outers who showed up on his church's doorstep. Nevertheless, he had never taken the time to develop any kind of relationship with Santori. Bethel Temple's worship style was a little too informal, and the church held a few doctrinal views that he disagreed with. All told, however, it was a good church.

A few minutes after the Santoris arrived, a tall Latino woman entered the station. Mr. Santori and Olga hugged her warmly and introduced her as Rachael Ramirez, a lawyer who had moved from Chicago two years earlier. She, her husband, and three children lived on a farm on the road to New Hope. Although she was tall and large-boned, dwarfing Maria and Olga, she was not intimidating, and she spoke with grace and gentleness. The seven of them sat in a small conference room close to the main desk.

Before they all settled into their chairs, Mr. Santori spoke. "We are all brothers and sisters in our Lord Jesus Christ," he said, "and we are here to uphold and sustain one another."

For Pete's sake, Santori, this isn't church. You'll turn Ellie off so fast she'll burrow into her tunnel and never emerge.

"I am here to listen," continued Mr. Santori, "and while I listen, I pray. I want you to know that whatever you say, I love you. If Jesus loves you, then I love you. I've asked Rachael to come because I trust her. She's a sister in the Lord. I don't know who wants to start—Pastor Loverage? Maria? Osvaldo? All I know is that the police have found some connection between a burglary and Osvaldo."

Ellie spoke immediately, and Clayton gave an inward sigh of relief.

"I know more about this than anyone else. I'll tell you what happened."

For the third time Clayton listened to his daughter describe going into Miss Merkle's house and being there when the burglary took place. When she came to the part about the shoes, Maria spoke up.

"Those are Osvaldo's shoes, but he hasn't worn them for a long time. The policeman found them under my couch."

"I wore them this summer when I painted with Mr. Pettigrew," said Osvaldo, "but I bought new ones for school."

Maria began to cry softly, and Olga handed her a handkerchief and put her arm around her.

"Ramon and Raphael?" asked Mr. Santori.

"Probably," said Maria, her voice so low she could hardly be heard.

"Why didn't you throw the shoes away, Osvaldo?" asked Rachael.

"I forgot and left them at the house. I don't live there anymore; I stay at the church."

"Do you ever visit your mother at the house?" Rachael continued.

"I did once. To get my things."

"Why don't you go to the house?"

Osvaldo looked at his mother, afraid to say anything about his brothers.

"They threatened him," said Maria. "I made him move."

"Why did they want to harm him?" asked Rachael.

Maria closed her eyes and bit hard on her lower lip. Rachael waited. Osvaldo took his mother's hand. After a while Rachael spoke gently.

"Don't be afraid, Maria. It's okay if it's hard and hurts. I understand. All of us here understand and love you."

Maria did not look at them but finally spoke. "They brought things to the house."

"You think they stole things and hid them at your house?"

"TVs, computers, stereos, other things. They put them in my bedroom, then took them away."

"Did you inform the police?"

"No. They're my boys. I didn't want them to get caught; I just wanted them to change."

"And they said they'd hurt Osvaldo if you said anything?" asked Rachael.

"And Ellen, and Mr. Pettigrew . . . or burn down the house."

Clayton listened to the lawyer. He didn't know how good a lawyer she was, but he sensed a genuine concern for Maria that would extend to Osvaldo and Ellie.

"And there's another thing," said Maria. "The policeman found a crystal angel in my drawer."

"One of your boys left it?" asked Rachael.

"Probably Ramon. He wrapped it in a napkin that said 'Mama.' The policeman took the angel."

"And you think it came from Miss Merkle's . . . ?" asked Rachael.

"Probably," said Ellen. "She was into that kind of stuff."

There was never any doubt whether Rachael Ramirez would counsel and represent Osvaldo. Clayton and Mr. Santori told Maria not to worry about the cost. God would provide some way to take care of it. Clayton figured that he'd end up being the way God provided, and wondered how much she charged. But he wanted her to represent Ellie. His daughter didn't clam up with her as she had with McAfee.

On the way home, Ellie told him she felt better now. She liked Rachael—already she called the attorney by her first name—and, yes, she would like to work with her.

"Father, I saw Mrs. Brandt's name and address on some magazines in Mr. McAfee's car."

To anyone overhearing, her statement would sound like a complete non sequitur, but Clayton understood. He'd always detected negative vibes between his daughter and Shirley Brandt.

S I X T E E N

Mrs. Archambeaux, the school principal, permitted Ellen and Osvaldo to miss the rest of the school week as long as they completed their daily assignments. It was a short week anyway, with Thursday and Friday being holidays. It would be better, she said, to let things calm down a bit before they returned. Mr. Wicker volunteered to drop off their homework assignments each afternoon and pick them up the next morning.

On Tuesday Ellen and Father went fishing again. She got up early, brewed coffee, and sautéed catfish Father had caught several months earlier. Then, on Jewish rye bread, thick mayonnaise on one piece, a thin film of hot jalapeño salsa on the other, she arranged paper-thin carrot rounds interspersed with raisins, blanketed them with spinach greens, sprinkled grated Parmesan cheese, and finished them off with the extra-thick catfish fillets. After slicing off the crusts and wrapping the sandwiches in Saran wrap, she scribbled out labels reading: *Captivating Catfish Canapés—recipe from Caddo Lake, TX, circa 1923.* She packed a large shopping bag with the sandwiches, Father's coffee, a couple of Dr. Peppers, two apples, paper towels, a book, and several CDs. This time she'd take her boom box. She threw in a ball of string in case Father forgot; their fishing rocks waited on the shore.

The morning went perfectly. They discussed the newly discovered sport of rock fishing and made a liturgy of various techniques for securing their rocks to their strings. They wouldn't want to lose their valuable bait. While they fished, absorbing the scarce warmth of late autumn sunshine, she played one of Father's favorite CDs followed by one of her own that she thought he might tolerate. Most of the morning they read. They had finished *The Hobbit* and started the *The Fellowship of the Rings*. Occasionally they pulled in their lines to see if they'd caught anything. Each time they were successful, for the rocks dangled safely from their strings, and the fish swam freely.

When they ate lunch, Father said grace and thanked God for the magnificent fall day and for his daughter. Later, he told her the sandwiches were delicious and then reminisced about fishing with his father and Uncle Claude at Caddo Lake. He had hoped one of his children would like fishing, but it had held too little action for Clay, Jr., Dan, and Linda, and they were quickly bored. He never dreamed that Ellie would be his fishing companion.

As they rode home after lunch, Father said that was the most relaxation he'd had in years. The fishing was magnificent, and the Tolkien trilogy promised to be even better than *The Hobbit*. He'd seen the books lying around the house for years, but hadn't bothered with them; now he'd have to extract himself from them to concentrate on his sermon preparations.

Ellen knew they needed to talk about more serious matters, and several times started to say something about Miss Merkle or the binder. They *had* to talk; they couldn't let it ride much longer. But how could she just start talking to Father about his former lover? They'd end up arguing. The morning had been too good to risk tarnishing and should be left untouched, preserved. They needed more fishing trips to serve as a healing salve before stress opened old wounds. She was grateful Father was not pushing her.

At the end of the ride home Father thanked her for bringing the boom box. "I enjoyed *all* of the music, Ellie," he said with a smile. He gave her a quick hug before hurrying off to church for an afternoon meeting.

ON TUESDAY EVENING Ellen and Father, Osvaldo, Maria, and Rachael Ramirez met at the Santoris' house for dinner, and Rachael updated them on her discussions with Brandt. He had spent Tuesday morning with Miss Merkle inventorying her stolen items. The teacher had presented him with a computer printout of her Hummels, complete with dates of manufacture and purchase, and estimated values. The Hummels, crystal figurines, sterling silver, music box, and jewelry totaled almost four hundred items with an estimated value of $60,000–$70,000.

Brandt still had a lot of questions. How had the burglars gained access to the house? There was no evidence of forced entry, so where did they get a key? Was the front door left unlocked, or open? Had someone let them into the house? Had Ellen ever told Osvaldo where Miss Merkle's key was hidden? Had Osvaldo ever gone into the house with Ellen? How did one of the burglars happen to be wearing Osvaldo's shoes?

Osvaldo was no longer a suspect in the actual burglary. A librarian, Mr. Delgado, said that Osvaldo had been at his usual spot on Friday afternoon and had checked out a book at 3:45. Furthermore, Mr. Pettigrew said that Osvaldo was working with him from four to six.

Osvaldo had positively identified the tennis shoes. The gray streak reminded him of a comet, and he knew which house he was working on when the paint had splattered his shoe. He didn't wear them anymore because they were sloppy, and his feet were growing.

Because of the tennis shoes and the angel found in Maria's house, Brandt was zeroing in on Osvaldo's brothers, but he needed more evidence before charging them. There were unconfirmed sightings of the brothers in East St. Louis. He'd learn more when they tried to unload Miss Merkle's things.

"But Officer Brandt's still not too sure about you, Ellen." Rachael cocked her head and raised her eyebrows.

Ellen wanted to reply that the feeling was mutual, but right now that seemed petty.

"The case would move faster if you'd work with him. He says he has to shake you by your heels to make something fall out. You don't have to *like* him to trust him, Ellen. He's not out to get you. And there's still the separate matter of your trespassing. . . ."

She did not reply. There was nothing to add to her recorded statement. She and Brandt were incompatible.

Then Rachael mentioned one other matter. "Miss Merkle seems quite upset about a missing binder that seems to hold special meaning for her. According to Brandt, she is more distraught about that than about the lost Hummels."

Ellen could tell Father was disturbed at the mention of the binder. He began rubbing his knuckles with his thumbs and sucking in his upper lip. The missing binder puzzled her. Was it the same one that had lain on the bed?

By the end of the evening, Osvaldo said he would talk with Brandt, but Ellen refused. She couldn't work with someone she didn't like, respect, or trust. It didn't matter if he was a police officer, or if cooperating might help her. In the end, Ellen agreed to consider the officer's questions if they were submitted through Rachael, but even then, she wasn't sure she'd answer them all.

EARLY WEDNESDAY EVENING Rachael stopped by the Loverages' house to give them another update. She'd asked that Maria and Osvaldo be there, and said she'd drop them by the Santoris' in time for dinner. Ellen greeted her warmly and ushered her into the living room, where Osvaldo and Maria were already seated. They chatted for five minutes before Father joined them.

Rachael described her day in Springdale, working out of Mr. Santori's office: lunch at the Megatronics cafeteria with Maria and Olga, ten minutes with Osvaldo after school, two trips to see Ellen at home, several calls to Father at the church, and numerous calls to and from Officer Brandt. He was the most difficult part of her work, the attorney said. She trusted him, but their conversations were always edgy.

"I understand Officer Brandt talked with you several times, Osvaldo," said Rachael.

"Six times so far. He even came out to Mrs. Ritchie's house this afternoon."

"What does he ask you?"

"About Ramon and Raphael. He thinks I'm like them because we're brothers."

"What do you tell him?" asked Rachael.

"Not much. I talk about New Mexico, but not our house."

"But he keeps coming back?"

"Yes, but I'll never say anything." He glanced at his mother, who had her eyes focused on the floor.

Rachael informed them that Brandt no longer connected Ellen with the burglary. Nothing he had uncovered contradicted her statement. One doesn't carry a science book when committing a burglary. He also recalled an incident earlier in the year when Miss Merkle's dog got loose. He knew that Ellen, as she claimed, was on good terms with the dog.

A possible explanation of how the burglars gained entry had turned up. Several weeks earlier at the mall, Miss Merkle had left her keys in the door of her 1950 Bel Air, but was relieved to find them still there when she returned after several hours. There had been ample opportunity for someone to copy the keys, put them back in the lock, wait for the driver to return, and follow her home—a common procedure for an opportunistic thief.

Finally, some of Miss Merkle's Hummels had turned up in Belleville along with descriptions of two men roughly fitting those of Ramon and Raphael, who were trying to unload them. Alerts for the brothers were issued throughout Illinois and Missouri.

"Ellen," Rachael continued, "the only thing you have to worry about now is whether Miss Merkle files a trespassing complaint. Because you took nothing, and Miss Merkle had no idea you'd been going into the house before the burglary, she might be persuaded to show some kindness toward one of her top students. I'll talk with her. Something might be worked out.

"In the meantime, enjoy a wonderful Thanksgiving. God is still in control, and even in the midst of problems, we all have a lot to be thankful for."

All her life Ellen had heard those sentiments, the be-thankful-no-matter-what way of thinking. It was supposed to be Christian, but sometimes when she heard those things at church, they sounded flippant or insincere. Expressions like "Praise the Lord" and "Alleluia" often stood for "Wow, that's great," or "Right on!" But she didn't mind what Rachael Ramirez had said. She did have a lot to be thankful for. What had happened was a major glitch in her life, but it wasn't going to ruin everything.

In a quick prayer she thanked God for Father, Osvaldo, and Maria, then added the Santoris and Rachael. And there were her books and her music, and her new joy of reading and fishing with Father. The world was good. Everything was going to be all right.

ON FRIDAY EVENING after Thanksgiving, Rachael Ramirez told Ellen and Father that she'd talked with Miss Merkle. By appointment they had met at the teacher's house that morning. Rachael explained to her how the case stood, that Osvaldo was not a suspect, and that Ellen had gone into her house to find a quiet place to read and had unfortunately been there during the burglary. It was now her, Miss Merkle's, decision whether a trespassing complaint would be filed, but the Loverages hoped that she would accept an apology and not file.

"Is there a chance of her doing that?" asked Father.

"When I went to her house, I was optimistic, but now I'm not so sure. After she heard what I had to say, she thanked me for coming and immediately ushered me to the door. All she said was, 'You can send the girl over anytime she's ready.' Maybe you should wait a week, Ellen, and let things calm down some more."

"I don't want to wait."

"Your father or I could go with you," suggested Rachael.

"No. I'll take care of it." This was something between her and her teacher. She wanted to go alone.

ON SATURDAY MORNING Clayton drove to New Hope for a meeting with Bill McAfee, at the lawyer's request. It was urgent, he stressed, and he needed to see Clayton alone, preferably in a location away from the church and their homes. He suggested The Pink Turtle, which appeared to be the attorney's favorite hangout. McAfee wouldn't reveal the purpose of the meeting, only that it was important church business. Occasionally McAfee reviewed church matters with him, but he had never asked to do it away from town. Clayton told him Saturday morning was free, and, yes, they could have breakfast at The Pink Turtle. He'd be there at seven.

As Clayton drove the twenty-seven miles to New Hope, he realized how much he'd rather be fishing with Ellie. The good weather was still holding, but any day Indian summer would surrender to a northern chill. By spring Ellie would be close to graduation. They'd have to find something else to do together during the winter.

He tried not to think about the approaching meeting with McAfee. It brought back childhood memories of his father sending him to the mailbox at night. Their section of Houston had no streetlights, and hedges bordered the sidewalk where he walked. He was so sure someone would jump out and grab him that he always ran in the middle of the street. Now he felt that same apprehension.

Maybe McAfee was going to insist that the church hire an associate pastor, the one destined to take over after he left. Brandt would feed him a handpicked name, made to order for the First Brandtian Church of Springdale. Perhaps McAfee was going to oppose the improvements to the gymnasium, insisting the church had more urgent needs. Clayton could handle that. He didn't always agree with his church leaders, but he knew how to compromise and work with them. But this meeting with McAfee felt different. He wanted to turn around, get Ellie, and head for Braxton Reservoir.

The hostess at The Pink Turtle directed him to an enclosed room at the back of the restaurant reserved for small conferences. Around a table, with half-filled coffee mugs, sat Bill and Susan McAfee, Jack and Shirley Brandt, and two young couples, Steve and Debbie Benchley and Mark and Vickie Unger. This wasn't one person jumping out from behind a hedge, it was an ecclesiastical ambush, organized and determined. Brandt, he knew, was behind the whole thing.

For a moment Clayton was tempted to walk in, stare them down, and then leave them in their war circle, but he needed to find out what they were up to. He wouldn't order anything. That way he could withdraw whenever he wanted without being indebted for even a cup of coffee.

Bill McAfee greeted him warmly. "Pastor Loverage, we're so glad to see you. We hope you don't mind sharing this time with the Brandts, Benchleys, and Ungers."

"How thoughtful of you to include other members of the flock, Bill. I might have invited a few myself if I had known."

He circled the table, greeting the men with handshakes

and the women with gentle hugs. He took a chair near the door. At least they hadn't cut off his escape route. Everyone ordered breakfast except him. He was sorry, he said, but he'd have to decline. He was fasting. Couldn't even have coffee. Some extremely important decisions lay ahead, and he needed guidance from the Lord. To avoid lying, he resolved to carry through on this instantaneous fasting decision, at least until that evening.

"You can be sure we'll uphold you in our prayers, Pastor," said Susan McAfee.

"Thank you, Susan." He scanned the group. "Now, I'm sure there's something important you have to say," he said. "We should get to that as soon as possible."

Everyone shifted nervously except Brandt, who had his head bowed as though in prayer.

"To put it bluntly, Pastor," said McAfee, "we believe it is the general consensus of our congregation that you resign."

That was blunt, like a cudgel.

"The effectiveness of your ministry has declined in the last couple of years, and this episode with your daughter has caused a lack of credibility. The Bible tells us that a man shouldn't be a church leader if he cannot control the actions of his children. Furthermore, let me summarize a few other important facts."

Clayton listened to the indictments.

"First, average Sunday attendance has declined 12 percent over the past two years."

True. Oh, so true.

"Offerings decreased by 19 percent in the same period."

True. We have major budget problems.

"You're losing the congregation. They're crying for relevant sermons on current issues, but all they get are expositions of Bible passages."

All the issues of the day are addressed in my expository teaching, if you would only listen.

"Our music is old-fashioned, or to be more accurate,

anachronistic. Organs belong in Gothic cathedrals. We should be on the cutting edge of church development, taking advantage of modern technology. We need synthesizers, guitars, and drums. Young families are moving to churches where they can relate to the music."

A valid point. I need to think about that some more . . . seriously. God knows I've tried.

"We all realize you're a highly respected speaker at marriage and family conferences, but word about Ellen has spread around the country, and it is doubtful you can maintain your status and reputation. I learned yesterday that your conferences at Pine Cove and Milwaukee have been canceled."

I canceled those myself for reasons I won't disclose. But again, you have a valid point.

"And, Pastor Loverage, this congregation is shocked that you have so little influence on your daughter. Your ministry at Springdale Church is so undermined by the Merkle incident that many are already planning to transfer their membership."

I wonder who the underminers are.

Mark Unger added that the church needed to be patterned after one he came from in St. Louis that now had almost two thousand members. That church had done away with their organ and choir and had a worship team of twelve that led the congregation in songs with a beat they could feel. Everyone could focus on the words as they flashed on two giant screens; there was no need to peer down at a hymnal.

Vickie added that the Sunday school at Springdale Church differed little from the one she had attended twenty-five years earlier. Bible stories, memorization, attendance pens, "Jesus Loves Me, " "This Little Light of Mine."

"My kids are bored," she said, "and they fuss to stay home and watch Sunday morning cartoons. We need modern ideas. This is almost the twenty-first century."

Steve Benchley mentioned foreign missions. "Why should we fund missionary efforts in Ghana, India, and Mexico? Is that our way of avoiding personal contact with the needy on our doorstep? Within twenty miles of Springdale there are enough problems to drain our church's resources. Furthermore, we should be starting satellite churches."

Debbie Benchley added that his sermons failed to reach her. Bible study could be done in small groups and privately at home.

Shirley Brandt said that no one doubted his dedication to Springdale Church or the fine work he'd done in the past, but that was all the more reason why he should graciously resign. There was still time to go out as a beloved, respected pastor, but if he held on, the issue would be forced and he would leave in disgrace.

Clayton was not about to respond to a group that had proclaimed its own authority. He needed to leave the restaurant; the walls were closing in on him.

"My friends, I appreciate your comments and concerns for my well-being and that of the church. You have made some valid points. I will give them full consideration. But surely, since I am only one among nine, you don't expect me to comment on specific issues at this time. I ask you to continue praying, and to examine not only my ministry but your own hearts."

"Pastor Loverage," said McAfee, rising to his feet, "I must stress that time is short. You must not let this matter slide. A month, maybe even two weeks, is too long. A church fight will damage everyone, and I assure you, you will lose. You know how to reach Jack or me, and we expect a call before next Saturday.

"And Pastor," the lawyer concluded, "I want you to know that I love you. Everyone here loves you. The whole church loves you. It is because of love that we urge you to resign. We are your brothers and sisters in Christ and have prayed about this long and hard. You know this is very difficult for us. For your own good, for Ellen's, for our church, it is time for you to step aside."

Clayton dismissed himself, leaving a five-dollar tip to cover the water the waitress had brought him, and drove to Springdale by the back roads. Joyce had always called them the "pondering roads."

Was he surprised at what was said? No. But he hadn't expected to meet an ad hoc committee. That was a cheap shot.

Were they right? That was always a possibility. He knew he resisted change, but he had made changes over the years. They were too fast for some people and not fast enough for others. He would think about everything they said. He didn't want to be a dinosaur trying to survive in Middle America at the end of the twentieth century.

But then there was Ellie, dear, wonderful, in some ways brilliant, frustrating-beyond-words Ellie, left with him three years ago to care for alone. Right now she was more dear to him than Springdale Church. Rimless, thick glasses. Hair as straight as uncooked spaghetti. Books growing out of her hands. Stubborn and immovable as Ayers Rock. But her stubbornness wasn't aimed at doing evil, just at doing things her own way.

When he thought about it, in many ways she had caused him less worry than the other kids. If she left home when she was eighteen, as she threatened to do, he'd miss her terribly. She was his bookworm, his sandwich girl, his rock-fishing partner, and yes, his antagonist.

Now she had become the principal issue in his staying at Springdale Church, the leverage Brandt and McAfee thought they needed to remove him. Maybe they were right, and the church had lost confidence in him. If that were so, he would move on. There were other churches he could pastor. Or he might retire. He was fully vested in the denomination's pension plan. But he didn't want Brandt to take control of the church, and he knew that could happen. Brandt, with all of his good intentions, would re-create the church in his own image, and it would slowly die. If he had to leave, he'd warn the denomination about what was taking place. Maybe they could step in and do something.

AT HOME CLAYTON pressed the replay button on his answering machine for the ever-present parishioner-to-pastor messages—what he lived for and what he dreaded. One was from Jack Brandt requesting a meeting with him. Just the two of them, he said. Perhaps on Sunday afternoon, anywhere Clayton desired.

Clayton left his own message. "Thank you for calling, Jack, but Sundays are reserved for worship and family; no church business. We can meet Monday evening after the Building Committee or early Tuesday morning. Your choice. My house would be fine."

"Tuesday morning at seven, if that's the soonest you can do it," was the return message later that day. Clayton wondered if Brandt were staging another ambush.

SEVENTEEN

Ellen dreaded her inevitable talk with Miss Merkle, but she knew her situation wouldn't improve without facing her teacher and apologizing. Even before Rachael had suggested it, she had come to this conclusion. It's what Father would want her to do, although he hadn't offered any advice since the burglary. But the more she thought about it, the more it felt right. It was probably something the Bible would tell her to do too.

She was still amazed at how she had rationalized what she had done. Sometimes in the middle of the night she'd go over her reasoning, mimicking herself. *It's okay to go into Miss Merkle's house because I'm not going to steal anything. I just want to borrow a little bit of space that's not being used anyway. I'm not hurting anyone—not Miss Merkle, Father, or myself.* She knew she'd gone in because Father irritated her, but it wasn't fair to blame him for her troubles. He might be guilty of bugging her, but she alone had made the decision to enter the house. She had no business going in and was truly sorry.

She hoped, even prayed, that after a week Miss Merkle had calmed down and would accept her apology.

She resolved to be honest with Miss Merkle, as she had been with Father and with Jack Brandt. She wasn't sure what to expect. Miss Caroline Merkle was everyone's mystery. What kind of person was she? Did she have a heart, or was she just an English-teaching automaton? Was there any empathy and compassion behind her facade? Ellen hoped so.

She knew Miss Merkle favored her from the way she called on her in class and the comments she wrote on her reports. Now, that was lost. Would she even be allowed back into Miss Merkle's class? Maybe she'd have to change to a different English teacher or attend school in Longwood or New Hope.

Ellen allowed herself to fantasize. After her apology to Miss Merkle, her teacher would scold her a little and then forgive her. Then they could talk about the books in her library. Ellen had questions about *Anna Karenina* and George Eliot and *Notre Dame de Paris,* and Miss Merkle was the only person in Springdale with answers. Maybe her teacher would offer her a cup of tea, and they'd sit in her living room and talk. She might invite her to join the book review club at the Kingswood Country Club.

But then there was the matter of Miss Merkle's relationship with Father, which Ellen wanted to keep off-limits. She didn't want to talk about the photo on the nightstand, and she'd be embarrassed to bring up the photo album or the white binder. All of that happened forty years ago. It was none of her business, none of anyone else's business, just private, ancient history between a young Father and a young Caroline Merkle.

What would she say if Miss Merkle asked her if she'd seen Father's picture on the nightstand? Her teacher knew she'd been in her bedroom, because that's where she was hiding when the burglary took place. The photo was in plain sight; she couldn't miss it. It would be easy to say that she hadn't seen anything, that she'd fled into the bedroom when she heard the burglars come in the front door, that there had been no time to look around. But she'd made a commitment to the truth. She recalled the words that came to her so clearly the night after the burglary. *Into your hands I commit my spirit, O LORD, the God of truth.*

LATE SATURDAY AFTERNOON Ellen told Father that it was time for her to talk with Miss Merkle. It was eight days since the burglary, time enough for her teacher to calm down and for Ellen to resolve issues in her own mind. Father backed her up and encouraged her, but insisted on a brief prayer before she made her call.

On the phone Miss Merkle sounded cold and distant, and said to come over, if she could find the way. Ellen had never heard her teacher use sarcasm before. It wasn't a good beginning, but she couldn't back out now. She walked around the block to 473 Starling, asking God to honor her commitment to the truth.

Before Ellen could ring the doorbell, Miss Merkle opened the door, and, with a dramatic wave of her hand, invited her into the house. Rolex was glad to see her, but Miss Merkle ordered the dog back to his pad by the fireplace. Ellen waited, hoping Miss Merkle would offer her a seat, but the teacher said nothing, and they stood in an awkward silence in the entry hall.

"I want to apologize," Ellen finally said.

"Well?" Miss Merkle answered.

Standing in the front hall was not the way Ellen had pictured this. They were supposed to be sitting at the dining room table or in the living room. She had come there with confidence; now she wasn't sure of herself. "I'm sorry," she mumbled. "I needed a place to read, and I took advantage of you. . . . I was wrong. I shouldn't have done it."

Miss Merkle stared at her, but still said nothing. Rolex

began a soft, pitiful whine, as though he too felt the stony silence that infested the house.

Say something, Miss Merkle, anything. Cry, scold me, curse me, throw me out, but don't give me the polar treatment. "I never took anything, Miss Merkle. I had nothing to do with the burglary. Honest."

"I don't believe you, Ellen Loverage." She said the words slowly, evenly, as though she were taking a solemn oath.

"I never took anything, not even a drink of water. All I did was read novels."

"You're lying."

This wasn't working. She was in trouble. "You must believe me. I'm telling you the truth."

"Ellen, turn around and leave my house. You may come back and apologize when, and only when, you are carrying my binder. You know which one I'm talking about. If you do not return it, I will not only file trespassing charges, but do everything in my power to connect you with the burglary. I know you've been hanging around with the Villanuevas. I might never see my Hummels, crystal, silver, or jewelry again, but I want that binder. Do you understand?"

"I don't have it." Now Ellen spoke firmly. Officer Brandt hadn't intimidated her, so why should Miss Merkle?

"The burglars wouldn't want it."

"But I didn't take it. I didn't take anything." She spoke boldly, meeting her teacher's flashing green eyes, wondering if she was furious or frantic.

"But you know what I'm talking about, don't you?"

This is it. Lie. Evade the question. Tell her you don't have the faintest idea what she's talking about. God, I want to tell the truth. I'm supposed to trust You, but it's so hard. Please help me.

Miss Merkle waited.

"Yeah, I saw it on your bed last Friday." She reminded herself to watch it. She shouldn't bait Miss Merkle, who never let her students get away with *yeahs*.

"And you looked through it, didn't you?"

"Yes, but I read only the last letter from Father." *I might have read more . . .*

"Did your father send you to get the binder?" she asked accusingly.

"Of course not. He never knew I was coming here."

Her teacher didn't answer.

"I didn't take it, Miss Merkle."

"That's enough, Ellen. Don't come back without my binder." She spoke softly, but edged her toward the door with the firmness of a bulldozer.

"Good-bye. Thank you," Ellen said as she stepped out into a cold breeze.

As she left, she heard Rolex whining.

She didn't go straight home, but walked downtown to Bud's Burgers and ordered a Pepsi. She needed time to think before she talked with Father. She had wanted to avoid the whole matter of his involvement with Miss Merkle. Now what was she going to tell him? He was probably pacing the floor waiting to hear.

As she sat in the booth, she wondered what it really meant to tell the truth. Did it mean she was supposed to tell everyone everything without any discernment? Was she supposed to tell Rachael and Brandt about the photos and the letters? It was Father and Miss Merkle's forty-year-old secret, not hers. Even to help herself out of trouble, she had no right to say anything. But if she didn't, would she still be telling the truth? Did Father know Miss Merkle had saved everything he'd written? Unless that love-letter binder showed up, Miss Merkle would file charges against her.

God, this is complicated. Help me figure it out. I don't have a clue about what to do.

When Ellen reached home, Rachael was there. She and Father looked at Ellen expectantly.

"Miss Merkle didn't accept my apology," she told them. "She's going to file charges. I can't talk about it today, so don't ask me anything. I'll be in my room." She didn't want to be rude; after all, they were on her side and cared, but her anger wouldn't let her talk rationally. She needed time alone to sort things out.

Who was she angry with anyway? Miss Merkle? Yes, the woman was a heartless block of granite. But it was more than Miss Merkle. Maybe she was angry at God. She had trusted Him and committed herself to telling the truth, so why hadn't He honored her commitment and paved the way with her teacher? What was the use in praying and promising? Her apology had bounced off Miss Merkle like a Ping-Pong ball off the Sears Tower. All she cared about was that stupid binder.

Going into the house wasn't just between her and her teacher; it had grown beyond that. Just like Pandora, she had opened a box she had no right to even touch. All she had sought was a peaceful place to read, but that was tampering with the box. She had opened it a crack, and a snake had slithered out. Now she couldn't get it back in, and it was going to bite her . . . and Father. It would probably poison him. She had to tell him what she knew about him and Miss Merkle, and it was only right to warn him about the missing binder.

The next morning at breakfast she prepared scrambled eggs and bacon for him. She did that only once a month, when she felt like it. Today her motive was not only to do something nice, but also to set a mood. They ate in silence, not an angry silence, but one that was tense and waiting. On Sunday mornings he was always preoccupied with his sermons, but she had to tell him what she'd seen in Miss Merkle's house.

Finally she took a big breath and began. "Father, about Miss Merkle. I—"

"We knew each other in high school," he replied sharply. "We even dated. I might talk about it someday. I can't do it now."

He rose from the table, strode into his study, and closed the door.

Ellen covered her eyes, glasses and all, with her hands. *Father, I'm more like you than I ever imagined.*

ON MONDAY EVENING Ellen, Father, Maria, and Osvaldo again had dinner with Rachael and the Santoris. Ellen thought Father was beginning to enjoy having dinner there, because he and Mr. Santori talked amiably of church matters —shop talk, he called it—and several times she heard them laughing.

Rachael again reviewed the case. The only item that concerned her was the trespassing charge against Ellen. Osvaldo was clear, and Maria, although acknowledging that the boys had stored stolen articles at her house, was not in danger because, fortunately, the police had never found anything there besides the angel. If she were summoned to be a witness against her boys, Rachael would represent her. They could worry about that later.

That evening Osvaldo told them what it was like returning to school. More kids had talked to him in one day than in the entire time he'd been at Springdale High. He was a temporary celebrity, subject to a barrage of questions.

"Was it true?"

"Did you really go into Merkle's house?"

"Ellen Loverage went in, didn't she?"

"Is Ellen ever coming back to school?"

"I thought she was one of Miss Merkle's pets."

"I just shook my head and jabbered nonsense in Spanish," said Osvaldo. "I wasn't supposed to say anything."

"Were they after you all day?" asked Rachael.

"No, by lunchtime they were talking about the next basketball game."

Miss Merkle had returned to school on the same day, acting as though nothing had happened. She was the same old English teacher who'd been at their school for hundreds of years. No one dared ask questions about the burglary. She might as well have posted a sign reading "English Only Discussed in Class." Don't talk vacations, politics, personal feelings, sports; stick to English grammar and literature.

During the evening Ellen noticed that Maria was nervous and unhappy. Once she saw her in the kitchen leaning against Mrs. Santori. Her eyes looked red, as though she'd been crying a lot. When she asked Osvaldo if his mother was all right, he shrugged his shoulders. He had always confided in her, or at least explained why he couldn't. Maybe Maria was worrying about Ramon and Raphael. It didn't matter if they caused her trouble; they were still her sons.

MONDAY NIGHT the first snowfall of the season blanketed Springdale with an inch of snow that soon turned to slush. Clayton woke early Tuesday, shaved, and spent a short time reading the Bible and praying about his dreaded meeting with Brandt. He was tired and had wakened several times in the night with a pain in his back and lower abdomen. Probably something he'd eaten. While he was praying, he heard Ellie shoveling snow from the front walkway.

"For our honored guest," she explained at the breakfast table. "We must treat him with the respect he deserves."

Jack Brandt arrived punctually at 7:00. When Clayton opened the door for him, he noticed a small, droopy snowman near the front steps. A black belt with a baggy cloth holster hung from its middle, and a maple leaf served as a badge. As he closed the front door behind Brandt, he saw that the snowman had two faces. The one facing the front door had close-set, beady eyes, bright red cheeks, and a distorted frown. He could see only part of the one facing the street, but he guessed it had bright eyes and a tortured smile. No doubt Brandt had noticed too. Clayton wanted to go to Ellie's room and scold her for her impudence and congratulate her on a job well done. Too bad it was melting.

He and Brandt exchanged the expected niceties. How are

you this morning? Do you think we're in for a cold winter? How are Shirley and the kids? How's Clay, Jr. doing with his church in Fort Worth? It was ironic how congenial they could be when discussing nonchurch matters.

"How's Ellen doing?" asked Brandt. "She's back in school, isn't she?"

"She's going to wait another week. Right now she's upstairs in her room."

Brandt glanced toward the staircase. "Do you think we could go someplace else to talk?"

Clayton could imagine Ellie with her ear pressed against the door or the furnace vent, taking in every word they said, but he felt ornery enough to make Brandt squirm a little. "I'm sure she's absorbed in a book, Jack. Doesn't even know you're here." He chided himself for not telling the truth, but these were extenuating circumstances. "Would you like some coffee? Just made it . . . better than JubiLatte's."

"No thank you, Pastor. I can't relax here. I'd feel freer if we went to my house or just drove around."

Clayton wanted to end their talk before it started; it was too furtive, too foreboding. He had hoped Jack carried an olive branch; now he feared a hand grenade. He could insist they stay at his house, but he certainly didn't want the poor man to be uptight. One way or another Brandt was going to have his say; Clayton might as well hear it now. They'd leave, but he'd insist on driving, so he could return home whenever he wanted.

When Clayton went to Ellie's bedroom door to tell her he was going, she gave him a hug and pressed a note into his hand. He read it as he got his winter coat from his bedroom. *Stay cool, Father. I love you.* He folded the note and put it into his wallet, next to his picture of Joyce.

Clayton had barely backed out of the driveway when Brandt began.

"First, Pastor Loverage, I want you to know I had mixed emotions about our meeting at The Pink Turtle last Saturday."

Clayton wanted to say that he understood what he meant —mixed emotions, such as the exhilaration of the chase, the elation of ambush, satisfaction of springing a well-prepared trap, the thrill of possible victory, and the anticipation of catbird-seat joy.

"You've been a wonderful pastor, and Shirley and I have grown under your ministry. I'm sorry things had to come down to this."

"Jack, I appreciated what you had to say, but I think it could have been handled differently. An eight-to-one advantage to deliver a message like that isn't—"

"Pastor, that meeting was called after much prayer. You don't realize how much we agonized over it."

"You have my deepest sympathy." *Be careful, Clay; that's not helping.* "Jack, I'm seriously considering some of the things that were mentioned. But that's not why you asked to see me today. Why don't you just come out with it, so we can both get on with our days. I'm sure you have work to do."

"All right. Two words should get us started: Caroline Merkle."

Clayton felt paralyzed. For several seconds he couldn't breathe, his eyes lost focus, and an electric tingle surged along his spine. Brandt must have found something at Cary's house.

"What about her?" he asked, trying to control his voice.

"First of all, I hadn't expected to find your picture on her nightstand."

Clayton had no doubt Cary had photos of him, but had never imagined them next to her bed. He said nothing, but clung to what Ellie had said in her note. The easiest way to stay cool was to keep silent.

"I've checked on her background and yours. Except for your time in Europe, you two have always lived in the same city, often within blocks of each other."

Clayton wanted to smash the car into the next light post.

"I'm sure I don't have the whole picture, Pastor, but I'm afraid of what would happen if this were common knowledge.

A man committed to the truth, as you are, wouldn't deny it. My first concern is for the work of the Lord. The church I love is on the brink of a disaster that only you can prevent. I didn't seek this information; it turned up as part of the burglary investigation. I'm sorry."

Did the whole police department know what Brandt knew?

Clayton made a U-turn and headed back to his house. No wonder Brandt wanted privacy. Jack might see himself as rescuing the church, but to Clayton this was tantamount to blackmail.

"I'm not going to reiterate what Bill McAfee said last Saturday, but this reinforces it. Pastor, for your own good and that of the church, you should resign. It can still be done gracefully without Merkle's name coming up. It's time you listened to reason. You need to step down as soon as possible."

Clayton spoke evenly, measuring his words, holding on to Ellie's *cool* and *I love you, Father.* "Jack, do you mean that if I do not resign, some gossip will accidently leak out to the public?"

"Clayton, this is not gossip, it is truth. For forty years you and your high school sweetheart have lived within minutes of each other. Remember, you're the one who preaches the importance of truth."

"You're implying something that's not there, Jack. Please trust me. A fragment of truth isn't the whole truth. And remember, truth must always be tempered with wisdom and compassion."

"I have compassion for a church that is about to disintegrate because of the actions of its pastor and his daughter, and wisdom tells me that I must act. This will be the last straw for most of the congregation. Even the denomination will have serious doubts."

Clayton pulled into his driveway. He didn't know how much longer he could hold his anger. "Your compassion is astounding, Jack. I'm grateful that you have the depth of character to warn me about this potential disaster. I couldn't ask for a truer friend."

"I had hoped we could have had a good, frank talk. I thought we might even stop by the church and pray together," said Brandt. "Pastor, I'm not vindictive, and I have no personal agenda; I just want to do what's best for Springdale Church and for the Lord. I appreciate your time. I wanted this talk to work out better than it has."

Instead of getting out of the car, Brandt sat silently, biting his lip and working his mouth as though he had one more thing to say.

Clayton waited until he could stand it no longer. "And . . . ?"

"I wanted to mention a trip Shirley and I are planning."

"A trip . . . ?"

"Yes, we're driving to Texas. Do you know anything about Galveston?" Brandt didn't wait for an answer, but nodded faintly and stepped out into the slushy snow.

Clayton said nothing, fearing he'd detonate. He stood by his car, hands on hips, and watched Brandt drive off, two blocks, three blocks, until the car finally turned left onto Sycamore. *This isn't church,* he thought. *It's politics, intrigue, espionage.*

If he didn't resign, word about something that happened four decades ago would leak out to tickle anxious ears nourished on a diet of sitcoms and soaps. He'd be in the headlines of the word-of-mouth religious tabloids. Jack was right; it would destroy the church. Some would switch memberships; others would simply drop out and have nothing more to do with Christianity. The pastor's involved with another woman! Been involved with her ever since high school! The hypocrite! What's more, his daughter's being questioned about a break-in and burglary!

He walked slowly into the house. Ellie was waiting. Now was the time to talk with her about Caroline Merkle. She probably already knew more than he imagined. She'd had the same opportunities as Brandt in Caroline's house. Maybe that's why she'd been going there so often.

What did Cary have there anyway? The yearbook . . . photographs . . . He remembered Ellie asking about his yearbook. He had destroyed Cary's letters, but she must have kept his. How else had Brandt found out about those weekends in Galveston?

God, forgive me. Help me not to hate him. Does my sin follow me into the third and fourth decade? Lord, I'm so tired of her. Forty years is enough. And God, I don't feel very good. Take this backache away. You know I have work to do. My Lord, my Savior, I love You.

EIGHTEEN

Monday evening, after dinner at the Santoris', Maria had accompanied Osvaldo to his room in the basement of Bethel Temple. For two days she'd hinted that they were leaving Springdale; now the time was here. She told him to gather up his things and carry them outside.

"Please, Osvaldo, no arguments. Just do it. We must go." Her own things and a stack of sandwiches were already in the trunk.

That morning she had withdrawn all her money from the bank and bought Mr. Pettigrew's Camry. The rest of the money, almost a thousand dollars, would get them to Texas or Florida. They would buy inexpensive food and take turns driving and sleeping. No one would know where they were until Osvaldo enrolled in school and needed his records from Springdale.

Now she had driven all night and was exhausted. They would head south, down I-55, until they got to I-10; then she'd decide whether to go east or west. All she knew was that she had to leave Springdale. They were almost to Memphis, heading away from the snow, away from Officer Brandt and her other boys. She wasn't tied to Springdale; she could go anyplace she wanted, except back to New Mexico. Brownsville or Miami, where they spoke a lot of Spanish, sounded good.

She didn't *want* to leave Springdale. For the first time in her life she had a good job and had saved a little money. Osvaldo was doing well in school and was happy. But Officer Brandt kept hounding her, driving slowly by the house, knocking on her door, asking questions, questions, questions. He was trying to get Osvaldo. Watch out when a policeman's got it in for you.

She looked at her son. He was getting tall, maybe five foot ten now, and had lost most of his baby fat. He was a good student—A's in art and Spanish. He was painting Mrs. Ritchie's mural, and he wanted to go to college.

But he looked so sad. Except for his brothers plaguing him and the last two weeks with Officer Brandt, he had been happy in Springdale. And there was Ellen. Was she being unfair to her son? Ellen was his girlfriend and had helped him with his schoolwork.

Osvaldo had tried to talk her out of leaving, and they had argued. But he was too young to see the whole picture. She knew the dangers of getting involved with the police. Once they're after you, you never find peace. They watch you the way a snake watches a mouse. You're always a suspect. The next time there was a burglary in Springdale, Officer Brandt would look for Osvaldo, and sooner or later he'd pick him up and pin something on him. It was best to leave, to start over someplace where there was no Officer Brandt, and no Ramon and Raphael. *O God, why didn't You change my boys?*

"Mama," Osvaldo said, "we shouldn't have left."

"Ossie, we had to go." He never argued with her. He was always obedient. "Please understand. I know about these things. This is best for both of us. Don't talk about it any-

230

more." She hoped he wouldn't mention Ellen again. She didn't like seeing him hurt.

"Just one more thing, Mama. Then I'll be quiet."

"Ossie, we've left. We're not turning around."

"There's something I don't understand, Mama. You, Mr. and Mrs. Santori, all of us, prayed to God. Did God tell you to leave Springdale?"

Maria didn't answer him, but drove straight on into the black Tennessee night. All she wanted to see were the white and yellow lines dashing past and the red glow of taillights. She didn't know whether God had told her anything or not. She just knew that Springdale wasn't safe anymore, and she and Osvaldo had to leave. She wished God would write messages in the sky or speak with a booming voice. He could send the angel Gabriel to tell her, "Take your son Osvaldo, leave Springdale, and journey to Florida. There a way will be opened to you, and you will find a job and Osvaldo will go to a good school." But God didn't speak like that, at least not to her. She didn't know how He spoke. She just did the best she could, and the best thing right now was to leave Springdale, and especially Officer Brandt.

"Maybe God would work things out differently," ventured Osvaldo.

"Please, Ossie, no more. I know it's hard, but we have to leave. God will take care of us wherever we are." She was tired of thinking about it.

"And one more thing, Mama."

"No more things, Osvaldo. You've already used up your one more thing. Forget about Springdale. We're going to live someplace else."

"I owe Mrs. Ritchie $800," he said.

"What?"

"Mama, the mural isn't finished. She trusted me to finish it. I promised."

"It's almost finished."

"Almost doesn't count. I feel dishonest."

Everything was so complicated. To keep Osvaldo from being arrested as a burglar in Springdale, she was leaving. Now, by leaving, she was making him feel like a thief. She would phone Mrs. Ritchie and explain why they had to leave Springdale. She'd apologize and send money back to her, maybe $100 each month. But she didn't even know Mrs. Ritchie. And such a call wouldn't make Osvaldo feel any better. He had more pride in Mrs. Ritchie's mural than anything he'd ever done, and now she was forcing him to leave it unfinished.

She pulled the car into a gas station. While Osvaldo pumped gas, she closed her eyes and rested her head in her hands. She needed time to think, to pray. Maybe she was making a mistake, not trusting God, trying to work things out on her own. She was leaving a good job and a warm place to live, and she was taking Osvaldo away from Ellen, his mural, Mr. Pettigrew, and good grades. Maybe God did have another way to work things out. She'd asked Him before to send His angels to help her, and He always did. Mr. Spike, Mr. Pettigrew— they were sort of angels, weren't they? Maybe she should go back to Springdale and wait for another one.

What does the Bible say? Something about *Your ways are not My ways, says the Lord.* She could see God shaking His finger at her, scolding her. *Maria, as the heavens are higher than the earth, so are My ways higher than your ways and My thoughts than your thoughts.*

They had traveled only three hundred miles. It wouldn't be hard to turn around, drive back to Springdale, and unpack their things. Not even Officer Brandt would know they'd left, only the Santoris and Ellen. As soon as they got to Springdale they'd call them.

God, it's all Yours now. I don't know whether to keep going or turn back. I want to hear Your voice like thunder, but there is no voice. Just questions. I'm going to go back now and see what happens. Do You have another angel to send me? I have no faith. I want You to show me.

"Mama!" It was Osvaldo. She hadn't heard him get into the car. "Are you all right?" He put his hand on her shoulder.

"I guess so, Ossie. I've decided to go back."

"Oh, Mama."

"I don't know what's right or wrong. We might as well stay where you're happy."

"Mama, I'm sorry."

Now she had made him feel guilty. Unlike the other boys, he never tried to manipulate her.

"It's okay, *mijo*. I'm scared. But I might as well be scared in Springdale with our friends than someplace where we know no one."

"I'm glad, but I don't want to hurt you."

"Ossie, you never hurt me. You are a wonderful son."

"Thank you, Mama." They sat in silence for several minutes. His hand on her shoulder felt good. Finally a car behind them honked—somebody wanting to use their pump and not understanding why they were just sitting there.

"Do you want me to drive, Mama? You look tired."

"Yes, that would be nice." She felt exhausted. "You'll be careful, won't you?"

They exchanged seats and drove back onto the freeway, heading north. Maria adjusted her seat so that it reclined a little and leaned back on her headrest. Her boy was driving, and he was going sixty-five, not ninety.

O God, thank You for Osvaldo. Is he one of the angels You sent me? Open my eyes so I can see them, Lord.

She woke four hours later when the hum of the engine changed and she felt the car slowing down. They pulled into a parking place under the blue glare from a sign that read Bonnie's Family Restaurant. The stark silhouette of a barren oak was appliquéd against the blue-vermilion glow of the early morning sky. A light dusting of snow covered the sidewalk and roof, and white ridges balanced on each branch and twig.

"Mama, it's time to wake up. Let's go in. I have to use the

bathroom. We'll have pancakes, and you can get a good cup of coffee."

"You deserve a good breakfast, Ossie. We'll be home before noon, won't we? I'll phone Megatronics. I wonder if Officer Brandt is waiting by our door."

WHEN FATHER LEFT for his meeting with Brandt, Ellen went outside and destroyed her snowman. It wouldn't have lasted much longer anyway. She thought she was so clever— making the holster, using the maple leaf for a star, using red food coloring for his cheeks, giving it two faces—but she shouldn't have done it. It could only antagonize the man who seemed to be plaguing Father and who now was hounding Maria and Osvaldo. She herself wasn't bothered by him; she just didn't like him. As she turned to go inside, she noticed an envelope wedged under the lid of the mailbox. *To Ellen* was written on it in Osvaldo's peculiar scrawl. He'd never left her a note before. On half a sheet of binder paper she read:

> *Dear Ellen,*
>
> *Mama says that we must leave Springdale and go someplace where we are safer. In New Mexico she had bad experiences with policemen, and now she is afraid of Officer Brandt. Almost every day he comes by her house to ask questions. She bought Mr. Pettigrew's car. I made her feel bad when we argued.*
>
> *We don't know where we are going. Mama says either Texas or Florida, but I will write to you as soon as I can. You mean so much to me. Pray to God for us.*
>
> *Love,*
> *Osvaldo*

On the bottom of the note he had sketched a butterfly.

A few minutes after she read the letter, Father returned from his meeting with Brandt and found her crying at the dining room table. She let him read Osvaldo's note, and then he sat with her a long time while she cried silently, her head resting on her hands. She thought he might tell her that everything was going to work out for the best because "all things work together for good to those who love the Lord." She knew all that, but she didn't want to hear it. Those words might be a comfort in some future tense, but for the present, right now, she felt terrible, and it was better to feel Father's touch than to hear his words. She glanced up at him once and found his eyes closed and moist. Maybe he was crying too. Lately things hadn't been going too well for him either.

Ellen was pleased when, late in the morning, Father asked her to go fishing. She could tell by a tightness in his face that he wasn't feeling well. He wondered if he might be coming down with the flu, but he might just be suffering the after-effects of his meeting with Brandt. In her distress about Osvaldo leaving, she'd forgotten to ask. Their meeting had been so short that it couldn't have gone very well. But now they were going to Braxton, and that was good. They always came home from their fishing trips feeling better.

While Father's coffee brewed, she prepared special sandwiches, something solemn to fit the occasion. Sourdough bread was perfect. Dijon mustard. No mayonnaise or catsup. Large rounds of dill pickles, scattered with a scant dressing of feta cheese paste in vinegar and a smattering of parsley flakes, sage, rosemary, and thyme. Finally, thick slabs of turkey breast covered everything else. She wrapped them in Saran wrap and printed a label: *Jerusalem Sandwiches, circa A.D. 70. Compliments of General Titus.*

Today she knew they'd talk, really talk. Maybe they'd start talking about Osvaldo and Maria or his short-lived meeting with Brandt, but sooner or later Miss Merkle would be mentioned. Father looked pretty bad, almost sick. His time with Brandt must have been terrible. She chided herself again for building the snowman. Now Father was pacing resolutely around the house, his mouth set in its tight anger line, or maybe it was his pain line. She wasn't sure, but something was wrong. She wasn't used to seeing him with sad eyes. She liked them better when they flashed with excitement, or when he was about to face down a charging rhino.

They rode to Braxton in silence, past the church and the school, past the police station, past Piney's Diner, past the low earthen dam and onto the dirt road leading to the backside of the reservoir. She could see the lonely shed at the end of the road. The half-frozen puddles crunched beneath their tires, and yellow-brown leaves swirled by in a mild breeze.

While Father hauled the boat to the water, she gathered perfect rocks from the beach. It was important that they have some striation and color, but they couldn't be too round or smooth. They needed notches so strings could grip them and they wouldn't be lost. Fishing rocks were precious, not to be wasted.

Father rowed to their cove, but stayed near the shore. A northwest wind and somber sky promised more snow before the day was over. Brown and yellow leaves, pushed by the rippling water, carpeted the near shoreline; a few stubborn leaves clung to their branches, performing a twirling death dance in the cold breeze. While birds darted overhead, chirping their warnings before retreating to their nests, the early afternoon sun struggled to sear its way through the ashen clouds. She pulled her heavy, down-lined jacket up around her neck to meet her stocking cap. Clumsily, with gloved fingers, they helped each other tie rocks onto their lines. Then they lowered them into the water, hunched over with their backs to the wind, and waited.

AS HE SAT in the tiny boat with Ellen, Clayton felt nausea crawling from his stomach through his chest to his throat. The ache in his back was increasing, and his stomach roiled. Most of the time those things went away by themselves, but this didn't feel like the beginning of the flu. Now his teeth chattered, he couldn't stop shivering, and bile flavored every swallow. The restless water rocked their little boat. It was foolish to be out on the lake. The warmth of his bed would feel good. He inched closer to Ellie, leaning his shoulder into hers, to gain a little more protection from the chill.

He had to talk to her today. He should have done it a week ago. He wished he knew what she'd seen in Cary's house. Did Ellie know as much as Brandt? Did Cary have his old love notes lying around the house for everyone to see? Of course, it was her house, she could have anything there she wanted. She couldn't have anticipated intruders and policemen. But forty-year-old love notes?

He kept his eyes either closed or fixed on the floor of the boat. If he looked up, the shore wavered and spun. He didn't need to look at Ellie. He was satisfied to feel her next to him, to absorb her warmth and know she cared about him. He knew she was waiting, waiting to hear about Caroline Merkle. It was necessary, inescapable.

He'd never talked to any of his kids about Cary. There had been no need to. He and Joyce had left it behind so long ago. Now it was Ellie—frustrating, stubborn, distant Ellie—whom he was going to tell. He forced the words out of his gut.

"Some things you need to know, Ellie."

She leaned her head toward his as though to say, "It's okay, Father. I think I'll understand. And I love you."

Clayton talked for a long time. He could not remember a time in his life when he did not know Caroline Merkle. Their parents were best friends; he and Cary attended church together and went to the same schools from kindergarten on. When their families got together, they always paired off, leaving the other kids to play. In the sixth grade, they had their first date, if you wanted to call it that, to their grammar school graduation luncheon.

Everyone took for granted they were meant for each other. Clay and Cary—it was natural, a match made in heaven. They were active, intelligent, talented—he could say that to Ellie because she knew he wasn't bragging—and in high school they were inseparable. They had other friends, of course, but most of their free time they spent together. He was on the basketball and baseball teams, and Cary was always there as cheerleader. They were in the same advanced classes, always competing for the top grades.

"Do you know that old Chevy she drives?" he asked. "That was mine all through high school. Cary and I went everywhere in it. Somehow, after I married Mom, she got hold of it."

Cary was beautiful, one of the most attractive girls he'd ever known. They were the envy of their friends. While others struggled with relationships, continually dating and breaking up, they were steadies. They were meant to be Mr. and Mrs. Clayton Loverage, as sure as the passage of time. Their friends talked about it. Their teachers predicted it. Their parents took it for granted. They would go on to do great things together.

They were engaged before he knew what had happened. He'd never actually asked her to marry him, although they tacitly understood they would marry someday. While Christmas shopping during their senior year, they had wandered into a jewelry store. Soon they were looking at engagement rings and Cary was trying some on. They each had saved a little money, and they decided to share the cost of a modest, inexpensive ring. They could purchase the wedding ring during the summer, Cary said, just before they got married.

During that winter and early spring they made some "indiscreet" decisions, he said, did some things they shouldn't have. That was the closest he could come to telling Ellie about those weekends in Galveston. He was sure she understood what he was really saying.

As he talked, he shivered, and occasionally his teeth clacked loudly enough he was sure Ellie noticed. She probably thought he was nervous. This wasn't like him, the Clayton Loverage who could mesmerize thousands with a sermon or a talk on marriage. He felt like a little boy confessing some wrongdoing to his mother. His nausea was getting worse. He shouldn't be in a rocking boat in a biting wind. He needed to go back to the car. But now that he had started, he had to go on.

"One Saturday in the spring of my senior year, I went fishing with Uncle Claude on Caddo Lake. I liked being with him because we could talk, really talk. He'd been a missionary in South America before Aunt Emma got sick and they moved back to Texas. We were eating catfish sandwiches in a dingy restaurant in Uncertain."

"Uncertain?"

"A little town on the lake. Uncle Claude told me about watching natives in Venezuela catch river ducks. First they floated large, hollowed-out gourds down the river until the ducks got used to them. Then they cut eyeholes, put the gourds over their heads, and walked on the river bottom until the ducks accepted them as normal. Over a period of weeks they edged closer to the ducks, sometimes within a few feet of them, without trying to catch them. Then one day they lowered their heads from the gourds, reached up and grasped the leg of a duck, yanked it under, and wrenched its neck. Some ducks flew away, others hardly knew what had happened.

"I couldn't forget that story, Ellie. I don't know if Uncle Claude told it on purpose to wake me up, or if he was just telling an interesting story, but I saw myself as one of the ducks, paddling along, oblivious to a danger that lurked within a few feet.

"When I went back to Houston, I saw Cary differently. She was beautiful, fun, intelligent, a good person, everything I should be looking for in a girlfriend and eventually a wife. But as we came closer to graduation and marriage, I became less sure that I wanted to spend the rest of my life with her.

"I tried talking to our pastor and made a feeble attempt at confiding in Dad, but they were both sold on the idea of our being the perfect couple. It was normal to have doubts before marriage, they said. I'd get over it. Our moms were ecstatic about a big church wedding. All I could think about were those poor ducks being yanked down under the water with hardly more than a feeble squawk.

"I tried talking with Cary about how I felt, but she was worse than Dad and Pastor Cline. I told her I wanted to wait a year or two before we got married, but she acted as though she didn't hear me. Just before graduation, I told Cary we had to wait to get married, at least until after our freshman year of college. I didn't break off the engagement, just postponed the wedding. We'd planned to attend Rice together. It was the only school she applied to, and she'd won a full scholarship. I was accepted at Rice and three others. I deliberately chose North Texas State to get away from her."

"And you met Mom the first year at a Christmas party?" asked Ellen.

"Yes. We were married in June of our sophomore year. She was from around Denton." His jaw was quivering, and now his words tasted strongly of bile. He felt as though he might throw up at any time. It was stupid to be at the reservoir. "Ellie, I'm sorry. I've got to go back. I'm so sick."

As he rowed back, he couldn't focus on Ellie or the shore-line, and in the biting breeze the sweat on his face felt like ice. His arms weakened quickly, and his stomach churned. A few feet from shore he stopped, leaned over the water, and vomit-ed, a hard, gagging heave that brought up nothing but coffee and bile. As he spit into the water and wiped his mouth with his handkerchief, Ellie took an oar and poled the boat onto the rocky sand.

Her arm lay around his shoulder as several more waves of nausea and retching hit him. She was saying things that only his mother and Joyce had said to him, comforting, encourag-ing words that reminded him of his childhood; only the name was different.

"It's okay, Father. . . . You'll be all right. . . . Just get it out of your system. You'll feel better. . . . Your coat doesn't matter, Father. We'll wash it when we get home."

They sat in the boat several minutes before he was ready to stand up. "If I can just make it to the car, I'll be okay. The heater warms up the car quickly. The cell phone's there; I might need it." He wished she knew how to drive. All he wanted to do was lean the seat back and go to sleep.

"I'll get you to the car and put the boat into the shed. It won't take long," she said.

He should handle the boat, it was too heavy for her, but his legs and arms felt like posts. He felt lightheaded and thought he was going to start retching again. He might even faint. They would leave the old boat in the water and buy a new one in the spring. He just needed to sit and get warm.

"Father," she said as they climbed the slight rise to the shed. Her comforting voice had changed; she wasn't his mother or Joyce any longer. "Father, the car's gone. We left it by the shed, didn't we?"

He looked up. There was only one place to park, and the car wasn't there, only the weather-beaten shed standing forlorn next to a bare willow. On the one-lane road that ran out to the highway he could see a double ribbon of dirty tire tracks. There was no place to hide the car. No one was playing games with him. His car was stolen, leaving them isolated out at Braxton with a storm moving in. And he was sick. The pain in his back and stomach was so sharp he couldn't hold still. He didn't want to walk, or lie down, or stand. He needed to vomit again, but couldn't. He doubled over, sank to his knees. With each breath he groaned. He felt Ellie kneeling next to him, her arm around his waist. She helped him up and walked him slowly into the shed.

He sat in an old director's chair, and Ellie wrapped a stiff decaying tarpaulin around him, tucked it in under his arms, and wound it around his ankles.

"I'm going to the highway to get help. Here, keep my watch. It's almost two o'clock; I'll be back as soon as I can."

She understood that he couldn't walk out, and it didn't make sense for them both to wait in the shed for him to get better. He insisted she wear his fur-lined hunting cap. She didn't argue; she could hear the wind whistling through the cracks in the shed. "I love you, Father," she said as she left.

He heard her latch the door, and then a pain stabbed him so fiercely that he doubled over and rolled onto the floor. Each groan was mixed with a prayer that shouted wordlessly for relief and help and protection for Ellie. *God, let me faint. I didn't think pain could be so bad.*

NINETEEN

The return of the Villanueva brothers to Springdale both astonished and pleased Jack Brandt. Within a few days he'd nab them; it was only a matter of time. They thought they had the world by the tail, but they were punks, petty thieves, stealing trinkets and dumping them in minor, out-of-town markets. To return to their mother's place was folly.

His break had come a few hours earlier when a big rig rolled into town, right down First Street past signs warning trucks over ten tons to keep out of the center of Springdale. Within four blocks of the city limits he had it pulled over.

A short, scrawny man dressed like a Hell's Angel climbed out. "You're just who I'm lookin' for," the man said, a cigarette drooping from the corner of his mouth.

"Well, you're just who I'm looking for, too," said Brandt. "No trucks over ten tons are allowed on First Street. You passed three warning signs."

"Yeah, I saw them. You'll hafta write me a ticket. But before you do, let me tell you something."

"I'm listening."

"Late last night I picked up two guys on the far side of St. Louis. Let them off at the Springdale interchange about five this morning." He nodded his head toward the freeway. Then he proceeded to tell Brandt about a Latino woman and her son he'd picked up the previous winter in Texas and let off at the same interchange.

"The boy's name was Osvaldo," he said, "and the two guys I let off this morning talked about roughing up an Osvaldo. I kinda remember the boy's mother mentionin' two sons who were giving her trouble."

"What's your connection to these people?" asked Brandt.

"I told you. Their car broke down near Amarillo, and the two brothers stole a car and left their mother and brother to hitchhike. No money. No warm clothes. When I picked them up, they were freezing. That's all I know, 'cept that I liked them."

"You dropped the two men at the interchange at five. It's nine now."

"I drove to Decatur, but I kept imagining those two guys roughin' up Osvaldo. I liked the kid."

"You could have phoned, or told the police in Decatur."

"Yeah, but you're listenin' to me real hard. It's better this way."

Jack Brandt checked and recorded the man's driver's license. Oklahoma. Milton Beebe, age 43, height 5'6", weight 127 lbs. Brandt looked over at the little man. Unshaven. Dirty leather vest. Tattoos. Bandanna. Ponytail. Cigarette dangling from his lips.

"Thank you for the information, Mr. Beebe, but I'm afraid I'll have to give you a citation."

"It'll be worth it. I think you know who I'm talkin' about?"

"I'll check around. Maybe I can find something."

"When you see Osvaldo, tell him Mr. Spike says hello. Don't need to say nothin' else."

Brandt looked over the trucker again. "Tell you what, Mr.

Spike." He pointed down First Street. "You pull into the parking lot at Giant Foods up there on the left, and get this thing turned around and out of here. If you disappear in two minutes, there'll be no citation."

"Thank you, sir!" Spike clicked his heels, gave a half salute, and climbed into his cab.

Brandt watched the truck until it was nearly to the freeway, then called for a backup and headed for the small house on Depot Street.

MARIA AND OSVALDO arrived back in Springdale around noon. She had phoned Megatronics from Bonnie's Family Restaurant just before the day shift began and said she couldn't make it in. It was the first day she'd missed since she started work, and Mrs. Garber, the receptionist, said she hoped Maria was feeling better soon.

At home, Osvaldo set her cardboard boxes inside the door and left for school in the car.

She offered to write a note for him, but he said no, he'd tell the school secretary that there was a problem at home and his mother had needed him.

Well, that was the truth, Maria thought. He did not need to tell her that they had driven almost to Memphis on their way to another life.

Maria was thankful for a son who wanted to go to school. That alone should be enough to keep them in Springdale. All her other boys wanted to do was cut classes and cause trouble. She wondered if it was the classes or Ellen that made Osvaldo like school. She hoped it was both.

After Osvaldo left, Maria didn't go into the house, but walked to the pay phone at the depot to call Olga Santori. Her friend hadn't wanted them to leave. She wouldn't say I-told-you-so, but Maria knew she'd be delighted to hear her news. Within minutes the two women were in Olga's car, heading for JubiLatte.

245

"How far did you go?" asked Olga.

"Almost to Memphis."

"What made you turn around? Yesterday you seemed so sure."

"Ossie and I talked . . . I don't know how to tell God's will, Olga. One minute I think He's smiling at me, the next minute He's frowning."

"By the time you got close to Memphis, He was frowning?"

"I guess so. I don't know anymore. I just want to do what's best for Ossie."

"Maria, it's easy to mistake our ideas and feelings for God's leading. It happens to me all the time. I must be so careful."

"So how does God talk to us?"

Olga nibbled on her biscotti and thought. "The Bible." She stirred her coffee without drinking. "And Christian friends we can trust." She dipped the biscotti in her coffee but didn't take a bite. "Then sometimes, Maria, there's a voice from deep within us that guides us. But we have to be very, very careful . . . and pray a lot."

"You think I shouldn't have left last night?"

"I don't know, Maria. I'm not the voice inside you. But I'm glad you're back. I didn't want you to disappear from my life."

When Maria returned to her house, however, she found that everything was not all right. The kitchen and living room were a mess. Candy wrappers, empty cracker boxes, half-eaten red licorice sticks, and beer cans littered the floor. In her bedroom, the bed was a mess, the toilet was clogged up, and the hot water was left running. In the refrigerator she found a half-eaten fast-food hamburger and a can of Dos Equis, Raphael's favorite.

O God, I don't understand anything.

She felt like a kitten that God teased with a string, back and forth, back and forth. She should have kept going instead of coming back to Springdale. By now they'd be safe, almost to Florida. But now she was home, and any second the boys would walk in and take the thousand dollars in her purse. She should have gone to the bank instead of coming straight home. At least Osvaldo had the car.

She wasn't going to stay there and wait for them to come. She'd walk to Olga's. Maybe she could stay with Osvaldo in the church. Maybe they'd go to Florida after all.

O Lord, do You have another angel for me? Help me. I don't know what to do.

As she left the house, two police cars pulled into her driveway.

"Mrs. Villanueva, I want to talk with you a minute." It was Officer Brandt.

She didn't want to speak to him . . . or even look at him. "I'm leaving now." She didn't look back, but kept walking.

"Wait. I have a few questions."

She stopped but didn't turn to face him.

"Have you seen Ramon and Raphael?" he asked.

She shook her head.

"Do you know where they are?"

"No. Go away. I can't talk to you."

"Have they been in your house?"

"Yes. I have to go." She started walking again.

"You can't leave yet. I'll need you when we search the house. Are they there now?"

"No."

"May we go in and look, or shall I get a warrant?"

"Go look. They aren't there. I'm leaving."

"Come in with us. That will make things simpler."

She hesitated. She didn't want to stay there any longer. But if the officers were there, the boys wouldn't come home. "Only a minute. I'm in a hurry."

Cautiously the officers searched the house, noting only the trash. Brandt said he might take fingerprints later.

"What's in these boxes, Mrs. Villanueva?" asked Brandt.

"My clothes and a few kitchen things."

247

"Are you going away?"

"Yes."

"Where?"

"Right now I'm going to Olga Santori's house."

"Bethel Temple?"

"Yes."

"I'll give you a ride," the other officer said. "Your boxes too?"

"Yes, but I have to go to the bank first."

"We can do that on the way."

She thanked God for providing a police escort for her money. "Just to the bank and Olga's house. Not the police station." She needed assurance.

"You have my word," said the officer.

"I have to let Osvaldo know where I am. He's at school."

"Write a note, and I'll make sure he gets it," said Brandt.

Officer Brandt and the other man loaded her two boxes into the squad car, and she locked the house. Brandt said he'd have to keep an eye on it for a few days. The backseat of the squad car reminded her of arrests in Albuquerque, Socorro, and Las Cruces, and she shivered. The fingerprinting, the questioning, sometimes the dirty comments and rough treatment.

She didn't know his name, but the officer driving smiled and was friendly. *Is he another one of Your angels, God? You answer my prayers so strangely that I'm afraid to pray.* She wondered if accepting whatever happened was what prayer and faith were about. God would have to teach her, because she was just a kitten.

The officer dropped her off at the Santoris', and she thanked him sincerely. Officer Brandt had her note to Osvaldo. She knew he'd look at it. It didn't matter; she had nothing to hide.

ELLEN FIGURED IT WOULD take about fifteen minutes to hike the half mile out the access road to Highway 22. She tried running, but the half-frozen puddles in the tire tracks made it impossible. The area between the tracks was strewn with rocks, and she almost turned her ankle. On either side of the road half-dead, foot-high grass rose from uneven mud clods. To her right wavelets broke onto the shore, pushed by an ever-increasing wind. On her left a forest of oaks and hickories offered meager protection from the wind and no promise of a quick route to the highway. She decided the rocky middle was safest and headed out.

She didn't know whether Father's condition was serious. Maybe all he had were gas pains that would vanish in ten minutes, but he might have food poisoning or something worse. What if his appendix burst? He'd need antibiotics and surgery as soon as possible. In any case she'd never seen him suffering so much. She fought an engulfing panic, her heart pounded, and she started running and shouting for help. Then she reminded herself to stay calm. No one could hear her, and she might trip and hurt herself.

Just walk fast. Stay in control. Think! Get to Highway 22. Flag down a vehicle. Hope they have a cell phone. If not, ask the driver to take her to the nearest telephone, probably the one at Piney's. She didn't know what she'd do if the driver looked like a scrounge. Should she dare to get in with him, or should she wait for the next vehicle? She couldn't plan it out right now; she'd wait until the time came. When she got to a phone, she'd call 911. After that she'd get back to Father any way she could. This was the first time in her life she'd faced a big emergency, one where she had to make decisions that counted. She had to use her head. *God, don't let me mess up.*

As she thought, she prayed. Prayers made her plan, and plans made her pray . . . for Father, waiting in the cold shed . . . for the storm to let up . . . that she wouldn't turn her ankle on the way to the road . . . for the right person to stop on the highway . . . for the doctors to do the right thing . . . that she could get back to Father soon. Like a cake made from scratch, her prayer was a concoction of hopes, wishes, plans, and panic.

About halfway to the highway, she saw a car turn onto the road and head toward her. As it came closer, she saw that it was Father's car—at least it was white and the right shape. She stepped into the woods. Why would a person steal a car and then return it? Maybe they'd just borrowed it, but they would have had to break in to do that.

As the car neared, it slowed down, and Ellen stepped back further into the forest. She'd seen two men inside, so they'd probably seen her as well. She wished her sleeves didn't have fluorescent orange stripes. When the car stopped and the passenger-side window rolled down, she saw a leering Raphael. The brothers had dared to come back to Springdale! She backed up slowly to get behind a tree as Ramon opened the driver's door and stood on the doorframe to peer over the top of the car.

"Hey, Osvaldo's girlfriend!" he shouted.

She said nothing, but stayed as still as the trees.

"I see you. Come talk to us."

She heard another car door open, and took another step back.

"Our mama's hurt. She's in the hospital. She wants to see you," yelled Ramon.

She remembered what Maria had told Osvaldo: Never be alone with them. You can't trust them. Neither one has a conscience.

"We'll give you a ride. Osvaldo sent us after you."

Osvaldo didn't even know where she was. She backed up some more, till she could barely see them.

"Hey, Osvaldo's girlfriend. Don't make us come after you. Mama's asking for you. She's dying."

No way. He's a liar. *God, make them go away.*

Like a shot Raphael jumped from the car and crashed toward the woods. Ellen didn't wait to see if Ramon was coming with him.

She ran zigzagging around the trees. The forest was thick with saplings; there was no straight line to run in for more

250

than two or three steps. Sometimes she had to squeeze between saplings and clamber over fallen trunks. She didn't dare
take time to see how close they were, but she could hear them
well enough.

The forest floor was soft, covered with newly fallen leaves
made slippery by the wet snow, and it felt as though she were
running on ice. Although her boots protected her ankles
against the logs and boulders, they felt like lead weights.
Where should she run? She had to get to the main road. There
was no future running into an endless forest. But it was easy to
get confused and lost. She tried to veer to her right when there
were openings among the trees. That would keep her close to
the access road. Maybe she'd come out on the highway.

She tripped and fell, landing flat on her stomach. As she
lay in a bed of icy leaves, she could hear them coming. In the
breeze that soughed through the nearly bare branches, each
step they took sounded like a drumbeat, each word had the re-
tort of a rifle.

"Over here, Raphael. On the ground. This way. You go to
the right."

She leapt up and ran, away from the voices, a doe fleeing
baying hounds.

She ran without thinking, always away from the voices,
toward any open space she saw. She resented the slippery carpet of leaves and the branches that snatched at her jacket.
Each large log was a barricade deliberately placed in her way.
And always there was the sound of running feet behind her.
Each time her jacket was snagged, she knew they had caught
her and would drag her down. Her legs were tiring and her
side ached. She took deep, hungry gulps of air, feeling it fill her
lungs. Her heart hammered so that it throbbed in her temples.

*God, they're going to catch me. You've got to help. Make
them blind. Cripple them. Make the road come. Why don't
You ever answer my prayers?*

*They'll drag me back to the car. No, they'll rape me right
here in the forest. Then tie me up, beat me, kill me . . . they're*

251

going to do something!! God, I can't get in much deeper than this. Father's sick, and I'm being chased by rapists. God, did You forget about me? You don't hear me! You don't care!

She stopped behind a large tree, waiting, listening. They were further behind than she thought, but in the stillness their voices carried.

"Raphael, let's go back. My shin's bleeding."

"No."

"Raphael, this is stupid. She's not worth catching. She doesn't have any money. We gotta get out of here."

"You go."

"Someone's going to see the car—"

"You go. I'll get her."

"I might not be there when you—"

"Go! I don't care."

She heard the footsteps start again.

Ellen waited, not daring to breathe, feeling betrayed by the vapor that drifted from her nose and mouth. Ramon was leaving. Only Raphael pursued her. He'd follow her trail in the snow. She reached into her pocket and took out Father's fishing knife. She'd use it if she had to. She gripped it in her fist and imagined plunging it into Raphael's face or chest.

The footsteps slackened. He was approaching her tree. She could run, but she wouldn't last very long. Her thighs ached, and her shins were starting to cramp. Behind the tree she held her breath and waited. Maybe he wouldn't see her. He'd go away. How much louder can footsteps get?

"You, Osvaldo's girlfriend, I see your jacket."

She stepped from behind the tree and glared at him, the knife clenched in her fist. "Leave me alone. Go back to your brother." The words didn't make sense; they were just something to say.

Arms out from his sides, he crouched, ready to spring. He was shorter than she thought, no bigger than she and probably not as heavy. But that look in his eyes . . . He breathed deep and steady, licking his lips. He had a small pocketknife too, but folded it and shoved it back into his pocket.

"Put the knife down. I won't hurt you." His words were even, firm, controlling.

Ellen said nothing, but stood ready.

He picked up a branch the size of a baseball bat and started toward her, swinging it with each step. She backed up. The branch would hit her before she could use her knife.

"Keep backing up and you'll fall down," he said.

Raphael kept coming, swinging the branch rhythmically back and forth. As she backed into a log, she instinctively put out her left arm to ward off the branch as he closed in. It caromed off her elbow and hit her side. Then he swung again, hitting her right arm. She felt her hand open and the knife fly out onto the ground. When he lunged for it, without thinking she attacked. She'd use her fingernails and teeth if she had to. He might win, but he'd know he'd met a wolverine.

As they fell to the ground, Ellen aimed for his eyes and felt her fingernails sinking into his face. His eyes! Jab your fingernails into his eyes! As his stronger arms grabbed hers and pulled them away from his face, she raised her head and blindly bit something, she didn't know what. His leather coat? No, it was warm. Then she tasted blood, and he jumped to his feet swearing at her. As she lay on the ground, he had the stick again and came at her. Blood dripped from his left wrist, anger and hatred oozed from his face. He was swinging the branch overhead as he would an axe, as though splitting a log. Between swings she kicked him as violently as she could in the groin, then she leapt up and started running wildly. If he caught her again, there was no escape.

TWENTY

Jack Brandt drove to Springdale High School with Maria's note. On a loose scrap of paper, not even folded for privacy, she had scrawled in block letters: *Dear Ossie, Ramon and Raphael came back. Maybe that's why God made us be away last night. Don't let them see our car. I'm at Olga's. Love, love, Mama.* He folded it neatly, sealed it with Scotch tape, wrote Osvaldo's name on it, and delivered it to the school secretary.

What had made the Villanueva brothers come back to Springdale instead of taking off for Miami or L.A. or Timbuktu? Didn't they realize they were wanted for questioning in the Merkle burglary? Every police officer and highway patrolman within a hundred miles had their descriptions. Were they so tied to their mother that they couldn't stay away? Maybe she was a money source for them, or perhaps she played a role in their operations. From the tone of her note to Osvaldo, however, that was unlikely. She was afraid of Ramon and Raphael, and she mentioned God. But she was also aware that he might read her note. Perhaps she was a chameleon-lady who assumed any role necessary to avoid the law. He couldn't trust her.

He was now confident of the facts in the Merkle burglary. Ramon and Raphael were responsible, but Osvaldo was covered by flawless alibis. Ellen was innocent of any part in the burglary, but was guilty of trespassing. In addition, Caroline Merkle strongly suspected that Ellen had taken the white binder, and was threatening to file charges if it were not returned.

What distinguished this case from any other petty burglary was how it impacted the situation at his church. Usually he could compartmentalize his home life, his role at church, and his job, but this incident overshadowed all three, and there was no time, no place, when it wasn't on his mind. Each night he went to sleep easily, but after a few hours visions of the binder, the Villanuevas, Ellen, and Pastor Loverage awakened him. Once he'd dreamed of lying facedown on the binder, shielding it from deacons at the church who were trying to pry him off, tugging his legs and yanking his hair. One night he spent over an hour in his easy chair, eating Triscuits, sipping grape juice, and reading the Bible, before he tired enough to return to bed. Despite the dreams, his resolve about Loverage's resignation never weakened. He firmly believed this incident, coming at this exact time, was a godsend to apply pressure on the pastor. He liked to think of it as holy pressure, but in the past few days doubts had seeped in.

The thing that gnawed at him most was Caroline Merkle's binder. Until the previous night, it had lain in a canvas bag in his locker at Goldie's Exercise Gym. He hadn't worked out since he put it there, for fear that someone would ask him what was in the bag. They might even grab it and run, or cut his lock and break into his locker. He couldn't control his imagination, and almost every day he dropped by the gym to check on it.

He shouldn't have taken it. In his profession, he prided himself on honesty, always carrying out his job according to the rules. It was unthinkable to have taken the binder, or anything else, during an investigation. Yet he had done it, and now he couldn't scrub it from his mind. He was trapped between being convinced that God had led him to the binder and the gnawing feeling that he'd stolen it.

Only he and Shirley knew about the relationship between Loverage and Caroline Merkle, and they had no intention of publicizing it. They weren't out to smear the pastor, but to get new leadership for the church. By mentioning Merkle to Loverage, he had hoped to arouse the pastor out of his lethargy and spur him to action. Every day he prayed that would happen. Now he waited for Loverage to get back to him.

Shirley, of course, was worried about his edginess. At home he couldn't sit still to work or read or prepare for the class he taught Sunday mornings, but paced and snacked and ran unnecessary errands. The previous evening, as they were getting ready for bed, she had finally confronted him.

"You're worried, Jack."

"Pretty obvious, isn't it?"

"Tell me about it." They sat on the edge of the bed, and she put her arm around his waist and leaned her head on his shoulder.

"The binder. I shouldn't have taken it. I've never done anything like that."

"Were you supposed to ignore it? pretend it wasn't there?"

"No. It was there for me to read . . . but I shouldn't have taken it."

"Why don't you send it back to her?"

"Fingerprints. Yours and mine. They're all over it."

"We'll wipe them off," she said.

"Hard to get them all."

"We'll do it together."

"We'll miss a spot."

"Carefully. Twice. Three times."

"I'd feel safer burning it."

"You might feel safer, but destroying it will haunt you forever. You should send it back. I'll help."

For the next couple hours they sat at the dining room table with hymns and praise songs playing on their stereo. They wore gloves as they removed each binder insert and went over both sides with lightly oiled and moist cloths. Next they went over the binder itself. Shirley felt there was no chance that fingerprints remained; Jack wasn't so sure.

After they'd gone over the binder a third time, Shirley spoke. "There, that should do it. Would you like me to mail it to Caroline Merkle? I'm driving into St. Louis tomorrow. I'll mail it from there."

"Thank you, honey, but this is something I have to do. You're a wonderful woman. I appreciate you more than I can ever say."

That night he dreamed of the binder dancing in front of him, as though it were an animated book on a TV commercial. As it danced and sang praise songs, he saw glowing fragments of fingerprints they had missed.

The next morning, after Shirley left for St. Louis, he was supposed to drive to Decatur to mail the binder. It was wrapped, addressed, weighed, and stamped, and all he had to do was drop it into a mailbox. He'd wear gloves, of course. But someone might see him. The package was the size and shape of . . . well, of a binder. It might as well have *Caroline Merkle's Binder* written all over it. Someone was going to see him with it. He began pacing the floor again.

Once during the morning he thought about taking the package to their cabin near Otter Lake. It would be easy to slip it into the large woodstove, to let it burn to nothingness, to watch it oxidize out of existence. No one need know, not even Shirley. But he didn't have half a day to spend away from Springdale. Besides, it felt so terribly wrong. Yet he had to do something; he needed to get it off his hands so he could sleep at night.

After lunch Jack wound eight layers of Saran wrap around the binder package and put it in a series of four plastic garbage bags, each sealed as a barrier against moisture and insects. He wouldn't destroy it *or* return it, but hide it in a place so improbable that it would never be found. Perhaps it would be needed someday. Years from now he might return it to Caroline Merkle.

He preferred taking the binder far away, but there was no free time on his schedule in the next three weeks. Kingswood Country Club was on the northwest side of Springdale, and behind it sprawled several square miles of virgin forest, once part of the old Schroeder estate, now designated as a future state park. For the next few years it would be off-limits to the public.

Jack parked on the far side of the country club, on the northwestern edge of the forest. Carrying the heavily wrapped binder and his G.I. shovel, he hiked in for about ten minutes. Near a triple-trunked hickory he dug a two-foot-deep hole and laid the binder in it. After refilling the hole and replacing the dense covering of humus, newly fallen leaves, and small branches, he viewed it from several angles. Not the slightest trace of human activity. No one had seen him. The binder was hidden, probably forever. Maybe a hundred years from now it would be unearthed by a bulldozer or a backhoe, but then it wouldn't matter. The binder was more secure there than if he'd placed it in a safe deposit box, and would remain hidden well past Armageddon.

On his way back to Springdale Brandt stopped at Piney's for a cup of coffee. He needed a quiet place to relax, think, and maybe pray a little. He took his Bible with him to go over the lesson he was teaching the next Sunday.

Gloria Pine, the owner's wife, was waiting tables. "Hello, Jack. Just coffee?"

"Make it decaf. I need to get some sleep tonight."

"Good storm's movin' in."

"Not too cold, but we might get two to three inches of snow."

"Headin' out to the reservoir?" she asked.

"Wasn't planning on it. Just wanted a quiet place to read."

"Al says there's a car out there."

"A car?"

"Yeah, a white one about halfway out the access road. Why would anyone stop there?"

"I'll go check. Make that decaf to go." He was off duty, but something told him he needed to investigate.

CLAYTON HAD WAITED in the old shed a thousand years. The pain spread from his groin up the middle of his back, and he couldn't lie still. He clutched his knees to his chest only to straighten out again, arch his back, and roll from side to side with deep, rhythmic groans. Something terrible was wrong. He writhed, trying to wring the torment from his body. A rack couldn't have been worse, or hot knives jabbing, twisting, and tearing his abdomen, searing his groin, stomach, and back. Appendicitis! That was it! *O God, don't let it burst.* No, it must be cancer! Lurking there for years, waiting to break out and ravage him. *O Lord, I can't stay still. Make it go away. Let me pass out.*

He couldn't control his lower jaw, and his teeth chattered like castanets. He tugged the stiff, rotting tarp around him, but it felt like a sheet of plastic ice. His shoulders quivered, and his hands and feet felt like stumps. The wind rocked the old shed and taunted him with its eerie dirge of freedom. He was trapped in a cold tomb, an icy sepulcher. Ellie had latched the door from the outside so it wouldn't swing open, so he couldn't leave if he tried.

The watch she left with him was broken and ran too slowly, probably affected by the cold. Low temperatures did that to watches. It was a law of physics that everything slows down as it becomes colder. Although an hour of real time passed, her watch lied and registered only five minutes. She knew that would happen when she gave it to him.

Poor Ellie! It would take so long to reach the road; she'd freeze to death. Maybe she'd already reached the road but hadn't called for help. She hated him and was getting even by sitting at home reading and listening to her blaring, syncopated music. He was forsaken. Alone!

God couldn't see through the walls of the shed and must have abandoned him too. The frigid wind had blown the Lord away. He didn't know that could happen. God was supposed to rule the wind and the affairs of men. If you were His child, He was supposed to care for you. But God wasn't doing anything. He'd frozen Ellie's watch and now was freezing him, slowly, while the cancer consumed him.

Maybe no one came because he was already dead. This was what death felt like—timeless, solitary, excruciatingly painful, and cold beyond imagination—and it would last for eternity.

O Lord, help me. I don't believe any of that junk. I still trust You. You're all I have, and I won't let go. But why don't You help? God, You make me so mad!

Several times he thought he heard a car drive up or a voice call to him. But it was the storm teasing, mocking, enjoying its charade of hope. Storms didn't care. In fact, they enjoyed killing people. They'd done it a million times throughout the ages.

BRANDT HAD A FEELING this wasn't a routine check. Fitch's shed was visible from Highway 22, and there were often cars parked near it. But there was no reason to stop at the halfway point on the access road; one either went all the way to the small beach or didn't go at all. Besides, he couldn't think of a good reason for anyone to go out there today, not with a storm moving in. Maybe someone was sightseeing and had run out of gas or gotten stuck in the mud. He radioed where he was going. A routine check, he told the dispatcher.

Before he got to the turnoff he could see the white car parked up against the woods. He knew instinctively that it was Loverage's. The right color, make, and model. There were two others like it in Springdale, but their owners wouldn't go to Braxton.

The fish on the bumper and the license plate, NTJ 316, left no doubt. For some reason Loverage had stopped at the halfway point instead of driving all the way back to Fitch's shed. He'd probably broken down and walked out, but why would he go out there with a storm moving in? Brandt got out and put on his parka. The hood of the car was cold and dusted with snow, so the car had been there at least an hour. Near the driver's door, snow lay in deep imprints made in the mud by street shoes. On the passenger side, dried weeds lay trampled. He peered through the window. Beer cans? Hamburger wrappers? Empty condiment packets?

He went back to his car to call the station. "Yeah, Sissy. This is Jack. I'm out at Braxton. Has Clayton Loverage reported his car stolen? . . . Well, it's out here at the reservoir, about halfway out the access road. . . . Check at his house and at the church. . . . There's a lot of junk in the car that doesn't belong to him. Better send someone else out and notify the state ranger in New Hope."

He had about ten minutes before anyone would arrive, time enough to inspect the old shed. The car hadn't made it that far, but he'd check anyway. The first thing he noticed at the shed was an unlocked padlock dangling through the latch. There was no sign of a break-in. Maybe someone was in the shed watching through the cracks around the door. They might be armed . . . but that didn't make sense.

Revolver in hand, Jack walked around to the back corner of the shed and listened. A faint moaning, guttural and drawn-out, blended with the soughing wind.

"Hello," he called.

The moaning continued.

A little louder he called, "Hey, in there!" He rapped on the wall of the shed.

The groan stopped, replaced by a feeble, "Help."

"Who's in there?"

A voice groaned and mumbled something, but all he understood was "Help!" It didn't feel like a trap or an ambush. Still, he had to be careful.

"Loverage?" he yelled at the shed.

"Yes. Help." The moaning continued.

Jack reached around the corner of the shed and lifted the latch, letting the door swing open. Feet near the doorway moved in rhythm with the moans. He stepped back from the shed and saw a man writhing on the floor. He stood in the doorway, looking down into the glazed eyes of his pastor.

CLAYTON HEARD A KNOCK, a rapping on the side of the shed. It was death coming for him. He wouldn't answer. No, no, it wasn't death; death would come through the walls, like the cold. It was Ellie. Why was she knocking? Why had she waited so long? He tried to call her name, but no sound came.

"Loverage?" Someone *was* calling his name. Was it God? No, God wouldn't call him Loverage. Probably no one was there; it was just the wind goading him. There was more rapping, then, "Loverage, are you in there?"

"Help." The word jammed in his throat like an iron wedge. He couldn't even hear himself. He tried again, "Help me."

The shed filled with light, and a silhouette stood in the doorway, outlined against the slate sky. He couldn't see who it was, only that it was a man with a gun. "Help me." He felt himself moving with his pain, back and forth, groaning faintly. "Please."

Clayton wasn't sure the man had come to help him. He closed his eyes and rolled onto his side as another wave of nausea hit him. When he looked up, the man was gone, but the door swung in the wind, and he saw the snow falling on a gray world. Help hadn't come. God was teasing him, scorning his prayers.

Then the man came into the shed, pulled the door shut, and knelt beside him.

"Pastor," a voice said, "I'm sorry you're hurting so much. I've radioed for help."

The black and blurry figure wrapped the old tarp around him, tucking it snugly around his neck.

"Here's an old life preserver." The man gently raised Clayton's head and rested it back on something cold and soft. "There. That's better. It hurts me to see you like this. Do you know what's wrong?"

All Clayton could do was shake his head. The dark figure had to be Brandt. The voice had called him Pastor. But maybe God had sent an angel to comfort him. Maybe nothing was real and he was hallucinating,

"The paramedics will be here soon," the voice said. "Try to relax." The man took off his parka and laid it over him.

"Do you want some Piney's coffee to rinse your mouth? It's still warm. I'll dip this napkin into it."

When the man put his wonderfully warm hands on his forehead, Clayton knew they were the hands of an angel. He still hurt so much and groaned softly, but he could feel himself relaxing. Somebody warm was with him.

After a while the voice said, "You're going to be all right. I'm praying for you. God talks to us in mysterious ways."

He opened his eyes again and tried to see the man's face, but it was no use. It was either Brandt, an angel, or his imagination. He couldn't tell the difference anymore. Whoever or whatever it was, the creature was warm and kind to him. But the voice said God speaks in mysterious ways. What did that mean? Did God send angels to deliver messages like that? But angels were bright . . . and they didn't carry guns.

Maybe it was a message from God. Ellie was doing poorly in school; an ad hoc committee had demanded his resignation; Ellie had trespassed into Cary's house; his high school relationship with Cary was about to be revealed. How could he minister to others when he couldn't solve his own problems?

Was he a stubborn old man, and this was God's way of telling him to leave Springdale?

And where was Ellie? She'd taken off, leaving him to suffer in a locked shed in a winter storm. She'd been gone for hours, no, it was days. He could remember at least two nights that had passed.

All right, God, I'll resign. I'll move to Washington or Florida or Maine. I'll go back to Texas. I'll be a missionary in southside Chicago, Papua New Guinea, Kabul, anywhere. Just make my pain go away. Keep me warm under Your wings, and fly me away from Cary and Brandt. Help me not to hate them. And take care of Ellie. She wouldn't abandon me. Something's happened to her. O God, be with my little girl.

ELLEN COULDN'T RUN any more. She struggled with each step, thinking about how to move her legs over this rock and around that log. She moved in slow motion, forcing her body forward as though running in cold honey. Soon her legs wouldn't work at all, and she'd sink to the ground. That would feel so good.

But Raphael was coming. She could hear him. She looked back. He was no more than ten steps away. He was exhausted too. His teeth were clenched, and his eyes narrowed to rye seeds. Dried blood stained his wrist where she'd bitten him. She'd do it again, dig her fingernails into his flesh and scratch out his eyes. She tried to break off a branch but got a stick no larger than a pencil, a useless, futile weapon. Her arm felt so weak she couldn't lift it.

She had only a few steps left in her. Then she'd stop dead still or fall down. And then what? Were these the last steps of her life? God was going to let Raphael rape her. Then he would beat her or kill her. *God, You don't answer prayers. You just let things happen. Why do I even bother to pray?*

She saw a root and thought she lifted her foot high enough to clear it, but her toe caught, and she fell into a tangle of brittle branches and leaves almost covered with snow. It felt good to lie down and rest her legs and her lungs, but Raphael was coming. She turned over on her back to see him lunging toward her. He gave a weak bellow, all that was left of what might once have been a triumphant roar. As he was falling on her, she raised her arms to protect herself.

Ellen knew something had happened because she felt a tearing and heard Raphael's pathetic bellow turn to anguish. He straddled her, flailing wildly and grunting, pounding her arms and face with his fists. Then, wailing miserably, he put his hands over his left eye, rolled off, and lay still on his side in the brush. As she crawled away, he whimpered like an injured dog. Her pencil-stick must have found his eye. Maybe she'd blinded him.

God, just get me out of here. He deserved it. God, You know I had to.

She grabbed a sapling, pulled herself up, and began to walk away. One lens of her glasses was shattered and the frames were mangled, so she slipped them in her coat pocket. Now the forest was blurry. Even her hand in front of her wasn't clear.

"Don't go," he whimpered.

She was leaving. Nothing, nothing would keep her there.

"Help me." He was pitiful, like a wounded rat.

Don't listen to him. Keep going. Her legs trembled, and she couldn't hurry. His voice was so faint she could barely hear it. What was she supposed to do, help the man who was going to rape and kill her?

"Please, don't leave me."

She wasn't going back. Even if he was injured, he was dangerous. The most important thing was to get help for Father. Let the police handle Raphael.

She trudged through the forest, away from Raphael, stopping every few minutes to rest. The wind had been coming off the lake, so she walked into it. It was only a guess, but she might make it to the access road. Raphael's distant pleas faded into winter's icy breath.

ON BRANDT'S WAY back from the shed to the Loverage car, the dispatcher informed him that Buzz Rossiter was on his way to the reservoir. By the time he met Rossiter back at the car, it was snowing again. A light gusting wind flung heavy wet snow over the late fall landscape. By morning there would be three inches of snow-cone slush.

While Rossiter tracked the shoe prints a short distance into the forest, protecting the deepest prints with pine branches, leaves, and twigs, and marking them with pink flourescent tape, Brandt checked the car again. He had little doubt that the Villanueva brothers had stolen the car at the reservoir and left Loverage in the shed. They'd probably seen the car from the road and considered it easy pickings. Maybe they'd left and then returned to get money from Loverage, but for some crazy reason ventured into the forest a quarter-mile from the highway. Maybe the car had broken down or run out of gas and they walked out, but he felt something else was going on. The instincts he'd developed over nearly twenty years of police work were seldom wrong.

A mile straight through the forest were the Hanchett and O'Keefe farms, and far to the left, several miles past the farms, was the backside of Kingswood Country Club. Jack radioed the dispatcher to check with the farms and the country club. The sheriff could patrol the highway.

A siren announced the arrival of the ambulance and paramedics from Good Samaritan, and he sent them on to the shed. He didn't know what was wrong with Loverage, but he felt sorry for him. He would keep the paramedics on alert in case anyone else was found in the forest. Tromping through the woods in a wet, cold storm didn't sound enticing, but if anyone was in there, his help was needed. Besides, he'd like nothing better than to meet up with the Villanuevas.

Within ninety minutes of finding the car, two more officers and eight county volunteers were crisscrossing the forest, all with two-way radios. Brandt did not participate in the search, but assisted Rossiter in its organization.

Ramon was located quickly, cowering in a depression behind a large hickory, afraid of being found and more afraid of not being found. He refused to say a word and was taken to the police station. Within an hour a volunteer stumbled over Raphael, unconscious, suffering from hypothermia, his face badly swollen, his left eye gouged. The paramedics took him to Good Samaritan.

No one was sure if Ellen was in the forest or not. Ramon refused to say a word. She was not at home, at school, or in the library, but no one had seen her go into the forest. One of the paramedics said that Loverage might have mumbled something about his daughter, but he wasn't sure. They'd continue searching for her until they learned differently.

Brandt left Buzz Rossiter at Braxton and drove back into Springdale to get his other parka. While he was in town, he'd try to find out if Ellen Loverage was in the forest. Perhaps Ramon or Raphael would say something, and he might even look in on Loverage. He needed a yes-or-no answer about Ellen.

TWENTY-ONE

Maria left Olga's house late in the afternoon to walk to the drugstore. Because of the approaching storm, Olga offered to take her, but Maria declined, instead accepting a blue and purple anorak.

She needed the time alone to think and pray. If she met up with the boys on the way, they couldn't do anything. She had only a few dollars with her, and at this time of day there was a lot of traffic on the street. Besides, she wanted to stop at Jubi-Latte for a cappuccino. She had time; Osvaldo was working with Mr. Pettigrew after school and wouldn't be at Bethel Temple until after six.

At JubiLatte she ordered her drink and found an old *Reader's Digest*. She could understand most of the words, and it had good stories. But there were no empty tables, and she didn't want to sit at the tall table by the front window; that was for men. In the corner away from the windows, a middle-aged woman in a green suit sat alone with a stack of papers, a large book, and a purse on her table. Maria could see she was busy. Were people supposed to share tables when cafés were crowded? She thought they should, if they didn't bother each other. All she wanted to do was drink her cappuccino and read.

"Excuse me."

The woman glanced up.

"Do you mind if I sit here? I won't bother you."

The woman nodded, moved her purse to the floor, and went back to her papers, writing on them with a long red pencil.

Maria settled at the table, laid her purse in her lap, and sipped her cappuccino. She thumbed through her magazine, looking for something to make her smile. Out of the corner of her eye she saw the woman mark a paper and then stare at her. If Maria glanced up, the woman's eyes darted back to her papers. Maybe it was impolite in Illinois to invite yourself to someone's table. She wouldn't do it again.

Finally the woman spoke. "You're Mrs. Villanueva." It sounded like an accusation.

"Yes," she answered weakly. She was puzzled; who would know her, except for people at Megatronics or church?

"Osvaldo's mother."

"Yes." The woman was obviously grading papers. Maybe she was one of Osvaldo's teachers. Should she ask? Maria moved her chair away from the table and tried reading an article about a six-year-old child abandoned overnight on a field trip.

The woman kept marking papers and looking up at her. After a while, she cleared her throat and said, "Your sons broke into my house."

Miss Merkle! Maria wished she hadn't come to the coffeehouse.

"I'm very sorry," she replied faintly. She stared blankly at her magazine, fighting an urge to run.

Miss Merkle didn't say anything more, but went back to her papers. Maria told herself to leave. She didn't want to talk to this woman. Did Miss Merkle know that Ramon and

270

Raphael were back in Springdale? She gulped down the hot cappuccino and closed the *Reader's Digest*.

"They gave you a crystal angel." Miss Merkle sounded bitter.

"Ramon left it for me," Maria said, almost in a whisper. "The police took it away. I know it's yours."

"Did they leave anything else with you?"

"No. Just the angel. It was beautiful." She stood up to leave.

"Please, sit down. I want to talk with you."

She should go away right now. She had no business talking with a teacher. Miss Merkle had gone to college and read all the books; Maria had never read an entire book, only magazines, and sometimes they were too hard. She sat down in what felt like God's judgment seat. She hadn't raised her boys well, hadn't loved them enough. Now they had hurt someone, and she was partly to blame. "I'm sorry about my boys," she said.

"Did they leave a binder at your house?"

"Only the angel."

"No binder? It was white and had a photo of a young man on the front."

"If they couldn't sell it, they wouldn't steal it."

Miss Merkle was regal, like a queen. Her auburn hair, which showed a few strands of silver, was braided and coiled into a perfect knot. Small emerald earrings matched her modest, tailored suit. She sat straight as a mannequin, her hands clasped tautly. Her green-brown eyes looked tired, as though she were very old or had never used her eyes for smiling. Maria had seen lonely, hurting eyes in bars and jails, but the teacher's eyes surprised her.

"I'm sorry about your binder," she said.

"If the boys don't have it, then the Loverage girl does," the lady said, not so much to Maria as to herself.

"Ellen's a good girl."

"She had no business in my house."

"No, but she didn't mean to hurt you."

271

"Sometimes eyes see things not meant for them."

"I'm sorry. She didn't deliberately—"

"All I want is my binder. When you see her, give her that message. Please." She placed her papers in a small briefcase and stood up. Her coffee was half finished. "I don't mean to be abrupt with you, Mrs. Villanueva, but I must go. I have a lot of work to finish."

"God bless you, Miss Merkle."

THE FIVE MINUTES Brandt spent in the interview room with Ramon were wasted. He was as silent as a tombstone, no words, laughs, scoffs, or groans, only an insolent stare that followed the officer around the room. When Brandt mentioned Raphael's eye, Ramon shrugged his shoulders. On hearing a list of possible charges stemming from that afternoon, he yawned. At the mention of Miss Merkle's burglary, he leaned back in his chair and finger-combed his hair. When Brandt alluded to other burglaries in the Springdale area, Ramon propped his feet on the table.

"Listen, Ramon, I need your help. Anything you say is off the record. Just give me one word. Is Ellen Loverage in the forest by Braxton Reservoir? No details. Just say yes or no, to save the girl."

Ramon stared at him, unblinking. He was playing staredown, but there was no time for such nonsense. "Just one word, Ramon. Off the record."

On the table Ramon traced big capital letters with his finger. *QUIZÁS.*

"What's that mean?"

Ramon raised his eyebrows and shrugged.

"I'll ask someone else. Get out of here." He signaled for Harrick to take Ramon back to his cell.

At the dispatch desk he saw Sissy Ruiz. "Do you know Spanish, Sissy?"

"A little. Did he swear at you in Spanish?"

"What does *quizás* mean?"

"I know that much. It means maybe."

Brandt turned abruptly and marched out, slamming the door as he left. He'd get Shirley, drop by the hospital, and look in on Loverage.

CLAYTON REMEMBERED the siren, wailing like a northern gale, and the door of the shed banging open. Then two, three, or was it ten paramedics lifted him onto a stretcher. He tried to say something about Ellie, but he couldn't talk. That was all he recalled until he woke up at Good Samaritan.

The next thing he remembered was that he was warm and cozy and an angel was singing to him. There were no words, just a humming sound. He listened intently. Yes, he knew that song. It was an old hymn, one of his favorites. *O God, our help in ages past, our hope for years to come. . . .* He repeated the words as the angel hummed. He peeked through one eye. Orange hair, dorsal nose, narrow face—Adele Ritchie hovered near his bed. He'd never considered her beautiful; now she looked like a white-uniformed seraph.

She bent down and peered into his one open eye. "I knew you were in there someplace," she said. "It's about time you came out."

There was no doubt about the angel now. He tried to ask how long he'd been there, but mumbled something incoherent.

"You've been a good pastor," she said. "Now I'll find out how good a patient you are."

He stared at her as she talked in a blur, then closed his eyes and pictured himself on a bullet train catching snatches of fleeting scenery. *Morphine . . . Kidney stone . . . Everything plugged up . . . Bad pain . . . The worst . . . Afraid you're going to die . . . Gets worse . . . Afraid you're not going to die . . . You'll be okay . . . Nothing life-threatening . . . Fluids . . . Try to go, Mr. Lovrage. Try real hard. . . . Need to pass it . . .*

Dr. Kirshner might have to operate . . . Ultrasound . . . More morphine . . . Someday lithotripsy . . .

It was good to hear a quiet voice instead of the mocking wind and creaking shed. But she should slow down. Her words came too fast. No time to sort them out. Piling up. He wanted her to stop talking; her humming sounded much better. He felt her gently rubbing his hand. He was sleepy again. Let her go on talking. Tomorrow he'd unscramble what she was saying.

Clayton didn't like waking up to the pain. Sometimes no one was in the room, and he watched the dripping of the IV bag and the dancing green line on the heart monitor. Other times Adele or one of the other nurses took his blood pressure or gave him a plastic bottle to urinate into. Once Dr. Kirshner and another doctor talked near the doorway, but he couldn't understand what they said. Most of the time the pain whispered in his back and stomach, but sometimes it screamed, and he fought the groans. It felt so good when morphine eased the pain and carried him off to sleep.

Once he woke to Jack and Shirley Brandt staring down at him. What were they doing here? Shirley held his hand; Jack's smiling, rosy-cheeked face was poised next to hers.

"Good afternoon, Pastor." Unmistakably the voice of Jack Brandt. "I want you to know the church is praying for you . . . We're behind you all the way . . . Linda's on her way . . . Clay, Jr.'s flying in . . . We're praying you'll pass that stone, and, you know, God answers prayer."

Clayton took a vow of silence. He ached to ask about Ellie, but he didn't want to hear news, good or bad, from the Brandts. He'd ask Adele, or Dr. Kirshner, or Linda. He didn't let them know their words registered with him, but lay like a corpse, staring far past them, never blinking. He wouldn't nod, say hello, good-bye, or thank you. That was his message to them.

"Pastor, we love you," said Shirley, lightly pinching his cheek. "You know, when you hurt, we hurt too."

Suddenly he saw Shirley through the eyes of five-year-old Ellie when she had grabbed her nose. *Get your hands off my face, lady!* he wanted to yell. His little girl had been uninhibited. Oh, for the honesty of a child.

"I think we should probably go, dear," Jack said. "He's pretty well out of it. Wouldn't understand a question I asked."

Clayton continued his sphinxlike stare.

"Should we pray with him before we go?" asked Shirley.

"He doesn't even know who we are."

They said their good-byes. "Praying for you, Pastor . . . Hang in there . . . Don't worry about the church . . . It's in good hands . . ."

He watched them walk to the doorway, never turning his head, his eyes glazed as though staring through the ceiling at the Milky Way. As soon as they left, his pain came back stronger than ever. He groaned softly, and pressed the call button. More morphine, please. *God, forgive me, but I enjoyed that. I wonder what they'll say about me at church.*

ELLEN DIDN'T WANT to feel guilty about leaving Raphael. Some of the kids at church wore WWJD wristbands—What would Jesus do? Good question! Just what *would* Jesus do?

Maybe she shouldn't have left him. Was he going to die? She had felt the stick tear into him. Blood was running down his face, and there was blood on her glove that she tried to scrape off on the trees. Was he lying there blinded? His jacket was thin, and he wore tennis shoes. He would freeze if he stayed there very long. But it wouldn't have done any good to stay with him. He needed help, not company, and she didn't want to be company with the man who'd tried to assault her. If it was right to leave Father alone to go for help, it was right to leave Raphael.

If she walked slowly, she didn't have to stop for rest. She needed to keep moving, to reach the road, the lake, or one of the farms on the far side of the forest. The forest wasn't that wide. It was less than a mile past the Braxton turnoff on Highway 22 before there were cornfields. Maybe she was going around in circles. When people wander in the desert, they walk in circles, passing the same places time and again. That's what she was doing, and soon she'd stumble over Raphael's body. God had removed all the colors in her world except gray, brown, and green, and whether she used her glasses or not, everything looked alike. The trees, forest duff, and soggy snow stretched on forever.

The wind whistled through the tops of the trees, but on the forest floor it was not strong. The wet, never-ending snow stuck to her jacket and cap as easily as it did to the branches. Now and then, snow loosened by a shifting wind caromed around her.

She was not frightened until the light began to fade slowly, like a theater before a play. It was five-thirty or six, over three and a half hours since she'd left Father! Why hadn't she come to something? What would she do when it was pitch black? She'd become a sleepwalker, reaching out in front of her to feel the trees, creeping along blindly to keep from falling into a pit. She was going to spend the night in a black, freezing-wet forest.

She hated the trees. They were dark and threatening, like those in an enchanted Tolkien forest, their faces terrible, their arms outstretched to obscure the light. The wind gave them voices to sing an arboreal anthem of doom. Roots tripped her and small arms snatched at her, trying to rip her clothes.

She determined to walk until she found civilization. Father called her stubborn, so stubborn no one could make her do anything she didn't want to. *Well, I'm not going to stop. I'll walk until I collapse or pass out.* She'd feel her way through the trees, holding her arms out in front of her like antennae. She took her shattered glasses from her pocket and bent the frames so they'd stay on. She couldn't see any better, but at least a branch wouldn't poke her eye out.

Soon it was pitch black, or pitch white, and she took baby steps to avoid the roots that waited in ambush. She knew she wasn't walking straight, because each tree forced her to change direction. She imagined the trees' elves laughing at her as she went round and round, back and forth, almost making it to the highway, coming within a few steps of the lake, walking within sight of the farms, almost returning to Wally's shed where Father lay unconscious. The trees had locked arms, forming an invisible fence to entrap her. She belonged to them now, and they were determined to imprison her forever in their chilling domain. Still, she would walk, and walk, and walk, until they gave up and let her go free. Maybe she was more stubborn than they.

Step carefully until you feel something, she told herself. Step over or around the roots. Break off the smaller branches, walk around the larger ones, try not to change direction too much. And keep looking for lights. *O God, light would be so wonderful.* She prayed for a car light, a light in a window, even a twinkling star. *Jesus, if You're the Light of the World, show me some light soon. Don't hide it any longer. If I see light, I will run. I'll sprint. I'll laugh and sing and shout.* As the wind gradually decreased and a finer, drier snow fell, no light appeared, and she plodded blindly on into the blackness.

THROUGH HIS FUZZY consciousness, Clayton knew he was still loaded with morphine. It made him nauseated and coated his mouth, but it was better than the pain. Strange thoughts masqueraded as reality, and he was never sure of anything. Right now he knew someone was holding his hand and talking to him in a soothing voice. A woman. Every once in a while she'd exchange comments with a man. He listened for a long time before opening his eyes. He had to make sure it wasn't the Brandts. No. It was all right. He was safe. It was Linda and Alan.

Springdale was a three-hour drive from Wheaton. They

must have left the kids with Alan's folks in Naperville. Linda was so dependable, always there when he needed her. He liked to look at her because she was a young Joyce. He liked Alan too, although he was a little stuffy. Tall, dark-haired, with a face that resembled Superman's in the old comic books, Alan was serious almost to a fault, nothing like the hotshots Linda had dated in high school. In the six years he'd known him, Clayton had never heard him tell a joke. He was impervious to humor, and smiled only when talking business. He was a banking executive in Chicago with character beyond reproach, and he provided well for Linda. They were devoted to each other and attended a good church. What more could he ask for one of his children?

"Where's Ellie?" He hadn't known that would be the first thing he'd say. He should have said hello, or that he was glad they'd come.

Linda glanced at Alan. Maybe something had happened to Ellie, and they weren't supposed to tell him because he was ill.

"Linda, tell me about Ellie," he repeated firmly. When he spoke like that she always obeyed him.

"They haven't found her yet, Father. They're still looking."

"What day is it? How many days has she been missing?"

"It's still Tuesday, Father, about six-thirty. They brought you in at three."

"Something's happened to Ellie." She couldn't get lost walking from Wally's shed to Highway 22. Maybe she'd caught a bad ride. He shouldn't have let her go.

"They're still searching, Father. They'll find her; the whole church is praying."

"God doesn't answer prayers." He shouldn't have said that. The darn morphine was making him crazy.

"Father!"

She sounded shocked, but it didn't matter. She didn't know what it was like praying in that shed, having prayers bounce unheard off the walls. They probably still littered the floor. When he felt better he'd go out there and sweep them up. He'd prayed for Ellie's safety and for his pain to go away, and God hadn't bothered to answer either prayer. Maybe Bella Belinsky was right: If God really loved you, He wouldn't let you suffer.

"She's going to be all right, Father," Linda tried to assure him. "They're going to find her."

He wouldn't let her lie to him. Her voice was taut, her words too well measured, insincere. He always could read her, even when she was a little girl. Something had happened to Ellie, and Linda was covering up. Alan was sitting there saying nothing. If she were telling the truth, Alan would back her up. Ellie was dead, or badly injured, and he was lying in Good Samaritan, drugged so he wouldn't know what happened.

"You can't make me feel better, Linda." He sounded crabby to himself. "She left Wally's shed hours ago. She's dead, isn't she?"

"No, Father. They just haven't found her yet. It's not good for you to worry."

He knew what they were doing. Adele had told him how she didn't let patients know the truth when she thought they couldn't handle it. So much for his sermons.

"I'll worry about Ellie if I want to, and you, Alan, Dr. Kirshner, or anyone else can't stop me." He had to be strong and insist on knowing everything.

But maybe he was being too harsh. Linda had turned away from him and was crying. He hadn't meant to make her cry; he only wanted to be firm and not let anyone lie to him.

Alan talked softly to her. "It's all right, honey. Morphine does that. He doesn't mean what he's saying."

Ellie was missing, probably dead, and he was nigh unto death, or whatever that phrase was. He couldn't find the right words in his head. Now he'd made Linda cry by talking crazy. His world was spinning out of control. Whether he believed in it or not, he knew only one thing he could do.

God, You who know the future and control all things . . .
He was being too churchy.

God, for Pete's sake do something. Do something! Don't let anything bad happen to Ellie. And let me pass this stone. I hurt so much. God, You need to help me.

He felt himself getting sleepy. *And one more thing. Be with my church. Show me if I should leave. I really believe in prayer. I've prayed all my life. I just don't understand why You don't do something!*

Through his drowsiness, he saw them leave. They were going for a bite to eat. From the hallway he heard Linda say that at least it was just a kidney stone, nothing serious.

TWENTY-TWO

When Mr. Platt called Maria into his office at Megatronics, she knew something had happened to Ramon and Raphael. Now she sat by Raphael's bed at Good Samaritan Hospital. All she knew was that he'd had an accident in the woods and hurt his left eye. Both eyes were bandaged for now, and in the morning a specialist from St. Louis would examine him. They'd probably take him to St. Louis for an operation.

She didn't know why they had shackled his leg to the bed, or why there was a policeman in the hallway. Her boy was lightly sedated and couldn't see. Did they think he was going to run away? Or that his brother would escape from jail and help him? Or that she'd sneak him out of the hospital? The police always overreacted.

He must have done something very bad, but she wasn't ready to know, not just yet. Her boys were in trouble again, bad trouble. Maybe this would teach them a lesson; maybe not. Nothing ever got through to them.

She would stay with Raphael. He needed her. There was

no one else. Anyway, she was partly to blame for the mess he was in. If she'd loved her boys more, spent more time with them, taught them about Jesus when they were little, they wouldn't do bad things. Maybe it was too late to help him.

As she sat by his bed, she read aloud from a children's Bible borrowed from the waiting room; it had big print and easy words. She read the story about the blind man Jesus healed. The authorities didn't believe he was the same blind man who had begged for years at the city gate. They talked to his parents and then to him. "Once I was blind," he told them, "but now I can see. And I know Jesus did it."

That's how she felt. Once she'd been blind and Jesus helped her see how to live right. Maybe Raphael would listen and realize his life could be different. He didn't need to steal, and sex wasn't important enough to steal from a girl. Oh, he needed so much help.

As she finished the story he said, "No more stories, Mama. Why do you read that stuff?"

"You need to hear it, Raphael."

"God won't make me see; He made me blind. I don't want to hear about Him."

She sighed and closed the book. At least he'd heard something. Maybe the words would reach deep into his soul. The Word of God was like little seeds that sprouted and grew. But she wouldn't force Bible stories on him.

"Tomorrow, Raphael. I'll read to you again."

"Maybe, Mama. Maybe not."

As she sat next to him praying, Officer Brandt came into the room. The man followed her everywhere. Couldn't he give her a few minutes' peace?

The policeman didn't greet her, but looked at her coolly. "Is he conscious?" He tipped his head toward Raphael.

She shrugged. "Talk to him. Maybe he'll answer you."

"Raphael, this is Officer Brandt. I need your help. Can you answer one question? Can you hear me?"

No response.

"You just need to nod yes or no. This is important."

Raphael rolled onto his right side, away from Brandt.

Brandt walked to the far side of the bed. "Listen, Raphael. I need to know if Ellen Loverage is in the forest. Just nod yes or no, and I'll leave."

Raphael rolled back onto his left side.

Maria wanted to grab the policeman and shove him out the door. *Get out of here! You . . . you policeman! He's hurting. You can talk to him later.* And she wanted to shake Raphael. *Just tell him, Raphael. If Ellen is lost in the forest in this storm, she needs help.* But she knew Raphael wouldn't say anything.

"It's time for you to go," she said. "He can't hear you; he's asleep."

"As much asleep as you are, Mrs. Villanueva."

She glared at him. He had no right to talk sarcastically. She knew his type—she'd seen it in New Mexico in the bars, the police station, even in church—people who wore law costumes and church costumes to cover up what they really were.

After her talk with Miss Merkle, Maria had thought a lot about the binder. Miss Merkle may want her other things returned, but what she wanted most was the binder. Memories were more important than things. She couldn't imagine her boys taking such a thing. They were as likely to take a binder as a cookbook.

And Ellen hadn't taken it. Three times she'd heard her tell the story of going into Miss Merkle's house; each time she'd insisted she'd taken nothing, not even a drink of water.

Maybe one of the policemen took it. She couldn't imagine why. But some policemen were sneaky. You couldn't trust them.

"Do you know a store that is open?" she asked. She purposely scowled at him.

"The Circle K at the freeway is always open. Why?"

"Do they have binders?" She shouldn't do this, but she had to know.

"I don't know."

"I lost a binder," she said, looking straight into his eyes. "It was white, and you can slip a photo into the front cover. Maybe you've seen it." It's best to catch sneaks when they don't know anyone is after them. She saw him narrow his eyes. Now they were opponents, and they both knew it.

"It has a photo of a young man, seventeen or eighteen, on the front. Have you seen it?" she asked again.

For a split second she saw the look of guilt, and knew. And he knew she knew. She had seen his jaw drop and his eyes widen. She saw terror and loathing. It was good they weren't alone.

"You're a policeman," she continued. "You see lots of things. If you happen to see the binder, please don't open it. It's very personal. Just give it to me. Please."

His rosy cheeks turned brilliant scarlet, his jaw tightened, and his temples pulsed like bongo drums. He looked furious and frightened at the same time.

Maria hadn't been mean to anyone for many years. She was not supposed to hurt people, even people who were sneaky and guilty. But now she knew, even though she couldn't prove anything. She stood defiantly in front of him, arms akimbo, watching him struggle to say something.

After a long pause he replied, "If I see your binder, I'll make sure you get it. Good day, Mrs. Villanueva."

"*Vaya con Dios,* Mr. Policeman."

AFTER GETTING HIS PARKA from the paramedics, Brandt took a roundabout route back to Braxton Reservoir; he needed a few extra minutes to think. He radioed Rossiter.

"Anything yet?"

"No trace. We've completed the eastern section where we found the brothers; now we're starting on the western end. I moved the car to the old shed. Did you learn anything?"

"Loverage is completely out of it, and the brothers aren't

talking. For the time being, we have to assume she's in the forest."

"I called for search dogs."

"Good. Any articles of clothing?"

"Sweater, tennis shoes, athletic socks in the trunk."

"Perfect. Be there in ten minutes."

As he drove, he couldn't concentrate on the search for Ellen Loverage. If she was in the forest, they'd find her sooner or later. All he could think about was the Chihuahua that had just nipped at his heels. If the Villanueva woman suspected he'd taken the binder, maybe others did too. But he didn't have to worry; nothing could be proven. He reminded himself that the binder was beyond finding, safe until Armageddon . . . and beyond.

He arrived back at Braxton just after sunset. Rossiter was doing his usual efficient job. His squad car was now in the open area near Fitch's shed, where he could better coordinate the search. He assigned a section to each searcher, making notations on a detailed map spread out on a makeshift table in the shed. He made sure they all had flashlights and extra batteries, knew who was on each side of them, and had functioning radios.

Brandt remained with Rossiter to help with logistics. Two heads were better than one in coordinating the search, and he would add little in the forest. As they discussed their strategy, the bouncing lights of a vehicle driving through the puddles on the access road approached.

"That must be Higginson," said Rossiter.

"Who's Higginson?"

"He has some dogs."

"We usually call Hugh Smythe in New Hope."

"Hugh's out of town. His wife said to call Higginson as a backup," said Rossiter.

His colleague had thought of all the details. When there was action, Rossiter was one of the best. When it came to writing up details, however, he was close to worthless. He'd be an asset to any police force, but he'd never go very high. He'd have to learn to keep records the hard way.

Higginson drove up in a new SUV, polished bright red, with enough chrome that it looked like a giant Christmas ornament. In a quick glance Brandt noted three antennas; racks for guns, bicycles, skis, and a boat; a large trailer hitch; and a power winch. Two dogs paced restlessly in the back.

The dog owner stepped out of his vehicle, and Brandt judged him to be about six foot six and 280 pounds, all of it muscle. A round face with a brown walrus mustache looked out from under the bill of a winter hunting cap. He'd probably played football in college.

"Came as soon as I got the call. Name's Higginson." He extended a bearlike hand, first to Rossiter, then to him.

Rossiter summarized what had happened and the status of the search.

"How much experience do your dogs have?" asked Rossiter.

"The bloodhound's the best there is. Been on a hundred searches. If the girl's in there, she'll find her." He opened a back door of the van, and two dogs leaped out. "The other one, that's O'Dell—he's a mistake. Half bloodhound and half whatever. Ol' Madam Arf got out one night, and you know what can happen."

The bloodhound stood at attention, awaiting instructions. The mutt, on the other hand, was yipping, whining, pawing, and pacing. He was the goofiest looking dog Brandt had ever seen, his compact crazy-quilt body propped up on four stilts. His ears were long, like a bloodhound's, but he had to have some Great Dane ancestry.

"Somebody told me once that the mutt looked like a cross between a Saint Bernard and a Chihuahua," commented Higginson. "I dunno about that, but once in a while he makes a hit."

At the word *Chihuahua,* Brandt froze.

"A hit?" asked Rossiter.

"Yeah. The only thing his nose is good for is sniffing new dirt. He can smell it a hundred yards away. Always thinks he's found a bone. If something's been buried less than a week, he'll find it. Let him loose in a newly plowed field, he'll go insane. Now where are the girl's things?"

Brandt stood petrified, looking back and forth between them as they spoke, hearing nothing. He felt as if someone had just told him he had untreatable cancer. He should have burnt that binder, thrown it in a Dumpster, left it in his locker at Goldie's forever. But no! He had to bury it in the safest place he could think of. Now a one-in-a-million mutt could expose him. Armageddon might be here sooner than he'd expected.

He walked back to his squad car, mulling over the possibilities. The mutt might not find it. The spot was well hidden and already covered by two inches of snow. And even if they found the binder, there would be no reason for anyone to think *he* had buried it. Even if his fingerprints were found, he'd be safe; he'd handled it during the initial investigation at the Merkle house. On the other hand, if they found Shirley's fingerprints, all was lost. In his wildest imagination he couldn't construct an alibi for that. But . . . there was nothing to worry about. Shirley's prints weren't on file, and that stupid mutt wasn't going to find anything.

Yet he couldn't relax. For ten years Jack Brandt had done everything perfectly at the police department. Not one lie, not one half-truth, very few inadvertent errors. Now one misjudgment was threatening to undo him. He told himself not to worry. He had done God's will, and God would protect him . . . wouldn't He? They'd find Ellen first; the dog wouldn't come within a hundred yards of the binder. He was worrying over nothing.

He went back to Rossiter's squad car. Still no trace of Ellen.

"We'll find her in the next hour," said Rossiter. "I'm willing to bet on it."

Brandt began a slow pace between the squad cars and Fitch's shed.

ELLEN WASN'T SURE of anything except blackness, cold, and fatigue. Everything else was blurry, gray-black uncertainty. Sometimes she wasn't sure that God existed, or Father, or Osvaldo, or her room, or her warm soft bed and down comforter. After convincing herself they didn't exist, she'd find herself praying again. Mostly she prayed to see light, any light, but she also prayed for strength to keep walking. Baby steps made her legs ache, and cramps gripped her shins.

God, don't let me stop, even if I have to take baby steps into eternity.

Sometimes she envisioned Father pounding on the wall of the locked shed, pleading for someone to let him out. She imagined him lying unconscious on the floor, then dying alone. She shouldn't have left him. His fur-lined cap had probably saved her life, but he'd frozen wearing a stocking cap.

O God, be with Father. Let somebody find him. Don't let him die.

At first Ellen wasn't sure she'd seen the lights. For several minutes something twinkled through the snow and the trees, but she could no longer trust her eyes. She'd imagined lights before and headed toward them, only to have them vanish. But this time there were two lights, and they weren't going away. Then three lights, and four. She closed one eye and peered at them through her good lens. She'd found a parking lot, but she had no idea where she was.

A light shone from a window, and several cars clustered around the far end of a large building. As she headed toward them, a car pulled into the lot. She tried to run, but her legs had forgotten everything except baby steps. Father needed help. She had to tell someone.

As she approached the car, she saw that it was Miss Merkle's green Chevy. She tried calling, but her voice broke.

She leaned against the rear fender as her teacher gathered her purse and briefcase. Ellen tried to call out, but couldn't. When she finally uttered a frail, delicate "Help," the wind and snow snatched it away.

She inched next to Miss Merkle and touched her shoulder. Her teacher jerked around with a frightened gasp; as she stared openmouthed, all of Ellen's words dissolved, and she began sobbing. She tried blubbering something about Father, but her words were swallowed by great gulps of air. Miss Merkle put her arm around her waist and led her to the passenger seat.

"Just relax. I'll get you to Good Samaritan faster than the paramedics can." She drove out of the parking lot while calling 911 on her cell phone. "Caroline Merkle here. I've got Ellen Loverage with me. Found her at the country club. . . . Bruised and exhausted. Glasses mangled. . . . No. Don't send them. I'll be at the emergency room door in six or seven minutes. . . . Yes, yes. I'll drive carefully."

"Father, he's—" stammered Ellen.

"Clay's already at Good Samaritan. The search parties are looking for you. Are you okay? Everyone's worried sick."

"Raphael's hurt bad." She hadn't thought about him for a long time.

"He's at the hospital too. His brother's at the police station."

"What time is it?"

"A little after seven. You should rest. You can talk later."

Ellen leaned back against the headrest. The car felt soothing and warm.

"Miss Merkle, I didn't take your binder. Honest. I read the last letter. I shouldn't have. I'm really sorry."

She thought Miss Merkle might have said something, but she wasn't sure. She tried listening, but it was so warm, and it felt so good just to lean back. And they'd found Father.

God, if You answered my prayers, thank You. I really do

believe in You; at least I think I do. I wonder whether Osvaldo's in Texas or Florida. . . .

She barely remembered arriving at Good Samaritan.

CLAYTON SPENT A FOGGY night at the hospital. The morphine took away his pain but left him nauseated, sleepy, and jumbled in his thoughts. He loved and hated it at the same time. When he was asleep, someone was continually waking him up, taking his blood pressure and temperature, checking the IV, and shoving the urine bottle at him.

"Wake up, Mr. Loverage," one young nurse had said. "Here's our little bottle. Let's see if we can go now, Mr. Loverage. I know we can do it if we just try real hard. We gotta pass that thing, ya know."

We? The nurses needed better training. He'd talk to Dr. Kirshner about it in the morning.

If he urinated, even the tiniest dribble, a nurse swirled the contents of the bottle and poured the liquid through a filter into another container. There were never any stones. He could have told them that. His stone was the size of the Hope Diamond, and Dr. Kirshner would have to operate in the next day or two. He'd tell the doctor to save the diamond. He could sell it to help pay for the church's parking lot improvements.

Sometime during the night a nurse came in and told him that Ellie was all right. They were keeping her overnight for observation. She'd been found at the country club! Why did she go there, when she was supposed to walk to the road to get help? The girl had a mind of her own. But it didn't matter; she was okay and safe.

When Clayton woke the next time he was feeling much better. The nurse checked his diaper and showed him a dull, cream-colored object with irregular edges about an eighth the size of a BB. That was it? That tiny thing caused all that pain? If he hadn't felt so much better, he would have been disappointed.

Soon he was sitting up in bed drinking orange juice and eating one of Good Samaritan's famous saltless, gourmet breakfasts. At nine o'clock, Dr. Kirshner came by and told him he'd had a minor kidney stone. If it hadn't moved, it wouldn't have stayed minor, but those small ones usually pass, he said. X-rays showed two larger stones that might never move or might move and give him the same problem someday. He should drink plenty of fluids. Some people thought cranberry juice helped. Dr. Kirshner wasn't too sure about that. Clayton could leave at one, the normal checkout time. The nurse would bring papers for him to sign.

"How's Ellie? Is she here?" he asked.

"Dr. Van Epp's handling her case. As far as I know she's fine. I think she's still sleeping."

Around ten o'clock Buzz Rossiter dropped by to fill him in on what had happened. He was surprised, but happily so, to see Rossiter instead of Brandt. Accosted by Ramon and Raphael Villanueva before she could reach the road. Chased. Ramon went back but Raphael kept after her. He tried to rape her, but she injured his eye with a stick. Wandered for hours in the forest before reaching the country club. Caroline Merkle found her in the parking lot. She seemed okay, but a little traumatized.

"Dr. Van Epp's with her right now; then she'll talk with a staff psychologist."

"When can I see her?"

"I have no idea. Orange Roughy will let you know."

"You mean Adele Ritchie?"

"She's the boss around here."

As Rossiter was about to leave, he added one more item. "I thought you might like to know. One of the search dogs found that binder Miss Merkle wanted so badly, buried in the middle of the forest."

Just after eleven, Linda, Alan, and Clay, Jr. appeared. Dan hadn't come, but wanted two calls a day to keep him informed. He'd come if needed.

They knew less than he did about what had happened at Braxton. Two men had chased Ellie, they said, but she'd escaped. Confused, she couldn't find her way out of the woods. One of the men had hurt himself and was under guard in Good Samaritan; the other was in jail. No one was allowed to see Ellie. Maybe in the afternoon. And of course they would drive him home at one o'clock. Glad everything had turned out all right. Maybe they could all go out for dinner that evening.

If they'd stopped chattering for a few seconds, he would have told them what he knew. Instead, he just lay there taking it all in. What he really wanted to do was talk with Ellie. These others seemed like outsiders, visitors to the world he and Ellie shared. They weren't serious enough. Their words sounded trivial and offhand. Dinner out didn't appeal to him, and he wanted to protect Ellie from their cross-examination.

Just after eleven-thirty, Osvaldo's smiling Mayan face appeared at his door. Clayton motioned him in and introduced him to Linda, Alan, and Clay, Jr. *Osvaldo Villanueva*—he liked the feel of the name as it rolled off his tongue.

Osvaldo gave them his water-pump handshake and said a few soft words to Clayton about hoping to see Ellen soon and being glad the kidney stone was gone. The boy didn't feel comfortable around the rest of the family, and they weren't doing anything to help him. Clayton had thought he was in Texas or Florida by now, and wanted to speak with him alone. After a few forced clichés and uncomfortable silences, Osvaldo excused himself.

"Who was that?" asked Linda.

"Ellie's boyfriend," answered Clayton.

"Him?"

"Isn't Villanueva the name of the guys who chased Ellie?" asked Clay, Jr.

"He's their younger brother," replied Clayton.

"He's Ellie's boyfriend?" Linda sounded incredulous.

"One of the finest boys I've ever met," replied Clayton. "I'm sure you'll like him."

Clayton was released at one o'clock. Before he left, Adele took him to Ellie's room while the others went to get the car. Both Dr. Van Epp and the psychologist insisted she stay overnight at Good Samaritan. She had a little frostbite on her toes and was dehydrated. She'd slept until ten, through all the prodding of the nurses, and still wanted more rest. Clayton was told that he could see her for a few minutes, but was not to talk about what had happened.

He knew he would cry when he saw her. He could usually control his emotions, but not now. Maybe he needed more sleep too.

He stood over her bed and looked down at her. Her eyes were red-veined and tired. She nodded her head slowly and smiled up at him. He kissed her forehead, then sat on the edge of her bed and laid his head next to hers, and they cried together.

In just a few minutes Adele was back. Clayton dried Ellie's tears with a Kleenex, kissed her forehead again, and left. He didn't hurry to meet Linda and Clay, Jr. He'd have plenty of time with them the rest of the day. He wanted to savor his time with Ellie. *That was the best conversation I've ever had with any of my children.*

JACK BRANDT DREADED the meeting in Chief Riley's office with Rossiter and Higginson. The first item of business was the binder.

Riley praised Higginson and his wonderful dog O'Dell. "I don't believe there's another hound within a thousand miles that could have located where that binder was buried."

They talked at length about two partial fingerprints found on the binder. One was Brandt's; the other was not identified.

"Someone, for some reason, has carefully wiped each page, obviously trying to remove fingerprints," said Chief Riley.

"I've ruled out the brothers. Nothing fits their way of doing things. They don't steal sentimental binders; they don't have the patience to remove fingerprints from forty-some pages; and they don't dispose of anything by burying it deep in a forest. I see no reason for Caroline Merkle to bury it. She's the one who desperately wanted it returned. Ellen Loverage is a possibility, since the contents of the binder might make people look unfavorably on her father. But she left the house before you investigated the burglary, and Jack, you said you saw the binder on Merkle's bed. Unless we're missing something, the only other person who might have taken it is you, but that doesn't make sense either."

"The binder was on her pillow when I left," Jack said. "During the investigation I picked it up and looked at it. When I saw what it was, I knew I had no business with it." As he said the words, he felt a sharp catch in his chest and could hardly breathe. In twenty years of police work, he had never deliberately lied. He had set the standard high and always kept it. "When I walked out of the room," he continued, "the binder was still on the bed. It had to have been taken after that."

"This is a minor issue," said Chief Riley. "If it were serious, I'd use the lie detector. But the Merkle woman is just happy to have the binder back and won't file trespassing charges against the Loverage girl. It bothers me to leave loose ends. Either someone is lying, or we've overlooked another person who's involved, but I'm going to let this drop. It's not worth pursuing."

Two hours later, Brandt left Chief Riley's office, relieved that the investigation was finished. He had no doubt the chief and Rossiter knew he had taken and buried the binder. And then there was the Chihuahua. . . .

How would he tell Shirley they had no future in Springdale?

Clayton sat alone in his study on Father's Day. It was his first Father's Day alone in sixty years. True to her word, Ellie left home when she turned eighteen. Graduation was on Thursday, June 12, her birthday on Friday, and yesterday, June 14, she left for Minnesota to work at a Lutheran camp for children with disabilities. Clayton wasn't too sure about the Lutherans, but at least she was working and in a place that was reasonably safe.

They'd never live under the same roof again. After this summer in Minnesota she'd go directly to Carbondale where, despite her mediocre grades, she had been accepted at Southern Illinois University. Mr. Wicker said that Caroline Merkle had written a strong recommendation for her. After a couple of years she hoped to transfer to the University of Iowa for its highly rated writing program.

He had thought Ellen might follow Osvaldo wherever he went, but they were content to write and then see each other during the summer. If there was anything serious between them, they'd soon get tired of long-distance courting. Clayton knew that if they ever married, he'd be closer to Osvaldo than to any of his other children's spouses.

Maria had thought about moving from Springdale, but she knew her sons would find her wherever she went. She had moved from the Depot Street house into an empty room at the Santoris'. She didn't have to worry about Raphael or Ramon for at least another year.

Four cards lay on the desk in front of Clayton's computer. He could have opened them earlier, but he'd saved them until after lunch, the time his family traditionally opened Father's and Mother's Day cards and presents.

Of course, he hadn't really been alone that day, having preached at both the nine and eleven o'clock services and shaken hands with hundreds of people. No one had invited him for Father's Day dinner. If they had, he would have declined; he wanted to be alone.

He had two more Sundays left at Springdale Church. On July 1 he would become pastor of a small church in Marshall, Texas. Between then and now he had a pile of details to take care of. He wanted to leave things in good shape for whoever followed him as pastor.

He had mixed feelings about leaving Springdale, but there was nothing holding him here now except memories, and he would take those along. Ellie would never live here again.

As he sipped the coffee he'd picked up from JubiLatte on the way home, he opened Dan's card—a picture of a pheasant among spectacular fall foliage, a verse thanking him for being a good father and passing on wonderful memories, and a short note. *Dear Father, Thank you for the great times and wonderful guidance. I love you, Dan.*

He thanked God for his close relationship with his children. Nearly every day he dealt with dysfunctional families. His children could all express their feelings. Now all he needed from Dan and Beth was a grandchild.

Clay, Jr.'s card was also signed by Cathy and the kids.

Amanda and Pepper had neatly printed their names, and one of them had added baby Joyce's. Praying hands adorned the front of the card. Inside was a poem telling how fathers reflect God's love; under that was a Bible verse. Clayton looked forward to more time with Clay, Jr. and his family, who lived only two hours from Marshall. Clay, Jr. had invited him to preach at his church once or twice a year. He wondered if the grandchildren would play games with him. They hadn't paid much attention to him the few times he'd seen them.

He finished his coffee and went into the kitchen to find something else to eat. He wished Ellie were there to fix him one of her sandwiches. She hadn't made a bad one yet, although some certainly were unusual. The last sandwich she'd made had a thick layer of butter from Pierson's Dairy on one slice of bread and grape jelly on the other. In between were slivers of cashews, pecans, and almonds, and a layer of green peas. She labeled it *Pea-nut Butter and Jelly sandwich. Created by your daughter, Ellen, June, 1997*. It was wonderful.

He found a bag of pretzels and poured himself a glass of cranberry juice. He was drinking a quart each day since his bout with the kidney stone eight months ago. He still remembered the intense pain and his embarrassment over some of the things he'd said. But despite his fuzzy thinking in Wally's shed and at Good Samaritan, two things had become clear to him on a very deep level.

First, he had resolved that as long as Ellie remained at home, she was his most precious possession. Since October, they had read together two or three times a week and discussed what they'd read. She read four times as many books as he did, but when there was one she especially wanted him to read, he finished it as soon as he could. He trained himself to talk on her terms and forget all the wonderful advice he thought he had to share. He tried to listen instead. She was not a little girl, but a young woman. He didn't squander the short time they had left together.

Several times they'd driven into St. Louis to used-book

stores—her idea of paradise. On each trip he gave her fifty dollars to spend, and she was absorbed for hours going through hundreds of volumes before she'd end up with one or two elegantly bound classics. He enjoyed watching her in her ecstasy.

The second thing he had resolved to do was to resign from Springdale Church. His resignation wasn't because of Brandt and his ad hoc committee, but because . . . well, he never could define why. It was time to move on. More and more over the last five years he'd found himself fighting brushfires that detracted from real ministry. Committees, meetings, reports, planning sessions, long-term goals, fund raising, financial adjustments, etc., etc. That might be ministry for some, but not for him, at least not anymore. Maybe God had been telling him for several years to leave Springdale, and he hadn't listened. But he knew that leaving felt right. He looked forward to the slower pace of the smaller church and the additional time to devote to his congregation.

He was pleased that the Brandts hadn't been around to gloat when he made his announcement. Just before Christmas Jack had accepted a position as police chief of a small town in Indiana. The church was more shocked by Brandt's announcement than by his own. A pillar of the church was leaving, someone had remarked. Clayton refrained from telling them the pillar was termite-infested; he might have a few termites of his own.

The McAfees and several other couples threw a church-wide bon voyage banquet for the Brandts, complete with gifts and testimonials of appreciation. His declining Bill McAfee's request to emcee the Brandt banquet had displeased many church members. Clayton thought of accepting and then faking a minor kidney stone so he wouldn't have to attend, but his good sense prevailed. After all, Jack and Shirley had served the church well.

At the banquet he was determined to remain silent, but Bill McAfee got even with him near the end of the ceremonies by calling on him to speak. "And now, Pastor, I'll turn it over to you to say a few words about our friends, the Brandts, and how much they have meant to our church."

Afterwards Clayton thought the Lord must have been proud of him for the restraint he showed. What he felt like doing was a jig—a toe-tapping, foot-stomping, hand-clapping jig complete with hoorays, praise-the-Lords, and hallelujahs—but there was more to telling the truth than showing his feelings.

He spoke admiringly of the Brandts' dedication to the church and of the time they devoted to doing something they considered worthwhile. The impression they left on the church, he said, was deep and would endure for many years. He didn't say that at times it was like the impression of a cannonball. He mentioned that, as they had at their previous church in Fort Collins, they were leaving behind a legacy that would impact the lives of hundreds, if not thousands, for decades to come. He spoke of new directions for them as they moved on to Indiana, and urged them to be faithful to the Word and to listen for the Lord's voice.

After his five-minute encomium, there was a long, standing applause. He was sure that only the Brandts, McAfees, and Ellen had heard what he *really* said.

Clayton settled back into his swivel chair in his office and opened Linda's card. It was large and ornate, one of those seven-dollar cards he refused to buy. Inside was a letter telling him how much she was going to miss the trips down to Springdale. It was the only childhood home she could remember, and soon there would be no one there for her to visit. She urged him to visit her and Alan in Wheaton. Alan would have a hard time breaking away from his job for any length of time, but there was a spare room in their house he could use any time. It was bad enough for Gregory and Allison not to know their Grandma Joyce, and she hated to think of their seeing Grandfather Clayton only once or twice a year. At the end of the letter she told him how much she loved and respected him.

Clayton got a Pepsi from the refrigerator and settled into his recliner, placing the can directly over a white ring that stained the end table. He'd deliberately left Ellie's card until last. He was already missing her.

He had known the time was coming when he'd live alone. Someday he might marry again, but he wasn't anxious. He'd be cautious, and it was all right if it never happened. Last night was the first he'd ever spent alone in his own house. He was beginning a journey by himself. He wasn't blaming any-one; life was meant to be like that. He was excited and a little frightened. He didn't plan to cook. In the mornings he'd have cereal, at noon he'd eat out, and in the evenings he'd fix sand-wiches or microwave a TV dinner. He wondered if that would be his routine for the rest of his life.

He opened Ellie's envelope. There was no card, but a lengthy handwritten letter. She wrote mainly about how much the last nine months had meant to her, the months since he'd asked her to read *The Hobbit* to him. She'd cherish those months the rest of her life. She alluded to their shared secret, but did not mention Caroline Merkle or anything that had happened so long ago. Ellie was glad it was finally over.

After he announced he was going to Marshall, he had re-ceived a short note from Caroline. It was not mailed, but slipped into his mail drop with *Clay* scrolled on the envelope.

Dear Clay,

I wish you all the best in Marshall. I will not follow you this time; in two years I plan to retire and move to Chicago.

Although living close to you has not been nearly enough, I am content knowing that I've been faithful to the promises we made to each other. I have never wavered in my love, but hoped and prayed you would return to me. I will never love anyone else.

Yours always,
Cary

P.S. I sold the Bel Air to an antique car collector in St. Louis.

One evening he had shown the letter to Ellie. Someone else needed to see it, and he knew she'd understand. They had both cried a little and then stayed awake until one o'clock talking, much of that time about the beautiful woman that Ellie knew as a teacher and he as his former lover. He'd been amazed at how freely their conversation flowed.

"What made her do that, Father?" Ellie had asked.

"I don't know, Ellie. Maybe she didn't know how *not* to be with me. We'd been together since we were infants, and those weekends in Galveston . . . to her that was the same as being married. I wasn't very smart when I was your age."

"Did you ever talk to her?"

"I tried, twice. In Dayton and Kansas City. But she never listened. It was always someday, sometime, somewhere we'd be together again. She would be faithful; she would wait."

"What did Mom think?"

"She hated it, Ellie, and so did I. For forty years . . . But Cary left us alone. Mom and I lived as though she wasn't there, yet there was always that presence, that green lady we caught glimpses of."

"I feel sorry for her."

"So do I. I can understand heartache, but poor Cary let it become an obsession. . . . She had so much to offer someone else. . . ."

At the end of her letter, Ellie wrote that his Father's Day present was in her closet in green-and-gold striped wrapping paper. He knew her money was tight, and as he went to find the gift, he wished she hadn't bought him anything. The box was flat and long, the kind used for a tie. He didn't need another tie, and besides, he wasn't sure he'd want to wear what Ellie might choose. She'd go for lavender with chartreuse polka dots and thin orange stripes.

When he opened the package, however, he found two pieces of string and another note.

Dear Father,

I thought we might use these the next time we go fishing. They might not look special, but if you examine them closely, you'll find they are unique. They are made of strands from the cord Rahab used when she helped the spies in Jericho, and from the rope that let the apostle Paul escape those in Damascus who would kill him. They contain strands of hair from the Queen of Sheba, Rapunzel, and J. R. R.'s Lady Galadriel. One strand comes from the cord that forever bound the mariner to the albatross, and one from the rope with which Quasimodo tolled the bells of Notre Dame. One comes from the Channel Islands where Galliatt used ropes to secure the engine of the wrecked Durande. I will not mention every source, but some other time I will tell you. If you look closely, you will notice a strand of mud-puddle brown hair. It is my own. I am sure it is the weakest part of the string.

I worked eighteen years on this string, most of the time diligently, sometimes carelessly. I give it to you with all my love. You are my wonderful father.

Love, Ellen

SINCE 1894, Moody Publishers has been dedicated to equip and motivate people to advance the cause of Christ by publishing evangelical Christian literature and other media for all ages, around the world. Because we are a ministry of the Moody Bible Institute of Chicago, a portion of the proceeds from the sale of this book go to train the next generation of Christian leaders.

If we may serve you in any way in your spiritual journey toward understanding Christ and the Christian life, please contact us at www.moodypublishers.com.

"All Scripture is God-breathed and is useful for teaching, rebuking, correcting and training in righteousness, so that the man of God may be thoroughly equipped for every good work."
—2 TIMOTHY 3:16, 17

MOODY
PUBLISHERS

THE NAME YOU CAN TRUST®

THE MENDING STRING TEAM

ACQUIRING EDITOR
Michele Straubel

COPY EDITOR
LB Norton

BACK COVER COPY
Becky Armstrong

COVER DESIGN
UDG DesignWorks

COVER PHOTO
Stephen Gardner/His Image PixelWorks

INTERIOR DESIGN
Ragont Design

PRINTING AND BINDING
Dickinson Press Inc.

The typeface for the text of this book is
Sabon